AN OUTLAW PASSION

The pampered daughter of a wealthy tycoon, Laura Hamilton has never been allowed to spread her wings . . . until now. Embarking on a transcontinental railroad, the sheltered young lady intends to enjoy her grand tour and her new freedom. But her adventure only truly begins when a dangerous man boards her train . . .

The ravages of war hardened Sam Duncan, and now the only person he cares about has vanished behind the heavily guarded gates of the Silver Spur Ranch. Claiming to be a bodyguard hired by her father, Sam intends to stick close to Laura only long enough to gain entrance to the fabled spread where Laura plans to visit a powerful family friend. But the handsome gunslinger is getting *too* close. And it's getting harder by the mile to keep his mind—and his hands—off the surprisingly passionate young heiress. Yet how long can he let this sweet madness continue when the only thing they have in common is this over-powering need for each other?

Avon Romantic Treasures by
Susan Kay Law

A WANTED MAN
A WEDDING STORY
MARRY ME
THE BAD MAN'S BRIDE
THE MOST WANTED BACHELOR
THE LAST MAN IN TOWN

If You've Enjoyed This Book,
Be Sure to Read These Other
AVON ROMANTIC TREASURES

A DARK CHAMPION *by Kinley MacGregor*
ENGLAND'S PERFECT HERO *by Suzanne Enoch*
AN INVITATION TO SEDUCTION *by Lorraine Heath*
IT TAKES A HERO *by Elizabeth Boyle*
SO IN LOVE: BOOK FIVE OF
THE HIGHLAND LORDS *by Karen Ranney*

Coming Soon

A SCANDAL TO REMEMBER *by Linda Needham*

SUSAN KAY LAW

A Wanted Man

An Avon Romantic Treasure

AVON BOOKS
An Imprint of HarperCollinsPublishers

This is a work of fiction. Names, characters, places, and incidents are products of the author's imagination or are used fictitiously and are not to be construed as real. Any resemblance to actual events, locales, organizations, or persons, living or dead, is entirely coincidental.

AVON BOOKS
An Imprint of HarperCollins*Publishers*
10 East 53rd Street
New York, New York 10022-5299

First Avon Books paperback printing: August 2004

Avon Trademark Reg. U.S. Pat. Off. and in Other Countries, Marca Registrada, Hecho en U.S.A.
HarperCollins® is a registered trademark of HarperCollins Publishers Inc.

Printed in the U.S.A.

10 9 8 7 6 5 4 3 2 1

Chapter 1

It was a hard thing to lose a friend. It was harder yet when you could number your friends using less than one hand. When, if it came right down to it, it took but one finger.

The fact that Sam Duncan called no one else friend was his own choice. It was a lesson he'd learned hard; when people around you dropped like flies in August it was far easier to remain alone than to get to know someone just to lose them.

But Griff . . . Griff had been the one who, just like Sam, hadn't died. He didn't know if they'd been too lucky or too stubborn or just too damn stupid to give in when everybody else had. Though he had to admit "friend" didn't really cover it. When you'd spent nearly half a year together in a hole too small for a grave and managed not to kill each other, you had a bond that most people—the lucky ones who skipped through life happily unaware of the really vicious things people could do to each other—could never understand.

He winced, gingerly probing his jaw where it throbbed to beat hell, despite the ice he'd slapped on it an hour ago when he'd finally stumbled into town and found himself a saloon full of people who barely blinked an eye when a fellow weaved in looking like John L. Sullivan, the Boston Strongboy, had used him for a sparring partner. Sooner or later he was going to have to wash out the blood matting his beard, but he was shooting for later.

When he'd crawled away from the Silver Spur, it would have been closer to head to Salt Lake City. But that was a Mormon town, and he'd known he was going to need a place where he could get some whiskey.

He downed another slug from the bottle on the table before him, noting that his hand only quivered a bit when he lifted it. The room was small and rough, and the saloon keeper had charged him too much for it because it usually rented by the hour. But Sam knew that once he dropped into bed he wasn't going to be able to haul himself out again for a good twelve hours.

Outside the single grimy window, the sky had grayed, as if the sun were too tired to keep shining, not going out in a burst of flashy color, but simply fading away like a harlot's henna when her hair had gotten too gray to soak up the red anymore. A piano squawked from the main room below. It was probably supposed to sound gay and cheerful but instead it was brassy and off-tune, setting his brain to throbbing behind his eyes. Now and then a spurt of laughter—the nasty-edged laughter of people trying too hard to convince themselves they were having fun—burst through and clashed with the tune.

He was obviously getting too old to have the shit beaten out of him. He felt every wound: the bruise that spread over half his chest and made him groan every time he moved, the kick that had caught him in the back, the swollen and split knuckles he'd earned trying to fight back. He couldn't open his left eye, and the fact that his knees still worked was nothing short of a miracle.

He didn't recall it ever *hurting* so much. Maybe a fellow was allotted only so much pain tolerance for his life and he'd used his up before he'd hit twenty, because he was doing a piss-poor job of tolerating the pain at the moment.

He contemplated the whiskey for a while. He had to work up to another drink, because the stuff set his split lip afire every time he touched it, a burn that was almost as bad as all the other aches combined. Maybe if he just didn't move, didn't twitch, didn't *breathe*, it'd be okay.

Lord, if anybody could see him now . . . *ow, ow, ow*. Chuckling was a *really* bad idea, he quickly discovered. But he'd spent all these years building up a reputation as a really ruthless piece of work, so much so that the mere rumor that he'd been hired had snuffed more than one strike and range war before they'd ever gotten started. And right now he doubted he could defend himself against a six-year-old.

Yeah, there'd been a lot of men coming at him. *Maybe a dozen*, he thought, though his vision had blurred early on, and that just might be his pride talking. And they'd caught him by surprise—but that was the whole point, wasn't it? Nobody had caught Sam Duncan by surprise in a good fifteen years. But it had all seemed routine. They'd answered his questions with such mild disinterest before cordially escorting him off the Silver Spur that he'd been pretty close to assuming that they were telling him the truth and that Griff had never gotten there in the first place.

But Sam hadn't gotten to be the highest-paid hired gun in seven states by taking anybody's word for anything. He'd nosed around the nearest town for a bit—no information to be had, the most close-mouthed bunch of ostensibly "friendly" people he'd ever met, and that *did* make him suspicious—before heading back toward the Silver Spur. They were waiting for him before he'd ever gotten close . . . and since there were at least four other routes he could have taken back, he wondered just how many men Haw Crocker, the owner of the Silver Spur, *had* sent out to make sure that Sam Duncan regretted it if he didn't go quietly on his way.

It had gotten dark enough in the room that he could no longer read the two papers he'd spread out on the rickety pine table. He gritted his teeth against the pain of moving his arm and nudged the lamp closer.

The first one, small and crumpled even though Sam had done his best to smooth it out, he didn't need the light to decipher because he knew it by heart: the last letter he'd received from Griff Judah.

They didn't see each often, not in years. Didn't need to—it was enough to know the other one was out there, alive and whole. Once in a while they wandered into the same town at the same time and spent a day or two in a place very much like this one, trying to prove to themselves and the world that, yeah, they'd survived, plunging into wild sprees that never seemed to be as much fun as they'd sounded no matter how hard they pretended they were.

But Griff's luck hadn't run as true as Sam's after they'd left Andersonville. He hadn't gotten his strength back as quickly. And, while Sam's six-shooters soon became as much a part of him as his hands, Griff would just as soon have never seen a gun again. Sam had tried to help him out more than once—he had more money than he knew what to do with, considering he had nothing and no one else he cared to spend it on—but Griff had too much pride for that.

But in Griff's last letter he'd sounded hopeful. Excited that he'd finally found a job that he might settle into. Haw Crocker's Silver Spur was the biggest, richest ranch between Denver and San Francisco, and there was plenty of opportunity for a fellow to get ahead. It was the biggest and richest, of course, because the vein of silver Crocker had discovered had allowed him to buy up another fifty thousand acres and handpick the finest stock from Texas to Wyoming. Rumor had it, Griff wrote, that the mine still produced darn near eight hundred thousand dollars of ore a month, and wasn't that something?

Not that he was interested in the mine. They'd both had more than enough of holes in the ground. But Griff liked the wide-open spaces, where the mountains flattened into a broad valley, and the cows and the horses and the fact that a man could work alone with them most of time. And all that silver could run a lot of cattle for a long time, couldn't it?

But then Sam had never heard from him again. Griff had been pretty regular in his correspondence if nothing else and when two months passed without a word Sam had sent his own letter to the Silver Spur. Six weeks later the unopened envelope, ragged as if it'd had a hard journey, showed back up, NOT AT THIS ADDRESS printed in hard black letters across the front.

So Sam had finished his current assignment—roust up a gang of bank robbers that the sheriff of Mill City hadn't been able to handle himself—and headed for Utah, straight for that unsatisfying visit to the Silver Spur and his brutal little meeting with the men who were supposed to ensure he didn't return and snoop around.

Not that they would scare him off. But it wouldn't hurt to heal up a bit first, he thought, and lifted the bottle again, noting a bit hazily that it was only half-full. The pain was finally receding, aching low beneath a warm, pleasant buzz, and the printing on the page was beginning to blur.

He squinted at the newspaper he'd picked up on the stage to Hell's Pass. The driver had balked at taking on a man who'd looked like he'd just escaped from hell instead of wanting to be driven there, but a wad of cash and pretending to be a tenderfoot traveler who gotten in over his head had done the trick. Sam'd called himself Artemus Kirkwood, a pansy-assed name appropriate for a fellow dumb enough to get himself clobbered. He offered an outrageous amount to get the coach to himself, then stretched out on the seat and passed out for the first couple of hours.

When he woke up, the now-friendly driver, undoubtedly eyeing a hefty tip from his clueless passenger, had offered him a copy of the *Utah Register*. Not much interested in anybody else's troubles at the time, Sam had intended only to give it a quick scan before using it to block out the vicious sun that had interrupted his nap. Instead, his gaze snagged on a headline halfway down page 1.

PAINTER TO VISIT THE SILVER SPUR

Miss Laura Florence Hamilton, the renowned panorama painter, is scheduled to traverse the length of the transcontinental railway in preparation for her newest project, *The Rails at 15*, a celebration of the fifteenth an-

niversary of the driving of the silver spike and a recording of the changes that massive achievement has
wrought along its path in the years of its existence.

Miss Hamilton, while famous in her own right, is
even better known as the only child of Leland Hamilton, the Baron of Bankers, a man who has taken his
place alongside such captains of industry as Vanderbilt
and Gould. One of his most profitable ventures has
been his partnership with Utah's own Silver King Haw
Crocker. As the railroad passes within three miles of
the Silver Spur, Miss Hamilton will take the opportunity to rest and paint at Mr. Crocker's luxurious abode.

Miss Hamilton's party is due to leave Omaha May
12 by private rail car, though their schedule from that
point is uncertain, subject to the demands of her profession. Certainly there will be much in our grand state
to hold the eye of such an artist. Perhaps, like so many
before her, she will fall under the spell of our lovely
landscape and never leave again.

The *Register* would like to extend our warmest welcome to such an esteemed visitor, and . . .

May 12. Sam calculated the distance between Hell's
Pass and Omaha, pondered his own healing rate, and
winced. It was going to be a damned painful trip. Planting both hands on the table, he pushed himself to his
feet and swayed there for a blessed moment before going in search of some wash water.

With any luck, Miss Hamilton liked her men a little
rough around the edges.

"I do believe," Mrs. Bossidy said, "that man intends
to rob the train."

"Who?" Laura Hamilton twisted around, her motion

cut off in midswivel when Mrs. Bossidy's hand clamped down on her knee, a hearty squeeze even through the layered poufs of skirts and petticoats.

"For heaven's sake, don't *look* at him," she whispered fiercely.

"At who?" Laura asked again.

"That one out there on the back platform."

Laura dropped her chin to her shoulder, peering as discreetly as possible toward the back of the car. The man stood framed in the window: an angled slice of sturdy shoulder, clad in dusty black . . . dark hair, too long to be contained by his hat, cropped unevenly at the shoulders, whipped violently by the wind, slashing across one cheek like a scar and disappearing into a beard of the same shade . . . a face made all of angles and planes, uncompromisingly harsh, the eyes deep-set, the right one surrounded by the purple-blue stain of a horrible bruise. She couldn't read their color from here, but she was certain his eyes must be dark. A sunny, happy blue simply wouldn't do.

He filled the frame well, she thought automatically. But the composition was all darkness, brutally severe. It needed some softness, some light, for contrast. But an interesting face, unforgettable, eminently paintable if one's talent lent itself to portraiture. If fact it would be almost irresistibly tempting to do so, even to Laura, who understood very well that her talents lay in another direction.

"I told you not to look." The grip on her knee tightened until Laura reluctantly faced forward again. "I don't know what's gotten into you lately. You used to be such an obliging child."

"I'm still obliging," Laura said, then allowed, "almost always." She'd been far too obliging for too long, she considered. It was past time for her to be a bit less reflexively obedient.

"When it's convenient for you. That's not obliging, that's strategy," Mrs. Bossidy said, softening her words with a fond smile.

Laura could scarcely remember a time when Mrs. Bossidy had not been in her life. For so many years as her nurse, then she'd become Laura's companion. Laura loved her parents, but Mrs. Bossidy knew and understood her better. When Laura had proposed this trip, Mrs. Bossidy had been the only one who'd supported the idea from the first.

Which did not mean, in any way, that Mrs. Bossidy agreed with Laura on every point.

"I would feel much better," Mrs. Bossidy went on, "if you would at least return to your own car."

Once Laura's father had finally agreed to this expedition, he had put forth many conditions—a *great* many, Laura recalled wryly, which he had required her to repeat word for word before he'd allowed her to step one foot out the door. Mrs. Bossidy's presence was a given, but he'd also insisted upon not one but two guards, Hiram Peel and Erastus Hoxie, a prerequisite that was fine with Laura, for their presence in her life was as much an accepted fact as Mrs. Bossidy's. Her party actually traveled in not one but two private cars, both built precisely to her father's specifications, the construction of which had forced her to delay the trip for nearly a year. She and Mrs. Bossidy had one to themselves; the men, all her equipment, and their supplies filled the other. One more car, which Leland Hamilton had allowed to be bought standard, carried their riding horses.

"I like it in this one," Laura told her.

Not that the public passenger car was nearly as comfortable as theirs. Green velvet worn of its nap sagged over the rigidly straight-backed seats, the cushions so thin they might as well have not been there at all. The lighting was poor, the car crowded and noisy. A pinch-faced woman swaddled in black, who perched stiffly in the foremost seat clutching a small leather case, had protested the chill when someone pried open a window, and now the air was overly warm, packed with too many smells—sweet, heavy perfume, a whiff of onions, a baby who needed a change, a dozen more.

"If you're uncomfortable," Laura said, "you're welcome to go on back."

"And leave you here alone?"

"I'm hardly alone."

And that was what kept her there. She didn't know where to look, what sight to drink in first. Certainly she should be studying the landscape outside, noting the wide sweep of land as they rolled out of Omaha, judging the light, the way buildings clustering around the city's center thinned as they pulled away. It was why she'd come there, after all, and it was all so different from anything she'd ever seen before.

It was not that her world wasn't lovely; outrageously beautiful, in truth, the envy of most. She would have to be almost criminally ungrateful not to realize she lived a privileged life. It had just been so very unchanging, carefully and precisely bounded. She understood that it was so because her family loved her, and that because they had come so close to losing her once, they'd been determined to keep her safe, wrapped in batting and boxed away like precious crystal. Understanding why it had been so had not kept her from longing to see other places, other faces, than the ones she'd memorized years ago.

And here she was at last. She couldn't keep from grinning ear to ear like a child at Christmas.

The shimmy and bump of the car over the tracks made it impossible to sketch with anything approaching the precision her project required. At Kearney they'd unhitch from the train for a few days, and she'd have plenty of time to study the landscape. But this particular train would go on without them, and she'd never again get to study exactly these faces.

Three seats ahead there was a dumpling of a woman, all soft hills under faded blue gingham, her cheeks round as rising buns, hair white as good flour. A keen-eyed pastor in black, his white collar in sharp relief against a jet lapel, scanned the car constantly, frowning, as if on perpetual alert for signs of sin and decadence.

So many interesting faces . . . In the far corner, almost unnoticed, a young man in a tan suit nearly disappeared into his seat. He had the blandest countenance Laura had ever seen, a perfectly round face topped with a thin fringe of beige hair the exact shade of his skin. Even this man's face, absolutely forgettable, interested her. How could it be so utterly without character?

So very unlike the man on the platform. Without thinking, she twisted around again. There was certainly nothing innocuous about his looks. A sculptor might have better luck than a painter, she decided, capturing that look of danger in hard, cold surfaces and edges so sharp they'd draw blood at a touch.

And then he looked at her—full on, no pretense of a polite, accidental grazing of gazes. The intensity simmering in his eyes stole her breath and froze her smile in place.

My goodness. The corners of his mouth curved up, not quite a smile, but enough to make her heart thump. She wondered what it would be like if he really smiled and decided it was best if she never found out, if just the promise of one was so potent.

"I'm not the least bit alone," Laura repeated.

"That's precisely what concerns me." Mrs. Bossidy followed Laura's gaze. "Laura!" she snapped. "The man is a rogue at best and quite probably a bandit. Just look at him!"

"Perhaps that is wishful thinking on your part?"

"Why ever would I *want* him to rob us?"

"Oh, I don't know," Laura said lightly. "A bit of excitement, perhaps. This trip promises to be less than fascinating for you. Just think of it—the dashing outlaw holding you captive, you obligated to do *whatever* he orders you upon pain of your life . . ."

"Laura!"

"He's *very* handsome, don't you think?"

Mrs. Bossidy pokered up immediately, pinching her lips together until they almost disappeared. "If you keep saying such things, I'm going to drag you home to Newport, the painting be . . . well, the painting would be of no matter. You've done all the others without visiting the places yourself. You can do it again."

"I'm sorry," Laura said quickly, unwilling to risk the slightest chance that they must go home before they had begun. She would rather not paint at all than continue to work off secondary sources alone. And if she stopped painting . . . her work was such a large part of her life, perhaps *most* of her life, that she couldn't imagine what she would do without it. What she would *be* without it.

"I didn't mean to tease," she went on. "It's just that—" She stopped, her gaze sliding over Mrs. Bossidy as she thought, not for the first time, that her companion must have been an extremely young bride and widow before she came to work for the Hamiltons. And a very beautiful one at that. She was still an attractive woman, if one looked past the severe arrangement of her hair, the perpetually pinched expression, and the dark, enveloping dresses that made a nun's habit seem bold. Laura doubted that most men bothered.

"It was very wise of you," Mrs. Bossidy said, "to refrain from saying whatever it is you were about to say."

"I was not being wise. I'm just enjoying myself too much to argue about how mourning was never meant to extend for fifteen years and how I'm certain that anyone who truly cared for you would not want you never to enjoy your life again."

"What makes you think I don't enjoy my life?"

Perhaps the fact that she'd never seen her companion laugh at anyone but her, and seldom enough at that.

When Laura didn't answer, Mrs. Bossidy bent and whacked her handbag across the burly, corduroy-clad knee of Hiram, who dozed comfortably in the seat across from them. He snorted, then settled back into his dreams, his thick chin dropping to a chest broad as the Missouri.

"Oh, for heaven's sake." She took a firmer grip on her bag, fisting both hands around the strings, and swung like Big Dan Brouthers, the home run champ.

"Wha—" Hiram sprang up like a nervous frog, head swinging wildly from side to side. When he realized every head in the car had turned his way, he lifted both his hands in a placating gesture. "Sorry. A . . . wasp.

Terribly annoying. Bad wasp." Scowling at Mrs. Bossidy, he gingerly lowered himself back into his seat, eyeing her handbag as if expecting another slug at any moment.

"I fail to see," Mrs. Bossidy said crisply, "how you properly guard your charge when you are dead asleep."

"Oh, yeah." He glanced around at the assortment of passengers, most snoozing, the rest, eyes glazed, staring out the windows. A young boy of perhaps four bounced down the aisle, heading for the ceramic jug of ice water in the far corner near the lavatory. "Looks really dangerous to me." He hooked a thumb at a crinkled woman who couldn't weigh more than eighty pounds, hunched in her seat with her hands gnarled around a mahogany cane. "I figure she's the one most likely to give us trouble. What do you think?"

"I think that you're paid extremely well to worry about such things, which you'd do well to remember if you wish to continue to enjoy such fortunate circumstances. Now, would you like to wake Mr. Hoxie, or should I?"

"Oh, be my guest," he said.

"Children, children," Laura chided them. "Surely there is no need to poke at each other in an attempt to entertain yourselves."

Erastus Hoxie, who was as compact as Hiram Peel was large but, rumor had it, twice as tough, not to mention twice as old, had dropped off to sleep within five minutes of the train pulling out of the station. His head dropped back against the deep green cushion, his mouth slack, a thin trickle of drool seeping from the corner. "And let Mr. Hoxie rest," Laura went on fondly. "He looks far too comfortable to disturb."

A series of muffled pops came from outside the

train: two, close together, a brief pause, and then perhaps half a dozen more in quick succession. Around her, passengers roused slowly, mumbling. Mrs. Bossidy stiffened, and Hiram jerked up, suddenly alert.

Metal screeched on metal. The train lurched, then slowed, the rapid blur of scenery outside coming into focus. Hiram swore, a word so foul Laura glanced at Mrs. Bossidy, expecting a tirade about Laura's tender ears. But she was flushed, her eyes wide and mouth tense.

Somewhere behind Laura a woman cried out, the sound dropping abruptly off into silence.

"Hiram?" Laura ventured.

"Shh," he said, his expression grim. "Stay right here. Don't move, don't draw any attention to yourself." He gently poked the slumbering Mr. Hoxie with his elbow, a prod that had no effect. Hiram sighed and this time rammed his elbow into Hoxie's ribs with enough force that Laura winced. Hoxie snorted like a rooting pig and blinked awake. "Wha—"

"Hold-up." His voice was pitched low, intended only for his partner, but the women caught it. Mrs. Bossidy gasped, and Laura instinctively spun to check the back platform.

It was empty.

"Turn around." This time Mrs. Bossidy's hand on her knee slammed down in a painful warning. "Don't move, don't say anything. Make yourself as inconspicuous as possible. If someone points a gun in your direction, give them whatever they want."

"But *who*, there's no one here." Laura couldn't seem to work up the edgy concern gripping the rest of the passengers. It was too unreal— only a few moments ago she'd joked about the train being robbed, and now, with no clear evidence she could see, everyone assumed they were smack-dab in the middle of a hold-up.

She couldn't help but catalog the details. All those faces were even more interesting now, the veneer peeled away to reveal naked fear or determination or shock. If only she knew how to portray that on paper, the core of a person, the essence of emotion stripped bare. Capturing that split moment of revelation was when a painter moved from faithful recorder to true artist.

Hiram eased up in his chair. She was so accustomed to him jovial and relaxed, lobbing thinly veiled—and sometimes not so veiled—insults back and forth with Mrs. Bossidy, that she couldn't help but stare. She knew perfectly well that Hiram and Mr. Hoxie were her bodyguards; she just never *thought* of them that way. She'd never required anything from them but companionship and sturdy backs, functions they performed with admirable cheer. The sudden transformation of his demeanor was so dramatic that a thin blade of fear sliced through her fascination.

His hands hovered at his waist, sliding slowly to attract no attention, looping beneath the baggy flap of his corduroy jacket. A *gun*? she wondered. Had Hiram been armed all this time, and she hadn't known?

Of course he had. Foolish of her not to have realized. She'd just never given it any thought.

"Stop right there." The command cracked through the air. The mousy, bland little man Laura had assumed no one would notice—well, everyone noticed him now all right, as he jammed his pistol in Hiram's lower back. "Lift your hands. Easy now, no sudden moves. I might not be the best shot in the world, but I'm thinkin' I'm pretty accurate from this range."

And there it was, the fear that gripped the rest of the

passengers finally taking full hold on her. *Painful*. She hadn't expected that, but it was—it burned in her extremities, needle pricks in her fingers, toes, even the skin of her face, like blood rushing back to a benumbed limb.

Hiram cut his eyes toward Hoxie, a quick instant of communication. *One of them, two of us . . .*

"Oh," the robber said mildly, "and I'd make sure your friend there doesn't move, either. Preacher, you got everybody covered?"

"Got 'em." Some preacher. Amazing how a clerical collar made anybody instantly trustworthy. It took the merest glance now to peg the preacher as trouble, with that wicked glitter in his eyes and a cruel grin that bordered on maniacal. He'd taken a position at the front of the car, back to the door, between the water jug and the lavatory. He carried two guns like he spent more time with them in his hands than without and kept them trained on the cabin.

Just for fun, he reached over and gave the water jug a shove with his forearm. It shattered as it hit the floor, ice and shards of crockery flying, the crash tremendous. People ducked and flung their arms over their heads. Several women shrieked. One, a plump and pretty middle-aged matron wearing a great wheel of a straw hat, cried out, her hand going to her face where a fragment had sliced her cheek. Blood trickled beneath her fingers.

The train, its massive momentum finally spent, rolled to a stop. The car gave a final lurch, unsettling the two men standing, causing the nearest bandit to fling out his hands in reflexive balance.

The opening was brief. Hiram surged to his feet, a quick *whoosh* of motion. An instant later the robber recovered, bashing Hiram's head with the butt of his pistol. Hiram went down like a rock, back into his seat. His arms flopped loosely, booted legs sprawling until one toe touched the hem of Mrs. Bossidy's dress.

Her lip curled. "One would have thought that noggin of his was too hard to be damaged by a mere rap."

The mild-faced robber *tsked*. "Shouldn'ta moved." His gaze flicked to the two women. "Well, now, I imagine the two of you will have somethin' for us, won't ya?"

Mrs. Bossidy flung herself sideways, pressing Laura back against the seat, shielding her with her body. "You'll get nothing from her without going through me first. And I vow to make that such a difficult task that it will not be worth your while. Not at all."

He flashed a set of even teeth. "Promise?" Then he raised his voice to carry throughout the car. "Listen up, folks. Pretty easy, here—anything you got that's worth anythin', toss it in the bag as the preacher goes up and down the aisle. Some of our friends are up front with the engineer, and stationed throughout the train just like we were, and all in all it'll be the smartest thing to get it over with as soon as possible. You can try and hide somethin', but I wouldn't. It'll only make us hafta look for it." He looked directly at Mrs. Bossidy as he continued, "Come to think of it, go ahead and try."

Laura tried to nudge Mrs. Bossidy back into place. No luck; she was a lot sturdier than she looked.

"Preacher? Get started."

Preacher slid one of his guns into the holster hidden beneath his black coat and pulled out a sagging canvas bag. He looked down as he shook it open . . . and never looked up. The door behind him burst open. He wheeled halfway around as a body rocketed through the door, driving him down to the floor. One of his guns fired, the blast deafening in the small space. Paneling shattered, bits raining down from the hole where the bullet slammed into the ceiling.

Impressions flashed, too many for Laura to capture: the bland-faced robber spinning to see what had happened at the doorway; Hoxie surging out of his seat, vaulting over the back, and tackling him in the aisle; men leaping from all directions as if they'd been awaiting the opportunity, now unleashed, shouting, arms flailing.

Unthinkingly, Laura shoved Mrs. Bossidy away and stood, craning her neck to see.

Preacher was on the floor, facedown and spread-eagled, a knee on his back and a gun to his head.

It was him. *Him.* The dark man who'd disappeared from the back platform had somehow come through the front door and subdued the robber in an instant.

Chapter 2

"**G**et *down*." Mrs. Bossidy yanked on her skirt.

"Don't worry," Laura told her. "Everything's under control."

And indeed it was. A half dozen men surrounded each robber, fists clenched, belatedly prepared to play the hero. It was entirely unnecessary; the dark man had the preacher thoroughly subdued, and Hoxie had apparently knocked the other one out cold.

"Need any help back there?" His voice was low-pitched, smooth as melted chocolate. Laura had expected it to be rough, as harsh-sounding as the rest of him appeared. But it was warm, carefully modulated, the kind of voice made to murmur of love and secret things, a voice that might recite poetry and issue orders with equal ease.

"Nope," Hoxie answered cheerfully, climbing to his feet. "Two jabs and a left hook and he went down harder'n Glass Jaw Gillespie." Rocking back on his heels, he cracked his knuckles, more energized than Laura had ever seen him.

21

The man nodded. "Anyone got some rope?"

No one moved, as if, in the lull following that eruption of intensity, they couldn't think clearly enough to understand the question.

"How about this?" Laura said at last, moving toward the aisle.

"Laura!"

"Oh, hush," she said, brushing past Mrs. Bossidy. She worked at the fastening of the sash wrapped around her waist as she threaded her way through the men crowding the aisle and stepped around the limp body on the floor, resisting the most unladylike urge to give him a swift kick as she passed. Now where had that come from? She'd never suspected she had a violent streak, and Mr. Hoxie would likely be more than happy to mete out a bit more punishment should it become necessary.

"Here." She waved the drift of turquoise silk when she reached the end of the aisle, more breathless than the brief walk warranted, even for her. But she'd had an unusual and exciting experience; an accelerated heartbeat should be excused under such circumstances.

"A scarf?" Keeping the gun in place, the dark stranger sat back a fraction, tilting his head so he could look up at her from beneath the brim of his hat.

His eyes were dark, so dark. Blacker than midnight, twice as compelling, giving absolutely nothing away. *I should have known,* she thought. She'd wondered about his eyes, conjured deep sapphire and gray and a warm, rich brown. And now she couldn't imagine them any other way. No wonder she never did portraits, if she hadn't pegged the inevitability of that color right off.

"It's silk. Very strong. It'll hold him, don't worry."

His gaze dropped to the swath in her hand, the vibrantly colored fabric rippling because it was so fine that the slightest breeze, even a breath, set it in motion. She held it out to him, waiting.

"It's too good to be wasted on the likes of him."

"Don't worry about it."

He lifted his head slowly, as if noting the thick cream silk of her shirtwaist, abundantly trimmed with hand-knotted lace her mother had imported from Brussels, pausing at the wide glint of gold that encircled her wrist and the swing of heavy sapphire drops at her ears. "Rich girl, hmm?" he asked, so mildly it held no sting.

"Yes," she admitted, just as mild. Though that knowledge often spawned strong reactions from others, from fawning obsequiousness to acid envy, it was merely a fact of her existence to Laura, holding no more emotion than that her hair was brown or that she was left-handed. She had nothing to do with earning her father's fortune and minimal control over the use of it. She certainly appreciated its existence, since she understood that it made her life much more comfortable than it otherwise might have been; but that was about it. His wealth made some things much simpler and others far more complicated, an immutable part of her life that she'd long ago decided was best simply to accept and otherwise think about as little as possible.

His expression lightened: a slight crinkle at the corners of his eyes, the barest lift of his mouth. About as near as he ever got to a smile, she figured, pleased all out of proportion to be the one who drew it.

His fingers brushed hers. Warm, the rough calluses easily felt through the gossamer fabric, the texture and heat so different from hers that it was hard to believe they were the same thing, just two human hands. And then he threaded the scarf from her grasp, a quick glide of gauzy fabric.

He glanced down at the prone figure on the floor, then back up at her. "You any good at knots?"

"Not good enough that I want to trust my continued future to it."

"Okay, then, here." He flipped the gun around and thrust the butt into her palm. She took it without thinking. "Don't shoot me."

"I—" Belatedly realizing what he'd given her, she held it as far away from herself as she could manage. The metal was warm against her palm— his heat, she realized, transmitting itself to her. "I might," she admitted.

And there was the warming of his expression again, like the barest flicker of sunlight through a cloud-clotted sky. It could be dangerously addictive, she thought, prying that hint of warmth out of him.

The preacher lifted his head an inch. "Didn't I tell you not to move?" The man put his hand on the would-be robber's head and shoved. The preacher's forehead hit the floor with a solid *thunk*. "While she might wing me, too, I really don't think she's going to miss you completely from there, do you? At least, I wouldn't want to bet my neck on it."

He looped his captive's hands behind his back, twisting and tying his wrists together with her scarf with such proficiency Laura could only assume he'd tied up a few men in his time.

"Thanks," he said, and climbed to his feet. "I'm sure we all appreciate the sacrifice."

Events moved swiftly after that. Someone proffered a handful of the golden cords that held back the heavy swoops of draperies— so they hadn't needed her scarf after all, she thought with a twinge of disappointment—

and her mysterious hero had the bandit trussed like a chicken in an instant. He didn't glance her way again, just strode down the aisle as if he owned the place until he stood over the still-unconscious thief that Mr. Hoxie guarded. Laura followed. No, not *followed*, she amended; she returned to her place. That he'd gone there first was merely a coincidence. Laura Hamilton did not follow men around, no matter how interesting they were.

"Nice job," he said, tossing Hoxie a coil of cording.

"Thank you." Hoxie tied up his prisoner, yanking his arms around so hard that Laura winced before she remembered the man deserved it.

"There're bound to be more of them in the other cars."

Hoxie stood up, more than a head shorter than the mysterious dark man. "Up front, too," he agreed. "Probably came on horseback." He inclined his head at the prone bandit. "He said so. From the sound of the shots outside, I figure he told the truth about that at least."

The man nodded once, unsurprised. Or completely unconcerned. Laura, on the other hand, was getting extremely concerned, if this was heading where she suspected it might.

"Are you with me?" he asked.

Hoxie popped his knuckles and grinned. "Wouldn't miss it."

"Oh, no you don't." Mrs. Bossidy inserted herself between the men, her skirts frothing into the aisle, and rounded on Mr. Hoxie. "You're not leaving her here alone."

"Alone? There're all kinds of people here."

"Two of whom fully intended to rob or shoot us or Lord only knows what else only moments ago."

"They're not going to be causing any more trouble," Hoxie said in the wheedling, petulant tones of a boy on the verge of having his fun spoiled. "And Hiram's here."

"He's unconscious!"

"Oh, not for long." Hopefully, he poked Hiram with his toe, drawing no response. "Probably not for long," he amended.

Apparently unwilling to wait any longer, the stranger spun for the door. Laura blocked his way.

"Excuse me," he said.

He intended to go charging recklessly into trouble. Alone. "Mr. Hoxie, go with him." Laura had no way to stop the stranger, but she could at least ensure he was not completely without help.

"Hoxie, stay right where you are." When Mrs. Bossidy issued orders like that, Laura had always obeyed without question. Gainsaying her felt as odd as it did necessary.

"Mr. Hoxie, which one of us is more likely to go to my father to get you fired?"

"Bossidy," he answered promptly.

"All right," Laura admitted. "But if she does so, I'll go to him and get you rehired. If *I'm* the one to ask, however, she can't veto me."

"Miss, there's no time for this. Please step aside."

Laura faced her stranger squarely. "Can you use him? No pride, no heroics. Tell me the truth."

"Yes."

"Then go," she said, and stepped aside. "Mr. Hoxie, you too."

Clearly torn, Hoxie shot a furtive glance at Mrs. Bossidy. It was perfectly obvious which of the two ladies frightened him more, and Laura made a mental note to work on a more commanding presence.

But then the stranger strode down the aisle. Hoxie trotted after him.

They stopped at the door. The man eased it open, peering cautiously out. He waved Hoxie through, stepped out himself, and they were gone.

Out there. Where there were horrible men with guns and knives and who knew what other kinds of terrible things.

"Do you think he'll be all right?"

"Of course he'll be all right." Mrs. Bossidy waved her hand in dismissal. "Hoxie's always all right."

"No, I—" How terrible of her. She'd known Mr. Hoxie for more than half her life, and she was worrying about a man she had barely met. Hadn't even *really* met, if it came right down to it.

And it would never do if Mrs. Bossidy got even a whiff of such a thing. If she ever suspected that Laura had a weakness for mysterious, wicked-looking men, she'd have her bundled back to Sea Haven and locked away until she was too old for her clearly lamentable taste in men to matter.

Not that Laura had ever suspected she had a predilection for men such as he. But then, she'd never known any. Novelty, she reflected, always had a certain allure. No doubt that was all there was to it. "But Mr. Hoxie's not as young as he used to be," she said, attempting to inject as much innocence and appropriate concern into her voice, failing miserably to her own ears. Prevarication, like flirting and tennis and kissing, was undoubtedly one of the things one must master as an adolescent or be forever poor at.

But Mrs. Bossidy wasn't attending close enough to notice. She stood, fists on her hips, over Hiram, still slumped in his chair but stirring. His head rolled from one side to the other, his sun-browned cheek speckled with the imprint of the crushed plush seat back, and his lids fluttered. "Wouldn't you know it," she said. "The first opportunity in years for him to earn his pay, and he *sleeps* through it."

"I don't think being concussed qualifies as sleeping."

"Sleeping, concussed. The end result's the same, isn't it?" She leaned over and patted him on the cheek, more firmly than was required. "Time to wake up."

"I think he's coming around, anyway."

"Sweetheart, don't spoil my fun," she said, and thumped more firmly. "Come on, Mr. Peel. You're missing everything as usual."

More gunshots. Five of them, maybe six. Enough to have Laura on the edge of her seat, hands clenched so tightly in her lap that her fingers went numb.

The men in the car had propped the two well-trussed bandits in the corner of the car, where they'd slumped against the wall and glared at the passengers. Now and then a child—brave or dared into it—would sneak up to poke at them, only to be shooed away by their mothers.

Hiram, once roused enough to understand what he'd missed, attempted to go after Mr. Hoxie and the stranger. But when he managed to push himself to his feet, he swayed as woozily as if he stood in a boat instead of a train. Mrs. Bossidy merely gave him a light shove, and he'd dropped back into his chair. "You stay right there. No telling who you might crush if you toppled over in an inconvenient place."

"Hey." Palms facing her, he lifted his hands. "Whatever you say. Wouldn't want you pushing me around."

"Hmm." She tilted her head, considering. "Laura, what do you think? I do believe he's got his hands in the *exact* same position as when he was meekly acquiescing to that horrible bandit. You know, the one that Mr. Hoxie dispatched so very efficiently."

He scowled at her. "Now see here—"

"Oh, just stop it," Laura snapped, her nerves frayed to a fine thread, her display of temper so rare that they stopped sniping and gaped at her instead.

"Miss Hamilton." Hiram patted her awkwardly on the shoulder. "Hoxie'll be fine. Heck, even if he did get popped with a slug or two, it'd take more than that—"

"Mr. Peel!" Mrs. Bossidy broke in when Laura paled. "If that's your attempt at cheering her up, God forbid you show up at a funeral and try to comfort the bereaved. You'd have people throwing themselves in the grave in no time."

He scowled. "I—"

The door flew open, and Hoxie staggered through with a gun in his hand. He'd lost his hat, his jaw was puffing up on one side, and blood smeared the back of his hands. There was a rip in his jacket, and he was grinning like a kid who'd just been shown the candy store and told to "have at it."

A hum of concern and excitement greeted his arrival. "Not to worry, folks." He stuck a thumb in his belt, as puffed up as a banty cock set free in a henhouse. "All safe and sound. We'll be gettin' under way again shortly."

Good as his promise, the steam whistle blast drowned out the questions tossed in his direction as he swaggered his way to the middle of the car.

"What happened?" Laura asked, as soon he reached them. She raised to her tiptoes to peer over Mr. Hoxie's shoulder, but no one else came through the door.

Surely he will come back, she thought. He'd originally been riding on this car's platform. And wouldn't he want to check on his captives? "Is everything all right?"

"It's just fine," Mr. Hoxie said, grinning, preparing to take his seat.

"Wait, wait!" Mrs. Bossidy sprang up and pushed him away before his hindquarters landed. "You're going to get blood all over the cushion."

"So? I practically saved the whole train. I don't think anybody's going to complain."

Mrs. Bossidy dug in the huge canvas bag she took with her everywhere, pulled out a thin dishcloth, and spread it over the seat. "There. Go ahead."

He dropped into his seat with a gusty sigh and slapped Hiram on his knee. "Hoo-wee, you missed it, bud! Haven't had that much fun since—" He stopped, shooting a guilty glance in Laura's direction. "Well, in quite a while."

"Is—" Laura raised her voice as the train picked up speed, clacking along steadily, an already-familiar sound. "Is everybody all right?"

"Everybody but a couple of the robbers." He shook his head. "There were at least ten of 'em, though a couple rode away when it was clear which way the wind was blowin'. Four came up on the engine, shootin' at the engineers, and the rest were stationed in the passenger cars." He chuckled. "All of 'em but these two are trussed up and stacked in a freight car."

"And he . . . he's okay?"

"Who?"

If she squeezed them any tighter Laura's fingers were going to be permanently welded together. But if she relaxed her grip, they were undoubtedly going to shake. "You know. *Him*."

"Oh, the dark avenger?"

"The *what*?" Mrs. Bossidy snapped. "What kind of a

stupid name is that? What kind of a man would call himself such a ridiculous thing? Sounds like something out of a penny dreadful."

"*He* didn't call himself that. *I* did." Mr. Hoxie smiled, clearly unoffended. "You should have seen him, bursting in with both guns drawn, like he thought being one against four was more than fair odds, bullets flying in all directions. Never seen anythin' like it." He rubbed his chin. "A novel, huh? You think I could write one of those?"

"No," Mrs. Bossidy said.

"Did anybody get shot?" Laura couldn't imagine that one man could face four ruthless train robbers and come out unscathed.

"Oh, sure." He shrugged. "Not bad though."

"*Who?*" Her voice quavered. Mrs. Bossidy looked at her sharply. Laura said back in her chair, affecting unconcern.

"One of the robbers. Big brute of a fella, almost as big as Hiram, here. Went down just about as hard, wailing like a girl." He chuckled. "Shot him in the shoulder, he did, even though the guy was movin'. Then nodded like he'd aimed there all along."

"Is that hard?"

"Hard? 'Bout as hard as pluggin' a quail on the fly with a pistol. Didn't anybody ever teach you to aim for the body?" He thumped himself on the chest. "Bigger target."

"No, I can't say anybody ever taught me that." Or anything else about guns beyond the fact of their existence.

"Remedy that first thing tomorrow, if you want."

"You most certainly will not!" Mrs. Bossidy had a grip on her purse like she was ready to swing for his head if he dared to try such a thing.

"Yeah, I suppose not." He sighed in deep regret.

"Spoilsport," Hiram mouthed at her.

Laura cleared her throat, trying to inject the proper note of casualness in her voice. "Did you find out who he is?"

"He wasn't the sort to volunteer a whole lot of information, if you know what I mean. And we were a tad busy."

"Oh."

"They're gonna be handing all the captives off to the authorities at the next station. S'pose he'll come back to pick these up, too."

"Do you think he'll get off with the prisoners?"

Mr. Hoxie shrugged; the fun was over and he wasn't much interested in what came next. "Don't know."

"You're awfully interested in that man," Mrs. Bossidy commented.

"Oh, no," Laura hedged. "I just . . . it would be only polite to thank him. Perhaps offer him a reward."

"I see."

"You always taught me one can never be too polite. Something you've demonstrated for me so wisely all these years."

Hiram choked.

"Did I? Perhaps I overemphasized the importance of that convention."

"Oh, no," Laura assured her. "I am certain that it would be unforgivably rude if we did not thank him properly for saving our lives."

"And what, exactly, would you consider the appropriate 'thank-you' for saving your life?"

"I—" There was obviously a wrong answer, Laura decided. Mrs. Bossidy watched her with all the suspicion of a headmistress who knew her girls were plotting escape. "My heartfelt appreciation?" she ventured.

Mrs. Bossidy shook her head. "Where you and that man are concerned, there will be no heartfelt *anything*."

Chapter 3

Once they left the station in Papillon, Laura had allowed Mrs. Bossidy to nudge her back to their private car. It was perfectly obvious *he* wasn't coming back, anyway, and at least in her own car she could stop constantly glancing at the door, drawing her companion's sharp attention.

Looking back on it now, she didn't know why she had been so certain he'd come back. She only knew she'd wanted him to. But it was not as if she was accustomed always to getting everything she wanted. Her parents had certainly tried, showering her with toys and dolls and pretty new dresses, but they hadn't been able to give her the two things she had really wanted: health, and freedom. Only time and patience had given her those.

Laura had from the first wanted to plan out as little of the trip as possible. She intended to follow her interests and instincts. The painting would be better for it. They had spent two days longer in Omaha than they'd

33

planned, allowing her to wait for one brilliantly sunny
day to capture the light on the Missouri River and the
broad, shimmering expanse of the mudflats north of
town. It took them the better part of a week to reach
Kearney; they'd pulled off at Columbus so Laura could
capture the meeting of the Platte and the Loup River,
and again at a small side spur line on the great, empty
stretch before Grand Island, an endless sweep of noth-
ingness like nothing she'd ever seen.

And so she'd considered chugging right through
Kearney. In those endless months that she'd waited for
the cars to be completed, Laura had pored over the
available photographs and paintings of the entire length
of the railway. Her concept for the panorama was to
record the changes that the railway had wrought in the
years since the Union Pacific and the Central Pacific had
met: new towns, reformed cities, civilization in the
wilderness, as well as to highlight the wild and magnificent scenery that was at last accessible to thousands
from the comfortable vantage point of a train.

In the photographs Kearney was raw, bustling, like
an adolescent boy who'd spurted up, awkward in its
own skin.

But Kearney was all grown-up now, crisp-edged and
decorous, the tumble of lopsided, hasty wood buildings
replaced by sturdy brick structures and whitewashed
frame houses. In the three days they'd been there Laura
worked her way along the street that paralleled the railroad, faithfully recording what she saw.

She chose a small park that day, pretty with clipped
green hedges and a white gazebo, filled with families
enjoying a warm Saturday afternoon, a full mix of ages
and sexes, another change from when the town had

been populated mostly by men—railroad workers and cowboys and those who owned the businesses that catered to them.

And she was working, for the moment at least, blessedly alone. Her three traveling companions had already gotten impatient with the tedium of watching her work, and so they were off to other activities today, Mrs. Bossidy, shopping, and the two men off somewhere that they wouldn't reveal. They'd all had to admit she was safe enough in a public square on a pleasant afternoon.

She had vastly underestimated the time that her preliminary studies would take, mostly because, having always worked undisturbed, she hadn't budgeted for the frequent interruptions of people who wandered by and stopped to chat.

She couldn't bring herself to mind. Even when her health had improved to the point that her parents allowed visitors, they were carefully selected and rigidly scheduled. She would not have been surprised to discover they'd been required to undergo a medical examination first. But it was such a joy to have people stop by merely to say hello, a motley, wonderful collection of young and old, fashionably dressed and intriguingly scruffy. She'd only vaguely known such a breadth of humanity existed, for in her ordered, privileged world even the servants were well kept and well dressed. To her starved eyes, variety was a heady, wonderful thing.

But this afternoon she'd had a stretch of uninterrupted time, and now she frowned over the resulting study. She'd roughed in the outlines of the square, the tall false fronts of the stores on the far side, the wedding-cake spear of the gazebo. The proportions were good. Not perfect, but good. She would have preferred perfect, but she would have had to spend another three weeks on the square alone to achieve that.

She sighed and pulled out her palette. The greens of the grass and the trees, a deep vibrant spill of impending summer, would be the most difficult to capture. She dabbed pure green on the page, then swirled in yellow, blue, a tiny bit of white.

More yellow, she judged. She picked up the tube and squirted, rewarded only by a tiny bubble.

Darn. If she didn't have enough paint with her, the light would be gone by the time she fetched some and returned to the square. Still squinting at the paper, trying to decide whether a smidge more blue would help, she groped for her canvas bag. She could have sworn she'd left it in reach, right there . . . there . . . she finally gave up and glanced to her right.

Her bag was a good three feet away, two scuffed black boots planted beside it. She looked up, and up, the full length of two very long legs. Past narrow hips encased in faded denim, a broad chest, truly impressive shoulders, and here she had to clamp her hand on her crown to stop the slippage of her straw bonnet.

My goodness. She'd conjured him up a dozen times since that day on the train. She'd battled the urge to stop scribbling the landscape outside her window and draw him instead, even though she knew that would be a terrible mistake and she could never do him justice.

But she discovered she hadn't been doing him justice, anyway, because he was ten times more arresting in person than he'd been in her memory.

He'd shaved. And yet she'd recognized him immediately, as if she'd known all along what he'd look like without the beard.

He wasn't skilled with a razor. A day's growth shadowed his very fine jaw, marred by a couple of nasty nicks from the blade.

"You're getting it all over your hands," he said.

"What?"

He pointed at her hand. "The paint."

"Oh. *Oh!*" Bright yellow smeared her fingers. She scrabbled for her bag, dug through brushes and pots in search of a cloth.

"Here." He handed her a thin, rumpled square of linen.

"I couldn't. It won't wash out, it's—"

"It's fine," he said. "I'll consider it my contribution to the art world. Lord knows it'll never happen any other way."

She shook out the handkerchief, hoping for a monogram, any hint at his identity. No luck. The yellow stained the white and smeared over her skin, and she finally gave up.

"It's only making it worse," she said with a laugh. "It's a losing battle, anyway." To prove it, she held up her hand. There was blue beneath her nails and a wide patch of red on her left thumb. "I'm sorry about your handkerchief. I could have it washed. If you want me to return it . . ." She trailed off, hoping he'd supply a name, an address.

"Keep it," Sam Duncan told her. He'd pondered how to approach her for days, what would be the best way to attach himself to her party. Try to get hired? Play the suitor and get himself invited along? Finally, he'd concluded he'd simply have to get to know her a bit to judge the right approach.

Laura let her hand drop to her lap, the cloth crumpled within, conscious all the time that he watched her with minute care. Did he suspect that she'd do just that? That she would hide it in a drawer, a keepsake like a young girl saving her first dance card? It seemed a terribly adolescent thing to do, embarrassingly so, but her illness had caused her to miss out on such things at the appropriate time.

She couldn't bring herself to discard the handkerchief. But she could hardly fold it up and tuck it safely away while he stood there, could she?

"You're healing." The bruise around his left eye had slid from purple to yellow-green. The scrape on his cheek was fading, and the shape of his mouth—what she'd been able to see beneath his beard when they'd first met—had changed, his lips thinner, as if they'd been slightly swollen before.

"Healing?" he asked. And then "oh!" He pressed two fingers beneath his damaged eye, remembering his wounds. They were minor compared to many he'd had, hardly worth thinking about. "It happens. Not as fast as it used to, though."

Laura couldn't imagine what had happened to cause him so much injury. He'd handled the dangerous situation on the train so competently. Surely it had taken more than a simple bar brawl. A riding accident, perhaps. Or maybe he was a prizefighter . . . he looked too lean for the ring, but he moved with such confidence and controlled strength.

She hoped he might volunteer the information but said nothing. It was too forward a thing to ask, but oh, she wanted to know.

A bird chattered in a nearby elm, making the silence all the more obvious when it flew off.

And here was another thing she'd missed at the appropriate time. She'd never learned how to make light conversation with a man. The rituals of flirtation were a mystery to her, imagined from novels, glimpsed through carriage windows.

"You were . . . I saw you on the train."

"I remember," Sam said, injecting some warmth in his voice, testing for her response.

She flushed, immediate and bright. Her skin, flawless, overly pale, hid nothing.

He'd expected her to be sophisticated, perhaps a bit jaded. She was the famous daughter of an even more famous father.

And yet she seemed flustered and uncertain, maybe a bit shy. Would she be that easily led? The thought was surprisingly bitter. He had no problem using others' weaknesses to further his own ends, and it was not as if she would be hurt by his simply attaching himself to her party until they reached the Silver Spur.

But it would have been easier to try and charm her if he thought she'd been a flirt who'd charmed a hundred men herself.

"Have you been standing there long?" she asked hesitantly.

"Maybe an hour."

"An hour." Oh, heavens. She knew she often got lost in her work; her mother used to say the house would tumble down around her while she was painting, and she would never notice. But she would have expected that somehow, *something* in her would have noticed his presence. For certainly she was aware of him now. Her skin tingled, her heart raced.

She tried frantically to recall if she'd done anything mortifying in the last hour. Scratched in unladylike places, perhaps. "That must have been terribly uninteresting." She waved her brush in the direction of her easel. "It is not an action-packed activity."

"I wasn't bored," he said, in that velvet-draped voice that was the only smooth, soft thing on a hard and rough-edged man.

The silence settled again, prickly and obvious. Laura tried to study her work but the colors and shapes only swam before her, a kaleidoscopic spin.

She sneaked a glance at him. He appeared utterly at ease with the silence. So many people were uncomfortable with it, rushing in to fill it with whatever sprang to tongue. She herself was digging for words, searching for a conversation that would sparkle and intrigue. And yet he also answered effortlessly, without any trace of the stultifying shyness that often afflicted those who preferred the silence. Finally, she asked, "Did you get everyone taken care of?"

"Everyone?" He wore his hat low, a deep line of shadow across his face. She wondered if his eyes changed in the sunshine, if the light drew any color at all out of the blackness of his irises. "Ah, our inept bandits. We put them off in Papillon. I assume the authorities knew what to do with them."

"You certainly did."

He shrugged it off. "They weren't all that good at it, if you want to know the truth. Your guards probably could have handled them just fine." Perhaps she was a flirt after all, Sam decided. The fluttering and blushes and shy, shimmering smiles had their own appeal. It was flattering to a man to think he could cause that reaction.

"My guards?" she asked.

"Weren't they? They looked like guards."

"I suppose they are, though I guess I don't think of them that way."

"And how do you think of them?" he asked.

"As part of my life," she admitted. For so many years she'd never ventured out. For months her world had been bounded by her bedroom, then the house, and, finally, for a very long time, the great iron fence that surrounded Sea Haven. But when she'd finally pushed and pleaded enough that her parents allowed her to ease her way out—just a few blocks at first, a brief carriage ride along the road and back, which had them both breathless with worry—either Mr. Hoxie or Mr. Peel or both had always been at her side.

"How did you know they were guards?" she asked.

"Makes sense that you would have guards." In Sam's opinion she should have had more. The ones she had were, well, not inept, exactly. More like complacent, as if they were accustomed to having the situation completely controlled. They treated her more like a sister than a job. It spoke well of her that they were so fond of her, but being overfond of your charge damaged your ability to make difficult decisions if they became necessary.

It would be a terrible shame if anything happened to Laura Hamilton. The thought caught him by surprise. It was no business of his, and if a man like Leland Hamilton could not protect his own, who could?

But she was . . . like sunshine. Open, happy, smiling. And the world held far too little warmth as it was. He liked the idea that it existed, even if he could never have it in his life again.

"Oh." A hint of disappointment discolored Laura's previous pleasure at his presence. What had she expected, really? That he had sought her out only because something about her appearance and manner intrigued him? "You know who I am," she said flatly.

"You don't exactly make a quiet entrance," he said.

"From the moment they hitched those cars up to the train it was buzzin'. For sure you were rich enough to need a couple of guards, at least."

"I suppose so." He'd stood there an hour, patiently waiting. Her father often spoke of spending his life ever-vigilant, constantly aware that the vast majority of the people he met desperately wanted something from him. He'd been very poor, then very rich, and claimed the fact that people were always hoping to separate you from some of your money was the only drawback to being rich. It was, he considered, a small price to pay.

But she'd been shielded from that all her life. He sorted through the few people she'd been allowed to meet, ensuring that anyone he introduced her to was either as rich as her father—and there were few enough of those, even in Newport—or hid their awe extraordinarily well in her presence.

Well, someday she would have to face the world without her father's shield. She had pleaded and cajoled and finally threatened to be allowed this trip, assuring her parents over and over that it was only about the work and completely necessary to it. But deep inside she'd been truly thrilled at the prospect of meeting the world without the filter of her position and her family's protection, for though her companions were meant to serve in her father's stead, no one could ever be as effective in that regard as Leland Hamilton.

She sighed deeply and turned to face him. She could have picked an easier man to practice on. Even her father, famed for his perception, might have had trouble reading this one. "What do you want?" she asked, narrowing her eyes, alert for signs that indicated the truth from the lies. Given enough practice, she should be good at this. As a painter she was accustomed to noting visual details: shadows, the slightest change in form, delicate gradations of color.

Interest flickered in his eyes, an avid heat. *Here it comes*, she thought, and steeled herself, wondering what the story would be. A dying daughter, an orphanage? Or perhaps it would be an irresistible investment; a mine to rival the Silver Spur, if only he could raise enough capital to start blasting.

He gestured toward her easel. "May I?"

"What?" She was certainly successful in her chosen profession, as such things went. And while she understood her talent's limitations, she'd never doubted its existence. But her preliminary studies weren't valuable enough to make it worth his trouble to ask for one.

"Do you mind if I look?"

"Oh." The sketch, with its imperfect outlines and blocky patches of colors, was extraordinarily rough. She wanted to say no; there was nothing there that would impress an untrained eye. But he waited so patiently, with that slight lift to his mouth, and she was curious to see what else he wanted. "Of course."

He moved around to stand behind her, studying the page over her shoulder. She leaned back to allow him a better view, and her shoulder brushed . . . oh, mustn't think about what she'd just bumped up against! She jerked forward, her cheeks so fiery hot that she was glad he was behind her, for she couldn't have faced him straight on. "I'm sorry!"

"Don't be."

Laura sat bolt upright on her chair, stiff as a statue, afraid that if she softened her posture even a fraction she'd brush against him again, for he hadn't moved a step. She'd no idea if he meant that the contact was so slight and insignificant that it wasn't worth thinking about, or if—oh, goodness!—he'd *enjoyed* it, and so she should not worry about it.

Clearly she'd left this—men in general, and specifically dealing with an attractive one—far too late in her life. Once the railroad project was out of the way perhaps she'd take some time to work on this skill. There was something not quite right about a woman of twenty-five having such a ridiculous and ungovernable reaction to the presence of a man, even such an overpowering specimen as this one.

So she took refuge in the one constant in her life, and turned her focus where it belonged: her work. It had been a steady presence as long as she could remember, company for a lonely young girl who had few playmates and was often too weak to keep up with them in any case, a soaring, unbounded outlet for hopes and dreams that were restricted in so many other ways.

"What do you think?" she asked.

He was silent behind her, which gave her time to collect her wits, and she dared a look over her shoulder. That must be what they meant by a poker face: hat low, eyes hooded, mouth set, any hint of emotion completely extinguished.

"Well?" she prodded.

It took a moment for Sam to collect himself enough actually to register what was on the paper. His head was swimming, caught up in that potent and completely unexpected jolt of heat from when she'd brushed up against him.

Well, this was a surprise. Not to mention a complication. It should have been too brief and innocent a touch to spark such a powerful reaction.

"Mister . . . ?"

He blinked. Her work, he reminded himself. And his. "Ah . . . it's very nice," he said neutrally, tiptoeing around the topic so as not to hurt her feelings.

Laura burst out laughing. "It's all right. I know it doesn't look like much yet. It's not supposed to."

"It's not?"

"No." She pointed with her brush. "The final product will look nothing like this. I need proportion, impressions, a sense of light and motion. Most of all color, because I can't ever get that from photographs."

"And when you're done, what'll it look like?"

"Do you know what I paint?"

He seemed to be pondering the question before he spoke. "Why don't you tell me?"

That wasn't really an answer but she was enjoying herself too much to worry about it. She felt much easier with him now, on familiar ground. Her work she knew. "I paint panoramas. Ten feet high, sometimes as much as three thousand feet long. Have you seen one?"

"A few."

She nodded. "I'm doing the Union-Pacific Railroad, fifteen years later. The full length of the railway, attempting to show how much it has changed the land it rolls through, the cities and lives it has touched." She smiled. "You need a grand subject. I can't come up with one much grander than this. Almost the entire country."

"How long will it take you?"

It was hard to believe that he was as interested as he appeared. But he gave no hint of boredom. His gaze didn't flit behind her, around the square, searching for something or someone of more interest; he remained fully focused on her as he stood unmoving, hipshot, arms loose at his side. The man was certainly not a fidgeter.

"The preliminary sketches? I'm not sure. I've not used this method before, and there's no particular schedule to keep. Perhaps four or five months. The painting, though, anywhere from a year to six. It depends. I've always been on the quick side, but this one . . ."

"That long? I'd never have the patience."

I'd never have the patience. She collected the words greedily. He'd been tossing questions her way, drawing her out, making her reveal herself, and he'd given her nothing in return. This was the first tidbit he'd revealed: he was not a patient man. And yet not *impatient*, she'd wager. He stood too still, too comfortable, without any of the simmering edginess of the truly impatient.

"You might be surprised," she said. "Some things are worth a large investment of time."

She thought that he was really going to smile this time. Amusement crinkled the corners of his eyes, tugged at his severe mouth, suddenly making him look years younger. Now what, she wondered, had she done to draw that reaction?

"Very true," he agreed. "Have you done one before? A panorama?"

"Oh, a few," she said airily. If he could be casually dismissive about his exploits on the train, she could pretend that she worked with effortless ease, too. "I did a collage of Revolutionary War battlefields." She frowned. "Not entirely successful, I'm afraid. It was my first, and I didn't have the stomach to play up the blood the way the public likes. The voyage of the Pilgrims. *That* was quite popular. The length of the island of Manhattan—"

"I saw that one."

Oh, wonderful, she thought. *That would have to be the one he saw.*

"In Kansas City. I remember it."

"That's nice," she said quickly, hoping he'd move on.

"It was lovely. Your work is very precisely detailed. Almost photographic."

"Not photographic enough," she muttered.

"Excuse me?"

She considered prevarication. She doubted *he* was ever less than perfectly competent at anything he attempted. But what was the point? The truth was the truth. And it was not as if it had not been splashed over every newspaper in the Northeast. "I made mistakes."

His brow furrowed in puzzlement. "It happens."

"No, you don't understand," she said. She believed in knowing your strengths and accepting your weaknesses. She'd had no choice. "You pegged it right off. That's what I'm known for, my precision and accuracy. But in the New York canvas, I made mistakes."

"What happened?"

She was glad he didn't shrug it off as if it were unimportant. Her parents had, and Mrs. Bossidy. What were a few mistakes? they'd asked her. Artists take license all the time. But she'd never considered it that way. She was bringing places to people who'd never have a chance to see them otherwise. And because she knew so well what it was like to long to witness a place you had little chance of seeing in person, she took that responsibility very seriously. "I hadn't been there since I was a child. Never been much of anywhere, when it comes right down to it, until now."

"Anywhere?" He lifted one brow in surprise. "How could you paint?"

"From photographs, from descriptions. Sometimes

I'd even send someone there to take detailed notes for me." She smiled. "There are some advantages to not having to worry about the expenses, you know."

"There are *lots* of advantages to it."

"True." Even now, her gut clenched at the memory. "It worked fairly well. But this time there were mistakes. A photograph I relied on had been printed backward, and I put St. Patrick's Cathedral—*just* finished—on the wrong side of Fifth Avenue. Not to mention the color of the Brooklyn Bridge was several shades off. I suppose I might have made similar mistakes before."

She scowled, hating the thought. For a month after she'd first learned of it, she'd considered pulling every panorama she'd ever done from tour, going out and comparing every inch of her painted landscapes to the actual ones and not releasing them again until she could ensure that they were absolutely accurate.

"People are not as familiar with those places, though. But this was New York, and the bridge and the cathedral are so new they are fresh in everyone's mind. The work had been on exhibition less than a week before I heard of the problems."

He listened patiently, his eyes level on hers. And suddenly she realized how she'd been blathering on with only the slightest encouragement from him. In all likelihood he was only being polite—whether it was a quality he held naturally, or because people were *always* polite to Hamiltons.

She dropped her gaze to the brush she still held in her lap. The yellow paint was drying on the sable, graphic evidence of just how long she'd been spilling her soul to the man. Was it some quality of his that drew it from her, his calm, patient encouragement, his well-timed comments? Or was she simply so unused to the attention of an attractive man that her mouth kept spilling out words in an attempt to keep him around?

More than attractive, she realized as she looked up again, no more able to resist studying him than she'd been able to forget a single word of the reviews about the New York panorama. She understood she had little to compare him with. The handsome men in her life tended to reside between the covers of art books. And yet she doubted that he'd have any less effect on her if she'd met every man on the eastern seaboard.

His face was not perfect. Far from it; there was a break in his right eyebrow where a half-inch scar bisected it. His nose had a definite bump and veered to the left. His hair was badly cut, longer on one side. And, of course, there was that fading bruise, the remnants of violence.

But absolute visual perfection was boring. One of the first things her painting instructor taught her was that the eye craved some tension. Beauty always showed to best advantage when contrasted with the ugly.

"I'm sorry," she said. "Going on about that. I know that, as problems go, placing a building, even a church, on the wrong side of the street in a painting is hardly life-shattering."

"You have pride in your work. I admire that."

Warmth bloomed, as if the sun had just stoked up the fire.

"How about you? I—"

"Oh, for heaven's sake!" Mrs. Bossidy clipped across the square, her skirts snapping with each determined stride, her voice carrying clearly on the spring breeze. "Did I not tell you to stay beneath the umbrella? You are unused to so much sun so early in the year, and it is much stronger here."

Laura jerked, then squared her shoulders. She had nothing to feel guilty about, she reminded herself. Not about getting perhaps a bit too much sun, which felt wonderful on her head, her shoulders. Nor about spending a few moments conversing with an interesting man, something Laura had no doubt Mrs. Bossidy would be addressing as soon as the "sun" issue was settled.

One wouldn't have thought Mrs. Bossidy could cover so much ground so quickly without breaking into a run. As soon as she gained Laura's side, arriving in a cloud of rosewater perfume and a rustle of stiff petticoats, she twisted the pole of the large umbrella out of the ground, moved it forward until its protective shadow covered Laura completely, and jammed it back into the pebbly earth. "You must promise to stay beneath it, dear, or I won't have you out here at midday again."

"It ruins the light," Laura complained.

Mrs. Bossidy fisted her hands at her hips. "Fine, then. See how well you hold a paintbrush when you've blistered the back of your hands." Her expression softened. "I'm not just protecting your pearly complexion, you know. You've spent so little time in the sun, Laura, it's more dangerous to you than most."

But it seemed like everything wonderful was more dangerous to her than most. Parties, travel. *Life*. She'd been healthy for a long time, something that Mrs. Bossidy and her parents and everyone else she knew often failed properly to consider.

She opened her mouth to respond. And then saw the fine lines of worry that furrowed Mrs. Bossidy's brow, the icing of silver that threaded her dark hair.

The days when her illness was the worst—the weeks,

the months, she admitted to herself—were mostly a blur to her, a murky drift of memories, spikes of pain softened by the numbing medicines they gave her, all blending into a feverish fog. Those who'd sat by her bedside had likely experienced it far more sharply than she had. And so that memory lived in their minds more fully than it did in hers, and therefore affected their actions more strongly, no matter how much she tried to convince them that those days were long behind her.

"I'll try and remember," she promised.

"Now, then." Mrs. Bossidy whirled to face a less immediate but more potent danger. "You are . . ." She bared her teeth, an approximation of a smile welcoming as a badger's snarl.

"Leaving," Sam said mildly, though inside he felt like doing anything but. *Damn.* Getting around the harridan-companion was going to be the trickiest part. He wondered if it was all men, or merely Sam, that she didn't like in range of Laura.

He had yet to discover what promised to be the most effective approach, though he'd been making excellent progress. He shouldn't be so annoyed at the interruption; usually he took minor setbacks in stride. And if he'd enjoyed the time with her, was it such a terrible thing?

No, it wasn't. It was only if he ever hoped for more than a pleasant but ultimately unimportant interlude that it became a terrible thing.

But her companion, who clearly had more of a guard's disposition than her official ones, was glowering at him as if she were ready to attack at any moment. He had time to wait and watch; at the rate she was working, they wouldn't be getting to the Silver Spur anytime soon.

He tipped his hat to Laura and sauntered off.

Laura watched her mysterious man walk away. He appeared in no hurry to get away, but she could detect no reluctance, either. He didn't have the long canvas coat today, and his clothing fit him well: old, much-washed, comfortable. He seemed easy in his skin, nothing stiff or awkward in his movements.

She figured she had more appreciation of a male form than most inexperienced women. She had studied art, both paint and sculpture. Her mother had objected briefly but she'd refused Laura so many things that she hadn't been able to deny her daughter this. And nothing she had studied, none of those famous works that depicted the perfection of man, had anything on this one. Except that they'd often worn far fewer clothes, a situation Laura couldn't help but regret.

"Ahem." Mrs. Bossidy placed herself squarely in front of Laura, blocking her view. Unashamedly, Laura lifted herself to tiptoes, craning her neck to see over her companion. Unfortunately, Mrs. Bossidy was taller, had no reluctance about raising to her own toes, and the view through the tufts of ostrich feathers on top of her hat was less than satisfying.

"Spoilsport."

"Leaving aside the appropriateness of ogling a man in a town square, Laura, you could certainly pick a better candidate than that one."

Laura gaped at her. "And who on earth would that be? I know my experience is limited, but my good-ness . . . are you telling me he's *typical*?"

Mrs. Bossidy struggled to maintain her sober nun's face, but her eyes danced. "All right, so maybe there are few of them that are as, um, interesting to watch walk across a square," she allowed, then frowned. "That does not make it appropriate. Nor advisable."

"Professional interest," Laura said. He'd finally disappeared around the corner of a building, and Laura
dropped back to flat feet with a disappointed sigh.

"Umm-hmm. And since you almost never paint figures in your landscape, and when you do they're small
and distant and purely for scale, as you've often told
me, does this signal a change in your career?"

"No," Laura said. Though if she'd ever been
tempted . . .

"He's not for the likes of you," Mrs. Bossidy said,
not without sympathy. "You know that your father—"

"I know." Oh, did she know. And even understood.

"What did he want?"

"I—" I don't know, she almost said. What had he
wanted? Surely not just to stand around on a pleasant
afternoon and listen to Laura babble. Yet that was exactly what he'd done. "He was interested." Mrs.
Bossidy's mouth soured. "In the *work*," Laura clarified
quickly.

"Hmm." She crossed her arms, encased in black
poplin edged with a wide white cuff, in front of her, as
if confronting a disobedient pupil. "Who is he?"

Drat, Laura thought. "I don't know." *But I certainly
hope I get the chance to find out.*

Chapter 4

Kearney was not a large city, as such things went. Thirty-four hundred and growing fast, the mayor had proudly told her, and sure to explode once the Kearney Canal was completed. He had gotten into the habit of stopping by to offer his assistance and, Laura surmised, to ensure that his town was painted in a flattering light.

But though it was not large, neither was it tiny. Yet Laura caught glimpses of her dark man with suspicious regularity.

He did not speak to her again even though, as Laura realized with wry amusement, she was making it easy for him to do so. She set up her easel on a daily basis in obvious and public places, so that anyone who made the slightest effort would have no difficulty finding her. Although he would have to fight through Mrs. Bossidy most of the time, for she stood guard with determination and a scowl that Laura doubted few men would be willing to brave. No more solo shopping trips for Mrs. Bossidy, at least for the time being.

But Laura saw him often. Once, through the plate window of a restaurant as she ate her creamed toast, she glimpsed him striding down the street on a cool, windy day, hatless, his great canvas coat billowing behind him like smoke clouds. He appeared in church, slipping into the last row as the organ strains of the first hymn faded away, catching her eye as she turned at the door's slam, with that quirk at the corner of his mouth that always made her wonder if he ever truly smiled. Riding by on a fiery red stallion as she worked in front of the courthouse, strolling in front of a saloon as she wheeled by in a rented carriage, arguing politics on the front porch with a storekeeper when she and Mrs. Bossidy arrived to purchase a new scarf.

Laura did not believe it could be coincidental. And the very unpredictability of his appearances kept her on edge, constantly anticipating the next time, the next place, never quite forgetting the possibility that he'd be around the next corner.

They should have left Kearney two days ago. Laura knew she was stalling. There was little else of interest to paint there, and she'd already done studies in more detail than the subjects required. At her present rate they would never finish the journey before the snows clogged the rails over the Sierras. And yet she couldn't bring herself to give the order to hitch up to the train due to steam through.

"That's enough." Mrs. Bossidy froze in midstep. More restless of late, she'd suggested an evening stroll. The sun hovered over the horizon, a coral haze spreading wide, the broad flat surface of the river awash in pink and gold.

"What is it?" Laura asked, still caught by the colors. How *would* she mix that hue? Some carmine, certainly, and—

Mrs. Bossidy snagged her by the elbow, halting Laura's forward motion. "Let's go back to the car."

"But it's so lovely out."

"Gnats." She flapped a hand in front of her face. "Most annoying."

Gnats? Laura hadn't felt a one. "You go ahead. The color's just so lovely. I wonder if perhaps I should have days roll by as the painting follows the rails to allow me to use different skies, dawn and dusk, stormy and clear. Perhaps even all the seasons. It would be a shame not to—" She turned to survey the wide sweep of the river, calculating potential scenes, and Mrs. Bossidy practically threw herself in the way. "What is the matter . . . oh."

He was far enough away that there should have been some doubt as to his identity. A dark spear of a figure standing alone on the bridge, the sunset behind him making it impossible to pick out any features—all she could truly see was a tall black outline in front of a brilliant wash of gold and red.

And yet she was certain. She knew the set and breadth of his shoulders, the way he stood with most of his weight on his left foot.

He lifted a hand, a salute that told her he'd been watching them, too. Was it mere politeness or did he recognize them from afar? It seemed impossible to her that he did not know her as easily as she did him. Impossible-seeming, but in reality perfectly likely— she understood her fancies were merely that. They were fun to indulge, had gotten her through many a lonely day, but were not to be relied upon. She was her mother's daughter in that she enjoyed the rush of heady emotions, but enough of her father's in that she would not be ruled by them.

She stretched high and waved back, by necessity a quick, broad motion because she knew Mrs. Bossidy would intervene. She did not disappoint, grabbing Laura's wrist and yanking it down with such speed that Laura couldn't help but smile.

"Mrs. Bossidy, you are ever predictable," Laura said.

She frowned. "If you would show a bit more decorum and restraint, I wouldn't have to be," she said as she steered Laura away from the river and back toward town.

"And how, exactly, is merely responding to a greeting—across a space of at least two hundred yards, I might add—unrestrained? I'm quite certain that, if I put my mind to it, I could be *far* more unrestrained than that."

Mrs. Bossidy scowled and marched steadily on, towing Laura in her wake like a miscreant child. As a matter of fact Mrs. Bossidy had dragged her home exactly the same way when Laura was twelve. It was the first time since she'd had the fever that she'd set foot outside the grounds of Sea Haven. She'd pleaded and begged for weeks to be allowed a bit of a trip, a walk down the rocky beach or a trip to the dry goods store. For a child who had once been very active being confined to her rooms but for a religiously monitored hour of fresh air in the garden once a day, and even that only recently granted, the confinement was torture.

It hadn't been easy. She'd awaited her chance with a patience she'd never before utilized until she'd slipped out the door while the household staff were in a flurry preparing for one of her mother's parties, this the first since Laura had fallen ill. And then the gate—she would have been foiled right there, except the guard had been distracted by an attractive kitchen maid who,

Laura was pretty sure, was supposed to be peeling rutabagas.

Mrs. Bossidy had caught her five minutes down the road. She hadn't listened to a single one of Laura's pleadings, and she hadn't been all that gentle while she hauled her home.

But she hadn't told Laura's parents, either, something which, Laura knew, would have garnered her two burly guards in the guise of "nurses" around the clock until she was, oh, ninety or so.

"I love you," she told her now, as Mrs. Bossidy hustled her into their car and flicked on the gaslights. "But you've gotten a lot more annoying over the past few years."

"I could say the same about you," Mrs. Bossidy returned without pause. "It's a normal part of a female's maturation, but it would have been better if it had happened when you were fourteen. I thought it fortunate that we'd skipped it at the time. Now it seems it was merely delayed."

Hands on her hips, she surveyed the beautifully finished car and sighed. "I wish you would have consented to move to the hotel."

"Why?" Laura untied the wide silk ribbons that secured her bonnet. "It seemed more trouble than it was worth to move. And Father went to such trouble to outfit this car."

"We're going to be heartily sick of it by the time we reach Sacramento." She shot an impatient glance over her shoulder. "And I thought the whole idea was for you to experience and see as many different things and places as possible."

"Oh? And that's why you shoved me away from the bridge as if it were dangerous?"

"It was."

"I hardly think it was likely to collapse at any second. Or perhaps it was who was *on* the bridge you found threatening?" She *tsked*. "I wouldn't have thought a mere man would scare you off."

"He didn't!" she protested, offended. "It can't be coincidental, how often the man keeps showing up."

"I didn't really believe that it was," Laura said, smiling despite her best efforts to hide it.

"Laura." Though it was quickly masked, Laura caught the flash of pity in Mrs. Bossidy's expression, and her smile faded.

"Are you trying to imply," Laura said, trying to make light, to prove it didn't matter, while an ache settled behind her breastbone, "that the man might have ulterior motives?"

"What man doesn't?" Mrs. Bossidy replied. "Laura, if you were just another girl—another girl *exactly* as you are, with your face and your smile and your sweetness—I am certain that many men would fall victim to your charms. But the bald truth is you are Laura Hamilton. And a man could no more ignore that fact and ensure that his heart was not influenced by it than he could miss noting if you had a blemish the size of a grapefruit on your nose."

"Point taken," Laura said, determined to ignore the remains of that stubborn ache. It was not as if that hadn't occurred to her before Mrs. Bossidy pointed it out. She had just enjoyed . . . overlooking it for a brief time.

"Laura—"

"I'm fine," Laura said, and found that it was true. "Fine."

Mrs. Bossidy shot a glance at the door—for at least the third time since they'd returned.

"Is something the matter?"

"I need to go shopping."

"Shopping? Now?" It had to be after nine o'clock.

"It's somewhat of an emergency." Her hands fluttered. "Female items. Things tend to get, um . . . erratic, after a certain age."

Hmm. If Mrs. Bossidy was on the far side of forty, Laura would eat her brushes.

"Nothing you need to worry about for a while—"

"I'll go with you."

"No!" She was going to leave Laura alone? Without being dragged away by a full-grown buffalo? "You stay here. Wouldn't want you to catch a chill." She grabbed her bag and dashed out the door.

Mrs. Bossidy was a reasonably good liar, Laura reflected as she pulled away the heavy drape of lush green velvet and peered out the window. The shadows in the train yard were too deep for her to follow Mrs. Bossidy's black-clad figure, but a few minutes later a light in the other car winked out.

She could do with putting a bit more effort into believably planning the lines she delivered with such aplomb, though. For while there was not a store in existence that had ever been closed to Laura Hamilton, she was not unaware that they typically kept particular business hours. Business hours which likely ended sometime ago.

Female problem, my easel, Laura thought, and let three minutes pass before she slipped out the door.

She found Mrs. Bossidy quickly enough, waiting—and not patiently—on the other side of the tidy brick station. She should have chosen to do her nefarious business farther from the train to ensure that there was no chance of any sounds alerting Laura. But Mrs. Bossidy was not the sort to go wandering around in the dark by herself.

There was little light. Only a soft sheen of moonlight that glanced off the tracks and was swallowed up in shadows and the faint, brassy wash of light from the saloon across the street that didn't quite make it all the way there.

Mrs. Bossidy didn't wait well. She paced, quick, impatient steps that grew more agitated with each passing second. She didn't wait quietly, either, punctuating the night with words that would have made Mr. Hoxie proud.

But it didn't really take that long. Laura hadn't expected it to be that easy for them. He'd handled himself on the train so well. She knew her father hired only the best, that Mr. Hoxie and Mr. Peel guarded her because he considered them fully qualified for the job. But still . . . it surprised her when three figures crossed the street no more than perhaps ten minutes after she'd first leaned against the cool, rough brick wall. One short, powerfully compact, another tall and broad. And one between them, just as tall as Hiram but leaner, his steps graceful beside Peel's lumbering tread.

"What took you so long?" Mrs. Bossidy met them at the edge of the street, drawing all four of them into a thin, cool slice of moonlight.

Laura swallowed a gasp. They had a gun to his head—no, two, one apiece, lethal glints of metal.

Not a flicker of emotion showed on his face: not fear, not anger, not even impatience at being dragged away from wherever they'd found him. Not even sur-

prise or curiosity, as if being accosted by armed gun-
men was as routine a part of his day as being offered a
cup of coffee.

He certainly wasn't protesting. He moved along
with that predator glide as if the guns to his head had
nothing to do with it, as if he was going exactly where
he wanted.

Mrs. Bossidy met him toe-to-toe. Given the same
situation, Laura didn't think she'd have that much faith
in the guards and their guns. He just looked too much at
ease. And it couldn't have just been that the bandits
were that inept, could it? Hiram had had enough trouble with them.

"What do you want with Miss Hamilton?" Mrs.
Bossidy's voice was clear and sharp, and Laura was
pretty sure she didn't want to hear the answer, whatever
it was.

Years of sneaking around her house served her well.
She slipped up behind Mrs. Bossidy without any of
them noticing.

"If you wanted to talk to him," she said over Mrs.
Bossidy's shoulder, "you should have told me. I venture he would have come along without nearly so much
trouble if I'd asked him."

His hands flashed out—a quick spike of movement
like a cobra strike, without his gaze wavering in either
direction. Moonlight flickered over the metal of the
guns, then he had them, one in each hand, pointing at
his captors instead of himself, in less time than it took
for Laura to suck in a breath.

"Christ!" Peel swore. Mr. Hoxie stood frozen, eyes
crossing as he tried to focus them on the barrel an inch
from his nose.

"Now then," he said, settling his gaze on Laura. He

didn't seem the least bit worried about the two men, not even glancing their way. But Laura suspected if one so much as twitched, he'd have them down just as efficiently as he'd stripped their guns from them. For obviously they'd brought him here so easily because he'd *chosen* to go along with them; he could have stolen their guns anytime he wanted.

"What do I want from Miss Hamilton?" he mused. Laura's heart stuttered into uneven rhythm. She didn't even know what she hoped he'd say.

Nothing? Everything?

"I want to do my job," he said. "Her father hired me to keep her safe."

Chapter 5

"What?" The word burst from her, an echo of the hurt that erupted in her chest. She wasn't sure what spurred it the most: the fact that her father, who she'd believed had finally, *finally*, trusted her enough to allow her this small venture into freedom clearly didn't trust her; or that her lovely stranger was, after all, arranging himself into her life only because he'd been paid to do so.

The first *should* be no shock. She'd even wondered at the time, hadn't she, about whether when it came right down to it her parents would be able to let her go. She'd even joked about searching the train car to see where he'd hidden his spies.

And the second . . . well, Mrs. Bossidy had warned her. Heavens, Laura had even warned herself. And so the pain was not so much true hurt as it was a wistful regret, she told herself now. Hurt required things such as trust and intimate knowledge. The capacity for betrayal necessitated that there be a relationship *to* betray. What she mourned right now was not so much *him* but the loss of a fantasy she'd nurtured even as she understood it was unlikely: that someday, in some way, she would find a man who could look at her without immediately thinking: Laura Hamilton, the Baron's daughter.

Foolish girl.

He studied her closely. Predatory eyes, cool and dark. He did not miss a detail, this one, his focus intense as a hunting cat on its prey. Except she was not his prey.

She was merely his assignment.

"I said that—"

"I know," she interrupted, wincing at her rudeness but unwilling to listen to him say it again, laid out bare. She forced a laugh; she could not allow this to be important. "It just took me a moment for my brain to catch up with my ears."

She stepped around Mrs. Bossidy. It brought her close to him, far too near for either propriety or wisdom, until the warm, dark scent of him entwined with the smell of the night, her nose level with his chest. She tilted her chin up, made her smile go cool and reserved. She had never been able to pull off haughty for any length of time, but it was an effective weapon in her mother's arsenal, wielded when her warmth and charm had been perhaps too effective. But in this case Laura far preferred being thought the spoiled rich girl than one wounded by her own ridiculous yearnings. It was not as if he'd courted her. He'd merely . . . been there, and her own imagination supplied the rest.

"For heaven's sake, Laura, he's got their guns, you've no idea if he's telling the truth. Get out of here until I can investigate the matter." Dimly, she heard Mrs. Bossidy speak behind her, felt her tug at her waist in an attempt to pull her away. But they were minor inconveniences, only barely registered, as if his nearness overwhelmed all else.

"I'm not going anywhere," Laura said. "Not until I've had the opportunity to get to know my new . . . bodyguard."

The last word came out with heavy emphasis, a seductress's purr of innuendo she'd never used, surprising herself. His teeth flashed, a quick smile that vanished a second later but left an impression just the same, so strong she momentarily forgot everything but that fleeting power. *My, my,* she thought. *It really is a good thing he rarely does that. It's too potent a weapon to be unleashed on the world on a regular basis.*

He flicked his wrists, spinning the guns in his hands so they were butt forward. They hung there in the air until he glanced briefly at his would-be captors. "Well? Don't you want your guns back?"

Hiram grunted, Mr. Hoxie yelped, scrambling to grab their weapons with such belated haste that Laura worried they'd go off in the process.

Once they'd retrieved them, Peel and Hoxie held their weapons awkwardly, as if they weren't quite sure what to do with them. Did they aim them back on him? Holster them?

He addressed Mrs. Bossidy. "Feel better now?"

"Not particularly, no." She was still behind Laura, her hands at Laura's waist as if she was prepared to throw her to the ground and cover the girl's body with hers at the slightest need. "Who *are* you?"

Laura sucked in a quick breath. She'd wondered a hundred times since she'd first seen him. And yet there was a part of her that didn't want to know. The more she learned of him, the more real he became, the less the fantasy man that she could build into anything and anyone she wanted.

"Sam Duncan."

Erastus Hoxie gasped, his arm slumping to his side. Afraid the gun would drop to the ground, Laura bent and rescued it. Then, realizing what she held, she turned and thrust it into Mrs. Bossidy's hand.

"Good move," Duncan said.

She refused to be flattered by his approval. Her father was paying him; she must not forget that.

"Are you really Sam Duncan?" Mr. Hoxie asked, as much awe written on his face as though President Garfield had just popped up in front of him.

"You want a demonstration?"

"I'd say we just had one," Hiram said, frowning, as he checked the loading of his pistol before holstering it.

"What am I missing here?" Laura asked. "Who *are* you?"

"I just told you—"

She impatiently waved off the rest of his answer. "Yes, yes, Sam Duncan. *What* are you, then. Why is Mr. Hoxie still standing there with his mouth open, looking as if he might start curtsying at any moment?"

"He's almost as famous as you, Miss Hamilton," Mr. Hoxie informed her.

"I don't know as I'd go that far," he said.

"Don't be so modest," Erastus told him. "Miss Hamilton, Duncan here's the most famous gun in the West! I read about him in *Frank Leslie's Illustrated Newspaper*. They say all he has to do is show up in town and all the penny-ante crooks go scurrying like cockroaches in the light. They say grown men, hard-hearted and battle-hardened, weep when they discover he's signed on for the other side."

Mr. Duncan rolled his eyes. That he could laugh at such nonsense rather than be puffed up by it was one point in his favor.

Unfortunately, it was a very minor point. He sold his gun, his honor, to the highest bidder. She'd heard of such men. Their scruples were nonexistent, their allegiance bought and paid for, as fickle as a whore, always drawn to the heaviest purse. If he were the most famous of his kind, then he was, by logic, the most villainous, for surely one did not achieve such a reputation by kindness and adherence to high principles.

He had lied to her by omission. He had flirted with her to gain access to do his job. No man spent as much time warmly listening to a woman's chatter as he had in the square without there being at least a bit of flirting in it.

"You could have told me the truth from the first," she said.

"Could I?" he replied, his voice low, pitched as if he made an intimate declaration. But there was no emotion in his eyes. "I learned long ago to hold my cards close, Miss Hamilton. I suppose I *could* have, but I didn't *have* to."

Well, that should be a good warning to her, shouldn't it? Never to assume he'd reveal anything of himself that he wasn't absolutely forced to?

Not that there'd ever be the opportunity to need to remember that.

She stepped yet closer, forcing herself to look steadily up into his face. Her palms were damp. Her heart thudded. Grown men might quail before him, but Baron Hamilton's daughter did not.

"I have no need of your services," she said.

"Your father doesn't agree." He smiled at her then, a

smile filled with charm but devoid of any real warmth, calculated to lure her into compliance.

"A hired gun, are you?"

"Sometimes a man must undertake whatever employment is offered," he said mildly.

"Interesting. A man sells himself out to the highest bidder and they laud his deeds in newspapers and novels. A woman does the same, and the name for her is very different."

His smile vanished. Good. It looked patently false on him anyway. If he ever smiled at her again she wanted it to be genuine.

Not that she ever wanted him to smile at her.

"Some of us, Miss Hamilton, have not had the luxury of parents who are able to indulge us. Sometimes necessity does not allow us to be so . . . whimsical in our choices."

"Whimsical?" He thought her spoiled? "You know *nothing* of me. You assume much."

"You mean that I drew conclusions of what and who you are by what was written and said rather than what I've witnessed by my own experience?"

Her retort died before it made it out of her mouth. "Point taken."

Mrs. Bossidy recovered her wits. "We don't even know for certain if your father did hire him, Laura. Let me cable before we leave Kearney."

"No kidding, Miss Hamilton," Hiram added. "It's not like me and Hoxie need the help, y'know. Another fellow in the way'd probably just muck things up."

"Apparently you do," the man said. "Or you wouldn't have lost your guns. *You* should hire me if he hadn't already." He shrugged. "Go right ahead and cable. If you don't mind bothering Mr. Hamilton with such things, that is. For obviously if I'd had wicked designs on Miss Hamilton, or anything of hers, I could have carried them out already, anytime I wanted."

Hiram didn't like that. But he couldn't honestly deny the truth of it.

"Oh, why bother?" Laura asked. "It's just like him, isn't it? To hire protection and a spy in one? He didn't want me to make this trip in the first place and insisted I do it on his terms. Not to mention that if Leland Hamilton is going to hire another bodyguard, would he employ any but the most famous and most expensive?" She slanted a cool glance at Duncan. "I assume you are expensive."

"Extremely."

"Well, since you can obviously be bought . . . how much would it cost to have you to stay behind when we pull out?"

"I'm afraid I can't do that. That reputation you continue to ramble on about rests squarely on the fact that once I accept a job I always see it through to a satisfactory conclusion."

"No one would have to know. We're not telling. You've not been traveling with us this far, so no one knows. I will tell my father you protected me with the utmost efficiency. Your reputation can remain intact."

"No. Despite what you might think, I do take my word seriously."

He was as stubborn as her father. She'd learned the futility of arguing with him years ago.

"We're leaving in the morning," she told him. "Be ready," she said, spinning to march away.

"Giving orders already?" he called after her. "Aren't you going to welcome me to the party?"

* * *

"He's an odd one, that," Mrs. Bossidy murmured, glancing out the velvet-draped window in the door at the back of their train car. They were alone—Mrs. Bossidy, bent over the knitting she'd taken up three days ago in bored desperation, Laura sorting through her sketches—as the train clicked through western Nebraska. Though they had, very briefly, dipped into Colorado at Julesburg.

They were two hundred miles, but eight long days, out of Kearney, for they'd unhitched twice to allow Laura to work.

It was in some ways hard to tell that Mr. Duncan had joined their small party. He preferred to take his meals alone and outside. He seemed to enjoy the food, packing away in brief periods of time an amount that rivaled Hiram's massive meals. He also declined to sleep in the car when they were stopped, instead choosing to lay out his bedroll beneath the skies. Mr. Hoxie, whose hero worship hadn't dissipated a whit, attributed that lamentable state of affairs to the volume of Hiram's snoring, an explanation that could be true. If the windows were open, Laura sometimes heard his rumbling from the next car.

If they traveled through the night, Laura was uncertain if Sam Duncan slept at all. Invariably when they were under way, day or night, he stood on the back platform of her car. His gaze constantly swept the land they rolled through, turning to locate her every few seconds, as if he expected an attack at any moment. It was ridiculous, of course. What could happen to them out here? But her father certainly seemed to be getting his money's worth.

One would think she'd have been able to ignore his presence completely. She was accustomed to having servants, guards, and nurses around her. He hadn't said more than half a dozen words to her, a reticence she *should* have appreciated. And yet . . . she was so vibrantly aware of his presence that often she was conscious of nothing else. He was always *there*, patient, intent, as if she were the most important thing in the world to him, so crucial that he could not bear to look away. It didn't seem to matter how many times she reminded herself that it was his job. Her heart refused to accept it. She even found it difficult to lose herself in her work, something she had always done with such ease that her mother despaired that she would ever find the real world as interesting as the one she created.

She tried to concentrate. On the color, the light, the slope and proportion of the land. But the knowledge that he was *there* hovered, tantalizing, so omnipresent it should have been suffocating, as she'd always yearned for privacy and freedom above all.

But she was terribly afraid that she was growing so accustomed to the situation that it would feel strange when he was gone. There was a certain comfort in knowing that, whenever she chose to look up, she would find him. Though it was far from comfortable.

She glanced his way now. Braced into the wind, the sky behind him so dark it appeared to be early evening instead of afternoon, his sharp, dark visage blurred by the light spatter of raindrops on the windows. She reached up to touch the glass of the nearest window and found it cool, unseasonably so. He had to be chilled but it seemed to bother him not a whit. Hatless, his collar open, a brisk flush of color across the dusky slash of his cheekbones. The moisture had brought a bit of wave to his hair, the wind blowing it back from his face. Automatically she reached for her sketchbook, brushing a couple of quick lines across the page before she realized what she was doing and set it aside.

"An odd one?" she echoed. "Is that what he is?"

"Standing out there in this weather. In any and *all* weather. Why?"

"Spent some time pondering this, have you?" Laura asked.

"Don't be ridiculous." The steel of Mrs. Bossidy's needles jabbed in and out of a snarl of bright scarlet yarn. The project was completely unidentifiable, but Laura had asked what she was making—*once*—and had no intention of making that mistake again. Laura knew perfectly well Mrs. Bossidy's only interest in Mr. Duncan was suspicion, but she bristled so easily at the suggestion Laura couldn't resist. "Someone has to keep an eye on the man, considering how closely he keeps one on you."

"Umm-hmm." The rain spurted against the glass and plastered his dark shirt against his chest. "What's ridiculous is that he's standing out there in this weather."

Mrs. Bossidy frowned over the wool, then bared her teeth as she tugged on a strand, ripping out the row of uneven stitches she'd just laboriously completed. "Maybe he'll catch pleurisy and save us all a lot of trouble."

Abruptly Laura set aside her papers and stood. "I'm going to invite him in."

"Come now, Laura. He's a big boy. I'm sure he knows how to come in out of the rain if he wants to."

"My father probably offered him a bonus if he remained on duty twenty-four hours a day." She headed for the door.

"Laura . . ."

"I'll not have him take ill on my account, regardless of what my father promised him. We're miles from anywhere, *every*where, and no one's lying in wait to kidnap me. You know that as well as I do. There's simply no place to hide out there. We'd see any attackers coming from ten miles away. It's not going to hurt for him to come inside and warm up."

Mrs. Bossidy frowned, setting aside her knitting. "I'll do it."

"Stay. I know how you feel about cool weather, and I could use a bit of fresh air." She sprinted down the aisle before Mrs. Bossidy could start warning her about the risks ahead, spouting about chilly air and locomotive smoke and dangerous men.

Rain stung her face the instant she opened the door. He turned to face her immediately, then shifted so that his breadth shielded her from the worst of the wind. The movement was subtle enough that she was unsure if it was by design.

He said nothing. Not unusual, she supposed; a wise employee always waited for his boss to speak first. But her tongue got tangled up in staring at him. She wondered if it was shallow of her to be so taken with his looks. Surely she was wise enough to see beyond the surface to take the true measure of a person. But the artist in her couldn't help but be intrigued. His face challenged her, the ever-shifting shadows in his eyes as the light changed, the hard angles that seemed to reveal the secrets and hardships of his life if one but knew how to decipher them.

"You should come inside," she said at last. "The weather's turned, and there are darker clouds ahead. It's likely to get worse."

He glanced at the sky. "I'm fine." So she'd finally decided to talk to him, Sam thought. He hadn't expected her to hold out as long as she had. The lively curiosity that shone in her face whenever she saw anyone or anything new had to get the better of her sooner or later. He hadn't been traveling with them but a few hours before that became obvious. "I'm used to the weather. This is nothing compared to the high desert on a winter night. You're going to get chilled, though."

"I like it." To prove it, she dropped the arms she'd hugged to herself. "Crisp. Invigorating."

"It is that." She'd start shivering in a moment, he'd wager. Fresh color sprang into her cheeks. The fine, thin silk of her shirtwaist, the color of pearls, nearly as pale as her skin, couldn't be much armor against the weather. The fabric was damp already, clinging lightly to the angle of her collarbone, the gentle curve of her upper breasts.

He shouldn't be thinking of such things. Beyond the fact that she was merely a means to an end, and that using her any more than he'd already planned to would be unconscionable, it was clear that she'd been sheltered and protected for her entire life. She was years younger in experience than she was in truth—and she had to be enough younger than he it should give him pause as it was.

But his thoughts were not that governable. He'd spent the better part of two weeks looking at her—if he was supposed to appear to be guarding her, he'd decided, he'd better put up a good show of it. And one could not look at her so much without gaining a certain . . . appreciation.

She was not conventionally pretty at first glance. Too pale, too thin, bland brown hair, and light blue eyes, nothing that caught one's attention and held it, and those beautiful, clever clothes she wore drew the eye away from her.

But she wasn't what he expected. How could the daughter of such privilege be so innately kind? She was thoughtful of her guards, her companion; she rarely asked them for anything, much less issued the orders he knew they'd have followed without question. She wore her luxurious clothes without a hint of preening, as if she had no pride in them, and they meant no more to her than one of his old flannel shirts did to him. He had yet to decide if that was a good or bad quality, proof that she was irretrievably spoiled and so did not appreciate them or whether it confirmed that the trappings of wealth were meaningless to her.

But it was hard to consider her spoiled when she took such delight in every new sight and everyone she met. It made no difference whether it was a grand sweep of landscape or a shack on the verge of tumbling down, whether the person was a mayor dressed in a high hat greeting her on a bunting-bedecked depot or a weathered, cantankerous old farmer who'd complained mightily about her arrival holding up his lunch. They all fascinated her, a lively interest that couldn't be feigned.

And that was when plain transformed into something else entirely. The warm brightness of her smile, turned indiscriminately and powerfully on everyone she met, and the vibrant light in her eyes were far more affecting than mere prettiness. He wondered if he'd ever again be quite so taken by beauty.

Like now. She wasn't smiling—hadn't quite forgiven him enough for that—but she gazed at him with fierce concentration, a pucker to her mouth as if she was pondering something vital. And it made him feel important, in the way the son of an Ohio farmer who'd never done anything but survived shouldn't feel.

"So . . . you're talking to me again?"

She shrugged. "The other options are limited. I've known the three of them almost my entire lives, and I've heard all their stories a dozen times, as they have mine. Once we reach another town I'm sure I won't be driven to such desperate measures."

She had a bit of the devil in her, this one, that peeked out at unexpected moments. Not often, just enough to keep Sam anticipating it. She hadn't had much opportunity to let that devil out, he decided, but if she ever had the chance to loose it . . . "So I shouldn't be flattered."

"You can be flattered if you want to. I don't mind." The train rolled into a wide curve, shifting the platform beneath their feet, giving the wind an opening that it tore through with vicious enthusiasm. She shivered.

"You're getting cold. You should go inside."

She shook her head. "I'm fine."

"You won't be for long if you stay out here."

But she didn't move. He could appreciate a stubborn streak. He had a wide one of those himself. More than anything else it was probably what had kept him alive when so many others died.

But he couldn't stand to watch her shiver, her delicate shoulders looking so fragile they might snap with the next quake.

He ripped off his old cotton coat and slung it around her shoulders. She startled as he did so, jerking away, her uncertain gaze flying up to meet his. His hands hovered at her collarbone, tucking the edges of his coat up beneath her chin. It swallowed her up, shoulders flopping halfway to her elbows, the hem nearly meeting the floor. "Your father hired me to protect you from kidnappers and thieves and reporters and other such undesirables," he said. "But if you die of lung fever, I'm thinking I won't be getting my bonus, either."

"Oh." Her shoulders drifted down, a relaxation of her stiff posture that seemed strained rather than natural, as if she'd forced herself to soften rather than truly being at ease. "I didn't mean to jump. You surprised me, that's all."

"I'll try to give you more warning next time." His hands should be back at his sides. Yet they remained, in that pocket of warmth beneath her chin. He could move them up, down, sideways—any direction but away— and there'd be something worth exploring.

And Mrs. Bossidy will fly through that door and shove me right off the back of the train, he thought wryly.

He pulled his hands back. But his fingers brushed skin on the way—neck, the underside of her chin— delicately warm, far more arousing than such a brief touch should have been.

"Mr. Duncan—"

"Sam."

"I—" She darted a glance back at the train car, where the dragon nun who masqueraded as her companion had left them alone far longer than he would have expected. "I couldn't. It wouldn't be polite."

"We're not nearly so formal in the West, Miss Hamilton. Certainly not when addressing our servants."

"Servant? Is that what you are?"

"I'm getting paid to perform a service, so I suppose I am. This week, at least."

"Does that mean I can give you orders?" In another woman, he would have been suspicious of that gleam in her eye. But from Laura . . . surely the orders she was plotting to issue weren't that wicked.

How disappointing.

She took his silence as assent. "Good. Then I order you to go inside and get out of this weather."

"You didn't employ me."

She tilted her head, as if scheming to come at the problem another way. "Please?"

He glanced at the doorway. He could go in for just a little while, maybe. To make her happy and deflect suspicion. He could handle going in there briefly. He could leave at any time.

Immediately his chest tightened, as if a grizzly had plopped down on top of him. Darkness bled into his vision.

He swallowed hard and shook his head.

"If you're uncomfortable coming into the women's car alone, at least go into the other car with Hiram and Mr. Hoxie."

"I'm not uncomfortable." That was a lie, of course, but it had nothing to do with Laura or Mrs. Bossidy. "I just need to keep an eye on things. Those cars are so well padded an entire war party could arrive before we ever heard it coming."

"War parties?" she asked skeptically. "I thought that hasn't happened in years. I was under the impression that the army clamped down rather thoroughly after Little Bighorn."

"It was just an example," he said. "Surprised you knew about that."

"When one is confined completely to one's rooms for two years, and nearly so for a decade beyond that, one can go through quite a lot of books and newspapers." Though the newspapers had been harder to come by, Laura remembered. Her mother had worried that the headlines would disturb Laura's delicate emotions, as she'd put it at the time. Laura had taken to wheedling them from a footman who'd a weakness for the chocolates her father brought her back from New York. When your access to the world was limited, you had to take it wherever and however you could get it.

She saw the surprise on his face—so rare, to shock

any emotion out of him, or at least any evidence of it. But she'd rather learn something of him than have to explain her illness.

Come to think of it, she'd never had to *explain* it before, for everyone in her life had always known of it, whether because they'd lived through every painful moment with her or because they'd heard it whispered in the circles her parents moved in.

"Why didn't you tell me?" she asked.

Anxiety pitched in his chest. "Tell you what?" he asked carefully.

"That my father hired you." The mist gave a sheen to her skin. "Back in Kearney. You could have told me. You didn't have to . . . pretend."

"Pretend? Pretend what?" It would be better, so much better, to distract her with another subject and leave this risky topic completely alone. But he hadn't expected her to ask outright. She seemed so much more the type tactfully to avoid any subject that might matter. "Pretend to be interested?"

"I didn't say *interested*." Beneath the fresh, damp glow, color rose into her cheeks. She wore it well. "Friendly, perhaps."

"I wasn't pretending."

That caught her attention. Her lashes flew up. Blue eyes. Pale, unremarkable blue, but the color was so light and clear that you could see right into her soul, if only she would allow it. "Your work, I mean. Listening to you talk about it. I've never known an artist before." If she could be straightforward, so could he. "Is that why you were so angry with me? Because you thought I'd pretended an interest that didn't exist?"

"Don't be silly. You give yourself too much credit. No, I was angry because I believed that my father had finally, *finally,* decided to trust me with some slight independence. I was not pleased to discover I was wrong." Her gaze narrowed. "Did he tell you not to reveal yourself?"

"No." Now why didn't he just say "yes"? It would have been easier.

Because he didn't want to lie to her any more than he had to. And wasn't that stupid? He'd never before been much constrained by inconvenient scruples. "I've just always found it helpful to get the lay of the land before I admitted my intentions."

"Oh." She huddled deeper into his coat, the collar gathering up around her ears where the pale curve was tipped with red.

"That's it." He reached out and spun her around until she faced the door. "You're shivering. Time to go in."

"I doubt I'm required to take orders from *you,*" Laura said. His hands were heavy on her shoulders, warm even through the fabric, which itself held a potent warmth. *His* warmth; she'd felt it the instant he'd draped it around her, penetrating deep, so much so she'd momentarily lost the train of the conversation.

"You do when you've lost every shred of common sense." He opened the door and shoved her through, closing it behind her before she had time to protest again.

Mrs. Bossidy was standing right inside, bent over as if she'd been peering through the window. "Are you spying on me?"

"I'd prefer to think of it as *protecting* you," she said. "What did he say to you?"

"Let's just say we've come to an agreement."

Chapter 6

Everyone but Sam protested Laura's plan to unhitch twenty miles west of Sidney, Nebraska. She'd been told of a small side yard there, an abandoned station for a town that had never taken firm root. It sprouted quickly during the years the railroad was being built, housing workers and supply stations, but the new town had no industry to support it once the nearby section of the track was finished. Most of the buildings had been ripped down when the crews moved on—lumber was too valuable to be left behind—but the side track remained, and the tumbled piles of fallen sod houses. Shallow, indented rectangles, long ago overgrown with grass, were all that was left of the other buildings that once stood there.

The weather turned the day after Laura tried to order Sam in out of the rain. The temperature shot up, the earth steaming like a wash kettle. It made sleeping out under the stars like Sam did appear to be the smart choice, although when Laura suggested it, Mrs. Bossidy threatened to haul her back to Sea Haven unless she stayed safely and modestly inside.

Clearly the trip was already lean on entertainment options for the rest of the party. They were Easterners, after all, bred in the city and residing in a glamorous resort town. The wide-open spaces held their interest for about a day. So the last place they wanted to stop was this abandoned wayside in the middle of the plains. No comforts, no distractions, it promised few amusements except twiddling of their thumbs. But Laura considered it important to record this as well, the dead, fading impression of a town left in the wake when the railroad moved on.

As for Mr. Duncan . . . Sam, she reminded herself; even Mrs. Bossidy called him that now, though Laura couldn't guess how he'd talked her into that. He alone made no complaints. In fact he seldom spoke to her at all, or anyone else as far as she could tell, but he watched over her with an intense patience that left her disconcerted and overly attuned to his presence.

She took one of the horses, riding out toward a tower of rock that speared out of the prairie a few hundred yards north of the town. With no interest in sitting around and watching her sketch, everyone but Sam had chosen to remain behind, taking advantage of the slight shade cast by the blue-striped awning they'd unrolled from the side of her car, one of her father's special features. Mrs. Bossidy frowned over another snarl of wool that she claimed to be a sweater, the two men settling into yet another game of extremely low-stakes poker, which was the only kind Mrs. Bossidy allowed.

That left Sam to go with Laura. He rode a few feet ahead of her, controlling his horse with expert ease. She was surprised that the others allowed him to escort her alone, but the warm day and slow, mind-numbing repetition of her work had apparently been enough to make them risk it, though Mrs. Bossidy and Hiram had both taken him aside, out of her earshot, and harangued him for a good ten minutes apiece. He'd listened attentively but made no comment.

She sneaked a glance at him now. He wore a thin cotton shirt, a pale silvery gray that was as close as she'd ever seen him wear to a color, his dark, wide-brimmed hat casting full shadow over his face. His eyes were never still; they swept the landscape with a quick, expressionless flick in her direction every minute or so before returning to their alert scan of the surrounding area. The intense watchfulness that never seemed to waver was his most prominent feature. Did he never get tired, never get bored?

"You didn't have to accompany me today," she told him.

"Yes I did." He slowed his horse, dropping politely back into step beside her. He was ever circumspect, attentive to her wishes. An excellent employee. Her father would be pleased. Except it irritated her to the extreme—she did not want proper acquiescence from him. "There are always dangers, even in what appear to be the most benign circumstances."

"I hadn't planned to go beyond earshot."

"Until you found out I was along to do all the heavy lifting, you mean?"

"Of course," she admitted, smiling.

"So that's why Bossidy's not on our tail," he said. "I wondered. Usually if I'm within ten feet of you, she's within eight."

Heat rose. He'd said it so easily, a comment as simple as noting the weather. But to her it held more, an acknowledgment that perhaps there was some danger in the two of them being alone, and not only in Mrs. Bossidy's overly worried mind.

She *had* never been alone with him, not completely. Had never been fully alone with any man. And she couldn't help the little shiver of anticipation and worry and excitement that the thought provoked.

Oh, nothing would happen. He was a circumspect employee who'd never hinted at the improper, never given her any reason to think that he wished their roles were not so properly conscribed. She should not lose herself in fantasies.

And yet . . . oh, he was a lovely man. If she'd known from the first that she would have to wait all these years to be alone with one, she would have picked one like him to be the first.

"It doesn't matter if you don't go far," he told her. "Things can happen quickly." The horse pranced beneath him. A squeeze of his knees, a slight shift of his weight, and it settled immediately. "And you have been known to wander farther than you realize when your attention is captured by something that interests you."

"I do not—" He pushed his hat back and bent a skeptical look her way. "All right, maybe I do. That does not mean *you* have to come with me. I am not solely your responsibility, you know. Mr. Hoxie and Mr. Peel would have taken their turns, if you had not made it abundantly clear that their presence would not keep you at home." Her own horse was an old, plodding creature, but her skills were close to nonexistent, riding yet another activity her mother considered too dangerous for her. "You can trust them, you know. They've kept me safe for many years before you came along. I imagine they could manage a few more hours."

"I've never abdicated my responsibilities to anyone, no matter how trustworthy." He lifted his hat, revealing dark hair, dampened in a circle where the hat had pressed it to his head. He swiped his cotton-clad arm across his gleaming forehead. So he was human after all. She'd felt flushed moments after leaving the shade, moisture trickling between her shoulder blades. She was certain her face was red as a poppy—not her most becoming color—and her hair hung limp. He, on the other hand, hadn't seemed at all bothered by the heat before.

But then he didn't seem bothered by anything, ever, that she'd been able to tell. Was there nothing inside him, then? Or did he simply hide it that well? She persisted in believing it was the latter, though she was well aware that might be sheer fancy. Unfortunately, it only made it all the more tempting to prod and poke beneath that handsome surface in search of what he held inside.

"Trying to get rid of me, are you?"

"Don't be ridiculous," she said, turning her gaze away from his perceptive one. Though she'd sometimes . . . not lied, exactly, but shaded the truth, to her parents, her tutors, with some success, she suspected he could see right through her.

And she *was* trying to get rid of him. Having him silently, constantly, watching her work was too unsettling. Too distracting. "I was merely trying to give you a break in your duties. Surely even my father does not expect you to work the clock around."

"I don't know about that." He plopped the hat back on his head, for which she was immediately sorry. It shadowed his face too well and made it all the harder to discern his thoughts and moods. "I'm sure he did not get where he was by working short and easy days.

He strikes me as the sort who demands the same from his employees."

She burst into laughter. "You pegged him so quickly, did you?"

"It wasn't hard." He shrugged. "I know his type well enough." He slowed the horse as they approached the rock tower. "Where do you want to set up?"

"This is fine."

An hour passed. Maybe two, while Sam sat with his back against a lone, stunted cottonwood that clung to the bank of a nearly dry creek, and Laura sat beneath a sheltering umbrella, perched on the little three-legged stool he'd lugged out there for her, ripping through page after page of sketches.

At least I make a good pack animal, he thought wryly. Laura was such a bit of thing she never could have carried all those supplies—an easel, a canvas, paints and pencils and chalks, the umbrella and stool and blanket and a gingham-lined picnic basket—by herself.

Because he certainly hadn't accomplished much else since he'd joined up with her party. Mostly, he'd sat on his ass and watched her.

Oh, there wasn't much else he could do. He couldn't hurry her on to the Silver Spur without arousing suspicion. But it disturbed him how . . . content he was with the situation. There should have been at least some impatience simmering beneath his calculatedly watchful facade.

He was not accustomed to doing nothing. He generally assessed a situation, acted quickly, and moved on. Waiting was not his style, though he could do it when circumstances warranted.

But being there with her held an undeniable appeal.

A breeze sighed in from the west, rippling the long, yellow-green grass, brushing his face. The sun beamed benignly, a shade too warm, just enough to remind you it was there. He tipped his head back. Above him green leaves shimmied, a summer dance.

He could never get enough of this, the simple, sweeping pleasure of sitting in the open air and admiring a lovely day. He'd spent so many days confined, space and light denied him, wondering if he'd ever have another opportunity, that freedom still felt new.

And then, of course, there was Laura. And therein lay a more complex problem.

He did not seem to tire of watching her. That was odd enough in itself. A particular woman rarely held his attention for long, and it generally required a bit more effort on her part than her mere existence. And it was not as if Laura possessed the kind of beauty that blared its presence from across the room, snagging your attention and holding it.

Laura's was a gentler attractiveness, quieter, composed of the constant flare of interest in her eyes, the kindness in her expression, the concentration with which she approached her work. And perhaps that is why it did not burn itself out so quickly: When you had to search for that beauty, await the fleeting, tantalizing glimpses of it, it never became stale but retained its freshness and fascination.

She sat right at the edge of the blanket, at the border where the umbrella's shadow ended, so that her pad on its easel received full sunlight while she remained in the shade. And even as he watched, she scooted her stool forward until the sunlight blazed on her hair, and she had to squint against its power.

"Damn." He sprang to his feet. She did not look up

until his shadow fell across her—either she was so lost in her concentration she did not note his approach, or she had been aware from the first and looked up a beat too late in an attempt to hide it. "You're out in the sun again."

"Are you going to scold me now, too?" She lifted her face full into the brightness of it. "I like it."

There was more color in her face than when they'd first met, a brush of pink along her cheekbones, a very faint sprinkle of brown-sugar freckles across her nose. Unable to resist, he brushed his finger across the delicate ridge. Her eyes widened. It was wildly improper, an employee touching the daughter of one of America's richest men. And that bare touch with her was a hundred times more exciting than far more intimate caresses with another. "You're showing some color already. You're so pale, you'll burn to a crisp in no time."

Her skin tones were prized in the East. The whiter, the more delicate, the better; the mark of a woman whose life did not require exposure to the sun, who had no need to work in the fields or the gardens. But she'd been beyond that, pallor instead of merely fashionably pale. She looked healthier like this, with a bit of color to make her eyes sparkle. "And I would not," he went on, "want to face Mrs. Bossidy if I bring you back marked by the sun."

She sighed in surrender. A sound he'd dreamed of, too often, drawing from her another way. It hit him like a roundhouse punch, driving the air from his lungs and restraint from his brain, and he took a step back in case he'd be tempted to touch her again. Because next time, he knew, he could not confine himself to her nose.

She left her stool, fluffed her skirts—frothy yellow things, frilly as a daffodil—and settled gracefully down upon the blanket in the shelter of the wide-striped umbrella.

"I'm taking a break," she said. "Join me."

Ladies did not ask their servants to join them. He might not know much about wealthy society women, but he knew that. Laura—Miss Hamilton, he reminded himself; it would be so much better if he could think of her in formal terms—did, however; she treated Mrs. Bossidy and Hiram and Erastus more like family than staff. But they *were* servants, all of them, even though he played at the role rather than assumed it in truth.

"But you never take a break," he said. For a lady of leisure, she worked steadily, putting in more hours in a typical day than a mill employee. Wielding a pencil and a paintbrush was not the same as swinging a hammer or a scythe, of course, but she was far more diligent than he would have guessed. She was not a dilettante.

"I do today," Laura told him. She saw no further point in attempting to work that afternoon. She could not concentrate when she knew he was only a few feet away, watching her with those predatory eyes. She could never quite decide if she were prey in truth or merely a curiosity. "Sit."

He hesitated. Odd, because Sam never hesitated.

"Oh, come on." She patted the blanket.

"I'd rather not."

"You're not a good employee, ignoring my requests."

"Never claimed to be. I am, however, an excellent bodyguard."

"I'll sketch you," she said. *Let it go*, she told herself. The man, for whatever reason, didn't want to join her on the blanket. But it was becoming all too clear to her that she would not be able to give her work her full attention until her curiosity was appeased. Surely it was primarily his air of mystery that kept her interested. Once that layer was stripped away he'd be exposed as just a man, like so many others, and she could stop thinking about him all the time. "I'm quite famous, you know. People beg for this opportunity. Are you really going to refuse me?"

Finally, he sat down, on the other side of the blanket, as if putting as much space between them as possible while still appearing polite. She would have been offended if there wasn't such a wary glint in his eyes.

But why should he be wary of her?

She propped her sketch pad in her lap, drew a long, sweeping line across it. "Where are you from originally?"

"Does it matter?"

"I suppose not." Charcoal rasped across the page, a bare whisper beneath the hiss of the wind.

"Ohio." It was ridiculous, he decided, not to tell her immediately. He was so accustomed to keeping to himself, to automatically withholding any information, *all* information, in case it might expose a vulnerability that his opponent could exploit. But what could it hurt to tell her? He was bordering on rude, and he knew it. His mother would have been ashamed of him. "Near Columbus."

"There. That wasn't so hard, was it?" She bent her head, her mouth puckering up in concentration. She wore that expression often, and it never failed to make him want to press his mouth against hers.

"No." And maybe, he thought, the conversation would distract him from things he shouldn't be dwelling on. Like the way the sunlight brought out the faintest glimmer of copper in her plain brown hair. "You?"

"I was born in New York. But I've lived most of my life in Newport."

"I've heard it's beautiful there."

Her eyes went soft and hazy as she glanced up from the page and looked over the broad, even sweep of the land, the spear of red rock thrusting abruptly up from the flats.

He could bring that softness, that wonder, into her eyes. It would be a lucky man who had the right to do so.

"Yes. It is. But so is this." She turned back to him. "Do you still have family there?"

"No." The word clogged in his throat, and he had to swallow hard to continue. Odd, because the hurt didn't usually rise that quickly; he didn't let it. But there was something about her, and the sympathy that welled into those soft blue eyes like springwater, that made it surge afresh. "Not anymore."

Oh, what Laura wouldn't give to follow up on that one. But pain flashed through the midnight of his eyes. He wouldn't want to share that with her. Not yet, she thought, then amended, probably not ever. And it would be wrong of her to push it merely to satisfy her rampant curiosity. For it was not as if there could ever be anything more between them than this.

"So . . . how many men have you killed?"

It had the desired effect. His head snapped back, the pain transplanted by surprise.

"What?"

"You're a hired gun, right? Mr. Hoxie says you're quite fearsome."

"I've lost count," he said flatly. It was not unusual for Sam to meet women who were titillated by his reputation, attracted to the supposed danger he represented. He just hadn't suspected she was one of them.

"I see." Her stomach dropped. She hadn't really expected him to answer and had asked only as a distraction.

He'd killed men. She supposed she'd known it from the first but had never really felt the impact of it. As far as she knew, none of her small circle of family and friends had ever taken the life of another human being. To think that they had would have appalled her. *Did* appall her. And it only served to point out how wide and unbridgeable the distance was between them, the difference in their lives so large they might have inhabited separate worlds.

"You look so shocked." He chucked her beneath the chin like one might a child, friendly, ostensibly asexual. And yet that instant of contact lodged in her mind. *He touched me again, bare skin to bare skin.*

Very few men unrelated to her had ever touched her, and those, circumspect and correct, with properly gloved hands at a party her mother arranged and supervised.

Dear heavens, but it was long past time.

"I was in the war," he said. "It's hard to keep count when there are bodies all around, and you're terrified as hell one of 'em is going to be your own. Tallying 'em up is the last of your worries."

"The war?"

She was finally beginning to read him, she realized. The moments he showed the least emotion, when his lids were pulled low over those near-black eyes and his mouth was tight, harshly inexpressive, was when things roiled beneath the surface, threatening to quickly break through.

He nodded. "Though I must admit I wasn't in battle that much."

"You must be a *lot* older than you look," she said without thinking, and could have clapped her hands over her mouth for her lack of tact. But she had thought him no more than a few years older than she.

"I don't know about that," he said. "I was young when I joined up. Just sixteen."

"Sixteen?" Their cook's, Mrs. Pratt's, son was sixteen, fuzzy-cheeked, narrow-shouldered, and prone to awkward giggling fits anytime a maid wandered by. She could not conceive of him raising a gun against another person, another person raising one against him.

"Yup. 'Bout what you are now, hmm?"

She laughed. "Is that a clever way of asking my age without having to rudely come right out with it?" She brushed a few more careless lines across the page. "You don't have to be tactful about it, you know. I'm twenty-five."

There. That should be enough to put paid to any stray thoughts about her. "A veritable child."

She laughed. "Nearly a spinster, and you know it."

"Then that would make me decrepit. You're a dozen years younger than I."

She shrugged, as if those years between them were no more substantial than if they were twelve days instead. "Far be it from me to suggest such a thing."

"Not to mention," he went on, "that there are years and there are years. Some of mine probably count for twice some of yours."

"Like dog years?"

He couldn't help but smile at her. Oh, she was not for him. She was too young, not only in age but in experience, sheltered and pampered and protected. She was an heiress, one born to privilege, raised to enjoy it, schooled to continue it.

But that did not mean he could not . . . enjoy her, did it? Take pleasure in her company? For all of his years, all his experiences, this was a new one. He could not recall enjoying a woman out of bed. Though he had to admit he'd given very few that chance.

"I wouldn't be too sure about that," she said. "I nearly died once. That must count for a few extra years at least." Her hand stilled over the pad, her expression pensive. "I may have been sheltered, but sometimes I feel very much older than I am."

Oh, he did not want this commonality with her, the two of them having both confronted their mortality and survived. He did not want them to be alike, for her to seem possible, within his reach in any way. He was using her for a brief time, then she would go back to her pretty, jeweled world, and he would be alone again. Which was precisely how he preferred it.

"What happened?" The words came out of his mouth before he could stop them. He never asked about others unless it furthered his ends. He had no curiosity; it had been ground out of him. So why did he want to know about her?

It had to be her fault. The rampant curiosity that simmered so strongly in her had become contagious.

"Rheumatic fever," she said. "I was ten. It . . ." She touched her chest, lightly, as if it still held some echoes of long-ago pain. "It . . . damaged my heart."

Hell. No wonder she looked so fragile, so pale. No wonder her family protected her so carefully. "What in damnation are you doing out here?"

She waved off his concern. "It was a long time ago. It took years to recover fully, and a few more before my family believed it, but I'm perfectly fine now."

Heart damage. It pounded behind his temples, a drum that couldn't be stopped. "Like hell."

No doctors, he thought. *No hospitals within a day's ride. Are her parents insane?* Could they not at least have sent a nurse with her? If she had . . . a fit, a seizure, an attack, whatever she was prone to, he wouldn't have the slightest idea what to do.

He'd watched enough people die. You could see the life in them go out, that instant when they changed from a human to a mere collection of flesh and bone and skin. He could not, would not, watch her light extinguish.

"I'm fine." Laura set her sketch pad aside, scooted closer, and dared to touch him briefly on the arm before she caught herself and pulled her hand away. He was solid beneath the thin cotton of his shirtsleeve, warm as sunshine, and she wished very much she could have let her hand remain. "Truly, I am." She was half-touched by his panic, half-irritated. She'd had her fill of people worrying over her. "It was years ago. *Years*. Five different doctors declared me fit before my father would even consider this trip."

Sam figured Leland Hamilton would kill him if he ever discovered that Sam had used her. But it would be slowly and tortuously, if he ever suspected the way Sam *thought* about her. And Sam wouldn't have blamed him a bit.

But she'd touched him, and he could still feel the imprint of her hand, the light, sweet weight of female contact. He had to think about something else. Anything else. "Can I see what you drew?"

Her eyes widened. "No!"

She looked panicked. And guilty. He really hadn't been all that interested, just looking for distraction, but now he really wanted to see what was on that pad.

"Why not?"

"It's . . ." She snatched up the pad and clutched it to her chest like a mother protecting a child. "I'm not happy with it. Too rough. Not . . . finished. Later. I'll show you later. When I get it right."

"You didn't object to my looking in Kearney, and you were far from finished with that."

"No. I didn't." She swallowed hard. "But that was just a landscape. People are different. They're . . . sensitive when it comes to their portraits."

"I'm not." Now he *had* to see it. What had she done, drawn him naked?

"They all say that."

"All right," he agreed cheerfully, and waited for her to relax.

She did. He lunged.

She jerked, tumbling back against the blanket. He was sprawled across her, the sketch pad crushed between them, the only barrier preventing full contact.

It was a blatantly sexual position, a woman pinned beneath a man who wanted her. He'd dreamed of this a dozen times, had resisted the pull of her hundreds more.

And now there she was. Beneath him. And she wasn't protesting a bit.

Chapter 7

He couldn't have said how long they stayed like that. It might have been a second, might have been a day. Longer, for all the clarity with which he knew he'd remember it.

She did not feel as fragile beneath him as he would have expected. His legs fell naturally between hers, in the hammock made by her layers of skirts. Damned sketch pad; the edge bit into the inside of one biceps, and its flat surface was the only thing that kept him from resting on the slight, delectable curve of her chest.

One of his hands lay on her shoulder; it fit naturally on that smooth curve, the heavy silk of her bodice impossibly fine, softer than anything he'd touched in his life, warm from her skin. And he knew that if he but moved his hand a few inches, slid it up to the elegant, exposed column of her neck, he'd stroke something even softer, finer.

Her eyes were wide. How could anything be so blue? A sky, a sapphire, a mountain lake, all would envy that color.

There was nothing remarkable about her features. What made the distinction between beauty and plain? Did only a fraction of an inch make so much difference? What convention got to dictate such things?

He knew that some would call her ordinary. But, right at that moment, he knew that he would rather gaze at her than anyone or anything else. And that, he thought, was the most frightening truth he'd confronted in years.

Her mouth . . . her mouth was amazing. Somewhere in his head he understood it was no different than any other woman's mouth. Lips, teeth, tongue. All the same parts, all the same functions. But the curve of it fascinated him, the rosy blush of color, the way the corners turned up as if she were always on the verge of a smile.

Her lips parted, her breath coming out in a stunned *whoosh*. He felt it brush him, moist, warm, sweet-scented.

If he kissed her, he thought, she wouldn't stop him. And God knew that once he started he wouldn't be able to stop himself.

"Sam?"

"Sorry," he said, and pushed up with his arms— away from her, away from heaven, away from the road to hell.

He sat back. She curled up slowly, her brows drawn together, her lips compressed into as close as she'd ever come to a frown. She looked dazed, uncertain, and damn, it was his fault. He'd remained on top of her too long—he shouldn't have been there at all, and should have sprung away with apologies and polite recriminations the instant he realized where he'd fallen. But he hadn't, because he'd been too drawn to her. Because he'd felt more alive in that second, on her, than at any moment since he'd marched off to war.

But she'd no experience with men. That was perfectly obvious. No experience with *life*. With anything, really, but a world as perfectly constructed and artificial as the ones she'd painted, and the fact that it had once included a sickroom didn't change that. She couldn't be counted on to keep brief, physical contact in its proper place any more than . . . well, than he could, he admitted to himself.

He had to divert them both.

The sketch pad lay forgotten beside her. He snatched it up.

He hadn't expected much. He didn't have the face for portraits, and she hadn't been working on it terribly long. But he hadn't expected *this*, either.

"Um. Laura?"

Her cheeks glowing—oh, if only he'd put that color there another way—she grabbed the pad from his hand with such force that the momentum almost toppled her backward.

"I know you said your initial sketches were rough, but really, even so, my hair's not *that* bad—"

"It's not you." She ripped the page off the pad and tore it into a dozen pieces. "I was sketching that tree."

"The tree," he said neutrally. "It's that much prettier than me?"

"It's a very nice tree," she allowed. "But that's not why I drew it."

She had her head down. He could see the clean line of her part, the smooth, shining swoop of her hair into a neat roll at her neck. Brown hair; there should be a better name for that color. It sounded so ordinary, *brown*. And yet there were a hundred gradations in it, cool and pale, rich, and dark.

"I never draw people," she admitted at last.

"Never?"

She shook her head and sunlight gleamed across the crown. Oh yes, he remembered vaguely, he was supposed to be getting her out of the sun. Good thing he wasn't her bodyguard in truth. He'd never failed at any job he'd undertaken in his entire life, but she was in danger—from *him*—every instant she spent in his company.

"Why?"

She lifted her head, shrugging carelessly, as if it didn't matter. But her mouth trembled. "I'm no good at it."

"I remember the panorama I saw. It was . . ." Oh, damn, he was so bad at this. Comforting words, speeches designed to uplift or inspire. He'd never cared enough. "There were people in it."

She smiled. But it was small and pained, not the warm and easy one she usually gave so freely. "Figures. Impressions, roughly blocked-in passersby. No need for detail there. Those weren't individuals. They were just a crowd."

"I could almost hear the streetcars, smell the stench from the river. Your talent . . . all right, I admit it. I don't know a damn thing about art. But I refuse to believe that someone who can paint that so beautifully couldn't paint *anything* well."

"One would think so, wouldn't one?" She still held a fistful of paper fragments. She lifted her hand and opened, let the bits flutter down like oversized snowflakes. "I've tried. And tried. I didn't like failing at it, you know. There were so many things I couldn't do as a child. Couldn't run, couldn't swim. Couldn't even sing, though I couldn't attribute that to my illness." Once piece clung to her damp palm, and she shook it off. It drifted down. "But painting—painting I could always do, as soon as I got strong enough again to hold a brush."

Her empty hand fell to her lap, joining the clutter of paper scraps. "But not that. Landscapes are about faithfully recording what's there. In my case, copying the photos, adding in the impressions of others. But painting people . . . if you only record the features, you might as well be painting a doll. Portraits are about emotion, about *life*." Her voice deepened, with a ragged edge as if she'd recovered from a cold. "The panoramas are easy."

There was nothing about the painting he'd viewed that seemed *easy*. The amount of detail made his head spin. Even the physical effort involved; he had a hard time imagining that a woman as small as she could painstakingly brush paint over a canvas that huge. He pictured her on a ladder, the canvas towering over her, dwarfing her, a task so large as to seem Sisyphean. How much could she cover in a day? There had to be many times when she would step back and look at the small patch she'd just completed, compare it to the great empty swaths of white, and wonder if she'd ever fill it all up.

He wrapped his hand around her arm, halfway between her elbow and shoulder, his middle finger easily meeting his thumb.

"What are you doing?"

"Checking your biceps. There must be about three billion brushstrokes in one of those things. Your right arm should be stronger than mine."

"No danger of that." She laughed, as he'd intended, and he thought: *Look at that. I made her laugh even though she was sad.* It seemed an accomplishment greater than surviving prison. "And besides, it's my left."

Her left. She was left-handed. Had he known that about her? Yes. He knew . . .

He knew more about her than he cared to admit. He

had spent the better part of the last twenty years *not* knowing people, and the fact that Griff was missing only reinforced in a vicious way why he'd chosen a solitary path.

For if you did not know someone, you could not miss them. Everyone he'd ever truly known, he'd lost, in the space of two years. His brother, his parents, anyone with any claim to friend . . . all but Griff, until now.

He needed her for entrée to the Silver Spur. And that was *all* he needed her for, all he'd allow himself to need her for.

For a moment he indulged himself, dreaming of what it would be like if she were another kind of woman. He would take her to bed in a heartbeat—he wouldn't *need* her, not even then, but want her, oh yes.

But then he wanted her already, ferociously so, in a way he'd never wanted another woman. Because if he'd ever begun to want too much, he left. Ran away like the coward he obviously was rather than take a chance on it growing into something more.

But he couldn't run away from her. Not yet.

And she was not another kind of woman. She was the most *not that kind of woman* he'd ever met. Her father would ensure she remained that way. He regretted it, but he did not begrudge her father that. Were Laura his daughter, and had he the resources and power of Leland Hamilton, he would have done the same—if he ever allowed her out of the house at all.

"Why'd you ask me to sit if you had no intention of drawing me?" he asked, as much for diversion as any real curiosity.

Color rose into her cheeks, a quick bright wash of rose-pink. Oh, but that pale, clear skin—invalid pale, he reminded himself because maybe, if he thought of her as ill, he'd stop thinking of her beneath him—revealed her emotions as quickly and easily as if she'd painted them on a sign.

"Because I wanted you to join me," she admitted.

She was honest. He had to give her that. But what reason would she ever have had to guard her thoughts? She'd been surrounded her whole life only by people who had her best interests at heart. Unlike Sam, she'd never learned to shield every single thought, even those that seemed completely innocuous, in case they might give someone else an advantage.

"We should be getting back. Mrs. Bossidy will be on a rescue mission soon."

"I suppose so." She'd drawn her knees up, one arm wrapped around them as she plucked at a thread on the blanket. "Sam? Were you going to kiss me?"

"I—" Damn her straightforward honesty. He'd almost—*almost*—managed to wrangle his inconvenient urges under control. But those words out of her mouth immediately roused his desire again, placed it front and center, unignorable, damn near irresistible. "I wasn't *going* to kiss you, no," he told her. Which wasn't a lie, though certainly a careful shading of the truth.

"All right then." She lifted her head and looked at him directly. "Were you *thinking* about kissing me?"

He was famous for his ability to shield his thoughts. And she'd seen right through his sidestepping as if it were glass.

"I was thinking about it," he admitted. "*Thinking.* A man can't get in trouble for thinking." Though Sam was starting to feel like he could. "It's *doing* that runs a man into danger."

She took a deep breath. "I think you should do it."

"Excuse me?" he croaked.

"I think you should do it."

"I—"

She glared at him, heat and anger and so damn appealing he would have grabbed her right then if shock hadn't kept him frozen. "And don't you *dare* tell me I don't know what I'm saying because I'll hit you, I swear," she said fiercely.

"Why?" he asked quietly.

All the fight whooshed out of her.

"Because I'm twenty-five years old, and I've never been kissed," she told him.

It wasn't a surprise. It was still regrettable. A woman like Laura *should* be kissed, often and well. "That doesn't mean it has to be me. It *shouldn't* be me."

"I don't intend to be alone the rest of my life." Her hands rested loose in her lap. Bits of hair pulled free of its neat knot. Loose tendrils, the color lighter when released from the mass of it, drifted about her jaw, sunlight glimmering through the fine strands. Emotion shimmered in her eyes, and it all twisted up inside him.

It cost him to hold back, and he knew he couldn't do it much longer. And yet he couldn't stop her from talking. Her words sank into him, sweet-painful darts of possibility.

"When this trip is over, I'll go home, and I'll allow my father to introduce me to . . . someone. Someone of his choosing, who will no doubt be kind and cultured and eminently suitable." She was composed as she said it, completely matter-of-fact, as if it had never once occurred to her that there should be more to the man she gave herself to than his *appropriateness*. As if she'd never considered there could be anything else for her.

Sam could conjure the scene so easily: a man comfortable in a suit and a drawing room, respectful, devoted. Not a man with blood on his hands and darkness in his soul.

His hands flexed, his vision hazed.

"But once in her life," she continued softly, "every woman should be kissed by someone *inappropriate*."

Damn.

He swooped. Hard and fast, his mouth coming on hers with fierce, unerring speed, so sudden she startled, emitted a yelp of shock quickly swallowed up in his kiss.

Her fists were at his chest, crushed between them. Pushing him away? And then her hands opened, the burn of her palm flat against him through the thin cotton of his shirt. Her fingers curled, grabbing fistfuls of his shirt, twisting to pull him closer though he was already as close as he could be.

Oh, she should have been sweet. Tentative, unskilled, uncertain.

Instead she was bold. Demanding and wild, her mouth hot as fire beneath his. Greedy, pulling him close, tilting her head to fit her mouth more firmly against his.

Her mouth opened. Of her own accord, or because he'd nudged her lips wide? He didn't know. They kissed as if they'd done so a hundred times, like lovers who'd been apart for too long and were finally, at last, together once more, who didn't know if this would be the last and so were determined to wring every drop of pleasure from it no matter the price.

His arms came around her. Her back was narrow, almost fragile, the line of her spine bumping against his palm, yet she twisted in his arms. Thin like a willow whip, misleadingly frail, tensile and limber and so much stronger than appearances promised.

He drew his hands around her sides, smoothing the fabric of her bodice beneath his palms. The fabric was silky, her body warm and elegantly lean. His thumbs brushed the side of her breasts, a gentle, barely there curve that yielded to the slightest pressure, and he heard her quick intake of breath. His own breath was gone—she'd stolen it from him, along with whatever sanity he'd once possessed.

He leaned forward, ready to push her back down to the ground. She took another quick sip of breath, a half hitch of surprise, and stiffened. Only briefly, but long enough to remind him who she was. Who *he* was.

He released her and sat back, rump on his heels, turning his head to one side so he didn't have to look at her and see it: alarm or accusation or, worse yet, open, wonderful, irresistible desire. He pressed the back of his hand to his mouth, as a boxer might dab away blood. She'd bloodied him, all right, but in places where the wound was hidden, and the scars wouldn't heal.

"Sam?" she asked, uncertainty breaking on his name. He felt her fingers tentatively brush his shoulder.

He should turn to her. She deserved some kind of support or consolation. What would a woman who'd never been kissed assume when the man who'd finally done so couldn't bring himself to face her?

But he couldn't. *Couldn't.* If he caught one glimpse of those wide blue eyes, that lovely mouth, he would never find it in him to pull away again, her father and her future and his past be damned.

And it would ruin all of them.

"*Inappropriate* enough for you?" he forced out on a rasp.

"Almost," she murmured.

Chapter 8

Desperate measures, Lucy Bossidy thought as she rapped on the door to the train car that housed the men. It went against her grain to have to go to them for help. Laura was her responsibility and always had been.

The door opened. Mr. Peel stood in the doorway—*filled* the doorway, as only a man of his . . . bulk could. He was shirtless, a pair of loose tan pants slung low on his hips. Not lean hips, she noted—nothing about Hiram Peel could ever be called lean—but there was nothing soft about him, either. Surely in a man of that size there should be some extra flesh around the middle.

Not that she'd ever thought about his middle.

But he was solid. Smooth-chested. And apparently just out of bed, his brown hair spiked like a cock's ruff.

"Yeah?" he asked.

She tore her eyes away, focusing on the iron-webbed lantern bolted beside the door. Dear Lord, what had gotten into her? Yes, it had been a shock when he'd opened the door barely dressed. Yes, it had been a long

time, more years than she'd cared to admit, since she'd
been confronted with a bare male chest. But to ogle *Mr.
Peel*, of all people . . . she'd heard tales of the prairie
driving women to madness, though those stories had
always held it was living isolated through the winter
that spawned such insanity. Clearly the land worked
much more quickly on her.

"May I help you?" she corrected.

"No, you can't help me. Nice o' you to ask, though."

"No. I wasn't asking you." Her temples started to
throb. Now *there* was the reaction Mr. Peel typically
sparked in her. "I was instructing you. It is impolite to
open a door to a visitor with merely a 'yeah.' 'May I
help you' is a more appropriate response."

"May . . . I . . . help . . . you," he ground out.

"Not with that tone of voice," she said, frowning in
disapproval. "Not to mention that that's hardly the appropriate attire in which to answer the door to a lady."

"Oh, so you're a lady now?"

Not really, she thought, the old hurt lifting its head
unexpectedly, now merely an echo of what it once was,
a wistful ache rather than the sharp slice of loss it had
been.

But he didn't know about that. No one did. "As far as
you're concerned, Mr. Peel, I most certainly am."

"I was sleeping."

"Sleeping? In the middle of the afternoon? You must
have terribly taxing duties, Mr. Peel."

"I've got the night shift tonight. Gotta be alert."

"Always good to know you take your responsibilities
so seriously," she said, voice heavy with sarcasm. She
flicked a glance at him. Still no shirt. The man had absolutely no manners at all.

She was an experienced woman. She should have

been able to stand there, unbothered, blithely unconcerned. If she'd been confronting anyone other than
this annoyingly overgrown lummox, she was certain
she could have.

"What do you want?" he asked.

Now *there* was a question. One she rarely dared to
ask herself. "Is Mr. Hoxie here?"

"No. He's out on one of those damned horses. Scout-
ing the area, he said."

"I didn't know he could ride."

"He's on the back of a horse. The horse is moving. If
you call that riding, he's riding."

"It's probably just as well," she said. She would be far
more comfortable dealing with Erastus, who under normal circumstances could be relied upon to be at least
somewhat reasonable. However, his ridiculous hero worship of Mr. Duncan made his reaction unpredictable in
this particular case. Mr. Peel was the only other person in
their little troupe who hadn't fallen under Sam's spell,
which put them, for a brief period at least, on the same
side. "I need to talk to you."

He leaned against the doorframe and raised one eyebrow. "Talk away."

"It's about Mr. Duncan."

"Christ. Not you, too." He crossed his arms before
his chest. Muscle bulged. "Okay, I understand that
Miss Hamilton's vulnerable to beauty. It's in her nature. And Hoxie's susceptible to fame. He can't help it.
But you—thought you had at least a little sense."

"Why, Mr. Peel, if that's not the sweetest thing you've
ever said to me." She fluttered her eyelashes at him. "No,
that's not it. Laura went out to work with him today,
and—"

"Don't know why you let her do that," he said.

"Aren't you supposed to be chaperonin'? Lettin' the child gallivant around the country with a guy like that with nothing more than a paintbrush for protection wasn't the brightest idea you ever had."

It stung. Stung even more because she knew he was right. "I let her go out with *you*."

He shot her a look of heavy disgust. "As if I'd be interested in a girl," he said. "Much less in Miss Hamilton. She's practically my—" he cast around for the right word "—niece."

A girl? She remembered when Mr. Hamilton had hired Hiram in the first place. He'd been a big, bumbling, angry youth, seventeen at the most, which made him at least a few years younger than her, as close to Laura's age as her own.

"I know," she admitted. "I was just . . . I was concerned that, if I didn't allow her to go out with him as I did the rest of you, well, forbidden fruit and all that." She frowned, regretting that decision anew. "Obviously I was wrong."

"All fruit's forbidden to Miss Hamilton," he said. "The Baron's made sure of it."

And there, thought Lucy, was the crux of the problem. "You're right. I miscalculated. I believed they would not go far, and I did not want her to think I did not trust her."

He straightened in surprise. "Never thought I'd hear you admit you were wrong."

"Yes, well, don't get fond of hearing it. It won't happen again." Back to the important matter. "She came back flushed."

"So? She flushes easily. Skin's so damn white it colors up soon as the temperature goes north of eighty."

"It wasn't the heat," she said. "At least, it wasn't the sun."

"I know you're fond of jumping to conclusions, but this is a big one."

"No conclusions," she said. "Suspicions. Oh, I'm not saying anything irreversible happened. Not yet. But something did. And I want to ensure nothing else does."

He ran his tongue over his teeth, pondering, and nodded. "I'll take care of it," he said. Then stepped back and shut the door in her face.

"You see that fence?" Sam asked her. "That's the boundary of the Silver Spur."

"There?" She put down the pencil she'd been using to sketch the scene in front of her: the lift of the foothills and the mountains beyond, bristling with a wild tangle of sage and bunchgrass, studded with Joshua trees and gnarled junipers, a classically un-tamed Western landscape, contrasted with the precise, constricting geometry of the fence that slashed hori-zontally across the bottom of the scene. "Are you sure? I thought we were some distance away yet." They'd de-tached from the train on a long-abandoned side rail in Utah that morning when the landscape caught her eye.

"Hmm. Pretty sure." He squinted. "We're on the back side. Silver Creek is at the northwest corner of Crocker's land. The spur line that runs to the mines takes off from there."

"How do you know this land's his?"

He shrugged. "It's the fence. Nobody out here much bothers with one. Cattle's always been allowed to graze free. But Crocker's never been one to share."

"Now, *why* do you know that?"

She looked so pretty, gussied up in lace and a straw-brimmed hat fluttering with pale blue ribbons. But then, she'd looked pretty every day of the last twenty-three; since that interlude when he'd forgotten all the very good reasons to keep their relationship carefully bounded and, instead, surrendered to the insistent press of need, he'd had a much harder time ignoring it. "I did some work around here once. Hard to do anything in this part of the country without learnin' about Crocker."

"For him? Or for the other side?"

"For whoever paid me the most," he said noncommittally.

"Hmm." Laura leaned forward and quickly sketched the burning globe of the sun. Not likely that it would end up in the final work, but she had to capture it while she could, a great white-hot ball far more potent than the benevolent golden one that beamed down on Sea Haven.

To eyes accustomed to the deep and vibrant green of the Northeastern summer, Utah wore restrained colors. The colors were there: gray in the sage, green in the juniper, a tiny burst of three-pointed white from a Sego lily, the rusty copper of the ground itself. But the landscape was anything but lush, and it took a while to become sensitive to it, to discern the beauty and life in the subtle shades of dun.

"So?" she asked. "How's our spy doing?"

In the guise of a yawn, Sam stretched and twisted, glancing back to where their chaperone—Mr. Hoxie that day—crouched behind the stocky bulk of a stunted bush.

"If he can get out of bed tomorrow after squatting like that all morning," Sam said, "he's a better man than I."

"Are we ever going to have a moment alone again?" She smiled at him. Maybe a bit flirtatiously, but if you couldn't flirt with a man who'd kissed you so hard and well until it curled your toes and kept you up at night, whom could you flirt with?

If a woman had to wait until she was twenty-five for her first kiss, at least she'd picked someone who knew how to do it right.

And it wasn't as if he'd been immune. It had taken him a full two minutes to get his breath back, she remembered smugly.

"Nope," he said, too cheerfully for her taste. Shouldn't he be unhappy about the fact that, since that lovely afternoon, they hadn't gone anywhere without Hiram, Mr. Hoxie, or Mrs. Bossidy trailing behind, trying valiantly, and failing miserably, to stay out of sight?

She certainly regretted their presence. He'd remained circumspectly distant from her ever since, a perfect guard, day after day. One would think the impact of their kiss would have muted over that time, softened in her memory. And yet it only grew and sharpened, as if the time from it gave her the space to separate each moment and sink into the sensation each one offered, until that brief interlude took up more space in her mind. She had only to see him, to think of him, and that *feeling* swept back, precise and immediate, no different than if he touched her in truth instead of merely in her memory and imagination.

And yet it seemed to have had no impact on him. Nothing in his manner, his speech, his respectful and careful and seemingly impersonal guarding of her gave away that he even remembered what had happened between them. Except once, two days ago, as she'd sketched a gorgeous sunset as they'd crossed the

Bear River near the Wyoming border, and she'd looked up to find him close, so completely focused on her that the world fell away. He'd touched her only briefly, a shivering brush of his fingers beneath her ear, along her neck, interrupted almost immediately by Mrs. Bossidy's timely—though it was most *untimely*, in Laura's opinion—call to dinner. She could still feel it, the warmth, the rasp of the callus of his fingers against her tender skin, the direct line he took down, and around, to where the lace of her neckline halted his exploration.

"Did she say anything to you?" he asked. "Two nights ago. When I touched you—"

"No." She shook her head. "If she'd really *seen* anything, if they knew that you'd so much as brushed one finger against mine, Mr. Hoxie'd be right here, sitting between us, rather than over there hiding in the foliage. No, she only suspects. That's why they're being so sneaky, hoping to catch us in the act."

"Why would they want to do that?"

She edged a bit closer to him. His jaw tightened, his eyes narrowed. There was far more fun than she'd ever suspected in exercising her feminine wiles. She leaned his way, he swallowed hard, and she smiled. So much power in it. "So they can tell my father what terrible advantage you're taking of me and get rid of you once and for all."

"They could tell him that anyway."

"Lie, Mr. Duncan?" she said in mock horror. "Would you do such a thing to gain an advantage?"

"I'd do *anything* to gain an advantage," he said, his voice deep and even.

"Are you warning me off?"

"Yes." He debated even bringing it up; they'd

avoided the topic quite nicely for weeks. And yet it was still *there* between them, big and bold and clearly in the way. In fact, it seemed to be gaining power in the memory. Perhaps, if they talked of it, they could put it behind them once and for all. "I should never have kissed you."

"Why not?"

"You're all wrong for me," he said carefully. "More importantly, I'm all wrong for you. What good could come of it?"

"What good?" she asked, her temper rising. "How about that we *enjoyed* it? Isn't that good?"

"It's not that simple, and you know it."

"Why can't it be?" Foolish man. "Sam, do you think that I'm so naïve that I must tangle up a simple, lovely kiss with all sorts of emotions and plans? Don't worry, Sam. I'm not planning to marry you."

"What?" *Why the hell not?* Was the first thing that sprang to his mind. And Lord, wasn't that by far the biggest jolt of stupidity he'd indulged in for many a day? Since he obviously could not look at her and think clearly, he swung his gaze around, as if he were on guard in truth, and then—"What the hell is that?"

On a long slope perhaps three hundred yards away, a man pelted down the hillside, heading straight for them. He ran wildly, looking behind him as he chugged through the tangled brush and past the spiky tufts of bunchgrass.

"Sam?" Laura climbed to her feet, rose to her toes for a better view. Beside her Sam jumped up as well, edging sideways to put the bulk of his body between her and the approaching figure.

The man stumbled, going down hard, his arms flailing like a loose-limbed doll as he tumbled twice down the hill, coming to rest against a large, reddish rock that thrust crookedly from the crumbled slope.

She gasped and ran forward, coming up against the fence. It was rough-cut wood below, tipped with a taut line of new, silvery barbed wire that snagged on the soft silk of her shirtwaist.

"Wait." He caught her arm. "That's private property. Crocker doesn't take kindly at all to trespassers."

"But he's hurt! He—"

"No, he's up."

The man staggered to his feet, weaved a few unsteady steps forward, and began to run again.

Sound rumbled. Low enough at first she couldn't identify it. And then—"Are those horses?"

He nodded, mouth grim, shoulders tense. More anxious than she'd ever seen him, even in the middle of the robbery on the train. Why would that be?

The man was getting close enough to pick out features. He was a small man, a long dark braid flying behind him as he ran. His loose, dark blue tunic billowed as he sprinted, and his pants hung on his thin frame, as baggy as if he'd lost a lot of weight since he'd first acquired them. Behind him, above the crown of the hill, a dust cloud rose.

Three horses crested over the top. The sound of their hoofbeats grew louder, louder yet, like the threatening drumbeats of an approaching army.

"Oh, God." She lifted the top wire of the fence, intending to crawl through. But her skirts tangled, and a barb pierced her finger. "Sam, they're going to run him down."

The man was no more than a hundred yards away by then: narrow eyes set in a wide face, broad cheekbones under dark skin. A Celestial, Laura thought in surprise.

Chinese, most likely. There were many of them in the West. She'd read about it in the papers. Thousands had been brought here to work on the railroad and the mines, welcomed at first because they were considered hard workers and less troublesome than the Irish and the Mexicans, but now despised because the unions were afraid they were stealing too many American jobs.

Her foot found purchase on the bottom rail.

"Laura, no!"

"We have to do *something*."

"Just how are you planning to stop them? Those horses can run you over as easily as him."

One of the men on horseback uncoiled a lasso, circling it into a wide loop over his head.

Laura's heart pumped as if she were the one running.

Two hundred feet. He shouted something at them, an incomprehensible burst of staccato language.

"Sam! Do something!"

"What?" he said grimly. "Start shooting somebody? I'm sure as hell not going to get in a gun battle with you beside me."

"But—"

"We have no idea what's going on. He could be a thief. He could be a murderer."

That made a certain sense. If this was Haw Crocker's land—and Sam was usually right about such things—the men on horseback probably worked for him.

But oh—she found herself hoping he'd make it to the fence. He was so close, a headlong rush for freedom. Though she understood the fence was unlikely to stop the men on horseback, and certainly not a bullet; if he got that far perhaps they could shield him—

A hundred feet. The horses were almost upon him. He

must be feeling their heat behind him, the vibration of the ground beneath his feet, and realize it was hopeless.

The man's gaze met Laura's. *Dear God.* Wild despair, desperation, a bitter hopelessness. He knew he wasn't going to make it. But he would rather be run down and killed in the attempt than be captured.

The loop of rope dropped around his torso. The man at the forefront of the trio of riders—tall, wearing a wide-brimmed tan hat—yanked back on the rope, and he flew back, landing flat on his back.

"Hey. *Hey!*"

They ignored her completely. One of them, this one younger, soft around the middle, leapt from his own horse. He checked the man on the ground, who was rolling slowly from side to side. Likely had the breath driven right out of him.

The young man clipped the Celestial on the crown of the head with the butt of his pistol. The man on the ground sagged immediately. The young cowboy grunted as he lifted the limp body and threw it over the back of his horse.

She couldn't believe they were letting them ride off. She'd never felt so impotent. "Sam?"

He had his face turned away. As if he, too, couldn't stand to watch, his eyes hooded, his mouth bleak.

"Sam, *please.*"

"I can't," Sam gritted out. He would have given anything not to have Laura look at him with that accusation in her eyes. His stomach clenched, acid burning through. He remembered the feeling too well—freedom just on the other side of the pine log fence, that terrible desperation to reach it, knowing you wouldn't. Hell, he and Griff had tried to *claw* their way out, digging through rock with their fingernails, not much car-

ing if they bled to death in the process. When the
guards had discovered their tunnel in a sheltered corner
of the crowded stockade, all of eight feet deep, they'd
forced them to stay there. But they'd added that section
to their regular patrol, checking on them every twenty
minutes or so, and if they suspected them of having
deepened it even a fraction, they kicked in a few more
inches of dirt, laughing as it rained down on their prisoners' heads.

Twice, they'd managed to scrabble their way out.
The guards had had a merry time searching through the
prisoners for them, and an even better time making
them regret their "impertinence" before tossing them
back in their hole. "You've dug your grave," they'd
said. "Now stay in it."

Griff and he had lived—if one could call it that—in
that hole for six months. Too narrow for them both to
sit at once, they had taken turns, one leaning against the
wall while the other curled up and slept. If one of those
guards had tossed him a gun and given him the option
of ending it by turning the barrel on himself, he would
have taken it without question.

His back, his shoulders, his gut all hurt, every muscle screaming to help that poor man who'd come so
close to escape.

No, not help. *Interfere*. The guy could be a rapist, for
all he knew. And even then, it was no business of his.

He thought he recognized the youngest hand. He'd
been with the group who'd jumped him when he'd tried
to sneak back in the north border of the Silver Spur.
Though that entire night was a little blurry, and his eyes
had swelled shut early on.

The guy was likely too occupied to notice Sam. And
he'd shaved since then and hacked off a good chunk of

his hair. Even so, Sam kept his face turned away. He preferred that, in any case, for if he'd watched any longer, he wasn't sure he could have kept from stepping in.

Which would probably lead to disaster. You couldn't take anyone who worked for Haw Crocker lightly. He'd had the bruises to prove it.

And he'd only put Laura in danger if he tried to meddle. Not to mention destroy any chance he'd ever have of finding out what had happened to Griff inside those fences.

But turning away from the scene forced him to look at Laura—Laura, and the disappointment and blame in those pale blue eyes.

She had been furious when he'd told her that her father had hired him. And even then she'd had an inkling of what his life entailed. She had accused him that first night of being without honor, without purpose.

But now she'd witnessed it with her own eyes. It twisted inside him, all the impotent anger and heavy regrets.

Well, he had never asked for her to like him, had he? He'd known all along that there could be nothing between them. After this, she'd never ask him to kiss her again, and wouldn't that be safer all around, for both of them? He ignored the screams of protests from his baser urges, the part of him that kept him awake at night, dreaming about how her mouth had felt against his. The part that insisted that that kiss was something more, and if he never had that feeling again with her, he'd never have that feeling again, period. And that would be a terrible loss.

"Why should I stop them?" he asked. "It's not my job."

She blanched, her already-pale skin going white as a blank canvas.

And then the anger surged, coloring her cheeks and snapping in her eyes. "I have money. How much do you need to step in?"

"You can't afford me."

"Two thousand dollars," she snapped.

It had taken him three years to earn that much when he'd first left Andersonville. "Not enough."

"Four thousand."

"Too late," he said, nodding in the direction of where the three horses were disappearing over the crest. The dust blotted their figures, as if they were half-erased in an unfinished sketch, a dirty brown haze soiling a clear blue sky.

"Yes," she said coldly. "It certainly is."

Chapter 9

He haunted her sleep. What little sleep there was. Laura lay on her bed—a comfortable one, her father made sure—and stared at the inky darkness above her. Moonlight trickled through the window so the gilding on the ceiling shimmered now and then, as if a starlit sky arched above her. She wondered idly if someone had planned that exact effect. Likely; her father famously hired craftsmen with an eye for the details.

Mrs. Bossidy slumbered easily in the cubicle next door. Despite the train car's solid build, the interior walls were thin, to avoid stealing precious floor space. Their doors were open and, if she were very still, Laura could hear her heavy breathing.

It was soothing. Comfortable. After six weeks of travel, familiar. The evening was cool, so her window was closed, the sound of the wind outside only a very faint whisper.

But every time she closed her eyes she saw that des-

perate running man. Such an unusual face to Laura's
eyes, his skin drawn and sallow. Terrified . . . no, past
terrified. Like a man who'd been terrified so long he'd
moved beyond it, into that desperate hopelessness
where he no longer cared whether he lived or died.

She sighed and gave up trying to sleep. They'd be
moving on in the morning—the train to pick them up
was due shortly after ten. She could nap then, if she
chose to, until they arrived in Silver Creek.

She tossed aside the light coverlet. The rugs beneath
her bare feet were thick, plush wool, tickling her toes.
She moved to the window.

She'd left the drapes open. Night interested her. She
was so accustomed to color, studying every shade and
reflection of it. Night washed away the vivid hues,
leaving only a thousand shades of gray, revealing the
lines of a place. There were a few scrubby Joshua trees,
silvery in the moonlight. A storage shed—empty; she'd
checked herself. Little else but for the looming bulk of
the mountains in the distance.

Ah, yes. There. Sam. The long lean length of him
stretched out on a bare patch of ground. He hadn't
bothered with a tent, not even the tarp he sometimes
pitched when bad weather threatened. He was barely
visible in the shadows, a man who seemed made for the
darkness, or been created from it. He'd certainly spent
a fair amount of time dwelling in it—if she'd learned
one thing about him, she had learned that.

As she watched, she saw him shift, roll from his
back to his right side, as if he, too, couldn't settle in to
sleep. Perhaps the same thing bothered him that ruined
her sleep.

It had shocked her when he refused to intervene to
rescue that poor man. Especially since he'd charged to

the rescue so quickly, fearlessly, on the train. But then, he'd been paid to do that, hadn't he? To protect her, though she hadn't been in any immediate danger. No doubt paid very well.

But it wasn't that simple. In hindsight, she could understand what she'd ignored when she'd been in the grip of the moment. Much of what he said made sense. There was a limit to what they could have done given the situation.

But she couldn't simply accept that that was all there was to it. There'd been a thread of fury running through him, a strong and detectable anger though he'd worked to hide it from her.

No use. There wasn't enough outside to occupy her mind, and mooning over Sam was hardly productive. She tugged the drapes shut.

A comfortable armchair was bolted beside a small table. She'd insisted upon its presence, though there really was scarcely room for it. But she'd spent too much time in bed in her life as it was and preferred not to be in one if she didn't have to. The lamp mounted above flared to life with the touch of a match, the soft glow warming the rich wood walls of her compartment, burnishing the rosette-gathered panels of red silk on her ceiling.

She collected her sketch pad, a dozen completed drawings, a couple of pencils. There wasn't enough light really to work, but she could sort through them, make a few notes, perhaps eliminate some ideas. Knowing what to leave out of a panorama was as important as deciding what to include.

If she weren't going to sleep that night, at least she could do something productive with her time.

She flipped through the sketches. Good, good, not so good . . . she'd missed something in that landscape, she considered, tilting her head as she studied it. The proportions of that valley they'd passed right outside of Aspen were off. It had been a murky day, and the mountains kept shifting in and out of the clouds, so their shape was not as precise as she would have liked.

She moved on. So many sketches, of which she'd use no more than 10 percent or so.

Before this particular trip, she was starting to get a bit . . . not bored, exactly, but restless in her work. It was the scale of panoramas that appealed to her originally. If she were destined to paint landscapes, well, by darn, she'd paint the grandest ones she could. That, and the opportunity to immerse herself in a place she could not travel to herself. For a girl who'd lived in a narrow world, the massive scope of them drew her.

But she'd struggled with the last one, the New York panels. Deep inside that bothered her most of all. Perhaps the reason she'd made mistakes was because she hadn't thrown herself into it with her usual enthusiasm. As she'd gotten healthier, stronger, she'd gotten more intrigued by the real world outside her studio window; the painted one held less fascination. And contemplating the next project was difficult, being confronted with those huge blank rolls of canvas. The enormity of the task, once so exciting and challenging—now that she truly knew how much work awaited her, the prospect merely made her tired.

So this trip had been crucial to her in more ways than one. She'd thought that it would revive her enthusiasm, giving her back the passion for painting panoramas that she'd once had.

Instead the journey had given her other passions. A hunger for travel. Not the least sated by the trip, all Laura could think of was how much more world there was to experience. And wasn't her father going to love that, when she went home and announced that she really, really, wanted to go to Italy or Africa?

And a yearning for new people, different people. The richness of experience that had been denied her, the absence of boundaries. It was a grand, wide world, so wide even a panorama could never capture it. Perhaps, she thought, she'd do better to concentrate on one small snip of it and portray it perfectly.

And a passion for him. For Sam. She could not pretend that it didn't exist. She loved the way she felt when he was near, the way her blood thrummed in her veins and her skin tingled and her senses were alive, not only her vision but all the other ones, too, the ones that had been mostly ignored until now. Smell and taste and touch— oh, Lord, touch. Her lips throbbed at just the memory, her skin heating. She would not go back to being ignorant of that feeling, even if she could. Surely, when this was over, she could find someone else to give her that. Someone more appropriate, who would fit into her life and be willing to allow her to take a central place in his. Someone who would *long* to have that joining with her—for she was not so blinded by desire that she did not realize that Sam did not *want* to feel anything for her.

Her hands slowed as she reached the final sketch: the edge of the Silver Spur Ranch, the half-finished study she'd abandoned when that despairing man came running toward them. She traced the path he'd taken, down over the hill, across the flat, scrub-studded land.

The next page was blank. A clean slate, a world of possibilities. Without conscious thought, her hand moved over the page. A quick slash, a slow curve, a brutal, arrowing line. She drew faster, and faster still, completely unlike her usual deliberate pace, while her breath sped up and her heart beat faster.

She was breathless when she finished, as though she'd been the one who'd run miles.

A face. She'd drawn a face. *His* face.

She hadn't tried portraiture since she was fourteen or so, under the tutelage of Mr. Aspinwall, her art teacher. She'd been a natural at nearly every other form of art, though sculpture had challenged her, especially early on when her body was weak. But as soon as they'd moved on to figures, her talent seemed to desert her.

Everyone she drew was stiff, lifeless. Like her model had been a doll instead of a human being. Oh, the proportions had been right, the shape of the features. But she could never seem to animate a face.

Until now. It was all there, the desperate, narrow eyes. A face that should have been round, if its owner had been sufficiently well fed. And most of all the emotion—she couldn't look at that face on the page without her eyes stinging.

Oh, it wasn't perfect. She was too demanding of her own talent ever to be completely satisfied.

It was rough, the lines slashing across the page, the background nothing but a rough scribble. She'd missed on the hair, completely, and put in nothing more than a suggestion of his clothing.

But the *feel* of it was right. There was power in it, and despair, and panic.

She'd drawn a face.

Sam figured the town of Silver Creek could be a problem. He'd changed his appearance as much as he could, even retiring his favorite coat and hat. But he'd asked a lot of questions there, enough to be memorable. He could only hope they wouldn't stay long, and try and stay out of sight as much as possible while they were there.

They pulled into town near sunset. Later than they'd planned; the Union Pacific had been a little tardy in picking them up. Sam wondered if the passengers were ever annoyed that they had to stop and wait for Laura's cars to get hitched up, or if they were too happy to have the famous Miss Hamilton aboard to overlook the slight inconvenience. They'd have a story to tell their mothers, their cousins, their sweethearts, whoever waited for them at the end of their journey.

And he was nearing the end of his.

Silver Creek looked more like a stage set than a town, Laura decided as she stood on the back platform of her rail car while they unhitched it from the main train.

They'd sit on the siding until Thursday, until the next train through would take them to the station, three miles from town, where the trains from the mines met the railroad. An engine ran back and forth to the mines twice a week, shuttling long strings of ore cars. On that day it would return to the Silver Spur with a couple of extra cars.

The town was neat, neater than any she'd seen in the West. It hadn't grown naturally, springing up living and haphazard along natural lines. Instead, it boasted carefully geometric streets, well kept frame buildings that all looked the same, a tidy brick schoolhouse, a white, spire-topped church that could have modeled for a Christmas card. Even the grass, small, perfectly square lawns laid out in front of the houses and all clipped to the same length were unnatural. Lawns were rare out here, and yards tended to go wild, bare dirt or choked with weeds, for there was no time for luxuries such as grass.

Silver Creek would be difficult to paint, almost impossible to make real. No matter how she did it, what feature she tried to dramatize, nobody would believe that the town actually looked like this. There should be some flaw, somewhere—a wall in need of a fresh coat of whitewash, a determined weed pushing up through the boardwalk, a withering bush.

"Isn't it cute?" Mrs. Bossidy said. "I spoke to the conductor before we arrived. Mr. Crocker gives generously to the town. That's why they can keep it so nice." She sniffed. "Not like some of the places we've been through."

Well, Mrs. Bossidy always did like things all prettied up. Laura, who had spent her life in a polished world, not a single brown petal allowed on a flower before it was replaced, had discovered that she was drawn to things that were a little rough around the edges. They told a story through their imperfections, revealed their life in their scratches and dents.

She apparently preferred her men a bit like that, too, automatically seeking out Sam. Very unusually for him, he wasn't standing on the back platform, either of her car or the men's.

The stationmaster, balding and beaming, took up residence on the platform before the train rolled to a full stop, with a little step and a hand to assist her descent.

"That was very efficient," she told him with a smile.

"Mr. Crocker told us to take very good care of you."

"Then I will tell him that you did so."

He grinned even more broadly, seeing her safely to the ground before turning to support Mrs. Bossidy.

"Welcome to Silver Creek, ma'am."

"Thank you," she said, stepping down with the alacrity of a child charging down to the parlor on Christmas morning. "And I'm *very* happy to be here. Where is the telegraph station?"

"The telegraph station?" Laura repeated. And just who could Mrs. Bossidy be telegraphing? She had a few friends amongst the staff at Sea Haven, but no one she'd ever seemed particularly close to. "Are you sending my father a report?"

"No," she snapped. "I do have business of my own upon occasion."

"I know you do. I just meant . . . of course you do."

Laura knew very little of Mrs. Bossidy's life before she came to Sea Haven. Oh, she'd asked, often in the early days, questions that Mrs. Bossidy deflected easily and Laura had been too young to know how to pursue. But she hadn't tried for a very long time, she realized. Hadn't even wondered.

"Oh, it's only a few blocks down that way," the stationmaster said. "But it's closed. Evening, you know."

Mrs. Bossidy frowned. "What time will it be open in the morning?"

"Nine, usually. Sometimes earlier, if he's been to bed early enough the night before."

"Oh, dear," Mrs. Bossidy said, clearly deflated.

"But that's all right," he said quickly. Obviously it wouldn't do for their honored guests to be unhappy with anything about Silver Creek. "I'm sure he'd be pleased to open it up for you."

She glanced at Laura, then shrugged. "No, no. I'm sure it's fine. Tomorrow will be soon enough."

Hiram and Erastus lumbered up to them.

"Whew. Glad to be off that thing," Hiram said. "All

that rockin' to and fro is unsettlin' to a man's stomach."

"Oh, no," Mrs. Bossidy said. "Can't have your appetite leaving you, can we? With so little flesh to spare you'd waste away in no time."

"Where's Mr. Duncan?" Laura asked before she thought better of it.

"In the car."

"In the *car?*" That was very unlike him. He was inside seldom enough if they were under way, and even then only when driven indoors by unfriendly weather. Inside on a lovely day when they were in a station was unheard of.

"Yeah, he said he was a little under the weather," Hiram informed her. "Seems like he was, too. He was kinda pale, and sweating like a sailor in the boiler room."

"Oh." Poor thing. Of course the man fell ill occasionally. He was human, after all, though he seemed so vital and healthy and perfect that she couldn't picture him succumbing to mere illness. "I'll go look in on him."

"I'm sure he's fine," said Mr. Peel. "Just a touch of the ague, maybe."

"No, no, I'm sure you're anxious to begin work, Laura," Mrs. Bossidy said quickly. "And you're useless in a sickroom in any case. Too many bad memories. I, on the other hand, am quite good at it."

"It's so good to know where your skills lie," Hiram interjected.

"As long as one has skills in the first place," she tossed off serenely as she headed for the second car.

"But—" Too late. Mrs. Bossidy was already halfway there, and Laura really couldn't protest without being obvious. And even if she followed, Mrs. Bossidy would be hovering the entire time. She wouldn't have an in-stant alone with Sam.

Besides, Mrs. Bossidy really *was* much better in a sickroom than Laura.

He'd fallen asleep. That surprised him. When he'd first entered the car, he'd been dizzy, his heart panic-knocking like it belonged to a fresh recruit in a dugout with shells flying his way.

He could go inside when he had to, he'd reminded himself. Was even—mostly—okay in big, airy places with lots of windows like churches and train stations. But small places, dark places . . . they gave him trou-ble. But he *could* do it if he had to, he'd told himself a million times.

He just preferred . . . not to.

But it had seemed eminently sensible to sequester himself in the car when they rolled into Silver Creek. There promised to be too much hubbub surrounding their arrival, too many interested, eager people mulling about, though most of them were there to get a look at Laura. Not that they weren't used to millionaires, given they had one of their own. But she was different, an *Eastern* one, famous in her own right.

He could leave the train car as soon as it got dark, he promised himself. Prowl and poke around, see what there was to see. Not that he expected much. He'd had no luck there the first time and wasn't likely to have any more now. Any trace of Griff was long gone if it had ever been there in the first place.

No, his only hope was to slip right on to the Silver Spur without anybody noticing. Who would ever look for him as part of Laura Hamilton's entourage? They thought they'd chased him off once and for all. He'd been gone for weeks. And he really didn't think they'd actually *looked* at him all that closely. He hadn't spent much time with any one person in particular, though there were one or two he'd questioned that he'd have to avoid.

But the plan was workable, he judged. Soon as they got to the Silver Spur, this mysterious illness was going to come roaring back and confine him to his room. There'd be guards at night, no doubt, but there was an awful lot of ground to cover, and he'd be careful, a lot more careful than he'd been the last time. And the moon was waning; he'd checked last night. Two more nights, maybe three, and you wouldn't be able to see your six-shooter when held in your own hand.

But he'd dropped off while those thoughts whirled around in his head, right after Mrs. Bossidy's strangely solicitous visit. Probably because he *hadn't* dropped off the night before, when the thoughts spinning around in his head had been of that poor captured Chinaman.

He could have been a thief or a murderer, just as he'd explained to Laura.

It just wasn't likely. He had well-honed instincts for such things, and he felt in his bones there was something very wrong on the Silver Spur.

But it wasn't his business. He'd learned long ago to ignore his conscience in the name of survival. He'd had little choice. But you could tamp down a conscience, discount it, be certain it was eradicated, only to find it stirring at inconvenient moments.

Discovering what had happened to Griff remained his primary goal. He owed his friend that much. Owed him more than that when it came right down to it. If in the process he found out what happened to that man, that would be a nice bonus. He promised himself that he'd help if the opportunity arose—if the man *needed* any assistance.

It wasn't all that late, he judged. Coming up on midnight, maybe? The other two men were likely still out. Certainly Hiram was gone; if you couldn't hear the man, he wasn't in the car. They liked to tip a few at the local saloon whenever they rolled into a new town.

It was a pleasant evening. The window was wide open—it helped keep his heart steady to have it open, letting in fresh air—and a breeze fluttered through, soft and sweet-smelling.

He couldn't lie in bed on such a night and not think of her. Was that such a terrible thing?

Nothing more would happen between them. Only a few more days at the most, and they would never see each other again. In the meantime she was well chaperoned, particularly lately.

And neither of them was likely to *allow* any further . . . exploration. He knew what place he held in her life. He was an experiment, a part of her adventure, a memory of her excursion into the real world. She would go home and find a man who fit neatly into her life and that her family would welcome. Someone who carried a far sight less baggage than he did.

Someone who was willing to love her the way she deserved.

But it wasn't so wrong to fantasize, was it? To dream about what it would be like if she were a different kind of woman, one who could do more than a little kissing and keep a physical relationship in its proper, safe place?

Or, even, what there might be between them were he a different kind of man.

The breeze brushed his face, bringing with it a sweeter smell. Something must be blooming—

"You're awake," Laura said.

Chapter 10

His breath seized in his chest. He sprang up, the light bedclothes falling to his waist before he realized he was bare-chested. Naked? he thought frantically. No, he had his pants on. Thank heavens—or hell—or small favors.

"What are you doing here?" He should have heard her coming and had a chance to prepare himself. He'd spent a lifetime on high alert, listening for a telltale footstep, a whisper of sound that betrayed someone's stealthy approach. And she'd slipped right beside his bed without him hearing a thing.

Perhaps because she'd already been there in his mind, ever-present, ever-tempting.

She hovered beside the bed, her fingers twisting uncertainly together. Not in a nightgown, the frilly confection he'd imagined she would sleep in. No, fully dressed, in the wide dark skirt she'd worn that day, a shirt that ended in a flutter of lace beneath her chin, pure and ghostly white in the dim moonlight. She'd left the short little jacket behind. *One less layer*, he thought dimly, through the haze of rising desire that blurred his thoughts.

"I didn't mean to disturb you." She hovered beside the bed, just out of reach, a dream he could not reach for.

"What are you doing here?" he repeated harshly.

"I'm sorry," Laura said, backing away. "I didn't mean to—they said you were sick. I know Mrs. Bossidy looked in on you, but I just wanted to make sure—" The man wasn't wearing a shirt, Laura realized. She tried not to stare—oh, it was so terribly wrong of her to take such advantage of the situation! But how could she not? She'd seen statues. Paintings. But not living, vibrant flesh. Dimension, motion . . . it added so much fascination to the form. And there wasn't an artist in the world who wouldn't have begged for the opportunity to paint that body, all sinew and broad muscle and long bones.

"Oh yeah. Sick." He flopped back on the bed, his arms wide. Surely that'd be safer, Sam thought. Unthreatening.

"Do you have a fever? I—" She laid her hand on his forehead. "I—"

He caught her wrist.

"Laura."

Her pulse beat against his thumb. Quicker, harder, as every nerve she owned vibrated from the bright sensation of that one point of contact.

"Leave." His thumb moved, slow circles against the vulnerable flesh at the inside of her wrist. "For God's sake, Laura, leave. *Now*."

"I just wanted to—"

"*Now*." He should release her. Sam knew it, dimly, in the small part of him that retained a fraying shred of sanity.

Laura didn't move. How could she move? Life thrummed through her veins, fizzy, bubbling, wonderful *life*. This was what she'd survived for. This was what she'd waited for, all those gray, confined days and nights.

Slowly, she lowered herself to the edge of the bed. Still they touched nowhere but where his fingers encircled her wrist, but she knew her hip was no more than two inches from his thigh. Was he bare there, too, beneath the linens? The idea reeled in her rapidly fogging mind.

It was so terribly wicked, the sort of thing she'd never thought she would do. She was in the bed of a naked man, a wild and terrible and mysterious man.

"*Are* you ill?" she whispered.

"Yes," he growled. "Terribly so. Contagious, too. *Extremely*."

"No you're not." She lifted her free hand and wrapped it around *his* wrist, *his* hand.

"Laura, you have no idea what you're risking here."

"Is it such a risk?" she asked. "Such an awful thing? I liked kissing you. You liked kissing me. Why would it be so terrible to do it again?"

"Do you think I can do that?" Every muscle in his body was so tight it hurt, a sweet, burning pain that he was afraid he would forevermore associate with her. "That we can just . . . play for a while, then I could let you go?" he asked savagely. "Because I can't. *Won't*. If you don't leave now, you may not leave at all."

There. He'd finally gotten through to her, Sam thought: a quick intake of breath, her eyes wide, glinting with fear. The woman wasn't stupid. Surely she knew enough to run, fast and hard, back to her safe, guarded life.

He loosened his grip in slow, incremental fractions,

regretting it every second, because he knew it would be the last time he ever touched her, and touching her suddenly seemed like the best thing in the world, the one thing that would make living worthwhile.

Possibilities hovered in the air between them, all the things that might have been and would never be. Regret wrenched him. He understood it was for the best. For both of them. But oh, he longed for it to be different. That his whole life would have been different, so this could be something other than what it simply had to be.

She let go of his wrist, and the skin was warm where she'd touched him. He could remember it exactly, the soft smoothness of her flesh, the narrow, delicate length of her fingers.

And then she reached out and placed her hand squarely on his bare chest.

Their eyes met. Time caught, held, ripe with choices and possibilities. Shadows flickered across his throat, his chest. Bedazzled, she drifted her fingers across his skin. His collarbone angled down, straight and strong. Dark hair, wiry beneath her touch, thickened toward the center of his chest. *I could spend a lifetime here*, she thought, *and never lose the fascination of touching him*.

Then he yanked, tumbling her on top of him. They lay there like that, breathing hard, gazes locked. There was a sheen of moisture on his forehead, a hard, harsh line to his mouth as though he hurt, deeply and irrevocably.

"Last chance," he said.

Was there really a choice? If she had one, it was buried low and deep beneath the need that crackled inside her, raced along nerve endings. He was hard beneath her, completely unyielding, and she lifted and fell with each breath he took, a rhythm that thrummed inside her belly, her heart, found its way lower.

"No chance at all," she murmured, lowering her mouth toward his.

Almost there. A breath away. One more fraction of an inch until . . .

He rolled her off the bed, shoving her away, setting her on her feet, where she wavered, disoriented and disappointed.

"What—"

"Hush." He plopped back into the bed, yanking the pile of covers up to his neck, and slammed his eyes shut.

The door banged open. Bodies jostled through—one, two, three.

Peel and Hoxie stood on either end of the bed, arms outstretched, their guns carefully aimed, faces determined—they would not take Sam's skills too lightly this time. They were three feet from the bed, far enough that he could not simply reach out and snatch their weapons, and the two of them were separated by enough space that he could not attack them both at once. Hoxie's hand shook.

"Easy there, Erastus," Sam said. "Those things tend to go off when you jiggle 'em around like that."

Hoxie swallowed hard, narrowing his eyes. "Shut up."

Sam lifted his brows in surprise. "So what do I owe the pleasure?"

Mrs. Bossidy hovered in the doorway, peering into the darkened room.

"Laura! What are you doing here?"

"I—" She shot a guilty glance at Sam, uncertain whether she was more unhappy about being caught or being interrupted. *Darn, darn, darn.* "You were all gone so long," she said slowly, letting the implication that they'd been remiss in their duties hover in the air.

"I thought, if Mr. Duncan truly were as ill as Mr. Hoxie implied, we shouldn't be leaving him alone."

"Move away from the bed," she ordered.

"Excuse me, I—"

"*Move away*," she said, with enough heat that Laura obeyed automatically. The tiny chamber was hopelessly crowded with four people in it. Laura bumped up against the far wall and stayed there, confused, curious.

"Afraid I'm gonna grab her and use her as a shield?" Sam asked.

"Yes."

"I don't need a shield."

Laura finally recovered enough to speak. "*What* are you all doing?"

"Laura." Mrs. Bossidy took her hand. "Laura, my dear, he's not who you believe him to be."

"Look." He started to sit up. The covers fell away again, exposing enough impressive musculature to make Mrs. Bossidy's eyes go wide.

"Don't move," Hiram ordered.

Laura couldn't look away. *Now* there *is a painting,* she thought, a gorgeous bare-chested man in a mussed bed, hair tousled, eyes sleepy, so blatantly sexual that men would drag their women from museums rather than let them view it.

She tried to read his expression. Over the days, she'd learned to discern what little hints he gave: a slight tension in the corners of his mouth, a darkening of his eyes, a fractional deepening of the furrow between his brows. But nothing betrayed his emotions at that moment, his expression wiped completely clean. He was still beautiful—nothing could mute that. But the vitality that set him apart was absent, the intensity in his eyes shuttered, as if he'd distanced himself from her, stealing back whatever fragment of himself he'd shared with her.

"Sam?" she asked, taking a half step toward him.

"No." Mrs. Bossidy's voice cracked through the room. "Laura, your father didn't hire him."

"What?" It *whooshed* out of her, hope and shock and disbelief, leaving her limp and confused.

"We cabled your father when we stopped in Bear River City. He didn't hire anyone."

Her gaze slid around the room, touching them each in turn—Hiram, so furious he looked as if his head might pop off; Mr. Hoxie, wounded and uncertain; Mrs. Bossidy, protective as a mother bear. And Sam, as remote from her as though he'd been painted by an artist with no feel for the medium, distant and detached.

"*Sam.*"

She didn't know what she wanted him to say. That Mrs. Bossidy lied? That Sam had?

"It was . . . closed," she said numbly. "The stationmaster said the telegraph office was closed."

"They opened it for me," Mrs. Bossidy said.

Say something. But what could he say that would make any difference? Her father hadn't hired him. He'd lied to her all along.

"What did you want from me?" she asked him.

Stupid question. She knew perfectly well what he wanted from her.

Money. Of course it was money. What else could it be?

She remembered the kisses, sweet as summer, as intoxicating as the first time she'd been allowed out of the sickroom and she'd stepped out on the terrace and the ocean overwhelmed her, the waves crashing, the briny air flooding her senses.

Oh, he'd reeled her in so easily. No mere loan or

large investment for him. He would have had her in love with him within weeks. She'd been halfway there already. And for the man who married Baron Hamilton's daughter . . . "You wouldn't have gotten any. Any of my father's money, I mean. He would have made sure of it."

"It's not what you—"

"I told you to shut up!" Hoxie shouted.

Sam shook his head slightly. His mouth lifted in a painful impersonation of a smile.

And then he dived for the open window. *Through* the open window, headfirst, fast as a falcon plummeting after its prey.

"Hey!" Caught by surprise, the men reacted a beat late.

Laura was faster. She knew what he was capable of.

But by the time she reached the window, he was gone.

"Not much out here, is there?" Mrs. Bossidy said.

The train from Silver Creek to Ogden had dropped them off at the tiny station three miles from town— they called it a station, but it was in truth little more than a large storage shed—where another line of tracks speared off toward the Silver Spur mines.

"We should have stayed in Silver Creek longer," she went on. "Now we have to sit here for three days."

Laura glanced up from her sketch pad. They'd had supper an hour earlier; a simple one, as it always was when they weren't in a town or hitched to a train, something about which Hiram complained incessantly until Mrs. Bossidy shushed him. He was of the opinion that they should have brought their own chef on the trip, at which point Mrs. Bossidy opined that they traveled with one too many people for her taste as it was.

They'd set up a table and chairs outside and ate in the lowering sun. Low mountains rimmed the narrow valley that the rail bed spiked through. Beyond the shed—simple, tin-roofed, the lumber gray with age—there was simply nothing else, not even a few trees. Scrubby brush struggled for life, giving way to tufts of prickly grass. Now and then a hawk wheeled overhead. Once a lone rabbit flashed by in a panic. Deep blue evening settled over the land. No lights flickered in the distance. If there was another person within miles, there was no sign of them.

"I like it out here," Laura said. The quiet, empty spaces matched her mood better than the smug bustle of Silver Creek. And she, who'd been so pleased with every new acquaintance, had finally met her fill. If one more cheerful, friendly, helpful person interrupted the work she was struggling enough with as it was . . . well, at least she wouldn't be interrupted in the asylum.

Her work was going terribly. Not going at all, in fact, despite her best effort. The blank page, glowing yellow from the lamplight, accused her.

She couldn't work up the necessary passion for her subject. Oh, the land was magnificent. She realized it intellectually, understood that it would make a wonderful subject for a panorama. But she was tired of painting mountains and trees, rivers and towns.

But that wasn't the only problem, and she knew it.

It was because he was gone.

A day without him. One endless day, and already the trip had lost its luster.

She couldn't let him strip her of something that had

meant so much to her. But she didn't know how to regain her pleasure in the journey.

Tomorrow, she decided. She'd give herself one day to wallow in misery, then she'd just have to get over him. He wasn't worth more than a day.

She flipped the sketchbook shut and stood. "I'm going to bed."

Her brow puckered in consternation, Mrs. Bossidy looked up from the scarf she'd been working on for three days. Considering she'd managed all of three inches, Laura figured she might produce a scarf in time for Christmas. "Are you all right?"

"I'm fine. I'm just tired."

She balled up her project. "I'll come with you."

"No, stay."

"Laura." She paused, debating for a moment, then plunged in. "You're better off without him."

"Mrs. Bossidy . . ." She didn't want to discuss this with her. Well-meant, sympathetic platitudes about the temporary nature of first crushes were the last thing she wanted to hear.

"Even if he was what he seemed," Mrs. Bossidy continued, "even if he hadn't lied, you'd still be better off without him."

"I was never with him."

His face swam above her, a soft, cloudy, heated dream. There was gentle concern in his eyes . . . concern for her? And she was so happy to see emotion there that she smiled.

His mouth moved, but she couldn't hear what he said. She reached up and touched his cheek; lean, prickly with beard, and it felt so real . . .

It was real. He was real.

Laura blinked and struggled to sit.

"Easy now," he said, one arm firm around her back as he helped her up. "Your head's gonna be muddled for a while."

"Where are we?"

"Nowhere, really."

She swiveled her head carefully until she was certain it would remain properly attached. She sat on a blanket on the ground. A thin sliver of moonlight ghosted the landscape with gray light: rocky ground, clumps of sagebrush, clusters of wheatgrass. A horse—one of *her* horses—was tethered a few feet away.

"You stole one of my horses?"

"Borrowed it."

Her muddled brain cleared in stages, like fog thinning in uneven patches over a marsh. She was angry at him. She knew it, felt it burn in her belly, but couldn't locate the reason at first.

"What are we doing here?"

"I wanted to talk to you."

And then the memories crashed back on her. She lurched from his grip, skittering back across the blanket until her hands hit bare ground, rocks biting into her palms.

He let her go, just remained crouched on the blanket. "Watch out," he said. "There could be scorpions out there. Rattlers. And it's dark."

She'd gone to sleep in her bed and awoken outside. They could be anywhere. Miles away from the train from the look of it. Miles away from anyone that might save her. Try as she might, she couldn't put this together with *him*, couldn't be as worried as she obviously should be. "You . . . *kidnapped* me?"

"If you want to be technical about it," he said calmly.

Chapter 11

Laura scanned the area, trying to pick out a path, somewhere to run or hide, or anything that could serve as a weapon against him.

"You can yell, but there's no one to hear you," he warned her. "And you can run, but you know I can catch you. You can try the horse, but I'm betting you don't know which direction to go. All in all you're best off if you simply stay put, hear me out, and wait for me to take you back."

Over the years she'd imagined what she might do if she were abducted. Fight back, certainly, or try to escape. Something other than meekly accept her fate. But he laid out her options so reasonably. And it was Sam. The darkness cloaked him, leaving only the deep glitter of his eyes, the flash of teeth as he spoke.

"Laura, if I meant to do you real harm, I could have done it weeks ago easily enough."

True. But still . . . "Where are Hiram and Mr. Hoxie? Mrs. Bossidy?"

"Still sleeping comfortably in their beds, I imagine."
He shook his head. "If I'd been in charge, I would have
made certain someone was on guard at all times, but
that's just me. Heavy sleepers, all of them."

"They protected me just fine until you came along,"
she protested, deeply offended.

"Evidently nobody tried very hard to get to you
before."

She touched her fingertips to her temple, willing her
brain to function. "I don't remember . . . I went to
sleep. I woke up here. How did I not wake up when you
took me from the train car?"

He winced. "Chloroform."

"You *chloroformed* me?"

"It seemed simplest. I didn't want to knock you out.
Didn't much like the idea of gagging you either." He
shrugged. "Didn't want you struggling and waking up
those clowns. Someone could get shot. Might've even
been me."

She shook her head. "I still don't . . . how much do
you want?"

"Want?"

"Yes," she said, briskly businesslike. "I have some
resources, of course. But that's all that's available. It
will do you no good to compromise me. My father long
ago made it clear that he would not force me into marriage in such circumstances."

"Would I have to force you?"

"It wouldn't matter," she hedged, avoiding the question. "Even if there's no force, he told me in no uncertain terms years ago that he would not settle a fortune
upon my marriage unless he approves it first."

"I don't want to marry you."

She would not let that hurt. "Why, then?"

"I told you. I needed to talk you." Guilt, untimely and unfamiliar, nagged at Sam. He'd chosen the most expedient solution. He'd gone over his plan a dozen times and hadn't come up with a better one.

One of the reasons for his success as a hired gun had been his ability to ignore extraneous twinges of conscience and go for the simplest and quickest solution. He wasn't going to allow whatever inconvenient . . . sympathy he'd developed for her to get in the way of doing what needed to be done. And yet . . . *damn*.

She wrapped her arms around her knees, curling up like a child in front of the fire. Her hair was braided and pinned back simply, leaving the pure lines of her face clear and unadorned. "Why didn't you talk to me, then? Why all *this*?"

"They weren't going to let me say anything. Not then. And I didn't want to . . . there was no reason for them to know. They didn't *need* to know."

"Still—" She wanted to protest. Wanted to hold on to the anger and the offense. And didn't want to be touched by the fact that he'd trusted her with his story when he trusted no one else.

But it did no good to ignore the truth when she heard it. "A bit extreme, don't you think?"

"I don't have that much time to waste," Sam said.

"All right." She nodded, then dropped her chin to her knees. Her nightgown was white and simple, far plainer than the beautiful and elaborate clothes she wore each day. Somehow it suited her better, Sam decided. Her clothes were always so extraordinary you noticed them first. In this waft of thin white, you noticed *her*.

But he'd always noticed her, hadn't he?

"Talk," she ordered him.

"It's a long story."

"Then you'd best get started."

Start. Where to start? He'd been so busy plotting how to get her away from her guards that he'd spent no time planning how he'd explain everything. Even now, he'd rather go to her, scoop her up in his arms, and continue what they'd begun in his bed.

He'd stood over her bed, the chloroformed rag in his hand and contemplated what he would do, how she'd slip deeper into sleep, and it had taken an act of will stronger than surviving prison to force his hand over her mouth. When he lifted her into his arms—light, limp, the soft curve of her hip bumping his belly, the narrow width of her back—he'd swallowed hard and nearly tucked her safely back into her bed instead of quietly slipping out the door with her.

And then on the horse—getting on had been a trick, flopping her awkwardly across the back in a way he knew she'd never forgive him for if she ever discovered it. She'd rocked in his arms with each step of the horse, that sweet floral scent—he didn't know flowers, was it lilac or rose or orange blossoms?—drifting up and clouding his senses, so much so that he'd almost ridden farther than he'd planned because she felt so natural in his arms.

"Well?" she prompted.

He'd never said it out loud, he realized. Not once. It clogged in his throat, as painful as a bone splinter. "I was in Andersonville."

"What?" Laura lifted her head in surprise. She'd heard tales of the place, stories her parents had tried to hide from her. She'd been too young to know of them then, of course, but there'd been a story in the paper, interviews with the tragically few survivors of the notorious Confederate prison.

Sympathy swelled. She cursed the night. What would she find now, if she could see more of his eyes than an expressionless gleam? Would she see the truth?

But he'd lied to her, she remembered. He'd *drugged* her. This could be calculated as well, a skillful play on her sympathy. "I don't see what that has to do with me."

"I'm getting to that." The grim line of his mouth softened. Recently it happened more often around her, frequently enough that it no longer surprised her. It still pleased her. Even now, when nothing about him should please her.

"I told you I was in the army." It had been stupid to lie about his age to join up, he realized now. But his older brother, Tom, whom he'd idolized from the first, had marched off in search of glory, and he always did everything Tom did.

Except die.

"I was captured two months later."

"Sam."

Her voice carried a whisper of sadness, a richness of sympathy that drew forth a fresh burn of memory. Was that why he'd never told anyone before? Because it was easier to ignore when you never spoke of it? Pretend it hadn't happened?

"Was it as terrible as they say?"

Worse. Nothing anybody ever said or wrote could come close to the terrible reality of it. Even now, though he'd lived through it—*existed* through it—he could scarcely grasp the horror. Perhaps the human mind rejected it, the way a stomach revolted against rotten food, because no one could truly know that and remain sane and whole.

Laura edged closer on the blanket and gently laid her hand over his.

"I didn't intend to play on your sympathy," he said. "Though I do appreciate the side benefits."

"What, then?" Laura knew she shouldn't touch him. But his flesh beneath hers, living texture, the hard bump of strong knuckles, the sinewy strength of a man who'd survived, was comforting and compelling and really, what did it hurt?

"I had a—" What to call him? Sam wondered. "Friend there." *Friend*. That was a pale approximation of what Griff Judah had been to him. Compatriot, brother, lifeline. Even a replacement for the family he'd just lost. "He kept me alive, all those months. I would have given up without him."

How many times had Griff talked him back from the edge? Had told him that he *couldn't* die because then Griff would be alone? "He got a job on the Silver Spur."

"I see." Her hand remained, a precious connection to the present, keeping the past from swamping him.

"I never heard from him again." When he looked at her in the moonlight, all pretty and young and clean beside him, a part of him wavered. Wondered if maybe he shouldn't give it up and simply get on with his life. Not with her, of course. But someone like Laura would be if she hadn't been born rich.

For if Haw Crocker was trying that hard to hide something from him on the Silver Spur, Griff was likely long past Sam's help anyway. Would just knowing what had happened to Griff be worth all Sam risked, all he'd done?

But no. *No*. He owed Griff, and himself, this much. He'd never be able to live with anything less. And if there was even the slightest chance Griff survived, he *had* to do this.

"Maybe," she ventured, "he . . . perhaps he did not *want* to get in touch with you again."

She'd said it so cautiously, as if afraid to make the suggestion, he couldn't help but smile. "Not too surprising to you, hmm, that somebody'd want to cut me out of his life?"

"No, no, I didn't mean—" And then she caught his expression, and her own discomfort eased. "Not surprising at all," she teased.

"I came here looking for him. No one knew anything, or so they said. They swore he never showed up here at all."

"Maybe he never did." Laura wondered if he even realized she touched him, so lost was he in his thoughts and the story he told her. Thinking of his friend, no doubt, a friend who was obviously more than a simple friend. Someone you'd survived that much with . . . clearly there was a bond there that others could not always understand. The fact that he could care that much for someone, remain so loyal to someone for what had to be a good twenty years, made him all the more appealing.

"I considered that," he said. He turned his head, gaze sweeping the shadowed land. "I asked around in town. They all swore they'd never seen him. But, I had to give it one last try before I gave up, and so I sneaked back onto Silver Spur land."

He fell silent, his jaw working, eyes narrowed as if there were something fascinating out there. Looking into memories, she thought, memories she waited patiently for him to share. Because he *was* sharing them, giving them to her—perhaps not freely, perhaps with ulterior motive, but far more than he'd revealed to her before.

"They were waiting for me," he said at last.

"Waiting—oh." She swallowed. "The injuries, when we first met . . ."

"Yeah." He nodded. "They said it was because I was trespassing. I wondered, for a while, why they didn't just kill me. I suppose my death would have caused more questions than they wanted to answer. For all they knew I'd told someone about my suspicions."

Anger exploded in Laura. If so much damage had been visible, there had to have been even more that she hadn't seen. She was furious at them for having done that to him. And if that's how she felt, she could begin to guess what it meant to him that Griff might have been hurt, too.

He turned toward her. His hand rotated in hers, face up, his fingers weaving with hers, though he seemed unaware of what he was doing. And that made it all the more stirring that he would hold her hand for support, thoughtlessly, instinctually.

"You know what that means," he said.

"That they had something to hide?"

He nodded. "I needed a way back in. *All* the way in. I read the article about you in the paper, and I figured you were my best chance. They'd never expect me to come as part of your party. I'd be just another one of your guards. They'd probably never even look at me all that closely."

It was an awfully big risk for him to dismiss as if it were nothing. "What if someone recognized you?"

He shrugged, tossing off his personal safety. "I wouldn't be any worse off than I was already, would I? I shaved off my beard and chopped my hair. It was worth a shot."

And if someone recognized him, this time they really might kill him.

If they had something to hide, she reminded herself. Haw Crocker and her father had done a lot of business together, and her father often spoke well of him and his acumen. She couldn't believe her father would be that wrong about someone.

But the Silver Spur was a massive operation. Likely Mr. Crocker didn't even personally know half of the people who worked for him, much less keep close tabs on them.

And if there was nothing to find, there was nothing to find. Either way, at least Sam would be able to get on with his life knowing he had done all he could.

"Was it really necessary to . . . lie to me?" It was a soft pain now, gentler than the bright stab of anger she'd first felt when Mrs. Bossidy had told her the truth.

She remembered the time they'd spent together. The way he'd looked at her, listened to her, and she couldn't sort out the truth from the lies. Had it *all* been a lie? She was afraid that it was. Clearly he wouldn't let a few minor points like truth and her emotions get in the way of what he considered necessary and expedient.

She'd known he was capable of that from the first. She'd just chosen to ignore it.

"Crocker and your father have done business together. For all I knew, he's your father's friend, too. You didn't know me," he said, his voice softening. "More importantly, I didn't know *you.*"

But she couldn't let her own wounded pride interfere and dig in her heels for spite. This *mattered* to him, and she could help.

"All right then." She lifted her free hand and brushed back the loose swath of his hair, exposing the strong, clean bones. A beard? He could have been covered in turf from head to toe and painted white, and she was sure she would know him.

But the men on the Silver Spur weren't artists, she reminded herself. And likely hadn't spent nearly as much time studying his face as she had.

"I'm going to need some things from the car—"

Surprise lightened his eyes. "You're going to help me?"

"Of course."

"Just like that?"

"Of course," she said. "Now then—"

"Wait." He captured her hand, drew it together with the one that was still entwined with hers. "It wasn't all lies, you know. Not when I talked to you. Not when I kissed you."

Hope lifted inside her, a heady, effervescent lightness that felt dangerously good.

"I did that because—" He paused, searching for the right words, settling on the simplest. "Because I wanted to. But I shouldn't've," he said. "You're too young. Too—"

"I thought we covered that already," she snapped.

"I know." Offending her pride wouldn't help. "How about too inexperienced? Is that better?"

Better, no. But true.

"I took advantage of your curiosity and your new-found freedom," he went on. "I knew that you would be likely to read more into our friendship than was there, and yet I—"

"Well, now, don't you think highly of your charms?" she said lightly, while her heart pounded so hard she was afraid he would notice the evidence of her lie. "I was curious. No more, no less. Don't make too much of it," she advised him, determined to follow her own counsel.

He studied her thoughtfully, as if trying to find the truth behind her words. She forced a smile and returned his gaze as steadily as she could, making herself open, light.

Finally, he nodded. "I just wanted to make certain you understood that taking advantage of your natural warmth was not part of my plan. It was anything but part of my plan."

She was not part of his plan, Sam thought. Oh, Laura Hamilton, painter, rich man's daughter, had certainly been central to his strategy. But this woman in front of him, who stirred him and challenged him and haunted his sleep, was not.

Though it likely would have been better for both their sakes to let her believe that he'd kissed her for no other reason than to blunt her defenses, deflect suspicion, and ensure that she would bring him along to the Silver Spur. Laura, furious and wary, would guarantee that nothing improper ever happened between them again.

But he knew he was the first man to kiss her—a thought that, surprisingly, he found wildly exciting. He'd never cared much one way or another about a woman's past, her experience or lack thereof. What business was it of his? He supposed there was some elemental drive involved, the need of a man to stake his claim, an instinct that kicked in whether it made any real sense or not. Because the things he felt when he looked at her certainly didn't make any sense.

"Speaking of plans . . ." She inspected his face, direct, impersonal, the same way she'd study a tree before she began to sketch. He should be grateful she was so reasonable about it all, not allowing emotion or hurt or residual attraction to get in the way of what needed to be done.

Except he wanted nothing more than to lean forward, kiss that detachment away, and make it all decidedly personal.

"I still need some things from the train."

"You won't be in any danger," he promised. "Even if they tumble to me, there's no reason to suspect anything of you. And if your father's reputation is not protection enough, I'll get you out of there the instant there seems to be any threat to you." He said it earnestly, with the weight of a solemn vow.

She wanted, too much, to hear vows from him, and so she retreated to safer topics. "*Lots* of things from the train," she warned him.

"I know you're used to having your things," he said, "but it'll only be a few days."

"No." She gripped his chin—warm, gentle fingers; soft touch, firm hold—and turned his head from side to side through the fall of moonlight, studying the angles. "You're *hoping* they don't find you out. I, on the other hand, have every intention of *ensuring* it."

"You do, do you?" he asked, amused.

"So there are several things—all right, *many* things—that I require from the car. We're going to be explaining why we're without entourage as it is. He's going to expect me to have a full complement of luggage."

"All right." He stood and drew her up in one quick motion. She felt the lift of it, the lurch of her stomach, as if she weighed nothing, and he would pull her right off her feet. Then he released her, and she couldn't help but be sorry for it. It had been so pleasant simply to hold his hand, as if that's what hands had been designed for in the first place, the comfort of another human's touch.

"This way," he said, heading off in . . . whatever direction he was heading off in; nothing around gave her a clue. But away from the horse that snuffled contently and patiently to her left.

"But—"

"To the train," he said cheerfully, striding off so quickly she had to hurry to catch up, for she had little faith in her ability to track him through the darkened, unfamiliar landscape. "It's barely two hundred yards."

"Two hundred yards?"

"Yep. Didn't think I'd stolen you off into the wilds, did you?"

He was true to his word. With only a few more steps she could see the low, blocky outline of the rail cars. And she wondered why being stolen off into the wilds by him didn't sound outrageous at all.

Chapter 12

⌒⌒

The shriek yanked him from sleep, a banshee yell that ripped Hiram from a lovely dream—Christmas at home, and Ma's apple pie, a whole one just for him—his heart knocking in panic before he even realized he was awake.

Indians, he thought. *Has to be, nothing else makes that sound.* They'd told him a dozen times there was no danger out there, but what the hell did *they* know?

He groped for his pants, his thoughts a useless jumble, though part of him decided that, if he was going to get scalped, he wasn't going to do it naked. A shirt, and then his brain cleared enough to recognize it didn't matter.

Okay, gun. That was the only thing worth looking for.

He kept it close and loaded, on the tiny table that folded down from the wall. He cautiously pried aside the roller shade that covered his small window, squinting at the brilliant early-morning sunlight. *Nothing*.

He tiptoed out of his cabin and through the main part of the car, past the boxes and crates and trunks that

165

jammed the space to within six inches of the ceiling. *Not a bad place to hole up*, he thought; *there's no way an arrow is getting through all of that*. Now if he could just get the ladies squirreled away before the war party arrived.

There was no sign of Erastus. Had they shot him already, then? Though, knowing Erastus, he could still be asleep.

Another shriek. An obviously female one this time, a blast of sound that curdled his blood.

No time to wait for Erastus. He braced himself in front of the door, took two deep breaths to steady himself, his gun at the ready, and kicked.

The door flew open, the jamb splintering.

Mrs. Bossidy stood there, openmouthed, eyes wide with terror. His gun pointed straight at her admittedly lovely, though he'd tried not to notice, bosom.

She didn't move. Didn't speak. He eased through the opening, scanning side to side for any signs of danger. Still nothing. Either someone had a weapon aimed at her from some hidden vantage point, or—

"For God's sake," she shouted, "don't point that thing at me!"

He moved the barrel a fraction, keeping it shoulder high but aimed a foot to her left. "What's goin' on?" he asked, still unable to detect any signs of trouble.

She flapped a piece of paper she held clutched in her hand. Her mouth worked, open, shut, and he wondered if she thought there were words coming out or if she was too terrified to form them.

"Ma'am?"

She shoved the paper at him. He grabbed her instead, yanking her into the shelter of the train, safely behind him, then backed inside himself.

Nothing happened. Whoever, whatever, had spooked Mrs. Bossidy was long gone or uninterested in shooting . . . yet.

"What's out there?"

"Nothing," she gasped.

Then why was she screaming like somebody was peeling off her fingernails one by one?

"There's gotta be something wrong. You haven't insulted me once." He couldn't imagine what might have shaken her customary self-possession. It had to be something truly terrible.

She waved the paper, a flutter of white in the dim light leaking around the stacks of boxes that blocked most of the windows.

"Read it," she croaked out, "if you can."

"That's my girl."

My Dear Mrs. Bossidy,

I am truly sorry that you had to awaken to this. I would have chosen another way had I been able to see one, but pausing to wake you and explain in person would have been a delay we can ill afford. Also, I doubt you would have understood, though I shall try my best to explain it someday, and perhaps you will forgive me.

Please understand that I have not been abducted, nor am I in danger of any kind. You know me well enough to know that, were I writing this under coercion, I would find some way to encode a warning in this letter. I am perfectly safe and have every expectation of remaining that way.

I simply have some business to attend to. I will tell you that I am with Mr. Duncan. I know that you do not trust him, but I have information that you're not privy to. I tell you this not to worry you further but to perhaps allay those fears, for while you may have questions about his character personally, you can have no doubt about his abilities to protect me.

It won't take us long. I am sorry that we had to take the horses, but I cannot have you attempting to follow us. Interference may well turn something that should be safe and simple into something else entirely. So please, enjoy your brief respite from duty. There are plenty of supplies and water. I'm sorry that we had to take the horses. I believe the next train is due in two more days.

There is absolutely no reason to trouble my parents with this event. It will only worry them, for by the time my father is able to take any action it will most assuredly be all over, and I will be back with you, safe and sound. Cabling him will only mean that I will be locked in a nunnery for the rest of my life, and the three of you will be without jobs.

I will meet you in Ogden in five days. That should be plenty of time. I suppose it is asking too much to ask you not to fret overly, but you have worried over me since I was eleven, and it is long past time you took a few days to yourself.

I must be off.

> *All my love,*
> *Laura*

P.S. I truly, truly am not eloping, so don't worry about that. I promise. It really is merely a per-

*sonal concern of Mr. Duncan's, and I am happy
to be of assistance.*

"Crap," Hiram said.

He pressed the letter back in Mrs. Bossidy's hands—
she really had plump soft ones, he thought irrelevantly,
and wondered why he'd noticed—and left her standing
in the middle of the car.

Erastus was still in bed, curled up on his side with
his fists tucked under his chin like he was all of five
years old.

"Get up," Hiram said, unceremoniously whacking
the side of the bunk.

"Wha—"

"Miss Hamilton's gone."

"Gone?" He sat up, pushing aside a pretty, flowery
quilt that some woman he'd never mentioned must have
made for him. The broad pegs of his hairy legs stuck out
beneath the drooping edge of his nightshirt. "How can
she be gone?"

"Stole off with that damned Duncan." He spun, leaving him to follow. "Or got stolen off *by* that damned
Duncan."

Mrs. Bossidy was right where he'd left her, standing
lost and motionless between a pile of crates that held canvases and the tower of trunks stuffed with the tiny fraction of Miss Hamilton's wardrobe she'd considered
adequate to the trip. Or rather, he thought, Mrs. Bossidy
thought necessary; Miss Hamilton never seemed to care
that much about her clothes.

"Come on," he snapped as he strode by.

"Come on?" Lucy Bossidy knew she was reacting
slowly, as if moving through syrup, trying to make
sense of it all with a sluggish brain.

Laura had been the center of her life for nearly fifteen years, filling a huge, gaping hole that she had thought forever destined to remain empty. Laura's absence now set her adrift.

She blinked at Hiram, trying to make it all come into focus. "Excuse me?"

"I don't know her things. You've got to go through them, tell me what they took with them. Maybe it'll give me a few hints as to where they went." He snapped his fingers in front of her face, trying to get her attention. "Come on, Mrs. Bossidy. I need you."

For a big, bumbling boy who'd always seemed to have far more muscles than brains, he certainly knew how to take command when the situation warranted. "And then?"

"Then," he said, "we go get Laura."

"Well?" Sam asked. "What do you think?"

Laura stood back to approve her handiwork. She'd forbidden him to wear a hat and clipped his hair neat and short. It lightened his eyes, allowing the sunlight to reach them, warming the color to a rich, deep brown. She'd left a trim slash of sideburns that visually softened the sharp angles of his cheekbones and jaw, shaved the rest of his jaw ruthlessly and instructed him to keep it that way.

"You must shave twice a day," she reminded him. "It should appear as if you can't muster up a good crop of whiskers."

He grimaced. "I don't know what's worse, the grooming or the clothes."

The pants were his own; they'd had no choice there. But she'd had him buff his beat-up old boots until they'd gleamed like new; at least the leather was good.

The shirt she'd "borrowed" from Hiram because Sam didn't own anything white. Even better, it hung loosely on him, like a boy playing dress-up in his father's Sunday best, hiding the breadth of his shoulders, his power camouflaged beneath the loose, rippling swags of fabric.

"Okay, walk," she ordered him.

He turned and clomped away.

"No, no! Hunch your shoulders a little. And take shorter steps. You look too much like someone used to being in charge."

He tried. You had to give the man that. His shoulders rounded, and he turned his toes in, hobbling forward like a man on the far side of sixty.

"Oh, forget it. You're trying too hard. It shows."

He spun, frustration written clear across his face. "You, Miss Hamilton, are terribly bossy."

She mock-scowled at him. "Yes, and don't you forget it."

"I'm ever obedient."

"Mmm-hmm." This was going to be more of a challenge than she'd thought. Tangible power surrounded him and she was having a hard time getting him to hide it. "You'd better be," she warned him.

He strolled toward her. *Prowled*, in a way that made her breath catch in her chest.

"Smile," she ordered.

"What?"

"*Smile.*"

He bared his teeth. "No, not like that. You look like a mad wolf. Give me something . . . benign."

He stopped a foot from her. He was every bit as handsome like this, all buffed and polished. Citified. A man her father might have approved of. Though she much preferred him the way she'd first seen him, real and rough and heart-poundingly compelling.

"Thank you," he said softly. "For doing this for me. You didn't have to."

"Yes I did." She tried to smile, but her lips trembled. Perhaps he would kiss her again. Maybe even a little bit more. It would be an appropriate token of his appreciation, wouldn't it? Because she really did not think she could go through the rest of her life without, at least once, feeling again the way she'd felt when he kissed her: shivery, glorious, *alive*.

Except wanting it, so badly, should be a clear, blaring warning in itself. She obviously could not have a small snippet of him without longing for more. If he kissed her again, she would only want another, and another. His kisses were addictive, intoxicating, more dangerous than opium. Because she knew full well he was only grateful to her, and that when he'd discovered what happened to his friend he'd deposit her safely back with Mrs. Bossidy and go on his way. On to another job, another smitten woman, and never think of her again.

And she . . . she could hardly consider the men she might meet in the future as it was. She could not spend her life forever comparing other men to Sam. The more she knew of him, the more memories of him she had, the more likely she was to do so.

No, better she keep their relationship carefully bounded. She would assist with his current project and be glad that she was able to do so. And then she would neatly pack the memory away, a girl's cherished keepsake and nothing more, and get on with the rest of her life.

"Will I do?" he asked, lifting his arms for her inspection, awaiting her judgment.

She tilted her head, considering. *She* would have recognized him in a heartbeat. But her eye was accustomed to seeing the angles beneath a beard, the line of a body cloaked by loose clothing. Most people were not. Few tried.

And the Silver Spur employees who'd attacked him previously were all men. That made a difference. Few women would forget Sam Duncan, but she doubted the men found him memorable, at least not in quite the same way.

"Wait." She dashed to her valise, rummaged through to the bottom, and came up with a couple of small silver pots, two brushes. "Don't move."

"What the hell—"

He backed away as if she brandished a sword instead of a brush.

"Think of it as paint," she said. "I'm very good with paint."

"But you don't use—" He squinted, peering closely at her face. "Do you?"

"Only when forced into it by my mother or Mrs. Bossidy. The rest of the time I don't bother." She approached him as if he were a nervous colt she expected to bolt. "Doesn't mean I don't know how."

She brushed a waft of pale powder over his face and he coughed, waving away the drift of white that clouded the air before his face.

"Sorry," she said. "But you simply look too . . . healthy."

He caught her hand. She felt his thumb against the inside of her wrist. Knew he could feel the hammertrip of her pulse there, that he would note the acceleration of her heart. "Why not?"

"Why not what?"

"Why don't you bother?"

She shrugged. "There doesn't seem much point in it." It didn't interest her. "There was never anybody to impress." And even if there were, she knew the limitations of cosmetics. Even at approaching fifty, her mother retained a pure and classic beauty composed of excellent bones and lovely skin and vivid coloring. Laura, however, favored her father. Oh, she was not ugly; she was honest enough to realize that. But she also understood that all the cosmetics in the world would not make her something that she wasn't.

"You're right," he said.

Her heart plummeted. Why had she, for even one second, thought it might be different? Oh, but she was allowing her fancies to run away with her sense. His thumb circled lightly, sending shivers of sensation down her arm.

"Why would you ever paint up that face, when it obviously could not be improved on?"

Her mouth fell open. "Sam?"

Abruptly he dropped her wrist, disappointing her more than was wise. "Powder away," he said. "I'll be brave."

Chapter 13

I t took them most of a day to reach the gates of the Silver Spur. They approached as the sun dropped to the horizon, the sharp horizontal lines of the fence dark and crisp against the long grass, glowing gold in the fading sunlight. Farther back low, crumpled mountains climbed higher, a few swathed with wide bands of dark evergreens, most bare and brown.

The day had been long for Laura, unused to extended hours in the saddle. He'd suggested once that they stop for the night but she, understanding how anxious he was, had refused. He looked over at her now, lines of exhaustion drooping on her face.

"I'm sorry," he said. "I should have insisted we stop."

She straightened, more steel in that narrow back than anyone who looked at her would have expected. "I'm the boss, remember? I said no."

"We could have gone back to the cars. Thrown ourselves on Mrs. Bossidy's mercy, explained the whole thing. Maybe she would have—"

"You know better than that."

"But—"

She scowled at him, more like Baron Hamilton's haughty daughter looking down on the foolishness of normal mortals than he'd ever seen her, and he shut up. "Okay, okay," he said. "You're right."

"But of course."

The shadow of the huge gate that guarded the ranch fell across them. The letters were two feet high, black iron, topped with a spiked star. Two guards, rifles in hand, flanked the gate, awaiting their approach.

"This is it," he said. "Last chance to back out. I could find another way."

Find another way that almost ensures you'll get beaten to a pulp, Laura thought. *Or killed.* "After I went through so much trouble to fix you up? I can't wait to see how my handiwork's received."

"Nice to know you've got such pride in your work." If Sam were a better man, he would rope and tie her and drag her safely back to her guards. Maybe Crocker's men assumed they'd chased him off for good, and he could sneak onto the ranch and investigate. Not nearly as well as he could in this guise, where he'd have freer access to the compound, but some. Probably not enough, he admitted, but he wouldn't need *her*.

But even if he were caught he could easily pretend he'd duped her, too, and she knew nothing of his quest. Plus the ever-present specter of her supremely powerful father was as much protection as any woman got.

No, she'd be fine, and appeared to be rather enjoying the adventure.

And, he admitted, he wasn't quite ready to say goodbye to her yet. Which was the stupidest reason of all, but there it was just the same.

"But of course," she said. "Now get behind me like a good boy."

She tapped her heels against the side of her mount, which provoked no more response than a desultory switch of its scraggly gray tail. "Darn it." She banged harder, prodding the disinterested horse into a lurching trot. "Yoo-hoo, there," she called brightly, waving at the guards as she approached the gate. "I'm here!"

He nudged Harry, the gelding he rode, after her, careful to stay appropriately behind her. Harry wasn't half the horse that Max, the fine stallion he'd regretfully left at a boarding stable in Omaha, was, but Laura's nag made Harry look like a potential Derby winner. The third horse, bundles of canvases strapped to its side, a pile of leather-bound luggage on its back, trailed reluctantly behind, as if its pride were damaged by being pressed into service as a packhorse.

Laura glanced over her shoulder at him, which pitched her too far over to one side and made his heart stagger before she righted herself. Then she frowned. *Don't ride so well,* she mouthed at him.

Darn it. He snapped his back into a stiff line, so his rump banged against the saddle with each trot, an impact he felt all the way up his spine.

"Hullo!"

The guards kept looking at each other, then back at her, as if they didn't know what to make of her. They were obviously not used to ladies bouncing up to the front gate of the Silver Spur, two horses and one "assistant" in tow.

She trotted right up to the gate before she reined in her old mare. Much too close to the men with guns to his way of thinking. He halted his horse a few yards behind hers, his head down, shoulders hunched. But he felt the weight of the pistol he'd insisted on against his side beneath his jacket.

"Open up," she said, a regal tilt to her head as if it never occurred to her that they wouldn't follow her orders. Finally, one of them sighed and ambled over to the gate, his rifle held crosswise in front of his body.

"Ma'am? Beggin' your pardon, ma'am, but we don't allow sightseers at the Silver Spur." He gestured with the rifle. "Now move along."

"Ma'am?" Her voice went high with offense. "That's *miss*. Miss Laura Hamilton, and I'm expected."

"Miss Hamilton?" He sidled over to another guard and held a whispered conference. Then he dropped his gun to his side. "We didn't expect you for another three days."

"I'm impatient." Her laughter trilled, the giggle of an accomplished flirt who knew her foibles were enchanting and that she was allowed a wider latitude than most.

"Beggin' your pardon, *miss*, but it was our understanding that our engine was to bring your cars back on the next scheduled trip to the switching station."

"I got tired of waiting," she said, an edge to her voice that any maid who served a mercurial mistress would recognize, and obey, immediately. "There was nothing to do out there."

Another whispered conference, while Sam slumped on his horse and hid his admiration. He didn't know she had it in her to dissemble like an experienced sharper, playing the indulged heiress like she'd been born to the part. Well, she had, hadn't she? He'd just never seen her use it before.

"Wait here," said the man who stood in front, apparently the one in charge. Big and burly and red-haired, he was hatless, very unusual in this country, and Sam was almost certain it was his oversized boot that had found its way into Sam's rib cage.

"Wait here? Oh dear. It's been *such* a trying journey," Laura waved her hand in its pretty lace glove in front of her face. "Can't you just let us in?" Her tones were perfect, wheedling and sly and just a little miffed that men so obviously below her station weren't immediately jumping to do her bidding. This was precisely the woman he'd assumed her to be before they'd met. It was more than a little unsettling to realize she could assume the role so well.

If this *had* been the Laura Hamilton he'd met, he'd have no qualms about using her for entrée and never giving her a second thought.

"Unless you think that we might be some"—she giggled—"*danger* to you."

Raw, angry red burned in the man's cheeks, clashing with the brassy orange of his hair. "Sorry, miss, but Mr. Crocker's instructions are very clear. No one's allowed in without prior authorization. And we weren't told to let you in today."

"Who are you, sir?" she demanded.

"Red Monroe, ma'—miss."

She pouted prettily. "Surely you're aware I'm expected? What difference does it make if it's not precisely when and how I'd originally planned? You do know a girl reserves the right to change her mind, don't you?"

Red exchanged glances with his second-in-command. "Jonce, here, will ride back and get permission, miss."

"How long do you think that will take?" Her voice quavered, as if she were going to burst into tears at any moment. Red gulped.

"Only an hour each way," he hurried to explain. "In the meantime, you can just rest up and—"

"Out *here*?" she asked incredulously. "Unless you've some sort of a structure here that I can't see that I can utilize as shelter, I'm afraid that simply won't do. Because I do think this sun is on the verge of doing me in. I'm sure my daddy—you do know my daddy, right? Leland Hamilton? Of course you do—will be ever so grateful if you take proper care of me. He's *so* good that way."

Sam coughed. He couldn't help it. It was either that or burst out laughing.

"And I'm certain," she went on, "that Mr. Crocker would *want* you to let me in. He came to visit us once, you know. Though he did *not* like the cruise Daddy arranged. Not an ocean man, he said. I recall that quite clearly. Of course, he always remembered me after that. Sent me a present nearly every Christmas. Once it was a pair of cow horns as thick as my arms." Her nose wrinkled. "It was very kind of him, I'm sure."

Red shot another glance at Jonce, who shrugged, clearly not inclined to be a party to the decision.

Red bent to one side, peering around Laura. "Who's that?"

Dangerous situations were part and parcel of Sam's life. He always faced them coolly, his breath steady, his heart calm. Mostly because he figured death had already had a good run at him, and any extra time he got from then on was a bonus. It was a good part of why he commanded such high fees.

A man who cared too much what happened in any given confrontation, who worried too much about living, was a man who made mistakes.

He'd rather have faced them flat out, guns drawn,

than like this. The situation was mostly out of his control, too dependent on Laura's charm—though she was doing a brilliant job—and the guard's stupidity.

He forced a smile, as wide and vacant as he could manage, and ignored the furious glances Laura was shooting his way, the frantic, furtive gestures intended to get him to hide behind her. But if they were going to recognize him, best to do it now and get it over with.

"Oh, that's Mr. Kirkwood. *Artemus.* He's my . . . well, I guess you could call him my new apprentice. Maybe my assistant? Which do you think sounds better? It's so nice to have someone to wash brushes and stretch canvases, you know."

"You can come," Red decided. "But he's gotta stay."

"I could *never* leave him behind!" she cried. "It just wouldn't do. Daddy would *never* let me go with all of you unescorted. It would be unseemly."

"Huh." He gnawed on the inside of his cheek. "Seems to me you already been running around with *him* unescorted."

"Oh, that's different." She tittered. *Tittered.* Dear God, what had he released in her? "Don't be ridiculous. Artemus is *no* threat. At least not to me."

Red frowned at Sam, who grinned at him so hard his cheeks hurt. He'd rather have pulled out a gun and started shooting.

Instead, he dropped one shoulder, leaned in Red's direction . . . and winked.

Red darn near strangled on his tongue. He scrambled back, nearly dropping his gun in the process.

"Collis!" Red bellowed at the youngest of the hands, a chubby, baby-faced boy all of twenty or so, dressed in solid black like he thought it would make him look tough. "Open the gate."

"But—"

"I said open the gate."

He scrambled to obey, though he clearly wasn't happy about it.

"Jonce, Collis, make sure they get to the main house," Red ordered.

Faces glum, they fetched two horses from the four ground-tethered twenty yards down the fence.

"Come on, then," Jonce said unhappily. He trotted perhaps ten yards before he looked back to see if they were coming. "Need help?" he said, lip curling in disdain.

"Oh, no," Laura said serenely, as though she could afford to be pleasant now that she'd gotten her way. "We got this far, didn't we? And truly, Artemus only fell off twice. He's really getting *so* much better. I'm so proud of him."

Collis gave Sam a disgusted look as he swung his bay around to bring up the rear. Sam tapped his heels against Harry's side, too hard, for which he mentally begged the horse's pardon, and lurched forward, clinging to the reins as if they were the only things holding him in the saddle.

The gate clanged shut behind him.

No going back now. His focus narrowed, the steady, intense awareness that came over him when he entered into a difficult situation, the preternatural alertness that kept him alive more than once.

If only he could have done this without Laura's help.

But then she turned in her seat and shot him a triumphant smile. The woman was having a wonderful time, clearly thoroughly pleased with her accomplishment. The instant he got her alone, he thought, he would thank her properly, and occupied himself quite nicely for a few moments planning the best way to do that. Until he had to shift uncomfortably in the saddle and remembered he most certainly could *not* thank her like that.

They were traveling south, the sun sinking beneath the high ground to their right, Jonce in the lead and Collis at Laura's side. The land they traveled rose and fell gently, but all around them it surged higher and higher, folding into mountains. They weren't high enough to hold snow at their summits, not this late in the season, blunt-topped instead of the brutal peaks they'd rolled past in the Wyoming Territories.

Sam tried to locate and memorize landmarks along the way. There weren't many—a line shack that listed against a narrow ledge, a cluster of sumac, a sharp, dry gulch. He supposed it was possible that Griff had simply gotten lost somewhere out here; there was a confusing sameness to the landscape, a dun monotony. But that seemed a lousy end for a man who'd survived the brutality of Andersonville. It should have taken a lot to kill Griff, more than just wandering around disoriented until his stamina gave out.

Besides, if it were that simple, why would they have tried so hard to keep Sam from looking around? Unless there was something else to hide. That was always a possibility. It would be a mistake to get so focused on Griff that he overlooked other explanations.

Laura kept up a steady chatter, bless her. A random spill of comments and complaints, tales of the East that the men could have absolutely no interest in, a torrent of words that had their eyes glazing over. But now and then she'd throw in a question, offhanded, careless queries that would never have aroused a moment's suspicion, the kind of things Sam would have asked if he could have done so without drawing attention.

And they answered, because she was such an obviously harmless bit of fluff, and they'd rather satisfy her curiosity than have her yammering at them about her last trip to Paris, which she'd told them about in such numbing detail that for a second even he believed she'd really been there.

"So," she said, just another question in a spill of words, "where's the mine?"

That's my girl, Sam thought. Laura obviously had an untapped talent for deceit.

"Oh, it's thatta way." Collis pointed southeast. "If you're quiet, an' there ain't much wind kicking up, sometimes you can hear the rumble of the stamp mill from the main house."

"A stamp mill?"

"It crushes the ore."

"Can I go see it?" She touched the glimmer of gold that encircled her neck. "I like silver. And gold, and diamonds, and . . . everything that sparkles, really."

"I—" He caught a warning glare from Jonce. "You'll have to ask Mr. Crocker about that, miss."

"Good." She clapped her hands as if it were already settled. "And where does the train go?"

"It parallels the road for a couple of miles, about a half a mile that way." He pointed east. "Then, of course, it curves south, toward the mine—"

"Collis!"

Collis cleared his throat. "I'm sure Mr. Crocker would prefer to tell you all about it himself."

"Well, he's not here now, is he? And I do so hate to wait for answers." She smiled prettily, and Collis grinned back, a boy lost to the charms of an accomplished flirt. "Do all you hands live together?"

"Sure. We've got a coupla bunkhouses right near the main house. But you'll be seeing that soon enough."

"And all the mine workers?"

"Oh, no, they stay out by the mines. We don't want *them* around—"

"Collis!" Jonce yanked on his reins, hauling his mount around. "You go on and lead for a while. I'll bring up the rear. Wouldn't want anyone falling behind."

That, despite Laura's best efforts, put paid to the conversation for the next twenty minutes, for Jonce was apparently not so easily led as Collis.

Smoke curled above a hill, the first sign that they were at last approaching the compound.

"I'm going ahead to tell 'em we're coming," Jonce kicked his horse into a furious gallop, rounding the hill in a cloud of dust as if he couldn't wait to get away from them. Or, Sam thought, they needed warning of an outsider's approach.

The compound nestled snugly into a small valley. A dozen buildings, maybe more. Sam located the bunkhouse, a cookhouse, the stables, all in excellent repair. The main house was a long, rambling, one-story affair, built of logs with a porch that ran the full length. It was the house of a man who wanted what he wanted and didn't much care what he had to pay to get it.

The horses in the corral were very fine. Someone had planted trees, spiky evergreens that clustered at the corners of the house but hadn't grown roof high as of yet. The yard was scraped clean, and he could see dozens of workers: a gardener in the vegetable plot behind the house; two washerwomen bending over a steaming kettle at the far side of what had to be the cookhouse; hands working with the horses, mending a fence that already seemed in good repair, whitewashing a tiny frame structure that was probably a well house.

Sam had been on many a working ranch. It always showed. In houses that desperately needed a whitewashing because that had to wait for a less busy time, and there was never a less busy time. A torn-up yard because a horse had gotten loose. Broken lumber piled beside the stables because wood was too valuable to throw away but nobody had found a use for it yet. A rusting plow in an overgrown patch of garden, or a drunken cowboy slumped in the shade. *Something*.

The Silver Spur was perfect, with the same eerie, unreal feel that the town held, times ten. A stage set of a ranch, where the people were props, not residents. A half dozen peacocks strutted through the yard, their jewel-toned feathers the brightest spots of color in the dusty brown complex.

"Miss Hamilton!" A man awaited them on the porch, smiling genially around a thin cigar. But he didn't come out to greet his guests, Sam noted, just waited on his porch for their approach like a king accepting the pilgrimage of his subjects.

So that's Haw Crocker, he thought. Not too tall, shoulders as wide as his house, a big mound of a belly that looked solid for all it was round as a hot-air balloon. His hat was broad, his shirt blinding white—too white for a man who worked the land. Obviously Haw Crocker had stopped dirtying those beefy hands a long time ago.

He waved to one of the young men flanking the broad stairway, who seemed to have no other function but to stand around and wait until Crocker thought up something for them to do. "Help Miss Hamilton down, would ya?"

Sam leaned toward Jonce, who'd jumped down and handed his reins to another boy who materialized from behind the house. "Aren't you going to help me down?"

Jonce scowled. "Swing your leg over and drop. I'm sure you'll manage." He jogged toward the porch.

He had to be more careful about tweaking the man like that, Sam decided. Or he was going to start laughing, and that wouldn't do.

Sam dismounted. Another boy appeared, to whom he tossed his reins. He'd much rather have seen to the horse himself than trust it to one of Crocker's minions, but Artemus Kirkwood wouldn't bother with such things.

He made it to the porch just as Laura ascended. Crocker condescended to take one step forward, and her pretty gloved hands were swallowed up in his.

"Miss Hamilton," he said, his voice deep, gravelly from too many cigars and too many years in the harsh climate. "I am delighted that you are here. I have not seen your father in ten years, of course—the distance is large, and we are both busy men—but I still consider him one of my dearest friends. And, of course, we've had several immensely profitable ventures together." He chuckled.

Laura adroitly slipped her hands from his. Her smile was proper, social, giving no hint that she was anything other than a friendly young woman. "It's very kind of you to have us. The trip was becoming quite tiring."

"I did not expect you for a few days. I had instructed the engineer to attach your cars. Surely it must be diffi cult for you to travel with so few of your things."

"Honestly, if I'd had to spend another night in that teeny little car, I was going to go mad. I'm sure I'll be much more comfortable here. And I'm confident that the Silver Spur will be able to provide adequately for my needs."

"I'm sure we will."

"Well, of course you will! And your birds are so *darling*."

"They eat the snakes." He turned to Sam, acknowledging his presence for the first time. "And who is this?"

"Artemus Kirkwood," she said, waving him closer. "My apprentice."

Crocker raised a thick eyebrow. "Your father allows you to travel alone with him?"

"Oh, well, what he doesn't know . . ." She trailed off, beaming at him. "No, don't give me that look. You have daughters, I believe?"

Crocker nodded. "Three of them. All safely married off. And one son that works with me here."

"There, you see? I'm sure it's a reflex reaction on your part, protecting young women from the attentions of men. I appreciate your including me in your concern. But don't you worry. Artemus has no interest in me beyond the painting."

She tugged on the loopy pink ribbon that secured her hat. "But the trip has been quite taxing." Her shoulders drooped tiredly, her mouth curving down. "Much more exhausting than I'd expected. I'm very thankful for the hospitality."

Haw turned toward the door. "Lupe! Please show Miss Hamilton to her quarters."

A lovely dark-haired woman in rich blue appeared. "This way."

"Thank you." Laura drifted across the porch to the door, then stopped, as if she'd just remembered. "What about Artemus?"

"Oh." Sam met Crocker's frown with a vacant smile. "We'll find . . . someplace to put him."

"You can put him with the hands," Laura suggested. "He'd enjoy the experience, I'm sure."

Behind him, Jonce and Collis shook their heads so hard they nearly snapped off. Sam had to bite down hard to keep from laughing.

Smiling, Laura drifted by.

Crocker had no idea what she was capable of, Sam thought.

But then, neither had he.

Chapter 14

Haw Crocker really knew how to set a table.

The dining room, a long, soaring rectangle of a room with stripped wood beams at least a foot in diameter, held a table that sat twenty-four with ease. Three young men in dark gray suits served and whisked dishes away with the kind of efficiency that only came from long practice and a drill sergeant of a butler. Platters of sautéed trout in almonds were quickly joined by a huge roast loin of beef, expertly carved and served with browned potatoes.

There were only seven at dinner, which seemed a terrible waste to Laura. Besides Laura, Sam, and Crocker, his son joined them. Ben was an entirely forgettable young man of about Laura's age who deferred to his father on everything and spoke only when spoken to, and sometimes not even then. Also in attendance were Crocker's ranch manager, Carl Fitch, and his wife Adeline, who had their own small house a hundred yards from the main; and a giant of a man introduced only as Clem, who'd mumbled "hello" and had not spoken again the entire dinner.

"This is lovely," Laura said, spooning up a delicious apple dumpling, "but you did not have to make such a fuss for us. We have been on the road for so long that anything would have been a great luxury."

"Oh, no," Crocker said. Candlelight gleamed on the smooth dome of his head. His face was deeply lined, as though at one time he'd spent a long time in the sun, but his scalp shone pink, as if it had been a while since he'd had to do so. "I simply enjoy a proper dinner at the end of a long day. Now that you're here, we'll begin plans for a special celebration. Saturday, perhaps."

She glanced at Sam, who'd been seated across the table from her, limiting their opportunities for communication. He smiled blandly at her.

"I'm not certain we'll be here that long," Laura said.

"What do you mean, you won't be here that long?" Crocker dragged his spoon across his plate, scraping up the last bit of cream. "Of course you're going to be here. I'd never want your Daddy to think that I didn't take good care o' you." He punched Sam, just to his right, on his arm to emphasize his point. Sam winced. "Her daddy and I made a lot of money together, son."

"I'm aware of that," Sam said precisely.

"Saw you poking around outside before dinner while Miss Hamilton was resting. Don't you like your room?"

"Oh, no, my room is quite acceptable." Crocker frowned, as if he'd expected something a bit more flattering than acceptable. "I'm just . . . restless sometimes. And curious. And, of course, it is part of my responsibilities to select possible vistas for Miss Hamilton's projects."

"New fellas—" Haw kept smiling, but his gaze had

sharpened. "*City* fellas, shouldn't be wandering around out here alone. Let me know next time you decide to explore, and I'll assign somebody to show you around."

"That won't be necessary."

"I insist," Haw Crocker said, in a voice that was accustomed to being followed without question.

"All right, then." Sam nodded. He could no doubt shake his "escort" easily enough if he had to. And perhaps he could pry a bit of information out of the man first.

"Tell me," Laura began, "my father is forever complaining about the difficulties in finding and retaining qualified workers. You are quite a good distance from the population centers, and I'm sure the work in the mines and the ranch is quite strenuous. Do you have similar problems?"

Crocker set his knife carefully across the edge of his plate, a blue-and-white pattern that must have been imported from China. He folded his hands together. He had big palms, fingers thick as sausages, hands that looked like they could bring down a steer or dig a mine.

"No," he said precisely. "Not to question your daddy's way of doing business—God knows he's done well enough for himself—but it's different out here, and I pay well for good work. We got no problem getting and keeping all the help we need." Then he chuckled, leaning back in his high-backed armchair. "Ain't that right, Carl?"

"Couldn't ask for a better boss," Carl said smoothly.

"Really?" Laura leaned forward intently, resting her forearms on the edge of the table, the snowy white cloth nearly the shade of the delicately feminine wrist exposed beneath a wide band of frothy lace. "Because my father mentioned something about the unions, that they've been causing terrible trouble in the mines, so much so that he considered terminating his investment—" She giggled. "Oops. I guess I shouldn't have said that, should I?"

Bless her, Sam thought. *Throwing out questions, prodding, poking, seeing if she can shake out something*. Not to mention encouraging Haw Crocker to view her as an empty-headed, innocuous fribble of a girl. By the next afternoon, he figured, she'd be stumbling into the mines, sketch pad in hand, her eyes wide and innocent if anybody objected to her presence, and nobody would be surprised.

Before this was over he was going to have to hogtie her to keep her out of trouble. He could see it coming already. And, if, while she was all neatly trussed, he was suddenly overcome by his baser urges, well, that wouldn't be entirely his fault, would it?

"What are you grinnin' about, boy?" Crocker asked.

"Oh." Sam wiped his mouth with his napkin, a luxurious rectangle of thick linen, and adjusted it in his lap until it lay smoothly. "My apologies. I realize it's most impolite not to share my amusement. It was merely a private reminiscence, however, and unfit for public consumption, I'm afraid."

Laura had both her eyebrows lifted almost to her hairline. She'd be haranguing him later, relentless until she pried an answer from him. And wouldn't it just serve her right if he told her the truth?

But then, he wouldn't be seeing her later. He planned to be out most of the night, looking for Griff or something that belonged to him. And it was not as if Sam could sleep in that stuffy room they'd given him anyway, with its deep, curtain-draped bed that would surely cut off his air supply.

They'd given him a room in a separate wing, the entire length of this monstrous house between him and Laura. And that bothered him. He'd spent more than a month with little more than a few yards between them at all times. Even in Kearney, before he'd joined her party, she'd always been in reach; he'd been closer to her most of the time than she, or her guards, had ever suspected, because he'd no intention of allowing her to slip out of town before he had an opportunity to attach himself to her party.

It was unsettling to have her that far away, even though Haw Crocker had every reason in the world to keep Laura safe. He'd be facing the wrath of Leland Hamilton if he didn't, and even Haw Crocker's considerable power faded to insignificance when compared with the Baron of Bankers. And yet . . . Sam was going to worry every single moment they were on Silver Spur land. Maybe every moment after that until he saw her safely back inside the gates of Sea Haven.

And maybe, he thought, his stomach sinking in dread, he might worry about her until the day he died.

"How's your work going?" Crocker waved over one of the serving boys, who quickly refilled his wineglass. He'd been doing that a lot but as of yet it'd had no noticeable effect on Crocker. Still, it was one sliver of information Sam hadn't had before: Crocker liked to drink, and he held his liquor well.

"Quite well, thank you," Laura answered.

"Care to share?"

"Oh, I don't think—"

"Please?"

Laura puckered up her mouth in thought, then her face lit. "All right."

She dashed out of the room in a swish of pale green silk. Moments later she returned clutching her sketch-book, her smile fixed and vacant.

The woman was up to something. She'd acquiesced too quickly, was trying too hard to appear shallow and feather-headed, as if her work was merely an entertaining hobby rather than something she put her heart and sweat into.

She tugged her chair nearer to sit at Crocker's elbow, pushing aside plates to clear a good space on the table. "Here you go," she said eagerly.

She leaned close to Crocker as he sifted through the sketches, spilling a torrent of commentary about light and shadows and proportion that had Crocker's eyes glazing over.

"And this," she chirped, "I started just yesterday. At the other side of your ranch, I believe, and this . . . oh. That's just some doodling, you don't want to see—"

"No." Crocker's beefy hand came down flat on top of the page. "I want to see it all. What's this?"

"Well." She flicked a delighted glance at Sam. Oh, but he was going to have to keep a close eye on her. She taken to this like she'd been born to the job. But she'd never had any experience with the darker side and the things that could happen when you took too many chances and pushed it too far. And so it would be up to him to protect her.

"It's the *strangest* thing," she said lightly. "I was just there sketching, minding my own business, and all of a sudden this odd man just started running toward us, shouting something we couldn't understand." She shrugged as if it were something vaguely interesting but ultimately unimportant. "And then some men on horseback ran him down as if he were a wild calf! Can you imagine? I meant to ask you about it, actually, but I forgot."

The broad charm vanished from Crocker's face, his expression unnaturally blank as he studied the sketch. He lifted it in his thick fingers, tilting it from side to side as if it might help jog his memory. Then he shook his head. "Nope. But I've got hundreds of employees, and dozens more come and go on any given day. I wouldn't recognize most of 'em."

He tossed the sketchbook in front of Carl, where it fell with enough force to raise a crumpled napkin on a *poof* of air. Ben peered at it out of the corner of his eye, his bland face paling.

"Carl? How about you?"

Crocker's and Fitch's gazes met, a warning flashing between them.

Carl cleared his throat. "Ah—" He barely glanced at the page. "Yeah, that's Chan. Hired him to work in our mines about a year ago." He shrugged. "Felt sorry for the guy. Most places won't take on a Chinaman these days. It was a mistake, though. He just went crazy one day. Attacked his supervisor, screaming at nothing. Stopped speakin' English, so we couldn't make a word out."

"Oh, the poor thing," Laura said. "What did you do then?"

"Wasn't much we could do. Called in the doc, but he said there wasn't anything he could do to help. So we rigged up a room where he couldn't hurt himself or anybody else and kept him there."

"You didn't institutionalize him?"

"We're short on sanitariums out here in the Utah

Territory, miss. And since we didn't know anythin' about him or his family, if he even had one, it seemed like it would be better to keep him in familiar surroundings. Maybe it'd help him come out of it."

"Oh, that's so kind of you," she said, beaming in admiration.

"We try to take care of our own here on the Silver Spur," Crocker said. They were lying. Sam was certain of it. But which part, exactly, they were lying *about* was a lot harder to detect.

The whole thing might have nothing whatsoever to do with Griff. But there was definitely something a bit . . . off about the Silver Spur.

"And yesterday?" she prodded.

"Yes, Carl," Crocker said evenly, "what *about* yesterday?"

"He got out." His voice rose on the last word, as if he were asking a question instead of stating a fact. "We didn't figure he'd last the night bumbling around outside. So we had to bring him in however we could before he hurt somebody. Or himself."

"Why wasn't I informed?" Crocker asked.

"Didn't see any reason to bother you about it," Carl said. Sweat beaded on his forehead. "He weren't gone but a couple of hours before we tracked him down. If we came to you with every detail, Haw, you'd be doing nothin' but hearing reports from sunup to sundown."

"True enough." Crocker nodded in agreement "All the same, Carl, if he gets out again, you let me know. I don't like the thought of the poor demented fella running around free. Maybe we'll have to hire a nurse, somethin' like that, to keep an eye on 'em."

"Sure thing, Haw."

"Oh, Mr. Crocker!" Laura's eyes were misty, so

richly admiring of Crocker's compassion that even Sam almost believed her. "That unfortunate lunatic is *so* lucky to have you."

Laura retired early to her room. Haw Crocker assured her that he understood her withdrawal; sending her off with a maid and profuse apologies that he hadn't realized the excitement of arrival and the strain of dinner was all too taxing for such a delicate creature on her first day.

Her father, she decided, must have described her in such a way that Haw thought she was teetering on the edge of death.

Laura knew she wouldn't be able to sleep, not for hours. But she'd retreated to her room early, pleading the strain of the day, because portraying a brainless twit was far more difficult than she'd expected.

Oh, it was certainly entertaining at first. Taking a bit of her mother's mannerisms, some of Mrs. Bossidy's, a good chunk of that silly maid at Sea Haven who twittered every time a man wandered by. She could see how playing a role, putting something over on everyone, could become addictive. Having to watch every move you made, every expression on your face, forced one to live in every single second, a rushing alertness that reminded you you were alive.

But the constant vigilance was tiring, an undercurrent of nerves thrumming painfully.

It certainly was a lovely room. Peeled logs, glowing soft gold in the lanternlight, formed the outside wall, centered with a big, shuttered window. The other walls were thickly plastered in cream and hung with gold-and-burgundy tapestries. Heavy, dark wood fashioned the furniture, the room dominated by a large, wine-velvet-draped bed with posts the size of tree trunks—which probably *had* been tree trunks.

The silently efficient maid had neatly stored away her things in a blink. Her dresses were freshly pressed, the skirts peeking out of an open armoire. Her canvases and cases had been stacked in the corner.

She wandered over to the window and pushed the glass wide. The sky was broad, deepening to indigo. A few brave stars winked on, along with a thin slice of bright silver moon.

A lovely evening, the kind of evening that was meant to be shared.

And suddenly she missed her parents terribly.

She'd never really been alone in her life. She'd had them, and Mrs. Bossidy, and guards and maids and nurses. She'd had so much company that sometimes she'd thought she was going to go mad with it, as if even her most secret thoughts did not belong just to her.

And she'd had him. *Sam*. Though he'd been in her life for a narrow sliver of time, it was an important few weeks, weeks when she'd learned a great deal about herself and what she truly wanted.

She wondered how long, when this was all over, it would take for her to stop looking up and expecting to see him there.

Her elbows on the wide sill of the window, she leaned out. There were lights in the bunkhouses, the squeaky wail of someone practicing a fiddle. Another light glowed, very faintly, in the window of a tiny cottage across the yard.

She breathed in. It smelled so *different*. All those years, she'd often dreamed of how other places would look. But she hadn't considered the smell. She'd been so accustomed to the scents of Newport, the brine of the sea, fresh-clipped grass, the lemon wax the maids used on the furniture, that she never really noticed them anymore.

Here she detected the smoky tang of sage. Smoke itself, from a fire somewhere. Horses.

She closed her eyes. Even if the rest of her senses were stripped from her, she would still know she was in another place because the air felt unique against her face. Warmer, drier.

When she opened her eyes he was standing right there outside her window, a mere foot away.

She smiled.

"You don't look surprised to see me," he said quietly.

She shook her head. Wasn't he always there, somewhere, watching over her? Or perhaps her senses detected his presence without conscious awareness: his scent, his warmth, a disturbance in the air stirred up by his potent energy.

"For a moment during dinner," she said, "I thought that you were going to call a halt to the whole thing and drag me away."

"I was tempted." His shirt was very white against the darkness of his skin. A fresh growth of beard shadowed his jaw. Unthinkingly, she touched his jaw, the stubble prickling her fingers, alerting her nerves.

"The most difficult part of your charade is going to be keeping a smooth face."

Time hung, frozen and potent as the moon.

And then he brushed her fingers away and continued as if she'd never touched him. "Next time you decide to pull something like you did at dinner, it'd be a lot kinder to my heart if you talked it over with me first."

"It was a sudden inspiration."

"Get those often?"

"More and more all the time." Even though they were alone, he still carried himself with Artemus's posture, his shoulders rounded and back hunched, making him appear both softer and shorter than she knew him to be. "I'm only sorry that I didn't seem to do much good. I thought maybe I'd bumble some information out of them if they considered me no threat."

"That's often the way it goes. You pull at threads all over the place, and none of them seem to lead to anything, then, when you're just about ready to give up, one tiny piece of information shows up that's exactly what you need." He smiled at her; he did that now so easily that she'd almost forgotten how difficult it had been to pull that from him once. "Of course, my usual approach is less patient and a lot more effective."

"I don't want to know about it."

His grin grew wicked. A rogue's smile, a pirate's smile. "Back to your illusions about what a fine, upstanding gentleman I am, are we?"

"No," she said. "But Artemus, now . . . that's my sort of man."

"Artemus is a ninny."

"Better a ninny than a chest-thumping, brainless gorilla," she said cheerfully, and he pretended to scowl.

Oh, that life could be this simple, enjoying a warm evening together, friendly banter and harmless flirtation. She had worried that he'd be angry about her unplanned investigating. Oh, he'd given her the obligatory warning, but his rebuke had been mild. Everyone else would have bundled her off for safekeeping and never let her out again. He alone did not treat her like an invalid. Perhaps because he'd never seen her as one, and so did not have that image in his brain of her weak and fragile prevailing over all others.

"I do appreciate what you tried to do tonight," he said. "This is not your fight, and yet you have thrown yourself into it. I don't know why you would put yourself out so far."

She opened her mouth to toss off something light. It was an adventure, it was the right thing to do, it was opportunity to investigate a new career—would the Pinkertons hire her, did he think? And though they were all some small portion of the truth, they were the least part of it.

"You know why," she said softly.

He went still, his gaze fixed on her. And then he transformed from Artemus into Sam. He straightened, his eyelids lifted from their somnolent state, his chest expanded. For a moment she thought that he might accept what she'd just offered, and they would go on from there, to someplace new and wild and wonderful. Her breath caught and held.

And then he shrugged, shifting his gaze across the broad, empty stretch of yard between the main house and the bulk of the outbuildings. "Anyway," he said, "we did learn something. They don't want us wandering around alone, and they were uncomfortable talking about the man you sketched."

So he would ignore her careful overture, and their relationship would remain light and so much less than it could be. Well, it was probably for the best. If they had begun down that path, where did she really think it would end? No place good that she could envision.

"It could be as simple as what they said," she pointed out reluctantly.

"Could be. But it's not."

"So what's next?"

"I'll nose around tonight. See if there's anyone who likes to talk. And we let some underling or another give us a tour tomorrow."

"Maybe we'll even get lost," she suggested.

"Maybe we will."

Over his shoulder Laura saw the door to the small cottage open, a flare of light.

"Does someone live there, do you suppose? It seems too small."

"Where?" He swiveled. "They pointed out every other damn building in the place to me this afternoon. Nobody said a word about it."

"Well, there's certainly somebody there now."

The light in the open doorway silhouetted a small woman, her hair loose down her back. A man, hat in hand, stepped up on the porch.

"You think that's Collis?" he asked.

"Yes. His left shoulder is always a fraction lower than his right." She stopped. "Well. Would you look at that." The figures twined about each other, and his head lowered.

"Guess Collis's got a friend."

She leaned farther out to get a better view. "You think they're going to do it right out there on the porch?" she asked matter-of-factly.

He lifted an eyebrow. "I suppose a proper guard would be covering your virginal eyes right about now."

"They're not virginal."

Forgetting the show on the porch, Sam snapped around to gape at her. She grinned at his shock.

"I studied art remember? My *eyes* aren't virginal."

"Mmm-hmm." His eyes gleamed with speculation. She couldn't hold his gaze. *The rest of me* is *too darn virginal, or I wouldn't have had to look away.*

"They're going in," she said.

"So they are," he said, as the door swung shut. "I think I'll go see what's going on."

"Sam! You know what's going on."

"Never know when a thread'll start unraveling. Until then you gotta keep tugging."

"Uh-huh." Curiosity sparked. "Maybe I'll come with you."

"Oh, no you won't."

Laura considered trying to brazen it out. The idea of being left behind to rest while Sam investigated caused an automatic kick of protest; it seemed like she'd been ordered to rest while others had fun for most of her life. But then she envisioned what he might see when he reached the cottage and knew she didn't dare.

"Take care," she called.

"Don't I always?"

"No. No, you don't."

He grinned and faded into the night.

Chapter 15

Lucy Bossidy had had some difficult days in her thirty-six years. Not that anyone knew she was thirty-six, though unlike most women, she hadn't been trying to pass as younger. Instead everyone thought her older. And a widow.

The worst of those moments had been many years ago, before she'd come to Sea Haven. It had been a dark time, one she remembered mostly in a blur of incessant terror and worry, and then a long plummet into grief.

Not again. No, not again.

She stood beside Laura's bed. Her empty bed, bare and accusing in the darkness.

When she'd first awoken to find her gone, she figured it had to be a mistake, another one of Laura's larks. It was not the first time the girl had gone hieing off in search of adventure and freedom. Laura had never seemed to understand how much danger existed for unwary young girls.

Intellectually she understood that Laura felt confined, desperate to break free of the restrictions that bound her. But Lucy *knew* what it was like out there. She'd tried over and over again to explain it to Laura. It became her primary goal to ensure Laura appreciated that safety and security and warmth were to be cherished, not escaped. Because the alternative was simply too awful.

She sank to the edge of Laura's bed, trailing her fingers over the pillow.

She hadn't taken her pillow. They'd taken a fair number of things, so many that Lucy had burst into a furious rant when they'd tallied it all up. How could that horrid man have stolen all that away, and Lucy, too, without alerting Hoxie and Peel?

But she knew it was mostly her fault. She *knew* Laura was susceptible to the man. Knew even more how young and blossoming women could fall under the spells of handsome and fascinating men with charmingly dangerous edges. It was a flaw in the character of many women that they were romantic fools over roguish and inappropriate men, the lure of reforming them darn near irresistible.

She'd known, and she hadn't stopped it. How could she ever have believed that merely getting rid of the fellow would be enough? Young passion just wasn't extinguished that easily. Forbidden desire was one of the most treacherous illusions on the earth, and if anyone knew that, Lucy did.

Oh, Laura undoubtedly believed what she'd written in the letter. She *had* gone of her own free well. That did not, in any way, ensure that she was out of danger. He could have her in bed right now—

No. The image was too terrible. She would not think of it.

The compartment suddenly constricted around her, the air becoming heavy and precious. She jumped up and dashed out of Laura's cabin, through the beautiful sitting room that she'd come to hate at least three hundred miles ago, and out into the still, empty yard.

The fresh air filled her lungs, settling her nerves enough that she no longer felt she might scream at any moment. Her gaze traced the horizon, her spirits rising, until she realized she was searching for a horse, a figure. Waiting for Laura to come home.

She started to pace, back and forth over the rocky ground.

Most of the day she'd clung to the thin hope that Laura might return momentarily. That she'd come to her previously reliable senses and realize what she'd done. If not for her own good, than for Sam Duncan's. Because if anything happened to Laura —and in this case *anything* could be something as minor as a hangnail—Leland Hamilton would ensure that Duncan never took another easy breath as long as he lived. If he lived very long at all.

But as the night descended, too soon, too dark, she'd understood that Laura wasn't going to show up with apologies so they could be on their way and forget that the whole thing ever happened—

She screamed as she went down. Pain stabbed in her ankle, her palms as they hit the ground. She lay there, stunned.

Stupid, lumpy, holey *ground*. In Newport they had a lovely, smooth lawn, and

"Are you all right?"

Hiram charged from his car, sprinting toward her like a bull in the streets of Pamplona. "What happened? Is it Duncan? I—"

"No, nothing like that." Oh, yes, *of course* it would

be Mr. Peel who saw her sitting ignominiously on her rear on the ground. "I just fell in a hole."

"Oh." He extended a hand. "I'll help you up."

"That won't be necessary." She hid a wince as she put a bit of weight on her ankle.

"Don't be stupid." He stepped about her, clamped underneath her arms, and hauled her to her feet with all the grace of a shearer wrestling a ram.

"Thank you," she said grudgingly. She whacked her gritty palms on her skirts as she turned to face him.

"What the hell are you doing wandering around out here in the night?"

"Couldn't sleep." She kept forgetting how big he was. If the ox had lumbered at her out of the dark when she wasn't expecting it, she would have been frightened out of her boots. "Suppose you didn't have that problem."

"I—Yeah, that's right," he said with enough edge in his voice that even Lucy felt a spurt of guilt. Absurd. It wasn't as if the man's feelings could possible be hurt. One must have them to hurt them. "I dropped right off, not a worry the world. It's not like I care the least bit for Laura. It's just a job."

"You're right." She touched him gently on the sleeve. "That was unfair. I'm sorry. It's just . . ." She felt the press of emotion high in her throat and swallowed hard. She refused to fall apart in front of people. Most of all, she refused to fall apart in front of *him*. "Where's Mr. Hoxie?"

"He left."

"What do you mean, he left?"

"He headed into town."

"But . . . Sam took all the horses!"

Hiram shrugged. "He decided to walk. It's only a few miles."

"But—but—" Did *everybody* around here plan to go

gallivanting around the countryside without clearing it with her first? "We talked about this: we were going to wait here in case she came back, then we were going to go on into Ogden, just like Laura suggested!"

"We didn't talk about it. *You* talked about it." He had his feet planted wide, sturdy and grounded. Solid. It would take a runaway coach slamming into him at top speed to get him to budge an inch.

"But we agreed!"

"Nope. We just didn't disagree. Not much profit in it. Easier to let you say your piece, then go ahead."

"But—but—" She was *not* unreasonable, dammit. Not obstinate and unwilling to listen. Why did they persist in treating her like she was?

"Why didn't you go?"

He opened his mouth. Closed it again. Red suffused his cheeks, the tips of his ears. His gaze skittered off into the darkness. "Somebody had to stay here in case Laura found her way back."

"Mm-hmm." All the fight whooshed out of her. *She* was here. And he'd stayed because he didn't want to leave her alone.

"What's Mr. Hoxie planning to do when he gets back to Silver Creek?" she asked.

"Ask around. Maybe someone saw them, or—"

"No one saw them," she said flatly.

"They could've."

"No. He's not that stupid. He wouldn't have taken her anywhere that they could be seen and noted." Worry again had her by the throat, a relentless squeeze. "Sh-she's g-g-gone."

"Aw, no, don't do that." He patted her on the back, nearly sending her back to her knees. "Don't cry."

"Too late." Dammit. She would have rather burst

into tears in front of the entire staff of Sea Haven than in front of Hiram. But it seemed she wasn't to have a choice. The tears rolled over her, unstoppable as a tidal wave, as elemental. It was almost a relief to surrender to them.

"Crap." He grabbed her by the back of the neck and hauled her up against him, driving an *oof* out of her as she slammed up against the solid wall of his chest.

"I can't lose her, too!" she wailed. Tears spilled out of her eyes, dripped out of her nose. Maybe she should be grateful that it was only Hiram witnessing this after all. She could feel her eyelids swelling, and it wasn't going to be a pretty sight. But since he already thought the worst of her, it shouldn't matter if he saw her looking like death warmed over. "Not another—"

"You won't," he said. One huge hand cradled the back of her head, gentler than she would have expected him capable of. The other rested at the hollow of her back, pressing her to him, his fingers widespread, so long that the smallest reached to the upper curves of her rump. With another man, in any other situation, it would have been a wildly sexual posture. "Wait. Another, 'too'?"

Had she said that? Fifteen years, and she'd never slipped once.

She opened her mouth to deny it. But she didn't want to. To deny it would make it seem unimportant, as if it had never happened. As if *she* had never happened.

"I had a daughter," she said.

She felt his surprise in the reflexive tightening of his arms around her. But he didn't comment, just waited patiently for her to continue. Who would have thought Hiram knew when to keep his mouth shut?

"It's not an unusual story, I suppose." The fury of

tears receded, leaving the deep well of loneliness. She was surprised how easily the story spilled out after so many years of being bottled inside. "I fell in love, and I believed him when he said he meant to marry me. He was so handsome, so charming. He was from a far richer family than mine, and I thought every wish I'd ever made in my whole life had come true when he began to court me."

When she stopped talking she could hear Hiram's heartbeat, she realized, loud and very steady. Comforting.

"I believed him when he said he had to prepare his family before they met me. And when he said it would be no sin to anticipate our vows a bit, and that he couldn't survive another day if he didn't have me." *Thump. Thump. Lovely heartbeat.* "I believed him a *lot*. Except when he said he didn't want me anymore. Or our child."

He bent down, his chin rubbing soothingly across the top of her head. "You lost her?"

"I—" Her voice shook. She took a deep breath and steadied. "I gave her away."

She waited for the shock. The recriminations. But all she got was the slow circle of his hand on the small of her back, the rise and fall of his chest beneath her cheek as he took a deep breath.

"I had no money. My parents didn't want to . . . didn't want to see what I'd done."

"Bastards."

Her shoulders lifted, fell. "No, they—" She started to say they were just parents, parents who were ashamed that their daughter had gone against everything they'd taught her.

But she *had* needed them then. She never would have

turned Laura out in a similar situation. If she—God forbid—came back from her adventure with Duncan in the family way, Lucy would move heaven and hell to help her. And she wouldn't say "I told you so."

At least not more than once.

"I couldn't take care of her. I had no money. I had no way of making any." She ran through the reasons, all those justifications that had played through her mind then, and every day since. Though she knew in her head they were right, *knew* it, in her heart they still felt like excuses.

"They were a lovely couple. I worked so hard to find the right ones. He was a doctor. She taught school because they hadn't been able to have any of their own, and she wanted to be by children. And when I gave her to them—" She squeezed her eyes shut. It hurt, the burn behind her lids, the ache in her chest. Hurt so bad that for a long time she'd thought she might die of it. "She said I was her hero."

He was swaying, back and forth with her in his arms as if he were holding a baby. The rhythm eased the tight twist of pain, if only a little.

"You are," he whispered gruffly against her hair.

She blew out a long breath.

He smelled good. Like sweat and horses and grass, but still good. Manly.

"It was two years before I found my way to Sea Haven. There wasn't much work, but I didn't care very much, either. But then I became a 'widow' and a nurse and went to work for the Hamiltons. Laura saved me."

"You're not the only one," he murmured. She remembered when Hiram had showed up at Sea Haven. He'd been young and wild when he'd come to work for them, angry at the world, and she really hadn't thought he'd stay. But he had, and after a while all the anger had seeped out of him.

"I can't lose her, too."

"You won't." His voice was absolutely sure. "I won't let you."

Heavens, but it felt good to have a man's arms around her. She'd blocked it from her mind. Had punished herself for ever having enjoyed it. But oh, that intoxicating oblivion that overwhelmed worry, blotted out hurt, swept away anything but pure physical drive—what a wonderful thing it was. At least for a while. She hadn't forgotten that, much as she'd tried to.

She turned her head and pressed her mouth—open, damp—against his chest. The cotton fabric was thin; her lips could detect the springy texture of the hair on his chest, the searing heat he carried within that huge frame.

"Mrs. Bossidy?"

"Lucy," she murmured.

"I don't know if I can call you that."

She arched her back and tilted her head up. The move pressed her lower regions against him, and the ache settled, strengthened. Heavens, but it felt good. Wonderful. How had she managed to ignore this for so long? "Try."

He cleared his throat. "Lucy." His head came down, closer, closer, until she could feel the wash of his breath on her lips.

"This doesn't mean anything," she warned him. "It can't. It's just . . . distraction."

"Mmm-hmm," he murmured. Which didn't really sound like agreement.

But then his mouth came down on hers, and she forgot everything.

Chapter 16

Laura didn't understand why she kept dreaming about men.

Sam, yes, that was self-explanatory. What woman wouldn't dream about Sam? And that Chinaman; that really wasn't that surprising, given how much she'd worried about him at the time.

But this one . . . big and bulky and unfamiliar, in her bedroom, moving around, clumsily ruffling through her things.

She blinked . . . blinked? And came to full wakefulness.

Reflexive self-preservation froze her in place, afraid to breathe, wishing she could turn her head to follow his movements.

He was in the corner of her room where her work supplies were stored. A mouth-breather, loud and heavy, as if he were under a great strain.

He dropped something. She heard the thud on the floor, the creak of his knees as he bent to pick it up.

She could just stay there, unmoving, and hope he went away. But those were her things, and . . . oh, she'd had enough of waiting and hoping.

And screamed.

He whirled, gaping at her. It was far too dark to see him well. A moon-round face, a build like a bear ready for hibernation.

He charged out of the room, the door slamming against the thick walls, the report like cannon fire.

She heard the thunder of feet. They burst into her room. Haw, Ben, Clem. Lupe, carrying a lantern that swung in her hands, throwing eerie undulating shadows on the walls. And Sam, only a few seconds later, skidding in behind them and pushing through the group to stand by her bed.

"Are you all right?"

"Yes, yes, I'm fine."

His face flooded with such relief that she softened inside; he must care for her, in some way more than merely a means to an end.

"What happened?" Crocker asked.

"There was someone in my room."

"Someone in your room?" He strode over to the bed. Laura yanked the covers up, glad she'd worn a high-necked, long-sleeved gown despite the warm evening.

Ben, Clem, and Lupe were in their nightclothes, too. Clem, a white nightshirt the size of a sail, the trunks of his legs sticking out beneath it. He was of a size to be her nighttime visitor, but there was no way he could have changed that quickly.

Lupe wore silk—creamy, shimmering, and surprising.

Only Mr. Crocker and Sam were fully dressed. Evidentally Mr. Crocker worked late. Sam wore black, giving him a dangerous edge. He'd been working, too, Laura thought, and couldn't help but worry.

And he was far more likely to be recognized in those clothes. She inclined her head to him, trying to encourage him to slip out of the room before anyone took too close a look at him.

"Didn't you see him in the hall?"

Haw and his son glanced at each other. "Nope."

"Then he's got to be *here* somewhere! You all arrived too quickly, maybe he ducked into—"

"That's ridiculous," Crocker interrupted.

Sam scowled and stepped forward. She shook her head, trying desperately to signal him with her eyes. *Get out, get out. Get safe.* Finally, he slipped out of the room and she flopped back against the pillows, releasing a relieved breath.

"Are you prone to . . . vivid dreams?" Crocker asked her.

"No, I—" They were arrayed by her bed. Clem had his arms crossed in front of his chest, threatening even in that ridiculous nightshirt. Crocker's face was suspicious. Only Lupe appeared sympathetic.

What good what it do her to insist? The man was likely long gone. Clearly Crocker had no intention of searching the house or calling an alarm in the yard.

"Well, perhaps," she admitted softly, lowering her lashes.

"There's a good girl." Crocker patted her awkwardly on the shoulder. "Would you like Lupe to stay with you until you get back to sleep?"

"That's very kind of you. But no. I'll be fine." Let Lupe get back to whatever assignation she was heading to—no woman wore a gown like that for herself. Idly she wondered who he could be; she could not picture the striking Lupe with any of the men in the house.

"I'm fine," she repeated, and yawned to prove the point. "I'm sure I'll sleep better now. If nothing else, I know how quickly you can all get here if I need you."

"I promised your father I'd take good care of you," Crocker said, just before he went out the door. "I intend to."

"Thank you," she murmured, as if she were already surrendering to sleep.

Lupe hovered by the door, the lantern in her hand. She was a lovely woman, with her vivid coloring and generous curves, and she appeared to be genuinely concerned. "Would you like something to drink? I'd be pleased to fix you something."

"No, thank you." Her curiosity got the better of her. And perhaps it would be useful to form a bond with the woman. Who saw more and heard more of what went on in a house than the housekeeper? "Your English is excellent."

"I've been here a long time."

"You must like it here."

"What's that got to do with anything?" she asked, and slipped out the door.

Laura wriggled her shoulders, adjusting comfortably against the covers, and waited.

"Nice lungs," Sam said.

She'd been expecting him. His voice startled her just the same, for he'd appeared at the window without a hint of sound, a breath of warning, slipping through in an instant.

"Thank you for noticing," she said softly. "You do have a way with windows."

"They're very useful."

He sauntered over to her, an innate creature of the night. If one of Haw Crocker's men saw him just then, he would recognize Sam instantly.

He sat down on the edge of her bed, which made her brows lift.

"Can't be too far away," he told her. "Gotta talk softly. Don't want anyone to hear us."

The walls were at least half a foot thick. Haw Crocker had built the house to stand long after he was gone. "Uh-huh." The mattress dipped beneath his weight, causing her body to sway his way. If she relaxed, she'd roll right into him.

"Where were you? You got here awfully fast."

He hooked a thumb in the direction of the window. "Only a little way out in the yard. Watching the comings and goings. It's a busy place out there, for the middle of the night." There was a hint of strain in his voice that gave her pause. Was he as unsettled to be on her bed as she was to have him there? And would it be wiser to ignore it or confront it?

"Oh?"

"Yup. The mill supervisors must live here instead of closer to the mines. Saw them all come back around midnight. Not to mention a whole fleet of guards. Seems strange that they'd need that many people to watch over the miners."

"Maybe they're a rambunctious lot."

"Perhaps." Half of Sam was attending to the conversation, shifting through the bits of information he'd gathered and the implications of someone breaking into her room. The other half was simply admiring. Her hair was braided, and her nightgown had more in common with a sack than a negligee. But her eyes sparkled with life, her mouth soft and animated. The line of her jaw was lovely, the curve of her ear pink and tempting. The fact that such simple things could stir him so deeply made him believe that, were he ever to see more than her gown revealed, maybe even *touch* more, he'd be captured more thoroughly than he'd ever intended.

And she was distracting him enough to allow him to remain in the room. He felt the strain of it, a hitch in chest, a pressure in his lungs. But if he concentrated on her, thought of possibilities and wants and yes, most of all, sex, he didn't feel like the walls were going to crush him.

"I know vaguely which direction the mine is now, at least," he said.

"Any sign of Mr. Judah?"

He shook his head.

"I'm sorry, Sam."

"I don't know what I thought I'd find." He'd never really considered the possibility of failure. Sam Duncan never failed. But what if there really was nothing to find?

No, there had to be. Men did not just vanish, not without a shred of evidence left behind for a diligent and motivated investigator to discover. "It's not like somebody's going to be wearing a jacket labeled with his initials."

"You'll find it," Laura said, with such absolute faith in his abilities that his worry eased. "How about the woman in the shed?"

"Ah. She's a busy woman, that one. Has a *lot* of very friendly visitors."

"Visitors." Realization dawned. "Oh."

"Yes. Oh." If she were . . . entertaining . . . all the men on the Silver Spur, she'd be a busy woman indeed. "And one more thing. She looks to be Chinese."

"Chinese?" She frowned in concentration. "That's rather a coincidence, wouldn't you say?"

"I would indeed."

She seemed so comfortable with him beside her on her bed. Oh, there'd been a moment of surprise at first, but she'd quickly accepted it, as if having him there was the most natural thing in the world. He couldn't quite decide whether he should be worried about that or insulted, because he was anything but comfortable there.

"Now. Tell me about your thief."

"You think he was a thief?"

"What else? You've got plenty to steal. And he'd have a helluva time kidnapping you from beneath all of our noses."

"You managed quite nicely."

"Yes. But very few people are as good as I am."

"Well, aren't you modest." She grinned at him, a flirtatious little curve of her mouth. He felt it settle into his gut, a warm kick of desire that left him a bit woozy, like he'd just downed a good slug of whiskey.

"Not a terribly useful virtue, I've discovered."

"What other virtues have you found useless?"

He wondered if she had any idea of what she was doing. Tempting him beyond reason, driving him beyond sense, with just some banter and a mischievous glint in her eyes.

He stood up, turning his back to her while he struggled for control.

"Sam?" she said, her soft voice a spur to senses excited to a fever pitch, attuned to the slightest stimulation from her.

"So tell me about your intruder," he managed. And sounded almost normal.

"I . . ." He heard her confusion at the change of topic, then she quickly rallied, businesslike and composed. *Always quick on the uptake, aren't you, my girl?* "He was big. I couldn't tell you much more about him than that. It was dark."

"That doesn't narrow it down much. Half of the guys who work for Crocker look like they were circus strongmen in a previous career."

"I don't think he was a thief," she said thoughtfully. "At least, he wasn't going through my wardrobe. He was over there. By my work supplies."

"Maybe he just hadn't found the good stuff yet."

"No. The armoire's right beside the door. My jewelry case is on that table. He had to pass them to get to the corner where I stored all my supplies."

"Well, let's see what might have interested him. You got a lantern?"

"Right here." She groped for the matches, lit it. He heard the creak as she climbed out of bed and should have anticipated the danger. Instead, he turned automatically at the sound.

She swayed by the side of the bed, the covers peeled back, white and inviting. A nice big bed, one made for a long night of loving. That, he thought, he'd stay inside for, and happily, too.

Her nightgown was summerweight, a sheer drift of white. Completely demure, but in the golden glow of the lantern he could catch hints of her body: the sharp indent of her waist, the slight curve of her hip, the long length of her narrow legs, and he had to close his eyes to tamp down on his passions, for it certainly wouldn't happen while he was looking at her. But it didn't help, for the image of her was burned behind his lids, imprinted in his brain.

She, however, apparently had no such problems. She brushed beside him—if she had any idea of how near the edge he hovered, she'd never have dared to come so close—and bent to the stack of books and canvases, the rolls of paper and cases that held brushes and pots of paint.

"Here. Let me." He took the lantern from her so she could search with both hands. Her shadow trembled on the cream-colored wall behind her, a graceful curve.

"It's silly, really, or he's very stupid. The jewelry's worth far more than any of these. In fact—" She snapped upright. "He took the sketchbook."

"Are you sure?"

"Oh, yes. It was right here."

"Maybe it just got lost in the shuffle as he was rummaging through things."

"No. It's really not that jumbled. I've got a smaller, blank one right here, and most everything else is still packed away. It's gone."

He knew how much work that sketchbook contained. He'd watched her create most of it. "I'm sorry, Laura," he said. If he hadn't *lured* her into helping him she wouldn't have lost it. "I'm sorry."

She shrugged, unconcerned. "So why did he want my sketchbook? Even an idiot must know the necklace I wore at dinner's worth more than all the work I've done in my entire life."

She looked so delicate in the lamplight, her skin so fine as to be almost translucent. Oh, she didn't belong here, with men breaking into her room while she slept and stealing her work.

"This is ridiculous," he said. "I'm taking you back tomorrow."

Laura was still pondering the theft, and his words penetrated slowly. "What did you say?"

"I said I'm taking you back tomorrow."

"You most certainly are not." Hands on her hips, she glowered at him, a fierce and threatening creature.

"I'll find another way," he said. "Now that I've seen the lay of the land, I'll find another way back in."

"Don't be stupid," she said. "I know it might be difficult, with that reflexive protectiveness kicking in, but listen to me. I do not *wish* to go back. I clearly was not in any danger—for heaven's sake, I screamed once, and there were enough people in my room to have a party. Not to mention I have utmost faith in your ability to keep me safe. And even if I did not, it is still my choice to make. Not my father's, not Mrs. Bossidy's, not yours. *Mine*. And I choose to stay."

"Laura." When did the most reasonable of women suddenly become rock-damn stubborn? "It's settled. I'm taking you back."

"And just how are you planning to do that without my cooperation? Chloroform me again and sneak me out without anybody noticing?"

"That wasn't what I had in mind, no," he said with only a twinge of guilt. "I could do it."

"I'm sure you could. But you're also going to have to stay with me and play jailor, or I'm going to come running back and ask Haw Crocker what happened to Griff myself."

"You wouldn't."

She merely raised one brow, coolly confident. "Try me."

"I'll sic Mrs. Bossidy on you," he warned her.

She laughed. "Darlin', do you think I've learned

nothing in the past dozen years or so? If I really want to, I can get around her like *that*." She snapped her fingers.

She was so delighted with herself, humming with anticipation and freedom, that he couldn't bring himself to haul her off and lock her up. Which was obviously what it would take to keep her completely out of trouble, now that she'd set her mind on it.

"All right," he said. Not because she'd badgered and threatened him into it, but because when it came right down to it he *wanted* to keep her around, though he was unwilling to examine that too closely yet. "Then get into bed."

"Excuse me?"

"If you're going to stay, I'm not going to have you collapsing from exhaustion."

The woman wisely decided not to push her luck. She meekly turned—ha! Like he was going to buy that now, after all her threats and temper—and climbed into bed.

She pondered the corner where her supplies rested. "So what do you think it all means?"

He dragged over a heavy chair, fashioned of dark Spanish-carved wood and plush red cushions, plopped into it, and kicked his feet up on the foot of her bed. "It means," he said, "until we figure out why you're having midnight company, you're going to have more. Because I'm going to have to stay by your side day *and* night."

Chapter 17

"They tried awfully hard to keep us from the mines this afternoon," Sam said the next night as he helped her through the window. "So let's make a trip over in that direction tonight, hmm?"

She swung her second leg over and gave a hop to the ground. His hands rested at her waist, and she was wearing . . . "What in God's name are you wearing?"

Lifting her arms, she gave a little spin. A loose black shirt swallowed up her torso, neck to wrist. "Bloomers," she said brightly. "Like 'em?" They sprouted from her waist, black—no, navy, huge gathering folds of fabric that billowed over her hips, thoroughly hiding her legs before gathering abruptly at her ankles.

"Where did you get those?"

"Once upon a time I had visions of bicycling," she told him. "I thought it best to be prepared when my father finally said 'yes.' She leaned forward, drawing him into her conspiracy. "It's best not to give him time to change his mind about such things."

"Understandably so."

"I thought so." She looked utterly ridiculous, swathed in as much fabric as a Bedouin, her face lit up like a child on Christmas morning. Without a doubt she was the most adorable thing he'd seen in his entire life. "I brought them along thinking they might come in handy. It seemed appropriate for tonight."

"Mmm-hmm." He struggled not to grin. She was too pleased with herself, too proud of her clandestine-operation clothes, and she would not take kindly to being the source of his amusement. "Very appropriate."

"So." She rocked back on her heels, an impatient gesture. "Where are the horses?"

"Tethered over by the corral. I saddled them already. But first—"

She sighed deeply. "Can we just skip this?" She turned and headed for the corral at a determined clip. He fell into step beside her.

"Skip what?"

"The obligatory attempt to convince me that the best solution would be to allow you to tuck me away someplace safe while you go on about your business."

Blasted perceptive woman. "No, we can't skip it."

She stopped halfway across the yard. All the outbuildings clustered in a broad, precise semicircle around them, blocky shapes in rigid alignment. No lights glowed in any of the windows, for they'd waited until past one. The second shift of mine guards had returned at half past midnight, and Sam had given them time to pitch into bed.

"Sam." She laid a hand against his jaw. Oh, she touched him so easily now, as if it were entirely natural. As if she'd touched him a thousand times and would do so a thousand more. And every time his stomach tightened and his breath seized and desire slammed into him like a cannon blast. Yet he couldn't bring himself to stop her. "I understand. I really do. I even know that perhaps you'd be more efficient without me. But I have a good eye. And, if we happen to be discovered, I can help you cover it up by pretending a lover's tryst."

"*That'll* surprise them," he said wryly.

"It'll probably relieve them." She smiled. "And the truth is, Sam, no matter what situation we go into, I'd feel safer by your side. I'd go crazy waiting here. And if someone stumbled upon me, if there's a snake or a cougar or an outlaw or whatever . . . I'd rather be with you."

I'd rather be with you. He was almost dizzy with it. He understood she meant under his protection, with his arm and his gun by her side. The weight of the responsibility pressed down upon him, substantial but not entirely unwelcome. And the sound of those words, that promise of trust, was heady.

"And I have an interest of my own here," she continued. "If I do not discover what truly happened to that poor man, I don't think I'll sleep properly again."

"Don't believe that tale about the crazy worker and Crocker's kind generosity, hmm?"

"Not for a moment."

He stepped back, gaze sweeping the length of her, her bright face and pulled-back hair and those ridiculous clothes. "I am *such* a bad influence on you."

"Yeah," she said, and grinned. "Isn't it great?"

She dropped her hand and headed for the horses. And for an instant he considered grabbing her hand and pulling her back, saying the hell with it all and asking her to ride off into the sunset with him, leaving everything and everyone behind. It didn't sound nearly as absurd as it should.

But the world was never made of two people, no matter how much one might wish it was. And what would he do when he lost her, too? To her father, to her old life, or, God forbid, something worse? She'd almost died once, and, while she certainly seemed strong enough now—and would have kicked him within an inch of his life for suggesting otherwise—there was always a chance the damage was more severe than they realized.

He wouldn't lose her after having her. He couldn't. And since he couldn't ensure he'd never lose her, then he just couldn't have her.

"Uh-oh," she said, and stopped in her tracks. "We've got company."

He tensed, preparing for action, his hands flying to his holsters. And then he relaxed again, for this couldn't pose much of a threat.

The Chinese woman who inhabited—worked?—in the tiny cottage stood perhaps fifteen feet from them, her hands folded in front of her, waiting. Her hair, dark as the night, was swept straight back and pinned. She said nothing, merely watched them with eyes so black as to give nothing of her thoughts away.

They took each other's measures across the small space, like gunfighters waiting for the signal to fire.

And still the woman made no move, said nothing, just stood there in her simple dark dress and impassive expression.

"Well. At least she hasn't cried an alarm yet," Laura said.

"Unless she signaled someone before we noticed her and now she's keeping an eye on us until they arrive."

"You're such a suspicious sort."

"You say that like that's a bad thing."

"Does she speak English?" Laura asked.

"How would I know?"

"I thought you investigated last night."

"She and her . . . friends weren't doing a whole lot of talking," he informed her. "And frankly, darlin', I'd think you'd be happy that I didn't investigate her that closely."

Laura *tsked* in disapproval. "Well, then. Enough." She smoothed the fabric gathers at her waist and took a step toward the woman.

"You'll never make a good investigator," he told her. "Not enough patience."

"I've got an idea."

The woman glanced around her as they approached, furtive, worried, as if afraid to be seen talking to them.

"Do you speak English?" Laura asked, her voice as gentle as if she were speaking to a painfully shy child.

The woman nodded. "Some."

She was a good four inches shorter than Laura, who wouldn't be called tall by anyone, and so slight a good breeze would topple her over. He'd be surprised if she could claim seventeen years honestly. And yet there was dignity in her posture, the hard-won steel that only a fellow survivor could truly recognize and understand.

"Would you speak to us?"

A barely perceptible shudder rippled through her—fear, Sam thought, and indecision "My house," she said. "Too late for visitors."

She spun and led them there without glancing back to see if they followed. Perhaps hoping they would not, thus relieving her of the decision of what to entrust them with.

Her feet pattered lightly across the porch. No squeaks on the board, nor on the hinges of the door as she pushed it open. Well kept, like everything else on the Silver Spur. Money and Haw Crocker's will went a long way.

It was very small in the house. Sam could make out none of the interior. He started inside, and his leg muscles seized. The air thickened in his lungs, his head going painfully light.

"In!" the woman snapped out.

"Sam?" Laura asked, wondering and concerned.

"I—" The night air was cool and fresh, but sweat broke out on his forehead, his back. "I should keep watch," he said. "Better I stay out here. Don't want anyone sneaking up on us if some randy cowboy decides on a late-night romp."

"We'll leave the door open a fraction, so you can hear," Laura said, "and—"

"No," the woman interrupted. "*Inside*, or no talk."

Oh, God. This was the closest thing to a clue—at least a potential one—that he'd had since this whole blasted thing started. And he was either going to have to go inside—inside that tiny, thick-walled, tight cabin that would surely squeeze the air right out of him—or he was going to lose out completely.

He'd been inside the train car. The dining room, Laura's bedroom. He'd been getting it under control.

But this place wasn't a fifth the size of any of them, scarcely bigger than a coffin, it seemed. The shades were down, and he just knew she was going to want to shut the door, trapping him inside.

He struggled to draw a full breath. If only it wasn't so damned *dark*, if only the small structure had more than one tiny window, if only—

"Please, ma'am, it'll be all right. No one will see him out here. He's really very good at that." Laura—what a wonder—was saving him. "And he's right. This way no one can come to the door unexpectedly."

The woman teetered on the edge, worry warring with trust. And then she slipped into the room, a silent wraith, and Laura followed her.

Sam hunched down on the porch, so the bars of the railing would break up his outline, and propped the door open a few inches.

Once inside Laura didn't dare move. Only a narrow line of light made it through the door, scarcely illuminating the space at all. The heavy air stung her nose, the scent of soap so strong her eyes almost watered.

"You've cleaned recently," she said, hoping a neutral topic would relax the clearly riotously tense woman.

"Smell the men afterward," she said, her tone vibrating with anger. "Don't like it."

Smell the men . . . ? "Oh," Laura said, her mind skittering away from the images. From Sam's comments she'd formed an idea of the woman's function on the ranch. In an isolated place populated mostly by men, she . . . serviced their baser needs.

But Laura hadn't given much thought to the reality of it. It was a world so alien from Laura's own that she couldn't quite grasp it.

She remembered that afternoon when Sam had kissed her. She'd embraced it, longed for it, recalled it with a sweet and piercing clarity. Yet she couldn't deny the uncomfortable intimacy of it. To do that, and a hundred times more, with strangers, to open oneself to a man—*men*—that you scarcely knew and probably didn't even like . . . Laura could imagine few things more horrifying. How did a woman end up in that place? Make a choice that this would be her life?

And obviously this woman regretted it. Anger and distaste vibrated off her small body.

But that meant she should have little loyalty to the Silver Spur. And that was what she and Sam needed, didn't they? Someone who would betray the ranch's secrets, reveal exactly what was happening here?

Laura felt guilty just considering taking advantage of this woman's misfortune. She vowed to herself that if an opportunity arose to help this woman, she would do so. And that promise helped.

"What's your name?"

"They call me Mary." She spat out the name.

"That might be what they call you," Laura said, "but what is your name?"

Silence. And then: "Been a long time since anyone bothered to ask me. It's Chen Jo Ling." Her voice strengthened. "Jo Ling."

"Jo Ling, how did you come to America?"

She shook her head. "Don't matter now. Collis, last night—" She swallowed audibly. "Collis visit me. Likes to talk, that one, much as likes to . . . well. Said you had picture of man who tried to escape. Can I see?"

"They claimed he was crazy," Laura told her.

Jo Ling made a sound of heavy disgust. "What else he be but escaping? Be crazy not to."

"Escaping from what?" Sam whispered through the crack in the door. Jo Ling startled, as if she'd forgotten he was there.

She clammed up, as if suddenly unsure she should be speaking about this.

"I see picture?" she asked again.

"I'm sorry," Laura said. "It's gone."

"They took it?"

"Yes." Is that what the intruder had been after all along, then? Why?

"You go now."

"Excuse me?"

Jo Ling pulled the door open and took Laura by the arm, steering her toward it.

"No, no," Laura said. "I've got some questions, we—"

Laura planted her feet and leaned into the pressure of Jo Ling's hands. The slight woman was a great deal stronger than she looked, but she barely came to Laura's chin.

"Miss, we do not wish to disturb you," Sam said. "But we cannot help you if—"

"Who says need help?" Using her shoulder as a prod, she leaned into Laura's back. "Dangerous for you to be here."

"Then we'd best get it over with quickly, hmm?" Laura said. "Do you have paper?"

She felt the weight of Jo Ling's shoulder in her back ease off a fraction. "You draw again?"

"I can try."

"Okay."

They left Sam outside, something which seemed to relieve Jo Ling to no end and which he protested less than Laura expected. Once the door was firmly closed and the roller shades over the window tightly fastened, Jo Ling lit a stub of candle.

For a den of inequity the room was disappointing. Laura had envisioned red velvet and flocked wallpaper, gold-leafed statuettes of naked bodies in lurid poses.

Instead it resembled a monk's cell, so clean as to hold no personality whatsoever, as if no one lived there. The walls were white and completely bare. The single room held a chair, a table with a wash pitcher, and a tiny trunk. The bed was barely big enough for one, much less two and adventures.

She flipped open the top of her trunk, which, from what Laura could see, held very little. It took her but a moment to locate a carefully folded scrap of paper, a pencil shorter than her thumb.

"Here." She thrust them at Laura.

What if she couldn't do it again? Laura had been so pleased with the original drawing; it had sprung from nowhere, from her dreams and her distress, forming on the page almost without her consciously guiding her hand.

This was so much more important.

She closed her eyes briefly, conjuring that face as clearly as if she were back there that day, in the sunlight, waiting, hoping, praying for him to get away.

Yes. Bent over the table, she drew rapidly, surely. The small scrap of paper limited her. The fragment of pencil was unfamiliar in hand, her fingers bent awkwardly around it.

And yet she was finished in moments. "Here. Do you know him?"

Jo Ling leaned over the table, bringing the candle close so she could inspect it, her expression intent. She did not touch it.

"No." She let out a long, shuddering breath. Laura could not tell if it was disappointment or relief. "Not him."

"Not who?"

Jo Ling straightened, but her gaze lingered on the sketch.

"Who?" Laura repeated.

The decision hung in the balance, as delicate and uncertain as a dragonfly wing. And then her expression closed off. "No one. No matter."

Hope deflated.

"You go now."

Laura nodded. She understood Jo Ling's fear. Why should she trust them? She was clearly in a precarious situation, alone on this ranch so far from her past and anyone who might help her, unhappy and hopelessly trapped.

And she would remain trapped, as caught in her situation and life as Laura had been in her sickroom, as Sam had been in Andersonville. If she did not take this risk, with them, she would be confined here for a long time. Perhaps forever.

"Jo Ling." Laura brushed her fingers over the surface of the cheap paper. "It really is very sad. He tried so hard to get away. We could tell that he was ready to sacrifice everything to escape or die trying. We could not help him then. I'd hoped we could help him now."

Jo Ling's eyes glimmered, liquid regret welling up.

"We could, you know. My father is very powerful, more so even than Mr. Crocker."

"Not true! No one bigger than Mr. Crocker."

"My father is." Laura nodded emphatically. "And Mr. . . . Kirkwood out there, he is very skilled at rescuing people. I should know. He rescued me once."

Jo Ling wavered, a tiny spark of hope flaring to hesitant life.

"We could help you," Laura said. "This may be the best chance you ever have, the *only* chance, to get out of here."

"Why you think I want out? Good food. Good house."

She recited them automatically, as if someone had

told her just that. As if someone had tried to convince her that she should be *grateful* for being forced into whoredom.

"Jo Ling, does Mr. Crocker visit you?"

"No." She chuckled, bitter and empty. "He have Lupe. No need to visit me."

Lupe. She should have realized. "Then what about the man in that sketch? And whoever you thought that man might be? We can't possibly help if we don't know what's going on."

Inevitably drawn, Jo Ling's gaze slid back to the sketch on the table. "Man Ho," she murmured. "Thought maybe . . . thought it Man Ho."

Careful, Laura told herself. Too many questions, push too hard, and Jo Ling would be scared off as easily as a frightened doe.

"Who's Man Ho?"

"My . . . friend. Met on the boat to San Francisco. Kind to me." She sniffled. "Did not see after they find out I was girl."

"After they found out you were a girl?" Laura frowned, confused, disturbed.

"Decide I would be more useful . . . here than in mines. But did not know about the mines yet then."

"Sam?" Laura said, a fraction louder. "Are you getting all this?"

"Yes." Just the sound of his voice steadied her, familiar and smooth, comforting and exciting at the same time.

"I think maybe you should come in here. I'm not sure what to ask anymore."

"I . . ."

Laura moved to the door—quickly, only two steps, and eased it open a fraction.

"Have you seen anyone out and about?" she asked him.

"No. It's been quiet."

"We'd better get you in and the door shut, though. It's either that or douse the light, and it's better to see her face."

She heard him take a deep breath. "All right."

The room seemed instantly smaller when he slipped in the door. He had to duck to enter, and his head must have nearly brushed the ceiling when he straightened, his shoulders as wide as the doorway.

He closed the door, leaning against the wall beside it. Jo Ling took a step back.

"It's all right," Laura promised. "You can trust him."

As she did. Unreasonably, given what she knew of him: that he was willing to put honor aside in favor of expediency. That he had traded his loyalty for money, his principles for comfort. That once they'd settled this he would ride off to his next job, his next hired duty, and she would never hear from him again.

And still she trusted him, with a bone deep belief, unreasonable but unshakable, that he would do his best for her during this time and that he would never hurt her needlessly or thoughtlessly.

"Why were you on the ship?" Laura asked.

The night ticked by, silent and waiting. And then Jo Ling nodded. "Parents sold me."

"Sold you?"

"To merchant who needed a . . . don't know the word." Her smile was bitter. "I become same thing anyway, but for more than one."

Horror washed over Laura. She understood that there were those in the world, *many* in the world, who were not so fortunate in their parents as she. They had confined her, yes, protected her so assiduously she sometimes thought she might go mad with it, but they'd always had her best interests at heart.

To sell your own daughter into what amounted to a repulsive and intimate kind of slavery . . . it was so far beyond her experience as to be incomprehensible.

"So I run away," she continued. "No place to go. But there was foreign man. *American* man. He take students to America. Young men only. I braid my hair and change my clothes and say I boy."

"Sam?" It made no sense to Laura. She looked over to Sam to see if he could sort it through. He leaned against the wall, his head back, and even in the flickering candlelight she could see his forehead gleamed with sweat. "Sam?" She took a step toward him. "Are you all right?"

He held up a hand to halt her progress. "Yeah. Yeah, I'm okay." His voice was thin with strain. "Just having a little relapse of whatever I had in Silver Creek. I'll be okay."

"Let's get you back to the house."

"No!" he said sharply, worried that, if they left now, they might never get Jo Ling to speak to them again.

"Do you know what she's talking about?"

"Exclusion Act," he said. "Eliminated all immigration from China except for a couple of exceptions. Mostly students."

"Yes!" Jo Ling said. "Said we could be students, come to America to study."

"How many?" Sam asked.

"Boat full." She shrugged. "Hundred? Two hundred?"

"What happened to them all?"

"Oh, there more. Many more than that, here already when we got here. Put us on trains, come here." Her voice slowed. "No school."

"Only mines," Sam said.

"Yes. Only mines."

"Sam, I don't understand. Why would they bring all those students here?"

"He's bringing them in illegally, Laura. Forcing them to work in the mines."

"But . . . but . . ." The picture was coming into focus, sharp, painful fragments of a truth she did not want to see. "But how?"

"Probably not that hard," Sam said. "Have to have somebody on the payroll at the docks where the ships come in, of course. Somebody else to look the other way at the rail yard when you load them up. A private train, most likely. But beyond that . . . it's pretty simple. And you've got all the cheap labor you need."

"Like *slaves?*"

"Yeah."

Sam's breathing grew labored, loud enough that it seemed palpable, taking up its own space in the small room. Anger, Laura thought, roiling up, blasting like a hurricane from within. Because she felt it, too, as powerful a thing as had ever gripped her.

She spurted for the door. Sam caught her arm, a quick strike of his own while he remained leaning against the wall. But despite the sudden reappearance of his mysterious illness his grip was strong, stopping just this side of painful. "Where are you going?"

"I'm going to go break Haw Crocker's miserable evil head, that's where I'm going."

"Yeah, that's a good plan."

"I thought so."

"Laura." He met her gaze. The strain of it showed on him. The sharp directness that usually marked his eyes was absent; instead they were glazed and unfocused.

His mouth was thin and tense, and a bead of sweat trickled down the side of his lean cheek. "You'll never get to him. And if you do, you'll never get *out* of here safely afterward."

Laura wasn't sure she cared, as long as she could make sure Crocker suffered along the way.

"It won't do them any good," he told her.

Darn it. "Do you always have to be restrained and reasonable and *right*?"

"I try."

"So what now?"

He sucked in a breath through his teeth, as though he had to struggle to bring in enough air, and pushed off the wall. "Jo Ling. There was a man who was here. Maybe six months ago. Griff Judah."

"I—" She hesitated. "Lot of men. Don't know many names." She frowned. "Why?"

"Please try to remember. He wasn't here long. He's tall, even taller than me, but thin. Brown hair."

She closed her eyes, as if mentally sifting through a pile of photographs. Faces, Laura thought. Faces of men. Faces she'd seen above her in the dark, men she'd . . . Laura forcibly shut down the images. If she dwelled on that she was going to be ill.

"Don't know," Jo Ling said. "Sorry."

Sam swayed. Laura stepped closer, afraid he might faint. And then he opened his eyes, looking directly into hers, and it seemed to steady him.

"That's it, then. We'd better be getting back."

"Yes, I—" She stopped as an idea bloomed. It was a long shot. A *very* long shot. But maybe . . . She dashed back to the table and flipped over the scrap of paper.

"Can you describe him to me? In detail?"

"I don't know," Sam said.

"It's worth a try."

Laura's hand hovered over the page as she waited expectantly for him to begin. And Sam just wanted to dash out of that cube of a room and keep going, out into the open range, where a man could breathe, where he could run a day, two, and never run into something that would cage him.

He closed his eyes, trying to conjure Griff. His image sprang up immediately, the details piercingly clear: a narrow, hollow-cheeked face, dull eyes sunken deep and encircled by purple, more dead than alive.

Griff, in Andersonville. But that wouldn't do any good; he didn't look like that anymore, thank God.

Nobody should *ever* look like that.

He struggled to recall the last time he'd seen Griff. It bothered him that he didn't know. Why hadn't he noted it at the time, just in case? How could he have forgotten that tomorrow was never promised?

He had vivid memories of the last time he'd seen his family. Of his brother, serious and determined, heading off to war as Sam and his parents waved from their doorstep, his mother gulping back tears, his father with his arm around her shoulders. And his parents, not long after, in almost the same position as he himself trod down that path.

But Griff . . .

Ah yes. Virginia City, the Red Garter saloon. Griff, laughing at him over a table as he laid down a full straight and hauled in a hefty pot.

"He looked—*looks*—younger than me. Though he's not. Got that kind of face, like a kid who grew too fast and never filled out all the way." He waggled his chin. "A lot of chin. His nose is sharp at the end. Deep-set eyes."

"Wait. Just a minute. I can't keep up."

He heard the furious scratch of lead on paper. In the small, steamy room, Laura's fragrance bloomed. Exotic flowers, kinds he'd never smelled before, no doubt gathered in faraway places that he didn't even know the name of, distilled to elemental sweetness just for her.

His breath came just a bit easier. It helped, to concentrate on her instead. She was so far away from prison, untouched by brutality and darkness.

"Hair?" she murmured.

"Brown."

"What kind of brown?"

Her voice reached him through the night, a soft and gentle tendril like a spring breeze.

"Dark. Ah . . . like turkey feathers? I'm not used to thinking about things like this. Do you study everything in such detail?"

"Mmm-hmm. Hush now. You're distracting me."

He could almost forget where he was when he concentrated on her, the sound of her voice and the scent drifting from her skin and the fact that she was mere feet away.

"Texture?"

"What?" If she'd studied him as carefully . . . what had she seen? He couldn't hold up to such scrutiny.

"Of his hair. Straight, curly, frizzy?"

"Oh. Peg straight. Clipped above his ears last time I saw him."

"Good."

He was not an artist, and yet he was certain he could describe her face down to the last freckle.

The scrape of lead slowed. One more quick stroke, then all was quiet.

"Might as well look," she said. "See if I'm anywhere close. It's an odd way to draw, and I'm not used to it. It might be very far off."

She held the paper tilted to capture the flare of the sputtering candle. And he had to stare at her for a moment first, her face a study in fierce concentration, her skin glowing in the soft, fluttery light.

"It's . . ." He squinted, trying to figure it out. "It's not that far off." But it wasn't that close, either, though it was very difficult for him to pick out exactly what was wrong. "His forehead . . . broader, maybe."

She'd no rubber, and so blurred the lines with her forefinger, drawing in sharper lines a fraction outside the originals.

"Better?"

"Yes." He could see Griff in the face now, a suggestion of his features in the pale gray lines. "Deeper hollows beneath the cheeks."

A shadowing with the side of the lead solved that.

"Hmm. Almost there. I —"

He'd almost forgotten Jo Ling's presence, hovering over Laura's other shoulder, until she interrupted him. "Ah. That one. I remember."

Dread and hope rose together, churning painfully in his belly. "You do?"

"Think so. Skinny man, yes?"

"Yes."

She turned toward him, her dark eyes grave. "Came to see me once. He did not want to . . . the other men send him. Welcome present. He said he only want women who *want* to. Told him Jo Ling did want to, but he say I lie. Ask me not to tell anyone we did not."

"That sounds like him." After months of having his

will beaten and stripped from him, Griff could never stand to think of someone else being forced into anything against their will. It literally made him sick; once, Sam had seen him vomit when they'd stumbled across a blacksmith beating his apprentice into submission. The blacksmith couldn't have beaten *anyone* for at least a month after they finished with him. "Where is he, do you know?"

"I . . . sorry, sir."

"Sorry because you don't know?" He had to force the words out, a staccato burst of one syllable at a time, all he could gather with each labored breath. "Or sorry because you do?"

And then he felt Laura's hand slip into his, a lifeline tethering him to the world, keeping him from slipping back into the void.

"Don't know why happened," Jo Ling said quietly. "Shouting. Lots of shouting. Dragging him off." Too much knowledge lurked in her eyes, the same knowledge, he knew, that others sometimes saw in his, and Sam went cold.

"Think they took him to the mines."

Chapter 18

Sam plunged out of the door seconds later. Because whatever sickness had gotten hold of him had finally got the better of him? Laura wondered. Or because he was headed directly for the mines?

She took a hurried leave of Jo Ling—a quick press of her hands, a rushed thank-you, a promise that they would find her a way to escape the Silver Spur. And then she dashed after Sam, her heart pounding, because if he were rushing rashly into danger, she did not know how she would stop him.

Any way you can, she told herself. She was resourceful. And she knew his soft spots.

But he merely stood in the yard, in a shaft of pale moonlight, his face uplifted, gulping air like he'd just surfaced from the depths of the sea.

"Good. You're here. I was afraid you'd . . ." She trailed off.

She watched him struggle visibly for control. And then he found it—of course he did; the only surprise was that he'd ever lost it, even for a second—and looked down at her, his feet planted wide, his hands clasped behind his back.

"Afraid I'd run off into trouble?" he asked. "Or afraid I'd gone off to have all the fun without you?"

So he'd recovered enough to twit her. Good. "The latter, of course."

"I want to. Dear God, I want to." His shoulders were rigid, and Laura thought perhaps he held his fists behind him because, if he did not, he would wrap his arms around her. "I want to go out there and rip the earth apart with my hands until I find him." And then he did grab her, his hands on her upper arms. Pulling her close, pushing her away—he seemed caught between the two, his fingers digging in, holding her with a foot of space between them. "And I want to leave right this second to take you back to Hoxie and Peel and beg them to keep you safe."

"I am safe, Sam," she said. "I'm with you."

He shook his head. "This is deeper than I thought. Illegal immigrants, forced labor for a mine that produces millions of dollars. People'll do a lot for that kind of money, Laura. Haw Crocker's got a lot to protect."

"I know that," she said quietly.

"Then let me take you back," he said, his voice ragged.

"Only if you come with me," she said.

"I can't do that, Laura. You know that."

He appeared a ghost in the moonlight. A black ghost, cloaked in regrets and remembered loss. But his hands on her arms were warm and strong, vibrantly alive.

"Let's go then. Right now." Fueled by injustice, fury pumping its energy through her veins, she tried to whirl for the corral.

"No." He held her in place. Stopped her, when she was so darn tired of people stopping her. "It's late, and we don't know for certain how long it'll take to get there and back. Better we have a whole night. Tomorrow."

"Silver Creek," she suggested. "We could go right now, tell everyone. When they find out what's happening out here—"

The shake of his head cut her off. "Do you think any of them give a good goddamn what happens to a bunch of Chinamen? All they care about is if that money keeps flowing into their town, building all those pretty gardens, that fancy school."

"You don't know that."

"Yes, I do."

"Were you always so cynical? So ready to believe the worst of everyone?"

"No," he said hoarsely. "I learned fast, though."

No one should have it all stripped from them, every illusion, every shred of faith in other humans. How did you go on every day, when you had no hope that something good might come of it?

"Then we'll leave right now," she told him. "We'll cable my father. He'll take care of everything. He'll contact . . . I don't know. The police, the army, the president. Whoever's the right person to contact. They'll come in and arrest that bastard."

It was a word she'd never said aloud. The bite of it pleased her, her anger surging in her veins until she shook with it.

Sam just stared at her, concern on his face and regret in his eyes.

"What is it?" she said. "It probably wouldn't even take that long. My father can work very quickly. I know your friend might have to . . . stay there a few days longer than if we could get him out tonight or tomorrow. I'd rather get him out right *now*, but you're right. We must be sensible about this, make sure we can do right by everybody. After all this time, a few more days—I won't say they don't matter, but they won't make a difference, and we can end it all in one swoop."

"They could make all the difference in the world," he whispered. "A minute could make all the difference."

All the difference when one is balanced on the edge between life and death, Laura thought.

"In case something . . ." She didn't want to suggest it; acid bit at the back of her throat. "If something goes wrong, though, it would be good to know we had someone coming behind us."

"Laura." He gave her a small shake, as if to ensure she listened. "You must promise me. *Promise me*. That you will not attempt to reach your father."

"But . . ." She jerked back, away from him. He hadn't expected it, hadn't released her, and her arms burned where she pulled free. "You think he already knows," she said flatly.

"They do a lot of business together. You said yourself that your father was one of the original investors in the Silver Spur. He's earned thousands, maybe *millions*, from his partnership with Crocker."

"No," she said simply.

"I can't take that chance."

"You don't know him." Her anger at Crocker mutated, expanding to include Sam. "I do. And you're just going to have to trust my judgment on this one. You've asked me to do that for you often enough."

He didn't answer. Because if he did, it would be no.

"You must believe me," she insisted. "I know him.

He could not do that. He could not stand by and see humans so vilely exploited for his profit."

"He has factories, Laura. He has mines."

"And that means he must abuse his workers?" she asked in a flash of scalding heat.

"Hush. You lift your voice any more and it'll rouse the hands and this entire conversation will be moot."

She hated that he had a point. She continued in a fierce whisper that would only carry to his ears but had the force of a shout just the same.

"I *know* him. He could not do that."

"I can't take that chance."

Couldn't take a chance on her word, he meant.

She whirled and stalked toward the main house, her head down, leaning forward like a sprinter seeking the finish line, quick enough that Sam had to step lively to put himself in her way.

"Wait. Laura, you have to promise me you won't go running off and—"

She stopped in her tracks, spearing him with a contemptuous glare. "So now not only do I not know and understand my own father, I'm devoid of logic as well? What do you think I'm going to do? Go running off in the middle of the night and try and bumble my way back to the train myself?"

Well, yes, that was exactly what he'd thought, but was smart enough to keep his mouth shut.

"I'll see you tomorrow," she said. "I'd rather not, but I will. I said I'd do this and I'll finish it. *My* word can be trusted."

"I never said it couldn't."

"Just my father's, is that it?"

Because there was no answer he could give that would not make her even more incensed, he remained silent. She resumed her march, bloomers snapping like sails in the wind, her narrow shoulders determinedly set as that of a boxing champion.

The window gave her pause. He waited for her to head around to the door. He'd have to stop her, of course. If she were seen, it would raise too many suspicions about why she was wandering alone in that getup in the middle of the night. She could likely talk her way out of it—her talent in that regard had become quite obvious—but still, they'd wonder. Plus he was pretty sure if Haw Crocker presented himself in front of her right now, she'd make a fist and start swinging. Sam counted himself lucky she hadn't started pounding on *him* already.

Maybe she'd be smart, swallow her offense, and request his assistance. And so he waited while she glared at the window with her hands on her hips, as if her gaze alone could bore a doorway in the thick log walls.

Then she put her hands on the sill and jumped up, hanging herself over the ledge by her belly. Her legs wheeled in the air, flailing wildly.

A gentleman would have helped. Except he was damned sure his assistance would *not* be appreciated, and he'd probably get one of those feet in his gut, or worse, if he tried.

She must have gotten caught, hung up there on the wide sill, the window too narrow for her to swing a leg around, too high off the ground for her to get a push from it. She rocked back and forth like a child's balance toy, kicking as if to gain enough force to propel herself over.

Then she tipped, feet pointing briefly toward the narrow moon before she tumbled into the room.

"Fool woman." He started to run. She could have landed on her head, she could have—

There was just sufficient moonlight to see her pop to her feet. She shook herself, affronted as a hen who'd had her feathers ruffled, then faded into the darkness of the room.

It had not been a great night, Sam reflected. They'd discovered they were in much deeper trouble than he'd ever anticipated, facing the kind of crime that governments threw army companies at to solve. There was only the slimmest chance that Griff still lived, and Sam didn't know if he should hope that Griff had survived thus far. For if he had, he was surely enduring hell again, and once was more than enough for any one lifetime.

And Laura was furious at him. So angry that she might have left him once and for all right then if she hadn't already given him her word.

Yet, as he stood in that weak moonlight, staring at the deeply shadowed rectangle that marked Laura's window, he couldn't help but smile.

Laura had that effect on him.

Ben must have drawn short straw, because he was clearly assigned to shadow them the next day in the guise of being their "guide." Or maybe he was just the person on the ranch who was the least likely to tell them anything, for even Laura was unable to pry more than a rare, inaudible mumble from him.

Sam had half expected Laura to lose her control at breakfast and bring the huge, moldering moose head hung over the stone fireplace down on Crocker's head. Her eyes had shot daggers at him the instant he strolled in. But then she'd gotten control of herself, smiled, and greeted him with as much fluffy charm as she'd displayed the day before. Crocker politely bid her "Good morning" and clearly dismissed her from his thoughts, underestimating her as badly as Sam himself once had.

She was almost as angry at Sam as Haw. She'd kept Ben between them as they rode that afternoon, never glancing Sam's way except to spear him with a fuming glare.

They did, however, find the rail bed that led to the mine, two gleaming silver arrows buried in a raggedy carpet of scrub grass. And then their eyes did meet briefly. Those rails could lead them to an answer.

Could lead them to finish this once and for all.

Sam waited one tortuous hour past sunset. He would have liked to go out sooner, but there was too much activity in the compound, hands crossing to a poker game, a maid beating rugs behind the house far into the evening. He sat on the porch with a cigar as a prop, battling the urge to prowl restlessly.

He'd waited for this for months. He was renowned for his patience, his ability to know when to bide his time and when to rush in recklessly. He'd never found it so hard to wait. The answer he needed was close; he could feel it. And he could not ruin it by being spotted saddling a horse.

Finally, it was time. There was almost no moon. It would make finding his path more difficult, but it also made it doubtful anyone would spot him.

He crossed to the corral, glancing once, regretfully, at Laura's window. It was inevitable that her father would wedge between them sooner or later. He just hadn't expected it to be like this.

He should be relieved. She'd sleep peacefully in her bed while he did the risky and messy work ahead. She'd be safe enough there. Crocker thought her nothing more than Hamilton's empty-headed daughter, and obviously her nighttime intruder had gotten what he came for. They'd only wanted the sketchbook. Crocker had probably decided that, displayed with the rest of Laura's art or worked into a panorama, it might have made an official somewhere suspicious as to where Crocker was getting his labor.

But it was still hard to leave her. Especially when he didn't know if he'd ever see her again.

He'd hidden a saddle behind a woodpile earlier, so he didn't have to rummage around in the tack room in the dark. Harry came to him quickly, quietly. "Good boy," he murmured. The other horses barely flicked an ear at his presence.

He was pulling Harry's cinch when he realized he wasn't alone. Whoever hovered in the darkness was impressively silent. Sam hadn't heard a single footstep, and Harry hadn't flinched.

But something alerted him. A whisper of sound his brain registered without conscious note? A shift in the electrical field that the scientists said surrounded all living things? All he knew is that, when the back of his neck tingled like that, somebody was near.

Slowly he ran his left hand around the horse's belly as if checking the snugness of the cinch, while his right crept toward the gun holstered at his hip.

"You're not really going to draw on me, are you?" Laura asked.

Harry nickered in welcome. Sam dropped his hand and straightened.

She was wearing her dark shirt again, her bloomers,

even a scrap of cloth tied over her hair so that she nearly blended into the shadowy bulk of the stables behind her. Only her face stood out, a pale oval that glowed brighter than the silvered remnant of moon overhead.

"I've been here almost an hour," she complained. "I thought it was the woman who traditionally kept the man waiting."

"I didn't—" He was rarely caught so unprepared. "You were angry at me."

"I *am* angry at you," she corrected. "Very." She moved forward to rest one foot on the bottom rail of the corral fence. "But this isn't really about you anymore, is it?"

How could the woman still surprise him? She shouldn't. And yet she did, with her strength and her honor and her quicksilver adaptability.

"Did you really think to leave me behind?" she said, a harsh edge to her voice that said she'd rather be shouting at him.

"It would simplify matters." He would not apologize for what he'd said. He was merely being cautious and logical.

Of course she trusted her father; she loved the man. But there were many men in the world who were loving fathers but bastards in all other ways. "You'll slow me down."

"I'll do a lot more than slow you down if you try and do this without me," Laura said through gritted teeth. She understood Sam's concerns, she truly did. But she also knew full well that the only person's word who could stand against Haw Crocker's was *hers*. She had to see for herself exactly what was going on at the mine before she did so.

For Jo Ling could have lied. She was an angry young woman. It was not, Laura had decided, an unlikely state of emotions for a woman in that profession. But for all Laura knew Haw might have thrown Jo Ling over for Lupe, and this was Jo Ling's revenge.

No, she must be certain. Then she would find her way to the authorities, Sam's objections be damned.

He said nothing, studying her with the unholy gleam of speculation in his eyes.

"Whatever you're plotting, just stop it," she said. "It's going to take chloroform this time, too, to keep me home, and I don't see any handy. And you'd better hope it knocks me out for the entire night, because the instant I wake up I'm coming after you. It's not like I don't know where you're going."

Finally, he nodded. Oh, how could she be so very outraged at him, justifiably so, and still be so drawn to him?

He did not trust her judgment. Did he really think that, if there was the slightest chance in the world that he was correct about her father, she would take the risk of contacting him? He should know her better than that.

And yet he was beautiful in the night, a dark prince, a dangerous predator preparing to go on the prowl. Her heart thrummed in her chest, that traitorous heart that betrayed her once, pumping strong and eager, the anticipation of what they were about to do threading with the excitement of *him*, the two emotions twined together so she could no longer separate them, and it tingled in her extremities, made her stomach flutter.

"We're going to have to move fast," he told her. "Can you ride something better than the nag?"

"Of course," she said bravely, and hoped fervently it

was the truth. Well, she'd had practice lately, hadn't she? She had to have improved.

"Astride?"

She hid her wince. "Why do you think I wore the bloomers?"

Chapter 19

⁓◦◦◦⁓

They led their horses out of the compound, lifting into the saddles only when there was a low hill and a hundred yards between them and stray eyes and ears. The wan moonlight barely penetrated the night; if Laura got more than twenty feet away from Sam and his horse, she couldn't see them, disorienting her completely, for she was a woman who depended upon her sight. She could hear them, though, the creak of saddle leather, the horse's snuffle, the soft metallic click that told her Sam had just checked the loading of his pistol, sending a shiver of apprehension down her spine.

She wondered—but didn't dare ask—how he planned to find the rails in the darkness. They could ride right by and never notice.

But she shouldn't have doubted. They'd been riding no more than ten minutes when he swung his horse to the left and picked up his speed slightly.

"How'd you find it so easily?" she couldn't help but ask, even though she'd promised herself she wouldn't talk to the man except when absolutely necessary.

"It's not the first time I've had to find something in the dark," he said before the silence, eerie and uneasy, descended again.

Riding astride was not as difficult as she expected. Her balance was better, once she found it, and Star, the neat little gelding they'd pressed into service as a pack-horse on the way to the Silver Spur, seemed perfectly content to follow Harry, as if he was already accustomed to it.

Starlight dazzled her. The moon, which appeared as if it might wink out at any moment, offered no competition, and so the stars burned bright and hot. The brisk, cool air kept her sharp, wide-awake, conscious of the fact that she had come very far, in many ways, in the last two months.

The boom startled her, a rumble in the distance that vibrated the ground beneath them and caused Star to shy until she soothed him with a soft word and a quiet hand. "What's that?" She squinted at the sky, clear and pure. "How can there be thunder? Behind the mountains?"

"They're blasting at the mines."

"Oh. Of course." Her stomach tightened. She thought, with Sam beside her, she wouldn't be worried. For all that she was furious at him otherwise, she trusted his judgment and his skills when it came to matters such as this.

Perhaps it was nothing, she consoled herself. They would get to the mines and find happy, well-paid workers and one crazy Chinaman compassionately locked away for his own good. Maybe they'd even find Sam's friend, so busy working and making money he hadn't had time to write.

That was the world she'd been born into, where people were kind, life was fair, and everyone got what they deserved. Her illness had stripped that comfortable illusion from her, and though her parents had tried valiantly to return it to her, she knew better now.

"How far away are we?" she asked.

"Not so close that we can't turn back if you want to change your mind."

"Oh, I'm so glad. Let's turn around right now."

He yanked his horse to a halt and swung around. "Are you serious?"

"No," she said. "Pretty surprised you bought it, though, even for a second."

"Yeah, well, even *I* am more ready to believe something when it's what I want." He nudged Harry back into a trot.

Is that what she'd done, she wondered? Believed that there was something there between them, something real and strong, because that's what she wanted to believe? She understood that she had a romantic nature, and that because he looked like a hero, acted like a hero, she might have placed him in that role because she so wanted him there, ignoring any evidence to the contrary.

It was something to ponder. She was certain she'd have plenty of lonely evenings to do so when this was all over.

"A half an hour?" she asked.

"Maybe," he said. "Maybe more. I can't judge from the sound. When we start seeing lights, though, it's time to slow down."

But a smell reached them next, drifting over a low ridge. Coal fires, wood fires, the rank odor of rotting refuse. And, oddly, a strong, stinging stench that reminded her of garlic.

And then the sound: a low rumble, too distant and

soft to pick out any individual sound, like muted heart-beats. But it grew stronger, the various lines untwining. Laura could detect a pounding, the groans of machin-ery and the steady chatter of loaded wagons rolling over rough ground.

Light rose above the ridge, a blare of low orange against the midnight blue sky, muting the stars' dazzle. They must have dozens of lanterns mounted around the mine camp to throw up that harsh glow.

Sam slowed his mount to a walk. The hoofbeats were certainly too soft to be heard above the clamor in camp—if this was what it sounded like in the dead of the night, imagine the din during the day—but Laura winced all the same. And so she was relieved when, at the base of the rise, he dismounted and motioned for her to do the same.

They let the reins trail on the ground; both of the horses were well enough trained to stay ground-tied. They crept up the long slope while Laura's heart thun-dered painfully in her chest, the rhythm echoed by the pounding she suspected came from the stamp mill.

"Get down," Sam said, as they approached the top. She did as he asked, crawling on her hands and knees, pebbles biting into her palms, until they lay flat on their bellies on top of the rise, peering through the screen of a dead bush.

The mining camp sprawled below them, a swarming infection of humans overwhelming the narrow valley.

It looked like another world from the ranch. The buildings were raw wood and unrelentingly ugly. Empty barrels and discarded machinery rusted in spare corners. Three railcars sat on the tracks, awaiting their load.

Lanterns on poles studded the camp, casting harsh

light on bare ground that was unsoftened by a single shred of living green. Tents spread out from the cluster of buildings, hundreds of them, dirty, sagging, no more substantial than if they'd been fashioned of old sheets.

"They can't live in those," Laura whispered, "all winter long. It must get cold up here."

"More than cold. And living's probably pushing it."

Maybe, when this was all over, the authorities would make Crocker live in one of those all winter long. It seemed an appropriate punishment. "Obviously they work shifts around the clock."

People swarmed below, waves of workers in loose dark clothes and long braids, streaming toward a large structure that clung to the side of the low mountain.

"Must be the entrance to the mine there," Sam said. "We're just in time for shift change."

"Sure have plenty of guards, don't they?" Laura was surprised that her voice was so even; her stomach shimmied like soft jelly. The guards were easy to pick out; they wore broad hats and strutted among the workers, showing off the rifles they carried. "It looks like a prison . . ." Her voice trailed off as she realized what she'd said. "Oh, Sam, I'm sorry."

"Didn't take your words to remind me," he told her. His were dark with devastation. "This place did. Even the posture of the workers . . . you can see the defeat from here."

"And were you defeated?" she whispered.

"Hell, yeah. They don't allow anything else," he said, his voice scoured clean of any emotion.

"How did you survive, then?"

The clamor from camp swelled into the night, filling the valley with harsh and painful sounds. Finally, he said, "Damned if I know."

"How can they need so many guards?"

"Lot of silver in there."

"And a lot of people who don't want to be working there," she said.

"Yeah," Sam agreed. "Even if a mine's losing half its ore to high-grading, they don't need that many guards."

"So you've no doubt that Jo Ling's telling the truth?"

"Enough of the truth to decide what to do from here based on what she told us," he said. He rolled to one hip. She'd seen him intent before, what she thought of as his hunting mode. It was nothing like this, though. Fury burned in his eyes, his mouth was hard and harsh, an avenging angel, as if he were restraining himself from running down that hill and taking out every single guard himself by only the thinnest thread. And anyone who saw him now would have believed him capable of doing so. She had no doubt that what Mr. Hoxie once claimed to be the truth was so: Men had only to see him coming to surrender.

"Come on," he said, gripping her upper arm to assist her. "Let's get you out of here."

"What? Now? We've barely—"

"Move it, Laura."

They were so close to the truth. His friend could be down there—working, voluntarily or forced. And he was planning to hustle her off to safety before he did anything about it.

"Sam, it's okay. I won't follow you, I promise. I won't try to talk you into taking me along. I'll stay right here, or by the horses. You can slip down there—look for Griff, hunt for records. Whatever you think best." If they missed their opportunity, and it was her fault because she'd insisted upon coming along, she would never forgive herself. "We're already here. I'll hide under that damn bush and not move a muscle if that's what's safest."

"You were right, Laura. There must be three dozen guards down there, maybe more. I'm good, but I'm not that good. There's nothing I can do right now. We need authorities, lots of them. The army, probably. We've seen enough to go to them. And if they won't believe me over Haw Crocker, they'll believe you."

His eyes, level, probing, met hers. "Can you do it, Laura? Even if you find out your father's known all along?"

"He didn't."

"I know you believe that, Laura, but I have to know that you can stand on this."

If she didn't say yes, God only knew what he might do in the name of finding evidence. "If he had anything to do with this, he's not the father I loved, anyway."

What did he see in her eyes? She met his gaze steadily, willing him to see the truth, to understand her determination to see it through and make it right. Apparently he found what he was looking for because he nodded.

"All right then. Let's go."

They crept down the side of the hill, as slowly as they'd made their way up, guilt dogging Laura every step of the way. If she hadn't insisted upon coming along . . .

She didn't see the hole, but her left foot found it. "Ouch!" she cried out, an automatic outburst.

"Gotcha." Sam's hand was there so quickly it was as if he'd anticipated her stumble, a firm support beneath her elbow. "You okay?"

"Let's find out." She put a smidgen of weight on her ankle, then a bit more. "I think it'll hold. I didn't mean to shout like that, though."

"It's okay. I'll gag you next time we go on a clandestine foray, so you won't have to worry about it."

"You keep threatening to tie me up. I'm going to start thinking you're all talk, no action."

He dropped her elbow, turning again toward the horses. "I—shit."

"What?" Her gaze followed his. "Shit."

"Well, what do we have here?" There was the cold, mean click of a hammer being cocked, the sound clear and chilling above the muted din from camp. Jonce stood no more than twenty feet to their left, just upslope. He had another man with him whom Laura couldn't recall ever seeing, a swarthy fellow with a nasty scowl. This one held a rifle like the rest of the guards down in the mining camp, hip high and angled their way. "Lookee here, Carver. All that yammerin' about how we're not supposed to be tipping one back on duty, forcing us to slip outta camp to ease the boredom, and here we find something so interestin'. They should be grateful that we was so thirsty, eh?"

She couldn't tear her gaze away from the guns, as deadly fascinated as a moth heading for the light. And then, blessedly, her stunned brain began to function again.

"Oh, thank *God* you found me," she said brightly, rushing toward them. "I had this absolute *need* to see the landscape at night, you see, to paint it properly, and then we were lost, and oh my goodness, we just followed the sound, thinking we'd find people, but then there were all those—" Her lips curled. "Those *men*, and—"

"For God's sake." Sam shoved her behind him, shielding her from the guns with his broad frame as if he were immune to the bullets. "Don't you ever run to-ward a gun again, or I'll shoot you myself."

"It could have worked."

"No, it couldn't have."

"You didn't give it a chance, and—"

"Shut up," Jonce snarled at them. "You think we're brainless saps like Collis? You're not going to distract us by bickering."

"You hear that, Laura?" Sam twisted around to look at her as he scolded. But his eyes flicked meaningfully toward the horses. She nodded in understanding. "No use in trying to distract them."

"That's too bad." She inched out from behind Sam, sliding downhill. But the men knew their business and kept the guns on Sam, for what threat could she be? They would not be duped into splitting their attention by a silly fribble of a girl. "I'm very good at distrac-tion," she purred.

"So," Sam said conversationally. "You gonna shoot us here, call for help, or haul us back to Crocker?"

"Oh, we'll take you back to Crocker," Jonce in-formed him. "You, you're no problem, we could pop you right now and save us the trouble. But I'm not makin' a decision on Miss Hamilton, there, myself."

"Well, we should get to the horses, then." Sam took a step toward them and Jonce jerked in reflex, the barrel of his pistol lifting an inch before he brought it back into line. "Easy, there, Jonce. Kinda jumpy, huh?"

"I'm thinking you two best be walkin'."

"Walking? It'll take us all night to get back, and Miss Hamilton's not likely to make it. You do know she has a fragile heart, right? If she drops over on the way there—well, can I be the one to tell Crocker you drove

Baron Hamilton's daughter to her death?"

Jonce and Carver exchanged quick, worried glances. "You're in charge, Jonce," Carver said.

"Oh, yeah, *I'm* in charge when it gets sticky, right?" He sighed. "Guess we'll have to go back into camp and snag a couple of horses before we head back to the ranch."

"We can grab a couple more guys to help us, too," Carver suggested.

"Good idea," Sam approved. "We'll stay right here with Carver, Jonce, while you scoot over that hill and fetch a couple of mounts. Get nice ones, now."

"When'd you turn into such a yappy sort? You were quiet enough on the way to the ranch." Jonce looked faintly puzzled. "You don't really think I'm dumb enough to leave you alone with Carver, do you?" He smiled, smugly pleased with his logic. "Naw, the both o' you are comin' with us. Since you seemed so interested in the camp and all."

"Okay," Sam said cheerfully, heading up hill. The guns swung around to cover his motion, leaving Laura momentarily exposed. *"Now!"* he shouted.

Laura didn't look. She just turned tail and ran for the horses, full pelt, her heart lodged in her throat and her stomach churning as hard as her feet.

She heard the *bang* of shots behind her but didn't dare look. The shots didn't bother Star, who lifted his head only when Laura snagged the reins and grabbed for the saddle horn. She jumped and pulled up, once, twice, before her foot found the stirrup and she dragged herself into the saddle.

Damn, she thought. She should have snatched Harry's reins before she mounted. She kneed Star closer, clutched the horn until her fingers hurt, and

leaned over . . . over . . . Harry's reins swung tantalizing out of reach.

"Got 'em," Sam said.

Sam. Thank God. Relief made her light-headed. He
grabbed the reins and leapt into the saddle in one smooth
motion, wheeling the horse around until they pointed due
south. "We're gonna have to ride. If you start falling behind, holler, and I'll slow down. Until then, we're going
as hard as we can until the horses start to labor."

He kicked the horse into a gallop, aiming him along
the base of the long, low ridge of the foothills. Laura
turned her own horse in that direction and prepared
herself to hang on for dear life. "Go," she said, thump-
ing Star's side.

As they rode away, Laura finally dared a peek over
her shoulder. She couldn't see Jonce and Carver.
Likely they were down, their forms lost in the dark
shadows on the ground.

"Did you kill them?" she called over the pounding
hoofbeats.

"No. Just knocked them out. They should be out for a
while, though," he shouted back to her. "If nobody
heard their shots, we might get three or four hours before anybody comes looking for us."

If they hadn't heard the shots. Big *if*. But there was
an awful lot of noise in camp.

"And what if they heard them?"

"Then we've got 'til they find our friends."

Five minutes? Ten? More? She hunched down, trying to relax, to fall into the rhythm of the horse. No
good.

But hang on   hang on she could do.

Chapter 20

The horses couldn't maintain the hectic pace for long. They were riding horses, town horses, meant for visiting and picnics, not for pounding over a rough landscape for hours on end. But those who chased them had horses bred for it, and Sam and Laura knew it.

Sam slowed his horse, waiting for Laura to pull up beside him.

"So what do we do now?" she asked.

"Head for Salt Lake City." He rode so easily, not the least bit winded, while she could already feel where aches were setting in, promising to protest harder if she kept up such foolishness. "It's a big enough town that there'll be people who aren't scared of Haw Crocker. Not to mention that most people there answer to a higher power than him."

"How long until we get there?"

He shrugged. "Depends how the horses hold up. Two days, maybe three. It's not that far, but we'll have to go through the mountains. That's better, anyway. We'll be

273

harder to track, the trees'll get in the way, and there'll be water."

Get in the way . . . of bullets? She gulped. "All right."

"We swung south at first to go around the mines, so now we'll turn southwest. It was out of the way to make a big loop around the camp, but obviously we couldn't gallop right through."

"All right," she repeated.

He studied her thoughtfully. "You can do better than that."

"Than what?" She couldn't seem to find her balance. Now that they'd slowed down, relieving her of the need to hang on for dear life, she found herself slipping and sliding in the saddle.

"Than that nice, meek 'all right.' Can't you yell at me? Rain fire and brimstone on my head for getting you involved in this? I know you're capable of it. You did just fine when we were discussing your father."

"Feeling guilty, are you?" This was the man she'd met on the train; unsmiling, intent, a man without softness or happiness or even hope. One who did what had to be done because there was no choice, not because he'd any hope of finding joy in it. "Perhaps this is my plan. I'd rather have you stew in it than relieve you a bit by a good verbal thrashing."

For an instant she thought he would smile at it. At *her*. But then she saw him swallow. "God, Laura, I'm so sorry."

"For what? For letting me make my own choices? For telling me the truth? For not locking me away to protect me?"

"Yes."

"You couldn't do that," she said.

"I should." No, he couldn't imprison someone, not even for their own safety. It was a weakness he should have overcome for her sake. "Ready for some water?"

She perked up immediately. "Water? Where?"

"Right here." He dug in the pack he'd strapped to the saddle before they'd left the main compound.

He handed her a skin of water and she gulped greedily. She wiped the back of her hand across her mouth, a wet gleam in the wan moonlight, and eyed his pack.

"Are you always prepared?"

"I try."

"What else is in there?"

"Ammunition, mostly," he said, sending ice down Laura's back, a chill she ignored.

"Tooth powder?" she asked him.

"That, too," he admitted.

"My hero."

For all that sharp moment of terror when Laura'd had a gun leveled at her, for the intellectual awareness of danger now, there was a certain pleasure in the moment. The air was cool and sweet, a breeze streaming off the mountains, carrying the scent of evergreens. The horse swayed beneath her, easing down from the sprint, the hoofbeats a soothing *clop*. They'd come far enough from the mines that the raucous din and harsh glow were fading.

"We could be the only two people in the world," she murmured.

"I—" He pulled his horse to a stop, waited until she noticed and halted her own mount. "I promised you I would keep you safe," he said.

"So far, so good," she said lightly, and nudged her horse on its way.

* * *

They alternated through the night, faster stretches once the horses caught their wind and the way in front of them was clear, then slowing to give them all a chance to recover and pick their way through rougher ground.

Not that Sam ever needed to recover, Laura noted. If he ever grew tired, it didn't show. She wondered where he'd learned that constant self-possession. Was that really how he felt in truth, in command of every situation, confident of his abilities and his choices, or had he merely learned that a good illusion of it was an effective weapon in itself?

They'd gained deeper trees, the ground rising in a steady slope. They had to choose their way carefully, and if they followed a trail, Laura certainly hadn't noticed it.

But Laura liked this landscape better than the open range. The trees rose on all sides, spearing toward the sky, a mix of evergreens she couldn't identify. They made her feel sheltered, safe; there were thousands of trees around her . . . how could anyone ever find them there?

She couldn't guess how long they rode. Long enough that the tentative pain in her legs and lower back gripped hard and stayed. The temperature plummeted as they rose and the night deepened but it kept her awake, the crisp air as heady as if they were breathing freedom.

The sky lightened above the pines when Sam looked back at her and swore. She tried to hide her grimace, but she'd been too late.

"You were supposed to tell me when you'd had enough."

"I'm fine," she insisted. "I can go a while longer."

"You're going to pitch right off that horse pretty damn soon, and you *would* have before you said anything, wouldn't you?"

He swung down from his horse. "Get off. Rest time."

"Heavens, but you're bossy."

"So?" Scowling, he lifted a brow. "You don't think I consider that an insult, do you?"

"I really can go a little longer," she said, "if you think it'd be safer. I'd as soon put as much space between us and the Silver Spur as possible."

"There's been no sign of anyone following us yet. They can't be too close. We can go faster tomorrow if we get some rest now."

Mute, Laura stared down at him.

"And the horses need a break if we don't want to injure them." Laura couldn't argue with that one, which meant she'd have to get off the horse.

She sighed. "All right." She leaned forward, attempting to use the momentum generated to swing her leg over.

"Need any help?"

"No." Pain speared through her hip. "I can do it."

He plucked her off the horse as if she were weightless. For that brief moment she thought of nothing but the feel of his arms around her. Then her feet met the ground.

"You can let go," she said.

"Umm." Now why had she said that? Pride? Independence? Who cared about such things compared to leaning against the solid bulk of his chest, his warmth chasing the chill, his arms holding her up so her legs didn't have to? "I don't think so. Not until the blood flows back into your limbs."

"I'm not sure I'm ever going to feel them again."

"Oh, you'll feel them. And probably wish you couldn't."

His hold loosened, and Laura stifled a regretful sigh.

"Are you hungry?" he asked. "We've more dried beef, some hardtack. Not exactly what you're used to, but it'll keep you going."

"No. I'm fine."

They'd eaten on the fly, washing down the dry food with swigs from the waterskin.

"There's no need to ration it, we've plenty to get us to Salt Lake City. You need to keep up your strength."

"No. I'm just tired."

He scanned the ground. "I don't have so much as a blanket." Why hadn't he thought to pack a bedroll? Sam thought. He always traveled as lightly as possible, finding speed and flexibility more crucial than comfort. But Laura Hamilton shouldn't have to sleep on the ground.

Laura Hamilton shouldn't have to do a lot of things she was doing that night, though, and he understood far too well where the blame for that lay.

"This looks like a good spot." She bent and brushed aside a clutter of twigs, needles, and stones. She sat down, glancing around as if she didn't quite know what to do next.

Hell. No pillow, no blanket, not even a cape to roll up in.

He knew what it was to sleep on the ground with no more than your clothes to shield you. The chill seeped through the fabric in no time, sank into your skin, your bones, until it took half the next day before you stopped creaking with every step.

"Wait."

He lay down next to her. Above him the stars were

fading, a listless twinkle against a charcoal gray sky. Clouds were blowing in from the west, tangling with the treetops. "Here." He thumped his shoulder. "Settle in. It'll keep us both warm."

She didn't hesitate. She hitched over until her hip bumped firmly against his. And then she lay down, snuggling up against his side as if it were the most natural thing in the world, her head pillowed against his shoulder.

His heart pumped, reminding him that he was alive. Not merely existing, *alive*. The softness of her breast pressed against the side of his chest, her belly cradled his hip as she lay on her side. He heard the catch in her breathing, the quick stuttering intake that told him she was not as blasé about their intimate position as she pretended.

"Comfortable?"

"Very." Her hand thumped his belly, and his muscles contracted at her touch. "Though you're not the *softest* mattress ever."

Oh, this was his punishment, wasn't it? To have her near, alone, *touching* him, her hand resting low on his stomach, and not being able to do anything more than keep her warm? The only question was whether she knew how much she tortured him.

"I thought you were angry at me," he said. "About not trusting your father."

"What would be the point now?"

Because she thought they might die? And Laura did not want to waste her last moment in anger? "I'm not going to let you—" He couldn't even say it. Refused to think it ever again.

"I've got other things to think about rather than be upset because we disagreed," she said. "Yes, I would have preferred that you trusted my judgment enough to believe that my father had nothing to do with this. But I don't imagine you survived what you did by trusting other people's judgments."

Try as she might, Laura could not fathom how she'd ended up here. Attempting to sleep in the open air, bad guys giving chase, curled up against the type of man she'd thought only existed in the books Mr. Hoxie was so fond of. And she *liked* it, every second of it. It was as if the world bloomed around her, expanding until there was nothing but space and freedom, giving her enough room to be . . . not a *different* person, but even more of herself.

"Yeah," he said, a catch in his voice that told her it had been a very long time since he'd trusted anyone, about anything. Griff, she supposed, which was why he was so driven to discover what had happened to him.

"I don't expect this to change your opinion," she told him. "And I know that my father has a . . . reputation. I realize he did not make all that money by allowing people to run over him, and that he can be ruthless. But he is also fair. He cannot take pleasure in winning if he does not believe he did so honestly. And what is happening to all those men is not fair."

His turn. The wind whispered through the trees, flowed over her face. She'd told him something of her family; now Laura waited for him to share something of his. She was wildly curious about what sort of family had formed him. Were they close? Did he grow so tough only in prison, or had his life been difficult even before then?

His breathing deepened; his chest lifted and fell lightly beneath her cheek.

"Are you asleep?"

"No," he said. "Though I'm leaning that way. Why aren't you?"

"I can't sleep." When she was quiet and still, she could detect the sturdy thump of his heartbeat. Did hers sound like that now, or was there still evidence of her weakness? "Oh, I'm tired. But I feel . . . jittery. Like everything that's happened is buzzing around inside my brain, and I can't get it to calm enough to let me sleep."

"It's like that after battle," he said. "At first you think that all you'll ever want to do is sleep. Every bit of energy has been drained from you, and all you want is oblivion. But then I would just lie there, staring at the sky, and no matter how much I begged for sleep, *prayed* for it, I could never force it to take me."

"So what do we do?"

It seemed a simple question on the surface. And yet the air hung heavy with portent, as if they faced a crossroads, where the path they chose could begin a different life for them, leading them to a future they could not forsee.

She held her breath, awaiting his answer. And yet she'd no idea what she wanted him to say, what fork she wished to take. That was the problem with freedom. Too many choices and too few answers. Confidently following a given path was much easier when it was completely laid out in front of you.

"You'll rest, if you can't sleep," he said quietly. His hand rubbed her arm—meant to be soothing, in truth anything but. "And you'll let me worry about everything else."

She closed her eyes, breathed in the scent and nearness and *existence* of him, and let the peace steal over her.

* * *

"Laura. *Laura.* You gotta get up, sweetheart."

She opened her eyes. "Why do I ever seem to be waking up with men looming over me these days?"

"Hey, you're the one who wanted an adventure."

She touched his cheek, her thumb scraping over the dense beard that seemed to have sprouted overnight. "Grows fast." His hair was mussed, his mouth sober, eyes too worried for her liking. Serious, dangerous, and so appealing she nearly lifted up and pressed her mouth to his, right then, without thought, without plan.

Above him the sky was charcoal and starless, disorienting her. "Did I sleep the day through? Or only for a few minutes?"

"Neither," he said. "It's midmorning. The weather's turning, and I don't like where it's headed."

A storm was coming. Now fully awake, she could recognize its approach, the air charged and heavy with warning, causing the hair on her arms, the back of her neck to stand up in anticipation.

"I'm going to have to leave you for a little while. It shouldn't take that long, I promise, but I heard shots—"

"Shots?" She snapped up. "How close?"

"Closer than I'd like." He sat back on his heels. He'd gotten ready to travel while she slept, she saw in a glance. The horses were bridled, his pack strapped to Harry. He'd swept the ground in the small clearing, erasing any trace of their presence. "God only knows what they're shooting at. Rabbits, ground squirrels, treetops. Each other, if we're lucky."

"Not us," she said flatly.

"Not, not us." *Yet.* He might as well have said, though she knew he never would. But it slammed her all at once, the danger she'd known existed but had never felt as an immediate and physical threat, chilling her down to her bones, lumping cold and hard in her stomach.

"It might not even be *them*," he said. "We're off Silver Spur land. But I need to find out."

Except it was them. Too much concern darkened his eyes for it to be random cowboys popping bottles off a fence. She could read his eyes now—dark, yes, but far from impenetrable. She couldn't believe she had ever thought them expressionless. It was all there to see, everything he thought and felt, if she only knew how to look for it.

"I know I told you I'd stay with you, but—"

"So why are you standing there chattering at me?" she said, adopting the imperious tone her mother used when someone got a bit above herself. "Hurry off and attend to the details so we can get back on our way and out of these mountains. There has to be a decent hotel in Salt Lake City, doesn't there?"

His faint smile told her he appreciated her attempt. He straightened, the creak of his knees surprisingly reassuring. He wasn't flawless. He was human, someone who'd survived long enough to have his body start to show the wear of the years, and she was the only one privileged enough to witness his imperfections.

He strode over to his horse, rummaged in the pack, and returned with his hands full. "Here." He handed her his waterskin, a small sack of dried beef. And then he hesitated. "This, too," he said at last, shoving one of his guns at her.

"Sam . . ." She eyed it with as much suspicion as if he'd tried to hand her a scorpion.

"It's not like you haven't held one of my guns before."

She lifted her eyes to his. "You might need it."

"I've got another."

"You might need them *both*," she said stubbornly. "And I don't know if I'd know what to do with it anyway."

"Not that hard. Point and shoot."

"All right, so I know *what* to do. I don't know if I *could*."

"You could," he said, his voice firm and sure. "If you had to, Laura, you could do anything."

Warmth bloomed over the chill. He believed in her; she could not doubt it. In her strength, her courage, her ability to perform in a crisis, all those things that everyone always thought she was too fragile for.

"Don't do anything stupid," she ordered him. "See who's there, delay them if you can, fine, then come back. Don't try taking out a half dozen of them by yourself." It was a hopeless bid that she couldn't help but make. If he thought he could stop them there, keeping them far away from her, he'd do it. "You were ugly the last time they got through with you. I prefer your face like this."

"Then I'll just have to stay pretty." His smile faded. "Laura, you're going to have to promise me. If you hear shots, you get on Harry and ride, as far and fast as you can. Don't worry about me, don't look back, just ride."

"Harry?"

"He's faster than Star, and he'll go longer."

"All the more reason you should have him," Laura said. "And besides—"

"I'm serious, Laura, you hear anything, and you get out. You'll only get in the way."

She recognized the ploy for what it was and refused to be wounded by it. "I don't even know where I'm going."

"Just ride west. You'll hit another ranch, a town,

sooner or later. All you have to do is tell them who you are, promise a reward, and they'll take good care of you."

He sounded certain. She didn't believe it for a minute. "You'll just have to hurry up and get back here, Sam, because I refuse to go on without at least one servant."

He studied her, regret and concern etched into his handsome face. She didn't want him to worry about her so much that it hampered his ability to protect himself. Because while he might have confidence in her abilities, she knew full well that, with Haw Crocker's men on her tail but without him, she'd never make it to Salt Lake City.

"Go!"

"In a minute."

He kissed her. No hands, no crushing passion, no impatience. Just a gentle meeting of their lips, soft, unbearably sweet. But it conveyed so much: *Keep safe, take care, I'll be back. And if I don't, this is what I want to remember.*

An ache hummed within her. It wasn't physical, the grinding drive that compelled bodies together, the simmering heat that had kept her awake so many nights. This settled in her heart, piercing deep, the tenderness more devastating than any passion.

She felt her throat clog, the burn in her eyes, the tears she didn't dare allow release. She battled them back, a sear of potential loss.

Finally, he pulled back—only an inch, so their mouths separated, but he was still so close she could see, even in the gloom, the flare of regret in his eyes.

"See you soon," he whispered.

"You'd better."

Chapter 21

Of all the things she'd left behind on the train, the one she'd never once considered she would miss was a clock.

Without the slide of the sun overhead she'd no way to judge the time. The clouds blotted the sky, robbing her of any hints.

She tried to be patient. Tried to conserve her strength, but she kept popping up and down like a jumping bean. Tried to fuel herself with food, but she couldn't choke down the beef through a throat that was still tight.

Every sound—the skitter of a rodent through the brush, the creak of a weakened branch—sent her dashing for her horse until her nerves felt as tangled and frayed as one of Mrs. Bossidy's knitting projects. The wind picked up, slapping at the trees, tossing the tops like whitecaps on the ocean.

And then he was back, coming through the trees like the sun breaking through clouds, leading her horse, the relief that flooded her piercing-sweet

"Let's go," he told her.

"Right now?" she asked him. "Because honest to heavens, Sam, I'm thinking I might want to throw myself in your arms and start popping off buttons."

He stared at her, open-mouthed, shocked to his toes.

"Hold that thought," he said when he'd recovered his voice. She hadn't meant it, not for a second, and he knew it, but it steadied them both.

"What happened?" she asked as he helped her mount Star.

"It was some of Crocker's men all right. Eight in this group, and they've got a good enough tracker that they had no trouble following us this far. But with so many men they got lazy, figuring at least one of 'em would notice if anyone was sneaking up while they were passing around a bottle and nobody was paying attention." He allowed a slight smile. "They'll be after us again, but they're going to have to catch their horses first. And those animals can *move* with the right incentive. They were too busy chasing them to notice me in the commotion."

He swung into his saddle. "Ready?"

"Ready," she said, though her legs ached, and her eyes were gritty.

Because Sam was by her side.

The weather had grander plans than cooperating with desperate travelers. Instead, two hours later, she decided to show off.

Sam and Laura picked their way up a mountain face, a zigzag path that hugged a slope far too steep to charge straight up. Gnarled evergreens clung to the rocky sides, their perch as precarious as Laura's felt.

The wind turned cold and mean. Thunder rumbled in

the distance, a deep, rolling boom that made the earth tremble beneath them and the horses skittish.

The rain began with a couple of warning spatters. Those were easy to ignore. But they didn't stay that way. Big, cold droplets, rescued from being hail by only a few crucial degrees, plunged down, heavier, and heavier still, until Laura and Sam were drenched. Sam offered Laura the only outergarment they had, a light coat he pulled from his pack, but she refused. She was already soaked; that would shield her for only a few moments, then it'd be so wet as to provide no protection, either. Better to save it for when it might make a difference.

The rain they could live with, though it made the trail slippery, the going slow. But it also washed out their trail behind them, the hoofprints disappearing into a swirl of muck. The best tracker in the world couldn't distinguish the few broken branches caused by their passage from all the damaged vegetation that the storm ripped free.

The lightning, however, was another matter, a bright, close flash that charged the air and bleached the world white, destroying their vision for a minute. It terrified the horses, unsettling them to the point that Laura and Sam had to dismount and lead them carefully along the narrow path.

It was safer that way in any case. They were lower, closer to the side of the mountain, its bulk providing some slight protection, muting the fierce battering of the rain. Sacrificed in the equation, however, were their shoes, quickly caked in a half inch of thick, coppery mud.

Tension coiled painfully in Laura. Bad enough to have armed, unscrupulous men on their tail; a danger-

ous storm on top of it seemed too much, as if the lack
of adventure and danger in the last dozen years of her
life had to be made up for in just a couple of short
days.

"We'll have to find some shelter," Sam shouted over
his shoulder at her, when another sharp crack of thunder faded. "But there could be a line shack twenty feet
off the trail, and I don't know as I'd see it."

A tree might offer some slight protection from the
rain. But Laura was far less worried about the rain than
a lightning strike shearing the trunk off right above her
so it crashed down on her head.

And then Sam paused on the trail, so abruptly she
nearly walked right into Harry's rump.

"What is it?" she said.

"I think there's—" He swiped at his eyes, squinted.
"There's something beside the trail just ahead. A hollow, maybe a ledge. Come on."

He hurried forward, leading Harry past the small
opening, leaving her space to come up behind them.

"Man-made," he said, his voice carrying over the
wind and the rain. But then, she could have picked his
voice out over a brass band, over the roar of the sea,
over the shouts of a thousand men. "There are hundreds of 'em, pocked all through the mountains. Somebody caught a glimmer and dug at it until they figured
out there wasn't a good vein there."

It was almost too small to call a cave. The opening
was barely four feet tall, considerably less wide, but it
spread into an arched area, perhaps three feet deep,
once Laura ducked inside. Then the space narrowed
abruptly, a hollow spike into the side of the mountain.
It was too dark for her to see how far it might continue,

but one would have to crawl to go any farther in any case.

"It's too small for the horses," she called back to Sam. Her voice sounded completely unfamiliar, hollow and harsh. "It'll even be a tight fit for the two of us."

No answer. The wind howled, the rain pounded; likely he couldn't hear her.

He stood just outside the entrance, staring into its depths, his eyes dark, unfocused. Water streamed over him, plastering his hair to his skull, his clothes to his body. Though she was right in front of him, he didn't appear to see her, his gaze aimed into the depths of the small cave.

"Come on," she said, voice raised over the clamor of the weather. "It's big enough, just barely."

He still didn't answer. It was as if she ceased to exist. Lines scored his face, drew harsh furrows between his brows.

Lightning flashed. Close to them this time; the sound exploded but a moment later, a charge of danger crackling in the air.

"Now, Sam!" Had something happened to him during that brief moment she'd ducked inside? He seemed stunned. Perhaps there'd been another strike, one she'd not noticed while she was sheltered by the stone, and it had frozen him somehow . . . memories of the thunder of guns in battle? She'd read of that once, that men who'd been in a war heard the cannons in other sounds for the rest of their lives, and it could throw them immediately back to the battlefield.

But either way she had to get him inside. She grabbed his arm and pulled. Her feet slid in the muck, and she couldn't gain good purchase.

"Sam." She put both hands on each side of his head, forcing him to look at her. "Sam. We have to get inside. It's not safe out here. You have to come with me. Please."

She wasn't even sure he knew her. There was no recognition in his eyes. They were empty, uncertain. *Afraid*. She would have sworn it was impossible for him, that nothing would ever put those anxious emotions there.

"Sam. *Please*."

He shook his head slowly. "I can't go in there."

Rain blurred her vision; his face wavered in front of her, unreal, indistinct. "You have to. *We* have to."

He stared at her like a drunken man, as if he knew he should recognize her but couldn't quite dredge up the memory. And then his expression cleared. "Come on."

Sam took Laura by the upper arms and steered her into the cave.

It closed around him immediately, driving the air from his lungs, the sanity from his brain, the last seventeen years from his life. It was as if he'd never left Andersonville, as if he'd been in that hole for months, he and Griff, the rain pouring down on them, collecting around their ankles, their shins, cold—so cold—wondering if the muck would just keep rising and drown them there, in that hole they'd dug themselves, their last hope corrupted into serving as their own grave.

"Sam?"

Her voice penetrated the past, like a needle prick of light after months of darkness, and he concentrated on it. On *her*.

"I can't stay in here. I *can't*, I'm sorry. It's not like that day on the train, I'm not going to argue with you about it. And I *will* tie you up to keep you safe if I have to." The words burst out of him, staccato-sharp. "But I can't stay."

"Sam, it's not safe out there."

"It'll just have to be. I'll stay close to the side. I'll keep the horses in front of me." It took all the air he had to speak; he felt himself gasping, still couldn't take in enough, his body becoming as starved for it as if he'd been underwater too long.

"Sam. What happened?"

"In Andersonville." The memories swept desperately over him, drowning him. He took a step to the side, to the border between in and out, between reality and memory, so that the rain washed over him, the cool sweet air filling his lungs. See? He'd had a choice. He could move. There was not a guard standing over him with a gun, demanding that he stay in his crypt.

"They kept us in a hole." The darkness in the tiny cave cloaked her, protected her. "Griff, me. We tried to dig our way out, and when they found us they made us stay there."

"Sam." He could see only the suggestion of her features; the cave was too dark, the rain washing through his eyes. It didn't matter. He knew her face, knew every expression that flickered through those eyes. There'd be sympathy there, and understanding, and the kind of rich compassion that made a man say all the things he hadn't intended to, believe in all the things he swore he never would. "You don't have to tell me."

"It's all right." He had never mouthed these words before. Even he and Griff, from the instant they walked out the gates of Andersonville, had never again mentioned those days. But wiping them away and trying to forget it had never worked, had it? Maybe, if he spilled it all, he could finally sluice it away, as the rain poured over him and rinsed him clean. "Six months. We could barely move. Couldn't lie down, couldn't even sit down at the same time. They threw us food. Sometimes poured hot soup right overhead and all we got to eat was what we could catch. Sometimes they threw in a shovel of dirt just to remind us how easily it could become our grave."

"Sam." She said his name again, as if she knew that her presence, her voice saying his name, were the only things keeping him in the here and now, the only things that prevented him from being sucked back into the brutal and tortuous past.

"We tried to crawl out at first. Scrabbled up the side—me on him, him on me. Sometimes they'd let us get almost all the way to the top before they'd kick us back in." He held up his hands; the little finger on his left hand was bent at the knuckle from when a guard had stomped on it. It ached in damp weather, and he'd wake up sobbing, sweating, until he saw the wide spaces around him and realized he wasn't back there.

She reached through the mouth of the cave, out into the rain, and took his hand. She brought it to her mouth, kissing the crippled finger, her breath soft and very hot, and the memories lost some of their power. Yes, there were terrible things in the world.

But there was also *Laura* in the world, and that made up for a lot.

She pulled his hand down, away from that wonderful mouth. But she still held it, her grip firm and sure.

"Ever since then, I can't . . . I can't be in small spaces. Dark, narrow—I'm going to suffocate if I go in there. I know I'm *not,* I know it's stupid, but if I go in there, I'm not going to be able to breathe."

There. He'd told her. He knew before now she had admired him, that part of her had built him up into a hero just as Erastus had. He'd spent years developing his reputation: the fastest gun, the fearless soldier-for-sale. He'd never allowed anyone to witness the thinnest crack in his armor, the slightest weakness in his facade.

And now she knew he was a fraud. He could ride after the most vicious criminal or walk into a strikers' camp with a dozen guns trained on him without the slightest twitch. But he could not enter a cave to get in out of the rain.

"In my room . . . you were in my room that night, after my sketchbook was stolen. How?" she asked, her voice conversational and curious, without a single hint of disappointment or reproof. She could have been asking him why he didn't like cream in his coffee for all it seemed to disturb her.

"It's a bigger space. Open windows, lights . . . sometimes I can handle it, for a little while."

"There were no lights that night."

"You want the truth?"

"Of course."

She still held his hand. He turned his wrist, curled his fingers so that he held hers instead. Her bones were long, narrow, and felt as fragile as a bird's. And yet they'd painted those landscapes, huge and magnificent, and gave him a lifeline through the darkness.

"You distracted me."

"Excuse me?"

He was about to shock her. She would know that, somewhere deep inside, no matter how many other things were going on around him, every second he spent in her company he was imagining her naked and beneath him.

"We were in your bedroom. You were in your nightgown. If I concentrated hard enough on what lay beneath that nightgown, what we could do in that bed, I could almost forget that there were walls around me."

Her hand went limp in his. Now she would surely pull away. He had to force himself not to tighten his grip, to hang on no matter how hard she tugged.

And then she stepped out of the shadows, joining him in the rain. It was marginally lighter outside the shelter of the stone. Her sopping clothes weighed down her slender frame. Her hair clung to her head. She was delicately formed, narrow shoulders, narrow face, her skin pale with cold. It made her eyes look huge and blue, so deep he could fall into them.

Maybe he would. It had to be a better place in there, with all that gentleness, all that warmth.

"You need to get back inside," he told her. "It can't be good for you to catch a chill."

"I'm fine," she told him. "Truly, I am. And I will. Get back inside, I mean." She stepped closer. Closer. "When you come with me."

"I *ca*—"

She stopped his denial with her mouth, full on, open, her tongue slipping in to blunt the formation of the word she didn't want to hear.

Her body fell tightly against his, the wet fabric no barrier between them. He felt the heat of her immediately, the swell of her breast and the dip of her waist, the press and retreat of her belly as she gasped into his mouth. The rain pelted his back, cold, persistent. But the fire she sparked was relentless, overpowering.

His free hand found her back. He swept it down the wet bumpy rope of her braid—she'd lost her kerchief hours earlier—and up again over the long, sleek track of her spine.

He tore his mouth away. Not to leave her—no, not that—but because there was so much more he wanted to taste. His lips roamed over her face, beneath her ear, along her neck, his mouth filled with the sweetness of the rain, her flesh, *life*.

She had started this for him. Laura truly believed she had begun it for his sake. But it couldn't be that simple, she realized dimly, not when the pleasure surged in her immediately, a tingling ripple of joy that followed the roaming of his hands and mouth.

She relaxed in his arms while his mouth fastened below her ear, his tongue swirling, hot wild circles against cold flesh, the contrast making the heat blaze all the brighter.

A sear of lightning, a bright bleach of the landscape, a dazzle flashing in her eyes. And then the crack of thunder, a whip strike through charged air, all her nerves spiking toward bliss.

Have to get inside. Have to get him safe.

She tried to cling to sanity. She had a purpose, beyond the drowning flood of pleasure, of the want that she'd never allowed more than the slightest purchase in her life until now. It swamped her, redoubled, a hundred times over, as if the pressure had only built while she'd held it in, tried to ignore it, and it exploded, a hurricane of need.

Walk. She inched forward, using her body to guide him back. But the motion brought her more firmly against him—her breasts hard against the unyielding slab of his chest, her hips against his pelvis, increasing and decreasing the pressure with each tiny step, a shifting, tantalizing rhythm that brought a moan to her throat, a sound the wind caught and carried into the storm.

Violence battered her. Not the storm—the fierce emotion, the brutal sweetness.

She retained enough sense to put her hand on the top of his head, the thick, soaked waves of his hair, and press it lower so he didn't bang it as they entered the cave. He took it as a sign to move lower; his mouth roamed down her neck to the hollow at the base of her throat, and she shivered—the cold? His touch? Impossible to tell.

She felt the difference as soon as they stepped inside. The only touch on her back was *his*, not the pelting of the rain. The sound muted, the temperature rose.

She kept nudging him forward. Deeper into the cave, deeper into the passion. Into safety? Into danger? She could no longer tell the difference.

Sam hit the wall. Cold, rough against his back. Distantly he recognized the texture of the wall, the shallow, scalloped indentations from some hopeful miner's chisel.

Laura was alive in his arms. Her mouth seared his cheek, the line of his jaw, darted over his skin, silver streaks of pleasure, never resting anywhere long enough for him to savor the feel of her there.

He captured her head in his hands, held her still for his mouth. His tongue plunged deeply. Sweet, so sweet . . . he could kiss her a thousand times and never get enough. Hell, he *had* kissed her a thousand times, in his dreams, awake and asleep, until he thought he might go mad with it, and he'd never come close to the reality of it.

She stole his breath. The wall was hard, unyielding behind him, the ceiling bare inches above his head.

And she pressed against him tightly, squirming close, the hard points of her nipples clearly detectable through the barely there barrier of their wet clothing. It pressed upon him from all sides, the brutal memories, the dream of her against him.

He tore his mouth from hers, let his head clunk back against the stone, hoping it would jolt the rising terror from him. Or blur his brain enough that he'd forget where he was and just enjoy her. Though he might have hoped for this, he'd never expected it, and oh, it was so much more than he'd imagined. *She* was so much more than he imagined.

He closed his eyes. It didn't help; dark was dark, and he needed the sunlight. His lungs burned, craving air.

Minutes ago Laura had been miserable. Cold, wet, and ruthless men with a penchant for guns on their trail.

Now she soared. His neck tasted of rain and salt and man. Her body arched against his, her hips circling without conscious thought, trying to get close enough, never quite managing, but gaining enough of a hint, a luscious taste, to drive her on.

But he wasn't responding. She felt it first as a faint frustration: Why didn't he kiss her back? Why weren't his hands on her? Why did he just *stand* there?

Soon she realized it was more. He held himself too rigidly, his breathing too labored.

She drew back. Hard to see him in the dark. But she could hear him, desperate gasps for air. She placed one hand on his chest—soaked cotton, no longer cold, the rock-hard plane of his chest beneath—as it bellowed in and out.

Distraction. She had to be his distraction, she thought, and went to work.

"I'm sorry," he rasped. "Laura, I'm sorry, I have to—"

Her hands tore at her blouse. When had the buttons gotten so damned small? They stuck stubbornly in their holes, and her trembling fingers didn't work nearly as well as they should.

Finally, she got enough open and yanked the front wide. She shoved her shift down, baring her torso to the chill of the air. She grabbed his wrists and placed his hands squarely on her breasts.

"Don't think about the cave. Don't think about the dark, don't think about the walls." She leaned into his hands, still and open against her. "Think about me."

"Laura." His hands rotated, the tough skin of his palms a luscious rasp against her tender flesh. And then he cupped her, lifting, testing their weight.

She should have been embarrassed. The thought winged in, far in the back of her mind, and tried to take hold.

But this was a different world than she'd ever inhabited. A different *skin*.

The darkness sealed them off from anything she'd ever known. The press of danger hard behind them encouraged her to forget about anything but this moment, this second, for it was all that the world promised them: *now. This*.

And so, shameless, aching, she leaned into his touch. Oh, if she'd have known, had even suspected what it could feel like, she'd have done this five hundred miles ago.

He bent his head and drew her nipple into his mouth. His hair, sleek and wet, brushed her skin, and she winnowed her hands through it, holding him in place, just in case he thought to pull away. He drew in strongly, causing a bright stab of pleasure that arrowed to her stomach . . . and lower still.

Sam tried to hold on to his talisman. *Laura. Just Laura.* Her nipple was hard against his tongue, the texture pebbled, the skin of her breast surrounding it velvety. He kept his eyes closed; it would be dark if they spent a night together, wouldn't it? He tried to tell himself that this was no different. But the press of the walls still threatened to crush him.

He straightened, feeling her fingers curl into his hair, hearing her disappointed moan as she arched into him. "I'll get back to that," he promised.

His hands strapped hard around her back, cupped the slight sweet curve of her rump through those ridiculous bloomers. He lifted, spun her so quickly she squealed, and pushed her against the wall so her feet dangled loose.

Better. No more wall against his back. There was air behind him now, a cool wash of wind coming in from the mouth of the cave mixed with a spray of rain. That helped, too, reminding him of the unguarded opening only a few feet away.

And *she* was in front of him. Laura, with her open heart and so many wondrous delights offered freely to him.

Her butt still rested in his hands. Her breasts were higher, more easily in reach of his mouth, and he bent to them again. They were lovely things, marble-pale and beautifully formed. Despite the strenuous day, that exotic floral scent still clung to her, and it was stronger there in the damp valley between her breasts. He nuzzled the curves, licked slowly over the nipple, then swirled his tongue until he heard her cry out.

This was supposed to be about Sam. The refrain pounded in the back of Laura's mind, a dim reminder, a fading lie. For this was for her, too, the sweet oblivion of a man's touch. She could no longer deny it, could no longer believe it was a rational decision that brought her here. How could anyone think when there was so much to *feel*? It overwhelmed her.

Desire. She'd heard the word. Knew people did crazy things in the grip of it, wild and stupid things, and had never understood why.

Now she did. This feeling had changed the world, had pulled kings and queens and generals helplessly in its wake, caused destruction and glory. She'd sometimes wondered if she'd had it in her, if somehow the capacity to feel this great passion had passed her by, if that was something else she'd surrendered with her youth before she'd ever had the chance to use it.

But oh, she hadn't. It had only required the right time, the right man. She reveled in it, gloried in it.

His hips moved against her, and she gasped. She pulsed back, tilting her hips, and found that spot, right *there*, where pleasure burst with each movement, intensified with each beat.

She wrapped her legs around his hips, opening herself to him.

"Laura." Oh, she would not survive this. How could she? Her nerves would shatter. She would fall into pleasure, and it would sweep her away. It was too strong, too overwhelming.

His hips went still, and she nearly sobbed. She tried to do it on her own, straining against him, the firm ridge of him hard against her, and oh *why* wasn't he cooperating?

"We can't do this."

"Of course we can." She rotated her hips. His hands were still clamped beneath her rear, holding her up, squeezed between the wall and him. She might never touch earth again. "We are."

"I'm going to put you down," he said. "And then I'm going to go outside—"

"No!"

"—and cool off."

Cool off. It was probably an excuse to get out of the cave, back into the storm.

Lightning flared, briefly flooding the space with painful brightness, throwing his face into stark relief. White, dark, shadows, pain.

Shocked at her own boldness, driven by fear and desire and concern, she reached between them and cupped him through his pants. And then was shocked again, for it wasn't at all what she expected—bigger, harder, hotter.

This was bold. Fascinating. So different from anything she expected that she had to explore further.

She dropped her legs to the floor to steady herself and scrabbled for his buttons.

Inside. She wanted inside.

There. God. Iron-hard, so hot it might have just been pulled from the forge, longer than her hand, thick enough that when she wrapped her fingers around it they barely met.

She drew the circle she'd formed of her thumb and forefinger down his length, and air hissed out him. But it was not fear that caused his reaction this time; she was certain of that. Surely the same feelings that gripped her held him, too; they *had* to. The feelings were too big to be contained in one human alone.

She leaned back against the wall, thinking it might steady her. But nothing would; her head spun, her stomach fluttered. And as lovely as this exploration was, her hands filled with him, it did nothing to assuage the ache that settled between her legs, and so she released him, sliding her hands around his hips to the hard curve of his rear, and pulled him close, back against her.

Each thrust of his hips made her gasp. Pleasure, pure and physical. Incredible.

Laura. All else had fled Sam's mind. She filled him, the sweet heady scent of her, the warm lithe curves of her against him. Her wet clothes chilled her skin, gooseflesh along her forearms; yet the warmth of her simmered through, her flesh, her heart.

Oh, she carried a faint scent of horse, her clothes were stained, her hair a wet snarl. But it only showed that she'd fought, first to do the right thing, then to survive. The fact that she'd battled by his side linked them together. And she bound him to her by this moment, a wild generosity that he could not refuse.

He balanced on the dangerous edge. Her hands upon him, and the way she'd spread her thighs and cradled his hips and ground against him . . . oh, God. Pleasure drove him hard. He was in danger of finding his peak right against her like the most inexperienced youth, propelled beyond his control by the first touch of a woman.

He shouldn't do this. Sanity called to him dimly from some whisper of conscience, immediately drowned out by the wonder of Laura against him, gasping in pleasure, urging him on. *Yes, yes, yes.*

He had to feel her. He sought the buttons at the sides of her bloomers, released them in an instant, and shoved his hands below her waistband.

There. Her bare bottom filled his palms, soft, skin

plush as velvet, and he squeezed once, quick and hard, before moving on.

He had to draw back a bit. She whimpered, tried to yank him back.

"*Not yet*," he whispered. "Only for a moment, I promise, but I have to—"

He slid his hands around. Probed gently, carefully, while he shook with the effort control demanded.

She was wet and hot and sleek, and she cried out when he touched her.

"Gently," he murmured against her ear. "Gently."

But there was nothing gentle about her. She pushed against his hand and grabbed his back, her nails digging in, her hips gyrating wildly. Her breath came quick, ragged and harsh.

And then she let go, struggling to push her bloomers and her drawers down, but they clung to her hips. "Help me," she panted.

He shouldn't. But what man could say "no" to a woman determined to strip? He told himself it didn't have to mean anything more than that. It was not an admission of what they would do next. Just a chance to glory in her bare and open for him.

The wet fabric was stubborn, and it took all four hands and a luscious wriggle to inch them past her thighs. But he didn't have the patience to work them over her boots and left them there, sagging around her ankles.

He wrapped his arms around her and lifted, leaning her back against the wall. "Come," she said. "Here."

"I—" She pulsed her hips against him, and he felt the glide of her against him, sleek and velvety, and he nearly blacked out with it, overexcited, overheated, overcome.

"*Inside me*," she demanded.

He tried to protest. But her mouth swallowed his words and her tongue swirled inside and she was right *there* and he slid inside her a fraction before he realized he'd moved. Maybe he hadn't moved. Maybe she'd done it, pushing herself forward, impaling herself on him.

Laura had forgotten her plan. Forgotten everything in the heated maelstrom of pleasure, in the feelings that swelled up inside and took her over and drove her closer, tighter, until she thought that, maybe, if she could be absorbed through his skin, that would get her close enough.

She would die if she did not have him inside her. Right now, deep and hot. It *hurt* to not have him there, and so she pressed herself on him, curving her hips until she couldn't go any farther without his help.

And then there was another kind of pain entirely. Stretching, burning, and she gasped.

"Laura?"

"Don't stop," she said. The storm roiled outside the tiny cavern, a violent burst of fury. She wanted him there, with her, in this shelter they'd made of pleasure.

He shook against her. Fear? Or need? Maybe both. She craved the need. He would want her more than he would fear the dark, more than he would hate the memories. She would make sure of it.

"*Now.*" The uneven rock behind her bit into her back. She tightened her legs around his hips, pulled at him with her hands. "Inside me. Now."

He hovered there, an inch inside her body, and she could feel each point of contact, thick and urgent, pain and pleasure a violent twin.

And then he gave in. He surged inside her, one quick, burning plunge. She bit his shoulder to hide her hurt, wrapping her arms around his back to hold him there.

"Laura, I can't . . ." he gasped.

"Then don't," she said. "I'm here."

He pulled back, thrust forward again. And shouted, his cry of release overtaken by a throb of thunder, a rumble that she felt in her belly.

He shuddered against her. His hips moved, slowed, a burst of pleasure. And each spasm twinged pleasure and pain where they joined. She couldn't sort them out, couldn't know what she felt except that she wanted him there, with her.

And maybe, she thought as she dropped her head to his sweaty shoulder, him still embedded within her, unmoving, not speaking—she was unsure if he was even awake or asleep, except that he didn't drop her—maybe next time in the dark, next time in the close spaces, when the hell of his memories tried to grab hold and suck him down, perhaps instead he would think of her.

Chapter 22

"Laura?" he whispered. "Laura, sweetheart, I'm sorry. It's time to wake up."

"Hmm?" She was curled up on his lap, just inside the entrance to the cave, as he leaned against the wall. She was comfortable. Warm. *Tired*. "Is it morning already?"

"No. But the storm's over. We have to go."

She tilted her head back. His face hovered over her, clear-eyed, alert, ready to move. She felt foggy and slow, wanting nothing more than to snuggle right up against that lovely chest and drift back into oblivion.

"Don't you ever sleep?" she asked, grumpy, the promise of a headache pushing at her temples.

He chuckled. "I do seem to be waking you up a lot, don't I?" Then he sobered. "I'm free, alive, and I've got you in my arms. Sleeping wasn't really high on my list."

Everything inside her went soft. *Uh, no, don't do that*, she thought. It was all right to admire him. To enjoy the way she felt when he touched her, to revel in the adventure of her time with him. To form memories of the man she couldn't keep that she would recall fondly.

But don't make me love you.

He gently brushed her hair back from her face, the stroke of his fingers soft and sweet. She must look a terrible fright. But his eyes were admiring, his smile appreciative, as if he gazed at the most beautiful woman in the world instead of a bedraggled and grubby version of a woman who was very ordinary to begin with.

And suddenly she didn't feel the least bit ordinary. Maybe she never would again. From now on she'd enter a room with that air of confidence that her mother wore with such glowing ease.

"I'm so—" he began.

"Oh, no, don't do this!"

His fingers rested at the side of her neck, a light touch that was enough to make her tremble.

"Don't do what?"

"Say you're sorry."

"But I—"

"No!" She cut him off. She couldn't hear those words from him. "It happened. It's over. I'm not sorry. I don't want to talk it to death. I don't want to muck it up with recriminations and regrets. I just want to let it be."

"But—"

She shut him up with a kiss. Closed mouth, hard, commanding. *Don't say a word.*

She drew back.

"If I keep talking, will you keep kissing me to keep me quiet?"

"Next time," she promised darkly, "I'll do something else to keep you quiet."

"We have to go." His hand slid around, encircling her throat, his thumb resting in the hollow. "Darn."

"Yeah," she said, her throat closing. The world, a particularly brutal and nasty part of it, was hard on their heels, and it was time to run again. "I know."

The train was late again. Lucy, buttoned to her chin in what Hiram thought of as her nun's dress, a great wheel of black straw covering every strand of her glorious hair, paced alongside the car, her quick steps jerky with impatience.

Hiram leaned against the side of the car and knew he was going to burn in hell. Because he'd never again be able to look at a black cloak of a dress without wanting to rip it off, and, if he didn't manage to avoid church for the rest of his life, he was going to commit a sin that even a kind and forgiving God wouldn't be able to excuse.

"Maybe they're not coming," she said.

"Oh, yeah, they've shut down passenger service between Omaha and Sacramento. We're going to be stuck out here forever."

She stopped pacing long enough to glare at him. A week ago that expression would have sent him running for cover. Now it made him horny. But then, for the last two days, pretty much everything was having that effect on him.

Her face crumpled. *Shit.*

"If we hurry, I bet we can bop off a quick one before the train gets here." He tugged at his belt. "What's taking you so long? Start stripping."

She gaped at him.

"Don't worry. We'll hear it coming, and I'll have

time to hurry up. Nobody'll see anything. Probably." He waggled his brows at her. "Unless you want. Some people like it that way, I hear. It could be arranged."

Then she frowned. "It's not going to work, Hiram. Distracting me by spouting offensive crudities is a weak ploy even for you."

He sighed. "You sure?" he asked. "Even if I promise to keep it under five minutes? Come to think of it, you wouldn't even have to get undressed. Just flip that skirt up and—"

"Okay, it worked."

For about thirty seconds. And then she went back to pacing.

"What are we going to do?"

"We're gonna get off at the next town, go find Erastus, see if he's found out anything useful, and figure it out from there."

"But—"

"That's one of your problems," he said. "Always trying to plan everything out in ridiculous detail. Sometimes things work out better if you just wait and see what happens and react. I mean, I sure as hell wasn't planning *us*, and see how that turned out." He grinned.

"Yes. Well." Lucy swallowed. She'd put this off as long as she could, but the train would be here soon, and she could not ignore it any longer. "About *that*."

"That? You can't call it somethin' that sounds better than *that*? Makes it sound like I farted in front of the Queen."

She—finally—knew better than to play word games with him. "I want to thank you very much for your . . . comfort and . . ." Oh, why was this so very hard? She'd practiced it in her head, and it surely would come as no surprise to him. Would quite probably come as an immense *relief* to him. "Understanding. This time was difficult for me and you made it . . . bearable."

"Bearable," he said flatly.

"Yes." She linked her hands together to stop them from shaking. "But whatever there was between us . . . it must stay here. You should forget it. We should *both* forget it."

"Excuse me, Lucy, but I don't think that's possible for me. And forgive my pride, but I don't think it's possible for you, either."

Her stomach lurched as the last two days rushed back. They'd been insatiable, both of them, barely stopping to eat or sleep, scarcely pausing to breathe. She would never have guessed she had that inside her. Obviously she'd bottled up a decade and a half of unused passion, and it erupted all at once.

She'd know better in the future. When they returned to Newport she would search for a lover, someone appropriate, and appropriately restrained, which would allow her to release her tensions before they built up to such an ungovernable level.

"All right, perhaps not *forget*," she said. He still leaned up against the side of the train, one leg bent, arms crossed in front of that wide and lovely chest. She was very fond of that chest. "But surely you understand it would not be possible for us to continue."

He lifted one brow. "It's not, hmm?"

"Of course not. You are too young. We are employed in the same household, and our positions are not . . ."

"I'm not quite up to your standards, is that it?" He said it without sting, but guilt twisted in her stomach just the same.

"No, not that," she rushed to assure him. "But it would obviously be a poor example for Laura were we to carry on right beneath her nose."

"Wouldn't do to shock the innocent miss, would it?"

"Of course not." He hadn't moved. Looked perfectly comfortable there, unsurprised, not the least bit offended. She frowned. Why wasn't he protesting? Not that she would change her mind. But a bit of dispute was only courteous when your . . . lover . . . was terminating the relationship.

"And so, while I will always remember this brief and unusual time with fondness and appreciation, it would obviously be best for us to go on as if it never happened."

She couldn't read his expression. His mouth was relaxed, not smiling, not frowning, his eyes clear. He looked like Hiram always looked, uncomplicated and at ease with himself and his world.

But there was much more to him than that; if she took nothing from the last two days, it was that he concealed a great deal beneath his simple exterior.

And then he pushed off from the train, tucking his hands in his pockets. "Okay."

"'Okay'? Just 'okay'?"

"Yup." A distant whistle shattered the quiet air. "There she comes. Finally."

"I . . ." It was precisely what she wanted. She should be grateful he was making it so easy on her, on *them*. "I guess I'll go check in the car, make sure everything's stowed away before the train gets here."

"You do that. Gotta have everything neat and organized, hmm?"

Nodding, she turned for the train and walked slowly toward it, head down.

Hoxie waited until she disappeared into the train car before he frowned, pulling his hands from his pockets where he'd jammed them to keep him off her.

"Like it never happened, huh?" he said. "Well, Lucy my love, we'll just see about that, won't we?"

The horses were laboring. They were game, but they weren't bred and trained for such things, and so, late morning, Sam called a halt in a small glen where a stream burbled through.

"We're going to have to stop for a while."

Laura was too tired to nod. She slumped in the saddle until Sam came around, and she pitched off into his arms. He set her carefully down and stepped away when her legs could hold her up.

"When this is all over I'm never going to complain about the train again."

"You never complain," he said. He led the horses to the side of the clearing because they'd been pushed too hard to be allowed to drink their fill.

Laura hobbled over to stand beside the stream. It tumbled down a slight rise, swirling merrily in a wide, shallow pond before running away. Narrow bands of sunlight fell through the trees, sparkling on the surface.

"Why don't you go in?"

Laura stared longingly at the water. She was sticky and hot, hair clinging to her forehead, and it was the best suggestion she'd ever heard.

Except for one minor thing.

"I don't relish the idea of being caught without my dress when the bad guys show up."

"*If* the bad guys show up, you mean."

Whoops. "Didn't I say 'if'? I meant to say 'if.' And

it's highly unlikely they'll find us, of course. A mere slip of the tongue because it's as fatigued as the rest of me."

"It's all right, Laura. I'm not going to hold your lack of faith in my abilities against you."

She gaped at him, scrambling to come up with a better excuse. "I *swear* I didn't mean——"

He chuckled, nudging her beneath the chin with his knuckle. "It's not an omen, darlin'. And I'm not that easily offended. I was just twitting you a bit. But now I'll make a note: all I have to do is claim injured pride, and you'll rush to console me."

His finger trailed down her cheekbone, and she shivered. "I'm very fond of the way you console me, Laura."

She turned her attention to the rush of water, knowing the glowing color of her cheeks gave her discomfiture away.

"Go ahead and go in, Laura," he said, his voice rich with amusement. Oh, how she loved his voice. "I saw no signs of them the last time I doubled back. We've got a half hour at least. The horses need the rest."

She unlaced her boots and tugged off her stockings. She needn't have bothered; they were shredded beyond hope, and she tossed them away.

"*Tsk, tsk.* Wasteful." He scooped them up, the filmy material drifting incongruously from his big, rough fingers.

"They're not much good for anything now."

"Oh, I don't know about that." He threaded them slowly through his fingers before grinning and tucking them into his pocket, a bit of silk peeking out against the black.

She lifted her skirts and waded in. The water was

clear as glass, cold enough to bite. It felt wonderful, washing away grime, soothing away the burning ache.

"Is that as far as you're going in?" he chided.

She glanced over her shoulder at him. "Excuse me, but unless my eyes have failed me completely, you're still on the shore."

"I'll get there."

The oval where the stream widened was no more than five feet across and shallow, barely coming up to her shins at its deepest point.

"Oh, go all the way in," he told her. "You know you want to."

She spun to face him. He should have looked the worse for wear. His black shirt was dusty from the trail, his hair hopelessly messy, and his beard was long past the point where it could be called a shadow.

He stood with his feet spread, arms folded, making no pretense of doing anything but watching her.

She'd been trying—and mostly succeeding—to put what had happened in that cave behind her. It had been born of unusual circumstances and was best kept there. Someday, when this was all over, she'd take out the memory and enjoy it. It would be her precious secret. No one would ever suspect how wicked and wanton she could be.

But it all rushed back at her now, as if a dam had been released upstream, swamping her with such sudden desire she shook with it.

She bent down to splash her face, hoping the cold water against her cheeks would shock her back into sanity. It didn't help. The sting of it against overheated skin only spurred her already rioting senses.

"Maybe I will wash," she said, breathless. It was not

an invitation, she told herself. She had mud on her shins, dirt on her forearms. She did not know when she would have another chance to clean up, and it only made good sense to take advantage of it.

"Need any help?" he asked cheerfully.

"No!" But her hands stilled at her buttons. "I can't decide. If I rinse out my things, they'll still be damp when we're ready to go on. But I can't stand the idea of washing up, then having to put these grimy clothes back on."

He didn't answer. His gaze was riveted to her hands on the buttons at her throat, his mouth set and eyes hot.

What could it hurt to play a bit? Laura wondered. They'd both earned it. And it was not as if she'd ever have the opportunity again. At least not with him, she thought, a tint of sadness coloring her desire.

She slipped two buttons through their holes, drawing aside her collar so a wedge of skin was exposed to the air and sunlight. Sam's mouth fell open.

"So? You're the expert on trail life. Wash or not?"

"Huh?" Sam had a vague notion she was talking to him. He saw her mouth move, the buzz of her words humming past his ear. But all he could do was watch, and wait, for her to open another button, to slide the blouse off her shoulders and reveal lovely, pale skin above the lacy edge of a simple shift.

Her cheeks pinkened, the flush spreading down her neck to her upper chest. But she didn't stop, stripping off her bloomers, swishing both pieces through the water before wringing them out and laying them over a nearby rock.

Laura couldn't go further. She tried. She'd taken him inside her. Why would she balk at being naked in front of him? She suspected the two often went together after all.

But the sunlight was strong, Sam too silent and intent, and she all too aware that her curves were barely that. And so she simply found a clear space and lay down, letting the water eddy and flow around her.

Sam hadn't moved because he *couldn't*. His brain had ceased to function, his limbs no longer under his control.

She wasn't naked. She wasn't conventionally beautiful. He'd found release in her body less than twelve hours ago. Yet his knees wobbled and his heart pounded and his head spun with her.

He knew there'd been no pleasure for her yesterday. That it had been as much about fear as passion.

Her first time should not have been like that. It should have been in a big, comfortable bed with clean sheets spun of the finest thread, a room heaped with flowers and candles, heady with the smell. There should have been plenty of time, a whole long lovely night of it, and a man who came to her with clean hands and a whole heart and her joy upmost in his mind.

He could never give her back that first night. But the pleasure that she should have had . . . maybe he could do something about that.

Chapter 23

❦

Sam's hands shook like a hopeless drunk's as he stripped off every stitch of his clothes and piled them beside hers. The water swirled around his ankles, the stones on the bottom of the stream smoothed by its rush.

She had her eyes closed and didn't seem to know he was there. Her hair spilled about her shoulders, waving in the rushing of the water, brown strands undulating like reeds. The water made her shift transparent, a white film over pale skin. He could see the indentation of her navel, the dark triangle of the hair that shielded her sex. The fabric puckered around the tight bud of her nipples.

Pleasure. Laura. Laura's pleasure. He tried to hold on to it. He had a goal, recompense to be made. But if merely looking at her was driving him over the edge, what would happen when he touched her?

Her lids fluttered open. And then her eyes went wide, her gaze attaching to the hard jut of his cock.

Laura had thought he could no longer surprise her.

She had studied him thoroughly in his clothes. Her imagination was good, her knowledge of human anatomy extensive. And her hands had explored him in the dark, measured the size of him, tested the width of his chest and the hardness of his belly.

But nothing had prepared her for this. She doubted anything could have.

Muscle swelled across his arms, his chest, ribbed his abdomen. And his sex, long and thick, angled out from him, brash and bold, as fascinating as it was frightening.

She lifted her head, water streaming from her hair. "Sam?"

"You have one chance to stop this," he said, harsh and low. "And it's now."

"I—" Should she protest? Lift her arms and welcome him?

It might hurt again. How could it not? she thought, unable to look away. And yet the desire hummed within her, growing stronger with each passing second, until she thought that she would even welcome the pain, *anything*, rather than letting the aching want burn on, unassuaged, until it consumed her.

"Time's up," he said, and knelt between her knees.

"Sam—"

"You had your chance. Now hush." He placed his hand on her belly, the heat of him a marked contrast with the bright, tingling chill of the water, his hand dark and male against the fragile, webby fabric. "I won't hurt you this time. I promise."

The pressure throbbed at the base of his skull. *Hurry. Stay alert. Stay in control. Please her.* But first he had to drink in the sight of her, for he knew that few men were ever presented with such a gift, and it would be the worst kind of sin to ignore it.

Her skin blushed pink, a reaction to the temperature of the water, a flush that reminded him of the color of a woman's skin when she approached her peak, when the blood raced through her just beneath the surface. Her shift came to just above her knees, a wisp of floating white, exposing legs that were miles long and lovely, delicately formed.

He hadn't expected her to be so . . . pretty. The color of her skin, the line of her waist, the slight round knob of her knees . . . he could spend days, weeks, merely enjoying the sight of her.

Though he would surely go mad in the meantime. For as much as he liked looking at her, every second made the desire pulse more strongly within him, taking him over, driving him beyond reason.

He bent and rolled the hem of her shift higher, higher, revealing the firm length of her thighs. She gasped. "Easy," he murmured. "You can see all of me. It's only fair."

Higher, while his hands started to shake. Higher, while the blood pumped in his temples and made the world start to swim.

And then she was bare to him, the sweet hollow where her legs joined her torso and the springy hair that hid her intimate flesh from him.

He slipped his hands beneath her, her curves fitting easily into his palms. Then he lifted her hips from the shallow water, beads bejeweling the mink brown hair. Laura struggled to sit up, making an inarticulate sound that he chose to interpret as encouragement. The motion made her legs separate slightly, giving him glimpses of gleaming, pearly pink, and he nearly plunged into her right then, driving for oblivion.

Laura. Her pleasure.

"Lie back," he murmured. "Lie back and let it come to you."

He bent and placed his mouth on her, holding still at first, sipping the cold water from her heated flesh, letting the feel and taste of her flood him.

She jerked against him. Shock, pleasure . . . both. He dragged his tongue slowly against her, and her hips jerked.

Laura did not do as he'd asked. Not at first. For she couldn't look away, any more than she'd ever been able to look away from a great work of art, an extraordinary stretch of landscape.

He had his mouth on her. *There*. The vision of it staggered her to her core, excited her just as deeply. Her skin was so pale, his so dark, a line across his waist separating the parts of him that had not been exposed to the sun. His hair, too, dark, wet, and gleaming in the dappled sunlight, against the white of her thighs.

She shuddered with each stroke of his tongue. There'd been pleasure that first time, interspersed with the pain and her concern for him. Brief, small waves of it, there and gone before she could truly experience it, tempting flickers of bliss.

That had been nothing compared to this. It rolled over her, threatened to take her down, swamping her in ecstasy. Her head fell back, her eyes closing because she no longer had the will to keep them open. Water streamed around her, sluicing softly over preternaturally sensitive flesh.

Was this, Sam wondered, what she'd felt in that cave? An excitement of your own, yes, an almost blinding one. But an even greater one to be found in witnessing *hers*, in knowing that you gave comfort, pleasure, joy.

Her moans rose, accelerating with the pace of his tongue against her, her hips circling. And she cried out, a keen burst of sound in the clearing, and shattered in his arms.

He gently lowered her hips and lifted his head. Her mouth was lax, her eyes closed, so spent she might have been asleep. He'd give her a moment, he decided. And then he'd drive her up again and again, until he'd squeezed a lifetime's pleasure into one brief, perfect interlude.

And then she opened her eyes and smiled at him, replete and joyful. "Come inside, Sam."

"Let me—"

"Now, Sam."

He grinned, sliding up the slick surface of her body. "When did you get so demanding?"

"About three minutes ago."

He lay upon her full length, resting between her legs, but he hadn't entered her yet. He fit his forearms along hers, entwining their fingers together. Her breasts were crushed between them, his sex hard against her.

There was not a single part of her that was without stimulation, either the water that rushed over every exposed surface or the hot press of his skin against hers, the heavy, lovely weight of his body on her.

She shifted her legs, lifting herself against him to urge him on. She'd only come halfway down from her peak, floating restlessly between satisfaction and hunger.

"Sam!"

He circled his hips, stirring up a current of water that lapped against her swollen, heated flesh.

He was beautiful above her, the full daylight allowing her to see him in detail, showing off the faint dazzle of gold in the dark brown depths of his irises, the droplets of water that sparkled on his face, the paler color of his skin in the lines that fanned out from his eyes.

She squeezed his hips with her thighs, trying to hold him near, to urge him inside.

"Sam," she repeated, more a plea than a command.

Sam knew that this would be the last for them. It couldn't be anything else. They'd reach Salt Lake City the next day, back to a civilization she understood, and her family would surely swoop down soon and sweep her away from him, taking her back to her own world, one as far away from his as the moon.

And he would go back to his solitary life, one he'd chosen with full knowledge of what he'd be giving up. It was a coward's way to sacrifice having a family and friends in order that you would never lose them. He understood that but could not change it. He'd lost too much ever to consider losing any more.

But he hadn't bargained on her, and admitted to himself that he was past the point that losing her wouldn't hurt. All he could do was hope to stem the bleeding as quickly as possible. And if she held some fond memories of him, if sometimes in the middle of a luxurious ballroom or a famous museum she remembered him with some nostalgia, it would be enough.

It would have to be.

But knowing this would be the last time, he drew out the anticipation, hovering at that point where he was almost . . . nearly . . . inside Laura. For if they did not begin, they could not end.

But then she arched against him, the tight buds of her nipples scoring his chest, her motion forcing him inside her a bare inch.

It obliterated his control. He drove inside her, gasping, the world narrowing to this place, this time, this woman.

They were apart from the world, disconnected from their past, exempt from the future. Here, right now, for a single, brief instant, what they could give each other was the only thing that mattered.

"We have to go."

He'd collapsed upon Laura, his softening cock still embedded within her, the taste of her still on his tongue and the smell of her in his nose. Perhaps it would never go away, he thought. He would move through his life with her presence a living thing, palpable no matter if she were thousands of miles away. She'd imprinted herself on him, scarred him, and he doubted the marks would ever fade.

Her hands drifted up and down his back. "Must we?"

"Yes." He kissed her, one last time, lingering over the sweetness. Then he pushed up, pulling her up with him, the water pouring off them as the future arrived. "Hurry."

They dressed quickly. Sam grimaced over the condition of his clothes, spattered with mud and streaked with dirt. Laura had a harder time with hers, the cold, damp fabric refusing to slide over wet skin. Sam helped her, and the determination with which he tugged on her clothes, the way he didn't pause even once to stroke or kiss a bare spot, told her that he'd meant the "hurry."

"Mount up." His hands at her waist, he lifted her into the saddle and immediately turned for his own horse.

And then, "Shit!" He leapt into the saddle, pulling hard on the reins and wheeling Harry around to face the direction from which they'd come. And then he dropped the reins and reached for his guns.

"What is it?" she asked, while her stomach lurched into her throat.

"There's somebody there." He squinted into a thick copse of pines. "Start riding."

"I don't see anyth—"

"*Ride,*" he shouted, and sent Harry flying off toward the trees.

A clump of brush shuddered. She caught a glimpse of a man in dark clothing, bursting out of the copse and sprinting away.

He popped a couple of shots in Sam's direction. It shattered Laura's stunned daze. *Time to do as you're told*, she thought, and sent Star off into the trees.

Sam bent low over his horse's neck, trying to stay loose enough in the saddle to keep his guns level.

Damn. Damn. Damn.

He'd known it was wrong from the beginning, and he'd done it anyway. Dragged Laura into this mess and, worse, let her distract him. And now they were both in desperate danger because he'd failed to adhere to the rules he'd set out so many years ago.

The man could run. Young, certainly, fit and healthy. He ducked around the trees, racing away.

Only one of them. Strange. Should have been more. Crocker's men always traveled in packs, weak jackals who knew their greatest safety was in numbers.

Just a scout, then. Probably sent a half dozen of them out in every direction, hoping one of them would get lucky.

And one of them had. Except his luck was about to end.

No use shooting in here. He zigged around trees, ducked under branches. Bullets were more likely to end up in a trunk than in the scout, just like the ones he'd popped off so wildly.

But then Crocker's man broke into a small clearing where a compact, spotted horse waited on the far side.

Sam took aim. And then Laura bloomed in his mind. What would she think of him, shooting someone in the back?

The hesitation cost him.

The man reached his horse and vaulted into the saddle. He twisted, sent a couple more wild shots in Sam's direction, and took off.

Good rider. Bad shot.

But the shots goaded him to his senses. Sam fired.

He got him in the shoulder. The man jerked when the bullet hit, then fell forward over the horse's neck before he pushed himself back up, guiding the horse with one arm and gaining the trees.

Fresh, Harry might've been able to get close enough to stop him. But after a day and a half of hard travel, he just didn't have enough left to catch a horse who was well rested and well trained for the terrain.

Sam swore savagely. If there was only himself to worry about, it would be one thing. He'd gotten out of worse situations before. And if he didn't, well, that wasn't the end of the world either, was it? His, of course, but he'd had a good many more years than he'd once figured he would, and there wasn't anybody around to be pained by his passing.

But with Laura in the equation . . . this was the one time he had to get everything right. Make sure he got her out safe and whole.

Could he lead Crocker's men away from her? Would they be satisfied with his capture and let her go?

No, of course not. And, Lord love her, though Laura was game and brave and willing, she simply didn't have the experience to find her way to Salt Lake City by herself.

They'd begun this together. They were going to have to finish it together.

She stayed low, hung on so tightly she thought her fingers would be permanently frozen in that position, and let Star go wherever he wanted. She figured there was a better chance he knew where he was going than she did.

Branches slapped at her. Star wasn't galloping full out, as the forest was too dense for that, but trees flashed by in her peripheral vision. She was dizzy with it, almost sick from the motion, her heart thudding as hard as Star's hoofbeats.

Then the pounding came from behind her, a rhythm that clashed with Star's. Someone was after her.

Sam? She dared a glance behind her and nearly slipped off her horse in the process. After a frantic grab for the saddle horn—she'd lost the reins—she hunkered down.

Okay, no more of that. It could be Sam, but she didn't dare slow down to find out.

If it was Sam behind her, he'd find her. And if not . . .

The horse behind her pounded closer. And Star was slowing down, laboring beneath her, while she thought her own heart might burst with panic.

"Laura." He was safe. *Thank God.*

Sam pulled beside her when the trees thinned. They settled into an easy trot because the animals needed it. "I didn't dare shout—I didn't want them to hear me—"

"He was one of Crocker's men?"

"Yes."

"Are they coming?"

"Not yet." His brown skin gleamed. Sweat, water from the river? The image rose, crystal clear, of him, naked, arching over her in the water. "Soon."

"You didn't kill him?"

He frowned, deep lines bracketing the mouth that she now knew could give almost unbearable pleasure. "No."

"Oh." She didn't know whether to be relieved or sorry.

"I tried," he told her, an honesty he'd never before felt confined by now driving him to tell her the truth. "I missed. I seldom do, but . . ." The slide of his Adam's apple up and down his throat was painful. "They'll all be after us as soon as he makes his way back to them. Good horse. It won't be long."

Her eyes widened, fear springing deep into the innocent blue. And then her mouth firmed, and she nodded. "Thank you for not shielding me from the truth."

Maybe I should have, Sam thought. Would it have been kinder to let her believe they were well on their way to freedom until the last moment? But he'd lied to her for weeks. He couldn't do it anymore.

She straightened, lifting her chin, mutinous, resolute. "Go on without me."

"*What?*" he burst out. "Are you insane? I—"

"Hear me out." The words gushed from her, as if she were determined to get them all out before he refused to listen to such madness. "If you don't have to worry about me, you've got a much better chance to escape. You're faster, you can shoot without being concerned that I'll get in the way of return fire, which I know has held your hand more than once. And maybe I can draw their attention long enough to give you a chance. And they're probably not going to kill *me*, anyway."

Probably not going to kill me. Veins throbbed in his temple, threatened to burst. "You *are*—"

"Not finished yet," she said. "And if you're free, then you can come rescue me."

She sounded so certain, as if it had never occurred to her that he might fail. She'd never questioned that he would come back for her, had not the slightest doubt that he would manage to get her out.

"Pick it up, Laura. Star's gotten his wind back."

"But—" She scowled at him. "It was a good plan."

"It is a good plan."

"Then why—"

"Because you overlooked one minor detail." He leaned forward, near enough that for a moment Laura thought he might drag her off the back of her horse and on to his. "I'm not leaving you."

Any other time, in any other circumstance, those words from him would have made her heart soar. "Sam—"

"Hang on," he said, and gave Star a slap on his rump.

Star gave out first. They'd pushed the poor animal past the danger point as it was, and finally he simply refused to follow the commands, planting his feet, sides heaving, head hanging low.

"Get off," Sam said, bending down, holding out his arm. "You'll have to come up with me. It won't be comfortable, there's no time to take off the saddle, but—"

"Shut up." She grabbed on, and he pulled, gritting his teeth with the strain, until he hauled her in front of him. He pushed back in his saddle, squeezing her into the narrow space gained. "Go!" she said.

Sam knew they were close. Not close enough for him to hear them riding up, but they must have caught a glimpse of Laura and Sam now and then, for they popped off random, ill-advised shots that had no chance of reaching their target but made Laura jump every time and allowed Sam to make a guess as to their direction and distance.

And they were getting closer. Close enough that he heard the impact when the last bullet slammed into a nearby tree trunk.

Grit burned his eyes. An insistent ache knotted at the base of his spine.

Both of which were nothing compared to the pain that churned around his heart and throbbed in his brain.

He was going to fail. Fail Griff, fail himself, and, most of all, fail *her*.

If he'd known it would come to this place someday, he'd have rather died in Andersonville than to put her in this danger.

Harry stumbled beneath them, then found his footing again. But he was done.

"Off you go." He dismounted, stretching up and hauling Laura off immediately. "Run," he said, and reached for his guns.

Their eyes met. *Don't argue*, he thought, hoping she'd see. That she'd understand. *Just run.*

Live.

She nodded.

"I'll try and send a horse your way," he said. "If you see one without a rider, grab it. Grab it and ride."

Another nod, her face grave, eyes shimmering. He memorized each line, each curve, each shadow. Would this be the last time he ever saw her? And would it be because this was his last day? If it was, he would hold her face in his mind until the last second, taking her memory into eternity.

She turned and ran. Not looking back, weaving around the trees, her legs churning in those stupid bloomers.

He turned, squinting through the screening of the vegetation, and brought up his guns. There, a flash of red. He shot. Missed. *Damn.*

A scuffle of sound to his left. He spun, shot again. Didn't miss this time.

There—

"Sam!" Laura's shout cut through his concentration. "Sam?"

He fired off a quick series of shots, no time to wait for a good target, hoping only to get lucky, to give them something to think about before they came charging through the trees. And then he turned and ran.

She hadn't gone far. He found her standing, stock-still, staring out in the distance. For a moment all he saw was her, his Laura, the relief at finding her whole and unhurt flooding him so quickly his head went light.

And then he saw the cliff at her feet.

It sheered straight down. Way down, a hundred feet, maybe more, to the wide, sluggish green-gray swirl of the river that had carved its plunge.

She reached for his hand as he gained her side. His gaze scanned the land around him. There had to be a way out. Somewhere, anywhere. A ledge, a rock, anyplace to stash her that would give her a bit of shelter while he fought.

She grabbed his hand in both of hers and brought it up to her chest, facing him squarely. "Tell me about your family."

"What?" he asked, barely registering her question. He'd have to go back, straight at their pursuers. Head them off before they got to her. Give her one clear path—

"Sam."

A man. There. A thin, young one, huddling behind the trunk of a tree, eyes wide with fear. Maybe another scout, or maybe he just had a better horse. The rest of them couldn't be far behind. He and Laura had a minute before the rest arrived, maybe only seconds.

"*Sam.*"

Too late, and he knew it. Another came up from the left, blocking that route; all Sam could see was an elbow poking out from a trunk.

And so he gave in to temptation and looked at her instead. Clear skin, brave eyes, soft mouth. "Oh, Laura, I'm so—"

"Hush. Tell me about your family. Alive, dead? Did you have one?"

"What?"

"I've been waiting for you to volunteer the information." Her eyes were wide, her hands shaking. But her voice was steady. "I want to know. Tell me now."

Tell me now before it was too late? She'd been patient before, curbing her curiosity because there seemed plenty of time. But if this was the end, she wanted to know this about him before it was over. Wanted as much of him as she could have.

He wanted to assure her it wasn't necessary. They'd

find a way out. But he couldn't promise her that, and so he gave her the only thing he was certain he could. "I had a brother. My hero, my best friend. Died outside Atlanta a month before I was captured, trying to cut off a supply line." He swallowed hard. "My father owned a dry goods store. My mother . . . loved us all, more than anything. They died while I was in prison. Influenza epidemic." Comfortable name that the doc gave to broken hearts.

She nodded, accepting, and drew in a long, shuddery breath. "Okay, then. I'm ready." Still clutching his hand, she turned toward the canyon.

"Ready for what?"

She glanced at him in surprise. "To jump, of course. To escape."

"Are you out of your mind?" he shouted. "No way in hell are we jumping off that!"

Chapter 24

❧

Sam and Laura were captured only minutes later, of course, the ranch hands scuttling up once everyone had arrived, approaching reluctantly despite all the guns aimed at Sam. They threatened Laura in order to get Sam to toss his guns away, making anger churn so fiercely inside him he'd barely heard what they said next.

Jonce came up first, wary and scowling, his head low like a turtle on the verge of pulling back into his shell, a pistol in each hand. "Don't move."

"Do we look like we're moving?" Sam asked him.

Jonce frowned at him, faint puzzlement marking his expression. "I know you."

"'Course you do, chap," Sam said, his voice as light as he could manage. He ignored the pain in his chest, the heavy responsibility for Laura's life that weighed on his shoulders. He considered himself cool in battle, unshakable in desperate situations. But that was because, he realized at last, the only life that had ever been in danger was his own. Hers, he discovered, was incredibly harder to wager.

But her hand still held his. How could she bear to touch him, knowing he'd brought her to this point? But there was no hint of recrimination. She squeezed, supportive, still convinced he'd find a way out.

She'd been ready to jump off a cliff with him, he marveled.

"I know!" Jonce said as the light dawned. "You're that fellow that was here looking for Judah." He sneered. "Thought we'd beat that outta you."

"No."

"Too bad for you."

"Where is he?"

The other hands, seeing that it was safe, were gathering, creeping out into the open, their caution easing as the number of guns pointed at Sam increased.

"Let's get movin'," Jonce said, gesturing with his gun.

"What happened to Griff?" Sam asked again. "Come on, Jonce. What difference could it possibly make to tell me now?"

"A dyin' man's request, hmm?" He bared his teeth. "Why not? But I'll do better'n tell you what happened to him.

"We'll give you the same choice we gave him."

So they weren't going to kill them yet. Jonce had made it clear, as he and his hands had surrounded Laura and Sam, the canyon's lip at their back and guns at their front, that Haw Crocker preferred to see to their disposition himself. But if they tried to run, they'd be shot then and there. Laura wasn't sure she believed Jonce. Haw didn't seem the type to give his minions a whole lot of autonomy.

It took them nearly twice as long to return to the Silver Spur than it had to flee. The horses were tired. They were two animals short, because no one had been able to chase down Star and Harry. The urgency was gone; the captives weren't going anywhere, and neither was the Silver Spur.

Laura found herself suspended in a strange, emotionless place between exhaustion and fear. She was in no immediate danger. After a day and a half of constant panic, pushing harder, faster, the constant press of knowing what followed them, aware they weren't going quick enough, she was drained, wrung of all emotion.

Now they moved at another person's pace, another's direction. Once or twice one of the hands looked at her with speculation and something that might have been lust, but it was clear they were far more afraid of Haw than they were interested in her.

She understood that danger awaited them but couldn't quite bring herself to *feel* it. She couldn't believe that it was over. That her life might be over. The fever couldn't kill her. The nightmare of Andersonville and years as a hired gun hadn't managed to kill Sam. How could someone like Haw Crocker do it?

And, in any case, they weren't there yet. So they plodded along on the back of the horses that the two youngest hands had been forced into giving up to them, separated by the entire group because Jonce didn't trust them anywhere near each other.

The world had been washed clean by the storm. They passed damage—broken branches, a stretch of meadow beaten flat, parts of the mountain that had been washed into a slough of muck. But the air was crisp, fresh, the sky scoured into a bright, clean blue.

She slept hard when they stopped, both nights,

longer uninterrupted stretches of rest than she'd had in days. The last thing she saw when she dropped off was Sam's eyes through the smoky little fire the hands had built to roast a partridge one of them had shot. He was the first thing she saw each morning as well, across a dead pile of coals, staring, brooding, worried.

She wanted to tell him it was all right. He couldn't have known. He'd given her every opportunity to back out. The world was full of dangers, and the most careful protection did not ensure one would avoid them. She could have died if her train jumped the track going around the curve as easily as she could have during their attempt to escape. Heavens, she'd been headed for the Silver Spur in any case. Even without Sam, she might have discovered something there that put her life in danger.

And, if her life were to end in the next few days, next few hours, after all, she was glad that she'd had Sam in it. For she understood that brief time she'd had with him was more than some people were gifted with in a lifetime.

And she couldn't help but believe that, somehow, he'd find a way to save them.

But then she heard the mining camp, long before they reached it. Near dusk, while a lead gray bank of clouds scudded in from the west, muddying up the colors of the sunset. A steady, ominous thudding, the grinding screech of gears, the earth groaning in protest of its invasion. And the fear began, a low, nauseous churn that grew with every step.

The corrosive orange glow of the mining camp rose above the foothills. It was midshift as they rode in, straight through the densely packed infestation of tents that held the workers.

A few of the workers slouched outside their tents. Finishing supper, sipping earthy-smelling liquid from small bowls that steamed into the cool night air. Others clustered around a game of dice, another small group simply slumped around a weak fire, staring blankly into the flames.

Only a couple even bothered to glance their way as they rode through, their eyes dark and flat, utterly drained of emotion. So exhausted they'd even given up on curiosity, Laura thought. Apprehension weighed on her, pressing down on her shoulders so that it became an effort to lift her arms.

She tried to pick out the man she'd drawn. Had they simply sent him back to the mines? Or had they killed him to discourage any other attempt at escape? She couldn't find him.

She'd believed his face was so clear in her memory, each detail so distinct, she'd recognize him in an instant. But they all shared that desperation, that palpable hopelessness, and she was no longer certain she'd know him amongst all the others.

They emerged from the tent city and gained the main part of the complex. There was an empty yard in the middle, reddish earth packed plate-flat by constant foot traffic, ringed by supply buildings and the poles that held the lanterns. The guards were more curious than the workers, but they'd been well trained, remaining at their posts around the perimeter. After a quick glance at the new arrivals they resumed scanning their assigned area.

Laura closed her eyes briefly, trying to draw in enough breath to steady herself. Her head had gone light, the world expanding and contracting around her, insubstantial, unreal.

"Off you go," Jonce said, signaling with his gun.

Laura's legs wobbled beneath her as she slid to the ground. *Dammit*, she thought, *be strong*. If an opportunity presented itself, she had to be ready to take advantage of it. Sam would never leave her behind, and she refused to slow him down.

He wasn't looking at her. Had rarely glanced her way during the entire trip back to the ranch, his concentration relentlessly focused on their guards, on the land they passed. She understood he was searching for the slightest opening. But right that moment she would have given anything to have had him beside her, her hand in his, his strength to lean on.

"End of the line," Jonce said.

Sam edged toward Laura.

"Oh, no you don't," Jonce said.

"Not even going to let me say good-bye?" Sam asked. He had a dozen guns trained on his head. But there was nothing in the way that he held himself, the set of his shoulders or the dark expression on his face, that betrayed any fear or concern. Instead, his eyes burned, his fists clenched, as dangerous as dynamite only waiting for the lit fuse to reach powder before the detonation.

"You'd better take good care of her," Sam said.

"Oh?" Jonce chuckled. "We'll take excellent care of her, don't you worry."

"Because you know her father's going to want to see her body."

"What?" Jonce's head jerked back, as if that was the last thing he expected to hear.

"We both know you're killing us. There's not much choice, is there, if you want to keep your little operation going? Me, it doesn't matter much." He shrugged, dismissing his death as if it were merely a tin of spilled milk. "But you know who her father is. Did you know that she's an only child?"

"So?"

"And did you know that Baron Hamilton's a good friend of President Arthur's?"

"So?" he said carelessly, but his brows drew together. "Why the hell would I care?"

"So you can't just have her disappear somewhere out here. If she's missing, he's going to have half the army crawling over this ranch until he finds something."

"So we give him a body."

Bile launched up Laura's throat, and she swallowed hard, perspiration springing out on her forehead. She understood Sam's intent. But hearing him discuss her death so dispassionately might just save them the trouble, because her heart threatened to give out at any second.

"Better not have an unnatural mark on that body," Sam said. "Or he's going to ask questions. And you'd better make sure that you pay whatever undertaker you use more than Hamilton can." He chuckled. "Though I don't know how anybody could do that. Because if there's one thing Baron Hamilton knows, it's how to get the answer he's looking for. Hell, how do you think he got a chunk of Haw's profits? You think Haw gave up part ownership in this place out of the goodness of his heart?"

Jonce exchanged quick, worried glances with his men.

"Better have a great story," Sam said, shaking his head sadly. "Heck, if I were you, I'd let Haw handle it himself. I wouldn't want Hamilton on my tail, y'know? I wouldn't sleep again if I knew he was after me. Man like that . . . he's not bound by laws any more than

Crocker is. Less, I'd wager. If he suspected someone of hurting his family . . . well, I'd take a gun to my own head rather than let him get his hands on me." He shuddered.

A couple of men shifted uneasily. Jonce's complexion went chalky beneath his tan.

Finally, Jonce jerked his head in the direction of a small, raw shack that huddled at the far end of the yard. "Put her in the office. Red, go fetch Crocker. He's the boss, after all. Might as well let 'im prove why."

Mac, who couldn't claim either five feet in height or less than sixty years, winced. "He don't like to be woke up."

"So wake Fitch and have him do it. He gets paid more'n we do, anyway."

Mac nodded and headed off in search of a fresh mount. The two youngest hands came up on either side of her. One put his hand on her upper arm to draw her away and she shook him off.

"Ma'am," he said softly, "come with us."

"What are you going to do with him?" She snapped out the question like the strike of a whip. "What are you going to do with Sam?"

"Oh, yeah. Sam." Jonce strolled closer, until the snub of his gun rested against the flat surface of Sam's belly. Sam didn't flinch. "You've caused us no end of trouble, you know that?"

"Glad to be of service," he said. "Looking forward to causing you a fair bit more."

"Don't get your hopes up."

Sam glared down at Jonce. If a man could have murdered with a look, Jonce should have dropped dead right then. Jonce leaned back a fraction, an inch of space sliding between the gun and Sam's stomach.

"Where's Griff Judah?" Sam bared his teeth, the feral snarl of a hunting cougar ready to bite.

Jonce's smile was cruel and satisfied. "'Bout three hundred yards west and six feet down."

Sam lunged, with a low howl of rage that froze the blood in Laura's veins. Jonce swung, his rifle catching Sam on the side of the head and knocking him to the ground.

He brought his gun to his shoulder, his finger on the trigger. "Try that again, and I'm shootin'. Not much sport from this distance, though."

A dark, shiny line of blood trickled from the corner of Sam's mouth. Laura took a step toward him but her guard held her back.

"What happened to Griff?" Sam ground out.

"He didn't like our . . . employment methods. Got a conscience, your friend."

"Inconvenient things, aren't they? Lucky I've never been troubled with one."

"We gave him a choice."

"How considerate of you."

"Thought so, too," Jonce said. "He could join those Chinamen he was so worried about down in the mines. Or we could shoot him right here." Jonce shrugged. "He picked the easy way out."

Laura's knees gave out beneath her. *Sam. Oh, dear God, Sam.*

No one else would have known how it affected him. His mouth did not tighten, his eyes did not well with tears. But she knew. As if she could feel his own pain, as if his heart howled out to hers in its agony, and hers answered, drawing in his pain. Perhaps it did; her body had learned to respond to his days ago. If an emotion could be that strong, whether joy or mourning, how could she not feel it, too?

"So," Jonce said. "How about you? You wanna work, or you wanna die?"

Sam rose slowly to his feet. Up, and up, his shoulders back, chest thrust forward as if daring Jonce to fire.

The mines. They wanted him to go down there, into that fathomless hole in the ground, where it was dark and cold and close. Griff Judah had chosen to die rather than enter that pit.

Sam would do the same. She knew it in her bones, in his face, in the way his body had trembled when confronted with the necessity of shelter in that cave. And this was worse, a thousand times so.

She could not watch him die. Watch them shoot him in front of her and leave him to bleed. Whatever they did to her from that point on, that alone would destroy her.

His gaze swung around to meet hers. And she saw it all there, terror and remorse and grief. And love? She did not know if she dared name it that. But he felt something for her, something strong and deep.

Don't die, she begged silently. He'd always been able to read her. Surely he knew this, too, could see it, *feel* it. *Don't die.*

And he nodded and drew a breath, long and shuddery, as if he knew he might not draw many more.

"Show me the hole," he said.

Chapter 25

He'd bought her a few hours. Maybe a few days. Himself, too, hours in hell, but hours nonetheless. Laura was determined to put them to good use.

The shed they'd shoved her in, slamming the door behind her, was eight-by-ten at the most, uninsulated, cluttered with chairs and boxes, a lone desk, and a small, unlit stove with a kettle plunked on top. It had two windows, both glassless, and when she rushed to one she was met with a guard's grinning face before he banged the shutters inches from her nose.

She stumbled around, collecting anything that might serve as a weapon, before pressing her face to a thin crack in the sloppily built shutters of the window that faced the main yard.

They'd stationed a guard right outside each window, too, she noticed immediately. Okay, no obvious way out, she decided. But that was three guards assigned to her, three guards who weren't watching the mines, and that couldn't hurt.

One could worry only so long, Laura discovered. It was impossible to remain on the razor edge of fear and alertness, particularly when nothing was happening immediately.

The night crawled by, so slowly that the passage of time was imperceptible, as if this night was now to be endless.

Little happened in the yard. Guards strode back and forth, their rifles held loosely in the crooks of their arms, rarely even bothering to greet each other because they'd obviously done this a thousand times before. The noise from the mines was constant, metallic and grinding, until her ears became accustomed to the assault and the drone faded into the background.

Finally, when she would have said they'd gone through two nights instead of merely half of one, the shifts changed, torrents of men flooding through the yards, heads down, silent. She searched desperately for Sam. Taller than any of the other miners, he should have been easy to locate.

He wasn't there. Had they killed him in the mines? Or was he still down there, huddled against a wall, thrown back into his own hell?

Her guard apparently found all the waiting hopelessly boring. He finally slumped against the side of the shed and slid down, firing up a thin cigarette, the smoke drifting lazily in the still air.

The clouds blotted out the moon, the stars, giving her no way to judge the incremental passage of time. Days of this, months of this . . . it would drive her mad, the constant, grinding wear of not knowing, waiting, helpless. Understanding nothing but death awaited you, trying to remain on guard for any sliver of hope, finding none.

She did not know how Sam had survived Andersonville. She tried briefly to sleep. Hopeless, but she had to try. Fatigue sapped at her and made the worry sink its claws in deep.

At last she thought the sky might be lightening a bit, a gray sheen thinning above the dark, opaque clouds, and dread congealed in her stomach. Was it morning already? Would she see another?

The guard dozed against the side of the shack. But he roused the instant she nudged open the shutters, no matter how quiet she tried to be.

Finally, Haw Crocker had arrived. A small group clustered a few hundred yards away, three men on horseback talking to two on the ground. The broad man gesturing widely, his back to her, had to be Jonce. Trying to explain what had happened without the blame falling on him, no doubt. He pointed in the direction of the office shed, and she tensed, muscles tightening all the way down her spine. But no one came her way.

Sound exploded, a blast that had Laura ducking automatically, her hands flying to cover her ears from the painful percussion.

When no more came she stood slowly, peering over the edge of the window. All hell had broken loose in the yard—men, guards and workers, running toward the listing building that guarded the main shaft head, all shouting, screaming, their rapid outbursts unintelligible whether in English or Chinese. The earth trembled beneath her feet, groaning as if in pain.

She shoved open the shutters and swung one leg over the sill.

"Oh, no you don't, missy," her guard said.

Shoot. She had to get the guard conscientious enough to hold his place when the rest went running. "What happened?"

Frowning, he shot a glance at the mouth of the mine, where several dozen men had gathered. "Shouldn'ta been blastin' right then. One of the charges must have gone off unexpectedly." He shrugged. "Probably caused a cave-in somewhere."

"A cave-in?"

"Yeah. They'll be pulling out bodies for weeks."

Fear speared into her throat. *Bodies. Sam.* She closed her eyes, curled her hands around the sill until the wood bit into her palms.

No. *No.* He was fine. He had to be. Fate could not be so cruel as to send him into his worst nightmare, the one he'd barely escaped, and crush him there.

And this bastard sounded more worried about the work involved in cleaning the mess than about the men who might have been lost in it. "Shouldn't you go help? See if some of them can be rescued?"

"You kiddin'? It's dangerous down there. I'm not risking my life for the likes of them. There's only a few guards down there, anyway." Anger raged through her like wildfire, a violent burn. If he'd just come close enough, if she could just get her hands on his gun, he'd be in far more danger from her.

"Of course."

"The other Chinamen'll go down there, see what they can dig out."

She ended up pacing. It was too hard to sit and stare out the window, waiting, wondering.

The sky lightened, casting a sickly pall over the ground where it mixed with the harsh light of the lanterns.

"How long has it been?" Laura asked, for at least the sixth time.

Her guard sighed and once again checked the watch

that swung from his waist. "Forty-five minutes or so. Should be . . . there!"

A half dozen men emerged from the building. Two limped painfully along, dragging a man with a bandaged head who sagged between them. One, bent over, his arm lashed to his side, shuffled out with a lifeless body draped over his shoulders.

And none of them was Sam.

They came out in spurts then. Sometimes only one, sometimes a few at a time. On stretchers, bodies draped in tarps. Men, hobbling, their clothes and faces coated with grime. Bandaged men dragging others, barely conscious, behind them.

Bodies soon littered the yard. So many men in that mine. Dozens of them. Hundreds? She couldn't even begin to guess. How many were still down there, trapped, dead or dying?

And nobody seemed to be doing a damned thing.

"Where are the doctors?"

"Ain't got no doctors," he said. "Them Chinese, they got their own kind of medicine, anyway. And if they're hurt that bad, no point in working too hard to save 'em. They ain't gonna be of much use to us anytime soon."

She'd been angry before. Furious, even, when she'd discovered what Haw Crocker was doing. But the rage that tore through her at the unfeeling guard's response was something entirely new, a murderous fury of the sort she would have thought herself incapable.

She'd wondered, more than once, how a human being could deliberately kill another. Now she knew.

The heaviest thing in the place was the coffeepot on the stove. She snatched it up, curling her hand around the handle until her fingers went numb.

A shot cracked through the air.

She flew back to the window.

Throughout the yard injured men were springing to their feet, throwing off slings. Dead bodies rose from beneath their tarps. Men who moments ago could barely stand ran. Streams of workers carrying pick-axes and shovels burst from the door and headed straight for the guards.

Crocker's men were vastly outnumbered. But they had guns, and the crack of shots punctuated the war cries of the miners and the screams of the wounded.

Two of her guards sprinted into the fray. This one backed away, shrinking into the camouflage offered by the dark bulk of the office.

Clang.

The kettle rang when Laura brought it down on top of his head as hard as she could, the handle vibrating painfully in her palm.

He wavered before sinking slowly to the ground. She wiggled out the window and hopped over his prone body.

It was impossible to tell who was winning, who was losing. More men poured from the tent village, most without weapons of any kind, throwing themselves into the conflict armed only with their fists. Somebody had shattered all the lamps, and gloom settled into the narrow valley. The pace of the shots slowed down . . . time to reload? Running out of ammunition? The battle was close, a chaotic churn of desperate men.

And Sam was in there somewhere. He had to be. Because someone had set this off.

Her brain spun frantically, trying to think of something, *anything*, she could do to help.

Nothing. She'd no weapon, no power.

The only thing she could do was run.

She hated the very idea. Leaving Sam behind while he fought for his life . . . it felt as wrong as watching that poor man be lassoed and being able to do nothing to stop it.

Sam would never leave her. But he would have been of more use.

If she could get away, maybe she could summon help. Probably not in time. But if . . . oh, she could barely think it. But if the worst happened, someone needed to be able to tell the truth of what had happened here. Someone needed to make sure that Haw Crocker was punished.

And nobody was paying any attention to her.

The horses Haw and his men rode in on were standing no more than three hundred yards away. She slipped along the edge of the camp, sprinting between buildings, pausing in the shelter their shadows offered.

Yes. She grabbed the reins of the nearest horse. He snorted and tossed his head, backing away from her.

"Easy, handsome," she murmured softly. "It's scary down there, isn't it? Let's get you away from here, shall we?"

She led him up the slope, leaving the chaos behind. She couldn't resist looking back. She needed to see him, just once, to assure herself that he was alive and fighting.

Though she searched until her eyes burned, she couldn't find him. A fire had sparked somewhere, and smoke drifted through the low line of the valley, blurring the individuals into one seething mob, a twisting mass of violence.

Take care, Sam. I . . . take care.

Time to go.

She dragged herself into the saddle, grimacing as

her rear quarters, still sore from the previous days of riding, hit unforgiving leather. She aimed her mount away from camp, back toward the main house. She'd swing around when she got close, then find her way into town.

A troop of riders thundered over the hill, heading directly for her. Panic flared. Run? Which way? Back into the thick of the fighting?

And then, as the morning sun finally burned through the thick, low clouds, she recognized the man on the lead horse.

"Daddy!"

It had been years since Sam had been in battle. Gunfights, yes; small skirmishes that he'd purposely chosen and controlled. They didn't count, and there were fewer of those than most people believed.

Battles were something else entirely. Frenzied, disjointed, the air thick with the scent of confusion and fear. But it all rolled back to him immediately, the instincts that drove him forward, the ability to concentrate on one small thing and block out the rest, the only thing that allowed one to function in the face of such danger.

And at that moment his focus was Haw Crocker.

Haw had found himself a good spot behind a pile of barrels, popping up to fire off a shot before ducking back to safety.

Sam cut to the left, leaving the heat of the fight behind, crouching behind the line of buildings. He taken a rifle off a scared, disoriented kid by the office—the kid had wasted all the bullets, firing madly into the crowd, but the heavy stock had proved damned effective when brought down on the top of a head.

He figured Haw would be turning tail soon enough. He'd been leaving the rough stuff to the hired help for a long time. And a man tended to grow more jealous of his life the nearer he got to the end of it.

The sounds of the fight covered Sam's approach. Crocker didn't glance away from the yard until the rifle prodded square in the middle of his back.

"I do admire a man who fights by the side of his men," Sam said.

Crocker stiffened. "I've done my share."

"Let's join the fun, hmm?" He jabbed Crocker's back. "Get up. Easy now. Wouldn't want me to mistake an innocent twitch for somethin' more aggressive, would you?"

Haw rose at a glacial pace. "I'll give you five thousand dollars."

"Is that all your life's worth?" Sam *tsked*. "Not nearly as much as I figured."

"Twenty. *Thirty*."

"How much silver you figure you take out of that mountain in a day, Haw?" He nudged him with the rifle to get him moving. "Enough to pay for all the lives you stole?"

"Just tell me, then." Desperation thinned his voice. "You've sold your soul so many times over, there can't be any left. Don't try and tell me that you're trying to do the right thing here. Just name your price, and we'll both get what we want."

What I want? No, Sam thought, with the wrenching ache in his heart that he suspected would be his constant companion from now on. *I'm not going to be getting what I want.*

"Move along," he said. "Let's see if we can calm things down out there before anybody else gets hurt, shall we? Anybody else but you, that is. Wouldn't mind that."

He walked him into a clear spot near the platform where the railhead ended. Two cars sat empty, awaiting a load. "Get up."

"I—"

"Get up."

He lumbered onto the platform, Sam right behind him, the gun never wavering.

"Okay, listen up," Sam shouted. "All you guards, drop your guns, or I'm shooting."

It took a while for everyone to settle down. Haw's men seemed willing enough to quit. The miners weren't so eager to end the fight; they had months and years of injustice fueling them, and more than one couldn't resist getting in one final shot. But finally the crowds gathered around the platform, faces uplifted, waiting, like a town come to witness an execution.

"Tell them," Sam said, jabbing at Haw to remind him that the gun was close, and Sam wouldn't mind using it. "Tell them to hand over their guns."

Haw remained silent.

"Tell them."

Most of Crocker's men reluctantly handed over their rifles to the nearest miner.

"I—"

"Now, now, let's not be hasty." The voice cut through the crowd, and it parted automatically to allow him through. A man—short, bald, his arm around Laura held tight to his side—strolled forward, in no rush, looking entirely comfortable despite the tense situation and all the weapons surrounding him. It helped, Sam supposed, to have a dozen huge men with their own flanking you.

It was over, then. The man had Laura, and that was all the leverage anyone needed.

"Be easier to sort this out if *everybody* puts down their guns."

"The miners just got 'em. Don't think they're likely to give 'em up soon. Can't say that I blame them. And most of them don't have enough English to understand, anyway." Finding miners who could grasp his plan had been as frustrating as hell. Especially since he'd been on the verge of blacking out every moment he'd spent underground. But after he'd knocked out the first two supervisors he ran across, they'd paid attention, rousting up three men who'd been there the longest and who'd gained a fair grasp of the language over the years.

"Looks like you're the leader of this little uprising to me," the man said mildly. One of Haw's partners, Sam wondered? A competitor, itching to use this incident to take over the mines for himself?

He didn't dare glance at Laura again. He had to *think*, and seeing her, frightened or angry and with blame in her eyes, would shoot his concentration to hell.

"So I figure," the man said, "if you toss yours down, the rest'll hand 'em over without much fuss."

"Sure." He tossed the rifle aside, causing everybody near to flinch, expecting it to fire. "It was out of ammunition when I grabbed it, anyway," Sam said. "Couldn'ta shot you if I wanted to, Crocker." He bared his teeth. "And I did."

Crocker struggled in his grasp, but the days when he could match a man like Sam were decades gone. "You're going to be very sorry you did this."

"Don't think so," Sam said. "Though I am a bit sorry I haven't killed you already. Save me from having to listen to you yap."

"You don't know who that is, do you?" Crocker chortled. "That's Hamilton. And he's made almost as much off of this place as I have."

"Hamilton?" Sam swung his gaze over.

Worry darkened Laura's eyes, drew her brows together, her mouth tight. But she did not fight the man's embrace, leaning against him as if to draw his strength, welcoming his support.

Back where she belonged.

"Got here mighty fast," Sam said.

Hamilton nodded. He was barely half a head taller than Laura, with the round middle of a man who'd been hungry once and now could afford to indulge every craving. Power sat well on his broad shoulders, as if he knew that he could stroll into any place, any situation, and take command. "Hoxie cabled me as soon as he hit a town. Good man, that. Amazing how fast you can get out here if you've got the train to yourself and pay 'em not to stop. Especially if you offer extra to clear the tracks out in front of you." He spoke mildly but his eyes were sharply focused, fiery with intensity. Exhaustion carved deep lines at his eyes, along his mouth. He probably hadn't slept since he'd gotten word that Laura was missing, and Sam liked him for it.

"Now that I'm here," he said, "Laura, you want to tell me what the hell's going on?"

"Now, Leland, you know that—" Hamilton gave Crocker a hard glare that had him swallowing his words before they made it out of his mouth.

"I'd rather hear it from Laura, Crocker."

"'Course you would." He gave a sickly chuckle.

"Father." Laura straightened, turned to face her father, her hands knotted before her. The last three days had marked her. Her clothes were ruined, her hair snarled, her complexion pale. The only wonder was that her father was asking questions first instead of shooting every single person who might have been the slightest bit responsible for putting her in that state. "It's a long story."

"I'd assumed it was."

"The important point is that Mr. Crocker—" Her hands twisted again, and Sam felt it as a physical thing, a pain that lodged high in his chest. He wanted to go to her, wrap his arms around her, and take her away from it all. "He was using these people as *slaves*," she bit out. "He brought them here, kept them here under guard, and forced them to work in the mines. No pay, no escape."

"That true, Crocker?"

Crocker made a show of jolly unconcern, but sweat streamed down his brow and dampened his shirt.

"I had labor issues." He tried to shrug, ended up twitching. "Kept wanting a raise, wanting shorter hours, wanting cages instead of baskets to get 'em down the shaft and all other kinds of expensive safety devices. You know how it is, Leland."

"I do?"

"Sure you do! Easiest way to keep the profits coming is to cut the expenses. And I never heard you complaining about the profits."

"I suppose not."

"There you go!" He tried to stride forward, winced when Sam yanked his arm higher behind his back. "Could you tell this asshole to let me go?"

"Well, I—"

"Daddy, you can't!" Laura cried. "He killed Sam's

friend. He tried to kill Sam, and he would have killed *me*. I'm sorry we worried you, going off like that, but it was *important*—"

"I was hoping not to have to tell you this," Haw cut in, a great gush of desperate words. "You know how it is with young ladies sometimes. Their heads get turned by the wrong men now and then, especially when their parents aren't around to point out the lies. They get so blinded by those sweet words that they can't even tell the truth when it's right in front of them.

Sam's grip tightened until Crocker yelped and sank to his knees.

Hamilton took Laura's hand—he wasn't letting her more than a foot away from him—and strode to stand in front of the platform. He was nearly level with Crocker and had to look up to Sam, but nobody would ever view it and think him subservient.

The poker face for which he was famous was firmly in place. "You telling me my daughter's *lying* to me, Crocker?"

"Not lying, exactly." He gasped out the placating words, breath shortened by the pain in his shoulders. "Who knows what lies he fed her? Had her pretty head in such a spin she's got no idea which end is up anymore. You'll straighten her right out once she's out from under the influence of—"

For a man approaching sixty, Hamilton still had a pretty good right cross. Crocker's head snapped back, and Sam's hold was the only thing that kept him from toppling right over.

"For God's sake, Leland!" His eyes watered, and blood trickled from his split lip. "We've known each other for damn near twenty years! Let's go back to the ranch, have a whiskey, and sort this out by the fire."

Hamilton turned his attention to Sam. "If I leave my men with you to help, do you have what you need to sort this all out?"

"I—" It was happening so fast Sam's brain scrambled to catch up. Hamilton regarded him steadily, giving Sam a glimpse of what accounted for Hamilton's immense success. He made up his mind quickly, acted decisively, and very few men could hold under that commanding gaze without quailing. Sam himself, who'd stood up to many in his day, had to force himself not to glance away.

But then, guilt niggled at him, too, making it harder to hold Hamilton's gaze. Sam *had* dragged the man's daughter into danger. He'd lain with her, and anything that Hamilton did to him was no more than deserved.

"You're Duncan, aren't you? You should be able to manage. Or is your reputation only that?"

"No, sir."

"Then I'm depending upon you to make sure justice is done here." When he drew Laura against his side his expression softened. Baron Hamilton might be one of the most powerful men in the United States, but Laura was obviously the center of his world. "Mrs. Hamilton was feeling a bit peaked—nothing serious, dear—so I wouldn't allow her to come along. We'll wire her at the first opportunity, but she won't rest easy until she sees Laura is safe and sound with her own eyes. So we'd best get back to Newport as quickly as possible."

"Leland!" Crocker tried one last time. "You can't mean to leave me here with *him*, God only knows—"

"Enough! I am a *businessman*, Crocker. Not a thief, not a bully, and most certainly not a slaver. I understand that many call me ruthless. And while it is true I have little sympathy for those who lose to me out of stupidity, arrogance, or their indulgence of their personal weaknesses, that is a *far* cry from taking criminal advantage of unfortunates. That, Haw, is not only cruel, it is simply *lazy*." He spat out the word as if it were the worst epithet he knew.

And then he steered Laura away.

"Father, I—" She stopped, looked back at Sam, softness shimmering in her blue eyes. "Could we have a moment?"

"Go ahead."

"Alone."

"No," he said cheerfully, continuing to hold her at his side.

Not like this, Sam thought. He did not want to say good-bye to her with hundreds of people around, some moaning in pain, a few lifeless bodies being carried away. Not with her father looking on, waiting, listening to every word. Not with Haw Crocker at his feet with the stench of fear roiling off him like sweat.

But what did what he *wanted* have to do with anything?

I'm sorry. You're the best woman I've ever known. Take care. Thank you. Thank you so much. Take care. Keep well. Have a wonderful life. Don't forget me.

I'm so very sorry.

How could he say all that to her, *show* her, make her understand, without ever saying a word?

"I'm sorry about your friend," she said at last, lamely, her free hand jerking toward him, as if she wanted to reach for him but knew she couldn't.

She loved him. He didn't know how he knew it; he just *did*, the awareness embedded as deeply in his bones as if he'd been born with it.

He couldn't let it matter. Her father would take her

back to the world she belonged in, and he would go back to the solitary life that had been forced on him so long ago. There was no other way.

The morning sunlight, gray and weak, misted over her. He tried to catalog each feature, score them into his brain where he could keep the memories safe. The precise shade of her eyes, the angle of her nose, the way the corners of her mouth trembled. But then he realized he already knew them all. She'd found her place inside him long ago.

He swallowed hard, struggling to keep his voice level. "I am, too." *Sorry about a thousand things. Most of all, sorry about saying good-bye to you like this.*

"Well. Then." He watched memories well in her eyes.

"Good enough," her father clipped out. Obviously considering the subject closed, the problem handled, he turned his back and dismissed them, marching Laura toward the horses.

Sam watched them go until his throat ached, and he had to blink rapidly. He turned to the nearest of Hamilton's men, a giant in black with enough ammunition for a regiment strapped across his chest. "You are?"

"Miller."

"Can you handle this one?"

Miller smiled at the ridiculousness of the question. Sam shoved Crocker at him and turned to the other men. "Come on, then," he clipped out. "We've got work to do."

Chapter 26

December

Laura squinted at the canvas propped on the easel before her.

Her studio was on the second floor of Sea Haven, at the back of the house, facing the cliffs and the ocean. It was supposed to have been her mother's salon, centrally located at the top of the grand staircase between the two wings that rambled off in each direction. But the light was best here, and so here was where she worked.

And that work was good, for all that she'd abandoned the panorama project. Better than good, the best she'd ever done. Though she'd probably never drum up the courage to show it to anyone.

She'd painted Sam from the shoulders up. It should have been an absolutely proper portrait. But it seethed with sensuality. His hair was tousled, his eyes slumberous, his mouth relaxed as if just coming from a kiss. She'd gotten every detail, each tiny nick and scar, the way his left brow curved slightly higher than the right, and his nose hooked a fraction, the likeness so precise it had to be either painted from endless sittings or the artist knew her subject in intimate and besotted detail.

There wasn't a grown woman on the face of the earth who could view that picture and not suspect its creator had gone to bed with her subject.

Sometimes, when working on it, the memories and the passion gripped her so strongly her hands shook and she had to stop and go on to something else to distract herself.

There were a half dozen other portraits around the room, in various stages of completion, each on their own easel, awaiting her moods. Jo Ling, a moody piece, far more impressionistic than the rest, the background a seething swirl of red and black. A blooming Lucy, who'd finally forgiven Laura, her hair around her shoulders, a soft work in pastel colors and sweeping sunshine. Her parents, laughing and relaxed, a canvas she had promised him she would never show in public before his death, because it would destroy his ruthless reputation.

She painted for the joy of it again, something she'd lost along the way, and she reveled in having it back.

But even that wasn't always enough. During the day, yes, while she worked furiously or visited with her family, she was happy. But at night, and despite her best efforts, her mood turned pensive and lonely. She wondered how long it would be, if ever, before she could drop off to sleep without feeling as if something was just *wrong* because he wasn't there beside her.

Outside, the wind blew in off the ocean, rattling the windows in the big French doors that stretched along the entire length of the room. Twin fires burned in the two fireplaces on either end of the room.

It hadn't snowed yet. But winter was threatening, the skies and the sea gray as pewter.

She picked up her brush again. A bit more warmth in the eyes, she decided. It hadn't been there when she'd first met him, his eyes cool, dark, and controlled, but—

Noise burst in the front of the house. Thumps, the crash of a vase, wood splintering.

And then "Laura! *Laura!*"

Her stool tumbled over as she sprang to her feet and dashed toward the source of the sounds. The marble steps that seemed as wide as a stable, spilled down to the grand foyer. A chandelier nearly the size of a carriage spangled star-bits of light over the floor.

A small table rested on its side, the shattered remains of a crystal vase strewn in a wide, glittering arc. The pink hothouse roses her mother favored were being ground to pulp beneath some very large boots.

Four of her father's biggest men struggled to drag Sam out of the house while he surged toward the staircase, shouting all the way. "*Laura!*"

"What took you so long?" she asked, while her heart lifted inside her until she thought she might drift up to the chandelier.

Her words froze everyone below her, a half dozen heads swinging in her direction.

Sam grinned. He looked much the worse for the wear, hair sticking up every which way as if he'd forgotten how to brush it, his dark shirt ripped at the shoulders, his boots tracking mud across her mother's gleaming floors. And he looked so wonderful she would have flown down the stairs and straight into his arms if she'd thought there was a hope in hell she would have made it there before her father got in the way.

Leland Hamilton stood in the doorway to his study, frowning so fiercely the corners of his mouth were nearly below his chin. "Get him out of here right now."

The men pulled, heaving their weight into it like cowboys trying to move a stubborn bull. Sam kicked in one direction, swinging in the other. He connected with both, two men dropping to their knees, yelping.

"Stop!" Laura shouted, and started down the stairs.

The two men who were still upright, wrestling frantically to maintain their grips on Sam's arms, looked to Leland Hamilton for confirmation. He jerked his head in the direction of the door.

"Father, if you have him thrown out of here, I'm going to be right behind them."

"I don't think it'd be much trouble to stop you," he replied.

"Then I'll try again tonight. And tomorrow. And the next day. Is that really how you'd like the rest of our life to go on?" she said. "Not to mention which you're making quite a mess, and if you insist upon having him bodily thrown out, it's going to get a far sight worse. I've seen him in action. Mother's going to be most unhappy with you if she loses any more furniture." She flew down the stairs, gaining the floor. "What could it hurt to hear him out?"

"It could hurt quite a lot," he said darkly. "Move him," he commanded.

"I *tried* to do it the right way," Sam called to her, panting, as they hauled him across the floor. "I tried to ask his permission first. I knew I should have just kidnapped you and been done with it."

Laura skidded to a stop in front of her father.

"Daddy, he loves me. I love him," she burst out. "You're not going to be able to change that by throwing him out in the street."

"Well shit." He scowled as if someone he trusted had just absconded with his entire fortune. "You *love* him?"

She nodded.

"Dammit!" he burst out. "Let him go. *For now*," he added meaningfully. "Stay close."

The room fell quiet. Waiting, as she did. She heard footsteps behind her, the easy, confident cadence she could have picked out of an entire army. "Laura," Sam said softly.

Suddenly unsure, Laura closed her eyes while her heart pounded frantically in her chest. She'd blurted out that she loved him. Even more, claimed he felt the same without his ever having said one word on the subject.

But he did. She knew he did. And if he did not understand that yet, well, she'd make certain he did soon enough.

Sucking in a shaky breath, she turned slowly.

Sam. Her Sam. He'd traveled hard to get to her. Lines of fatigue hugged his mouth, his eyes, and he'd lost some flesh. He hadn't cut his hair since the last time she'd seen him, and he had at least three days of growth on his chin. No wonder her father wanted him out. He looked like the worst sort of outlaw, dangerous and utterly without conscience.

But the light in his eyes took her breath away.

"I love you, do I?" he asked.

She swallowed. "Yes. You do."

He took a step toward her, his trembling hand lifting toward her cheek. "You always did have the best of me."

"Enough of that," her father said, knocking his hand away. "I said you could *talk* to her. I didn't say you could touch her."

"Shouldn't that be up to me?" Laura asked.

"No. It shouldn't. Now, Duncan, I assume you got things sorted out in Utah."

His gaze never wavered from Laura's. "Can't that wait? I've got a few other things on my mind right now."

"You're pushing my tolerance as it is."

He sighed, then spoke as fast as he could. "It took a while. The sheriff, the army, immigration. The government in Utah and in California—they all wanted their piece of it. Jonce is awaiting trial for Griff's murder."

"Sam," she said softly.

"It's okay," he said. *Later. Later, he would let her hold him while he said his own good-byes to his friend, then they could go on and live the life that Griff never had the chance to, and do it twice as well because they did it for him, too.* "Crocker was convicted of deliberate violation of the Exclusion Act, transporting immigrants illegally."

"That's it?" Laura asked.

He nodded. The necessity of staying to testify at Crocker's trial, arguing until he was hoarse for more charges, was part of what had taken so long.

"They don't care what he did to those people, only that he brought them here?"

"That's pretty much it," Sam admitted. He'd moved past the initial fury that had raged when he'd first discovered the charges, but not the frustration. "But he's in jail, Laura, and he's going to be there for a good long time. I suspect the territorial governor got a cable or two that ensured that." He glanced at Hamilton, who met his gaze impassively, neither confirming nor denying Sam's suspicions.

"The miners?"

"On a boat back to China. I saw them off myself."

"All that, and they're ending up back where they started."

"They seemed happy enough to go," he said. "They'd had more than enough of America."

"I suppose so," she agreed sadly. "Jo Ling?"

"Disappeared into Chinatown in San Francisco with her friend. I couldn't find her."

"Chan?"

He shook his head. "He was dead before we reached the Spur."

Laura took one moment to mourn all the lives destroyed, the justice that would never be enough. Then she put it aside. She could tell their stories through paintings, and maybe a few people would understand. Until then . . . *Sam is here. Here.* The joy bubbled up, a frothy, swelling champagne of elation that tingled in her fingers and went to her head.

"I'm sorry it took me so long," he told her. "Most of it was the work. But some of it was . . ." How did he explain it to her? That he'd tried so hard not to love her, tried so hard to forget, and finally had to acknowledge that the feeling was stronger than he was, that *she* was stronger than he was? That it had already been far too late for him to get out without being hurt?

But she was Laura, and she'd ever understood what he'd been unable to say. "You're not going to lose me," she told him. "Not ever."

"I know." For even if he'd never seen her again, she would have been with him, in every breath he took, every beat of his heart, for the rest of his days. "Let's go get married."

"Now?"

"If you had a preacher in the next room, it wouldn't be fast enough for me." Every second that was keeping him from being alone with her, and knowing she belonged to him, was one second too many. It felt like he'd been waiting too long already. That he'd been waiting for her his whole life without ever realizing it before.

"I've got plenty more guards," Mr. Hamilton said. "And I've got no problems with calling them. You're not marrying her."

"Not to get off on the wrong foot, sir, but don't you think that's up to her, too?"

"No. If the touching's not her choice, do you really think I'd let the *marrying* be?"

"But—"

"Father." She stepped between them, the two men she loved most who were nose to stubborn nose, eyes blazing, each one as hardheaded and determined as the other. Laura knew if she waited for them to sort it out themselves, she might be too old for babies by the time it got settled. She put her hand on her father's forearm. "Please, Daddy. You've raised me well. I've got more than a good dose of your good sense. I'm hardly a child."

"Yes you are," he said. "You're *my* child. You could be tottering around with a cane, and you'd still be my child. What do you think I've amassed all this fortune and power for if not for my family's protection? You can't expect me to hand you off to some ruffian with a bad reputation who dragged you into no end of trouble without using what I've built to stop it."

"Daddy," she said softly.

"Sir, I love her," Sam said, such richness and conviction in his voice that Laura's eyes stung. It was physically painful not to touch him, to let him wrap his arms around her and simply hang on, letting all that love flow between them.

"Well, that's easy enough to say, isn't it?" her father scoffed. "What's not to love?"

"What's not to love, indeed," Sam agreed. "You're not going to stop me without locking me up. And probably not even then."

Hamilton frowned at Sam. "There'll be not a penny of it for you, you know. I've made certain of it. If she marries without my approval, she'll never have any of it, whether I'm alive or dead. *Not one cent.*"

"Okay," Sam said cheerfully, and reached for her hand. "Can we go now? There's got to be a church open somewhere."

"You, too, Laura. You don't know what it's like to have nothing. I haven't worked my whole life for you to suffer in poverty, but you will if you do this. Be sure you understand what you're forfeiting if you marry him."

"Daddy. He's not poor."

Leland eyed Sam skeptically. The lowliest stablehand at Sea Haven was better dressed than he. "Sure he's not."

"He's not. And, even if he was, it wouldn't matter. Heavens, it's not as if I couldn't make a living if I had to, too."

"I'll not have you— "

"Sir," Sam said quietly. "You have my word. If I thought for one instant that Laura would suffer by marrying me, I wouldn't be here. She understands what I have, and what I don't, and she's never been shy about telling me what's on her mind. If she asked me to go, I'd be out that door before the final word left her mouth."

"And just how do you plan on taking care of her? Hiring out your gun, leaving her home to fret and worry while you put yourself in the way of men who hold life in no more value than the cost of the bullet that ends it?"

"No, I'm done with that. I've saved up over the years. I probably couldn't buy the rug in your office, but it's enough to live in some comfort. I'll buy some land, run a few horses, maybe some cows." He shrugged. "I don't care where we live. Laura can choose. Somewhere she feels like painting."

"Oh, *crap*." Blinking rapidly, Hamilton covered Laura's hand with his own broad paw, still bearing the scars of the years he'd worked the docks. "Why is it that the only two people in the entire world I can't say 'no' to are the two women in my family?"

"Daddy." She threw her arms around his neck so tightly he nearly strangled. But he didn't say a word of protest, just wrapped his own arms around her back and hung on.

"Duncan," he said, after spitting out the hair in his way. "You consider Utah?"

"Utah, sir?"

"Stupid mine's still there, and there's a fair amount of ore left in it. Somebody's gotta run it." He grimaced. "Ben wants a chance, his father's still got as many shares as I do if the government doesn't find a way to take 'em away. But I'd feel better if there was someone there I trusted to keep an eye on him."

Trusted. Sam's throat threatened to close. "I won't let you down, sir."

"See that you don't." Hamilton frowned because it was expected. "And, of course, we'll have to be running out there frequently to check on things."

"We'll be happy to have you." *We*, he thought. Marveled. *Laura and me. We.* He'd never planned it, never once considered that he'd be more than just one. A unit of two, both stronger for their bond, facing a sometimes cruel world together.

But oh, for all that that world could be harsh, it could also be immeasurably rich.

Of all the things he owed Griff, including his life, he owed him this most of all, for without Griff he never would have found Laura.

"You'd better be." And then, after one more last squeeze while his eyes screwed shut and he hung on to the last time his daughter was his little girl and his alone, he released her to her man. "Mrs. Jones!" he bellowed to his housekeeper. "Go find my wife. Go find Lucy. Hell, go find everybody. Laura's getting married!"

Sam barely had time to take Laura's hand and smile into her eyes before people began to arrive, troupes of maids and clerks and assistants and footmen, pouring from every corner, more than it seemed even that huge house could hold, all beaming with congratulations and happiness for Laura before turning Sam aside and threatening several delicate body parts if he didn't take proper care of her.

Her mother appeared in a rush of silk and lace and streaming tears. She managed one quick "I'm so happy," enveloping her daughter in her arms, before turning to sob noisily against her husband's chest.

Sam and Laura stood back to back while one person after another gushed by. He was aware of her presence there. He heard her speak, her joyous laughter. When he leaned back their shoulders brushed, a hint of her warmth making his knees weaken and his heart pump. It was a terrible, wonderful anticipation. They were finally together, and yet he couldn't touch her, couldn't kiss her . . . but he knew he would, soon, and for the rest of his life. He couldn't wait much longer.

Mrs. Bossidy waddled down the stairs, her belly so large it looked as if she might give birth at any moment.

"Laura?"

"Hiram," she told him over her shoulder. "He said it was the easiest way to get her to marry him."

"Smart man," Sam said. "I was going to try that if my first plan didn't work."

"Sam!" she exclaimed before she was surrounded by three young maids tittering about wedding dresses and flower arrangements.

"How long do we have to stand here and accept congratulations?"

"Oh, two or three hours," she said airily, laughter lifting her voice.

But she pressed against him, hard enough that he could feel the sweet curve of her rump against his upper thigh, and his blood, hot, demanding, pumped in his veins.

"We're not going to be able to get married if you make me have a heart attack first," he said, low, only half-kidding.

"So get me out of here."

"What?" He distractedly shook the hands of two men in severe black, who mouthed good wishes while glowering at him, and spun. He grabbed Laura by the shoulders, turning her to face him.

"It's not as if we're going to get one second alone together if you don't," she told him. "My father might have approved our marriage, but he'll still ensure that we're properly chaperoned every single second until we're properly wed." People mouthed words around them, but they faded into an unintelligible murmur. She inclined her head toward the door to her father's study. "See?"

Hamilton leaned against the wall, consolingly patting his wife's shoulder, scrutinizing their every move as a storm cloud gathered between his brows.

"Damn," he said, and he'd never meant it more.

"So kidnap me."

"What?"

Her eyes sparkled with mischief and happiness. "Kidnap me. You've done it before, and this is for a good cause."

He scanned the swelling throng waiting to congratulate them—just how many people *did* Hamilton employ?—the broad sweep of staircase and the tall, open doors at the top of it.

"Up there. Does that room open onto the terrace?"

She nodded.

"Are you afraid of heights?"

"Nope."

"All right, then." He swept her up and dropped her over his shoulder. Her hands dangled at his butt, and her delighted laughter bubbled above the crowd.

Sam charged up the grand staircase. "You ready for this?" he said, putting his own hand on the sweet curve of her rump to hold her safe, ignoring the yells behind him. He would bring her back soon enough, after he'd had her naked and alone for a while.

"Ready if you are," she said, and squeezed his rear.

Maybe not so soon, he amended quickly, and ran toward their future.

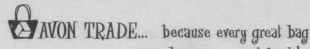